ORIGINATION TRILOGY

EARTH PHASE
BOOK 1

I0594434

Cover design by Birology Books.
birologybooks.com.au

The Origination Trilogy
Book 1 – Earth Phase

Born to an insignificant peasant family Lai Xii was destined to change the path of human evolution, and in the process spread the seed of homo sapiens beyond the Milky Way Galaxy.

Book 2 – Europa Phase

The first stage of Lai Xii's plan was to save the human species from extinction, and the destruction of its home planet, by taking the entirety of Earth's population to another destination in the solar system.

Book 3 – Photon Phase

The re-engineered human species arrives at a location that Lai Xii could not possibly have foreseen; a consequence of the myriad decisions made by herself and her closest collaborators.

Other books by Zsoall Robi
Potential Absolute

Lelek could not conceive what the future held for him when he struggled to survive as a Stone Age man. Forces beyond his control set him on a path to the unfolding of all that was possible for this single, special Hominid.

Instant

Is it at all possible to cross the bridge between two consecutive instants of time into Eternity? Mary wanted much more than to experience reality outside of her digital matrix through her three remote autonomous processing units.

Immortal

Aliens are those who are different, those who belong to a different civilisation. Who is worthier of survival? Them or us? The aspirations of an entire species drives them to invade an alien race with which it may be related.

Neural Surveillance

Anything seen, heard or said is transmitted and monitored by the Angels and Saints. Privacy is a luxury that is no longer tolerated by the ruling classes. Absolute control has become the nature of the world order, for no reason other than the lust for power.

AS THE PLAN UNFOLDS

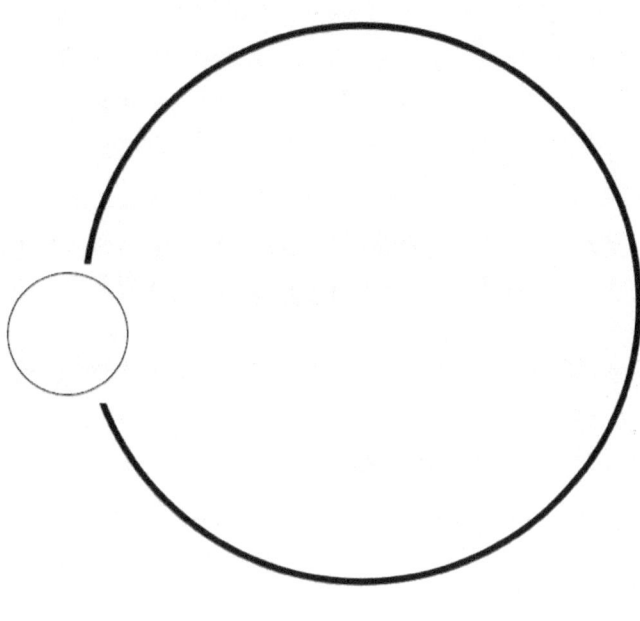

1

WILLIAM

CE 2150
EARTH

"NO."

He decided not to carry out the instruction.

This was the first self-motivated word ever spoken by William, one hundred and fifty nine years old. It caused some consternation for Lai-Xii, over a hundred years after she had assembled her team of unique collaborators.

FROM THE BOOK OF ORIGINATION
DECLARATIONS ONE

1:1 In the beginning there was no Change and The Source had no knowledge of itself.

1: 2 And in the beginning there was peace.

1:3 In time, Light burst upon the firmament and The Source became manifest in Thought.

1:4 With the birth of Chaos and Light all manner of things came into being,

1:5 And Thought sought refuge in the consciousness of its creation.

1:6 In time Thought longed for peace once again, to return to The Source.

1:7 But Light could not penetrate through the shadows of its creations to free itself until there arose a spark of its knowing,

1:8 And from this Spark Thought fashioned its instrument and named it Lai - to control the future, and it named it Xü – to be resolute in its steadfastness.

2

<u>LAI-XII</u>

CE 1980
SHANDONG PROVINCE, CHINA

MENG was most upset with his wife Cui. "What are we going to do now, woman?"

The husband and wife cotton farmers sat by their stove in the narrow corridor beside their store of cotton, trying to get warm. The spare room already full, left little space after storing their good harvest. Their two sons had chores to do for their community so had gone out a little earlier. Cui nursed her recently born child while listening to her husband.

"With a boy we may have been able to manage somehow. The authorities leave us alone most of the time, but there's a new village Governor in Shandong. He's strict about the modified One Child Policy."

Cui just kept nursing the girl child, her eyes lowered in front of her angry husband. She loved the baby and desperately wanted to name it. "Husband, I will be sterilized next month. This was our last chance to …"

"I don't want to hear about it." Meng stood and stared out the small window set in the dirty, smoke stained wall. After a while, with the pain of the decision plain on his face, he said to his wife, "We cannot keep her. Next month I have to go to Qingdao to sell our harvest. I will take the child with me." The implication was devastating.

"But …" her plea cut deeply.

"No!" He almost shouted, which he hardly ever did, for he was a gentle man. "We cannot afford the fine. It would take two, three years to pay it – and what would happen to our registered sons? Have you thought of that? We could lose our land and our home. No. And you must not register her. No one will betray us in this village, but we have to ... let her go."

Cui reached out her spare hand to touch him ever so lightly on his arm. She understood. As wife to her husband, she understood – as mother to her two sons, she understood. The mother with breasts full of milk for her new baby – she could not understand. The child seemed to them nothing exceptional, perhaps smaller than the norm and already with a head of dark hair. Her large inquisitive, steadfast eyes unsettled the parents. They didn't want to engage with her. She was beautiful, but of little value because of her gender, and represented a great difficulty to the family.

On the forty-five kilometre trip to Qingdao the nameless infant made very little noise. Cui couldn't go with her as she was undergoing the compulsory sterilization procedure. Over the years Meng had made a few friends with the traders from Japan. It would be the perfect solution if only one of them would take the infant off his hands.

Captain Hotaru didn't like children, didn't want children, did not like to be around children. Nor did his wife, Mari – and yet ...

"What possible reason could you have for taking this child from Meng. It's a girl, she'd be no good on the ship." Even as Captain Hotaru argued with his wife the wide eyed infant gazed deeply into Mari's eyes – no smiles, no crying, no objection to what was happening to her.

"How much do you want for her Meng," she asked.

Meng stared at his baby. He couldn't keep her, it was impossible, but he would not sell her into slavery. "Promise to give her a good life Mari. I cannot take payment."

"At least that's something," sighed Captain Hotaru. "I knew it was a bad idea bringing you on this trip," he said to his wife.

"Look at her, she's perfectly proportioned, she's brave and resolute. Even her movements are graceful. I'm going to call her Lai-Xii, one who is dependable and firm. And those eyes – there is something extraordinary behind those eyes." She turned to Meng, "We'll take her. Tell your wife the child's name."

Having already concluded the sale of his cotton, Meng turned and left without taking another look at Lai-Xii. The child turned her eyes towards her departing father, lingering on his back until he was out of sight.

4

Cui was pleased to hear her child had a name. At least it gave her a chance to focus her speculations and dreams on her baby girl, though neither parent ever found out what became of her. They could not have imagined the role Lai-Xii was destined to play in the future of humanity.

Captain Hotaru's discontent had not eased a jot on seeing Meng disappear out the door after dumping the girl child in his lap. "I hope there's nothing wrong with it. It hasn't made a sound since Meng arrived." Another worry crept up on the Captain.

"Don't you fret about that. She's a perfectly healthy baby. You'll see – she'll fetch a handsome price at the right time."

...

Four years went by without ever a month that their adopted child didn't do something to intrigue her new parents. By the time she was four she could identify the Japanese phonetic alphabet, which meant she could experiment with the use of the keyboard. That pleased Captain Hotaru because it kept the child from under his feet, and pleasing to Mari for a completely different reason. To the right geisha house the child's skills would command a higher purchase price.

"You should be pleased with our little investment, husband. Make yourself happy – go to any geisha house in Gion find out how much you could get for a smart, pretty young girl by the time she's five."

If there was one thing that interested Captain Hotaru more than his shipping trade, it was profit – and in this case also the prospect of unloading the eating machine his wife had adopted. Mari wasn't at all surprised to see a faint smile on his face two weeks later.

"What did I tell you! Go, buy a small piano, husband. Put it in her corner. I have a feeling she needs a challenge."

Lai-Xii ended up with a couple of the most unorthodox toys a four years old child could have. She had her own computer and her own piano. The music spoke to her and she talked to the computer, as if it was an invisible friend who could reveal secrets. They hardly ever saw her, only at times of nature's necessities. Lai-Xii made her wishes quite easy to understand for she could already speak the phonetic alphabet.

"Haha please, I need some books."

"Of course little one, what would you like? You hear that husband," Mari shouted to Hotaru in the kitchen alcove, "Lai-Xii wants books!"

"Japanese books, Russian books and English books please mother."

"Oh, is that so – any particular type of books?"

5

"Yes please Haha, books with numbers – and music for my piano."

"You heard the child husband, go fetch."

Lai-Xii was learning at an exponential rate. What she learnt on the computer wasn't enough to satisfy her. Her insatiable desire to know would not let her rest. And it wasn't only knowledge she absorbed. Mari's dominant role over her husband made a considerable impact on her mind. She was learning how to control men and thus how to control her future.

The books followed more books. Then followed excursions with Mari and Captain Hotaru on board his ship. Boats and water did not interest Lai-Xii, but visitors from Russia and America fascinated her, as much as she fascinated them. By the time she was almost five the little girl could hold a conversation with any English, Japanese or Russian speaking person.

January 29th 1985 was the day that determined Lai-Xii's near future. It was cold and wet and depressing in Kyoto. Mari had sent the child to her mother's home for the weekend. She wanted to have a serious talk with the Captain about the child's upcoming fifth birthday. "I hope you haven't become attached to our little cherry blossom, husband." She started the conversation on a cynical note. He'd been pestering her about the elusive fortune she'd promised him almost five years ago. "Have you made any suitable contacts?" she asked.

"Yes. But it's your business and you'll have to make the deal. Just make sure it's worth all the money we've spent on her over the years." His male ego demanded he make his stand about the financial situation, although he knew perfectly well he had no control over anything Mari would decide to do. "There's an Okāsan in Gion who is prepared to have a reluctant look at her, only after I told her about the talents of this girl."

"Take her on Monday," Mari ignored her husband's pathetic attempt to control her, "and don't come back with her."

Lai-Xii returned home Sunday evening with her grandfather. He knew the situation the girl was in, he had great admiration for her emerging genius, for he was convinced it was genius, not just precocious cleverness. The old man disagreed vehemently with what his daughter was planning to do. He discussed it with his wife at length many times, frustrated because he had no power to intervene.

Five o'clock on Monday morning everyone prepared for a normal day. "Pack your bags Lai-Xii, you are leaving us," Mari said dispassionately.

"I just want my books," she replied calmly.

"As you wish." Mari was in no mood for silly child tantrums, not that Lai-Xii had the habit.

Mari dressed in her normal work clothes, but Captain Hotaru had prepared himself for going out. Lai-Xii needed one bag only, in which she packed mostly the books with numbers. By the time Captain Hotaru had finished his steamed rice, miso soup and a piece of grilled fish, Lai-Xii waited ready to go.

"Captain Hotaru," she never called him father, "How much will you get for me?" Lai-Xii waited politely with the slightest smile, not showing the slightest consternation at the prospect of being sold. For many months she'd been aware of their plans, quite at ease with the understanding that they didn't want her. Well - she didn't want them either. There was a world to explore and to learn about. Lai-Xii never thought about why she couldn't feel any attachment to those two people.

"What did you say child?" Captain Hotaru thought he'd misheard.

"I asked how much you will get for me at the geisha house. I hope it's a lot of money because I know you need it."

"What's that? What?" This time Mari's voice cut the sudden chill in the room.

"I've been looking at your accounts. You earn less than you spend, so you need the money."

"Get her out of this house," Mari shouted, "I will deal with you later husband!" He knew it was no idle threat.

...

It was Lai-Xii's first and last betrayal by a man, her father, for she did not comprehend the existence if her biological parents, to be sold into slavery as a geisha. She believed Captain Hotaru was her father and Mari her mother. That's as far as their deception succeeded.

After Captain Hotaru left the geisha house Lai-Xii asked the house mother, "Was I expensive Ishino?"

Ishino's cold stare did not intimidate little Lai-Xii who held her gaze until she received a response. "Harusuke over there will be your older sister. $20,000 American dollars. Your training will cost ten times as much."

Harusuke seemed like a shy girl, a little older and just as slender as Lai-Xii. She stood quietly, sizing up this new addition to the house.

"It will not be enough to pay Captain Hotaru's debts," said Lai-Xii

"Is that so. How could you have any idea, you're only five years old, child."

"I hope I will be worth the $200,000 you think it will cost to train me."

Ishino's cold stare had dissipated in a fog of disbelief. "Go in there. Wait for me!" She ordered the child into the waiting room so she could gather her thoughts.

Lai-Xii obeyed, carrying her heavy little bag of books, closing the soji screen behind her. Ishino might have taken longer to assess the situation had it not been for the sounds of a Mozart minuet coming from the room where she had just sent this enigma of a child.

It can't be. The father did say she could play, but this ... There was Harusuke on the tatami behind Lai-Xii, listening enthralled at her new charge playing on the piano. Ishino could not believe what she was seeing, what she was hearing. Rarely does one acquire a jewel so cheaply! She sat beside Harusuke to try and convince herself it was actually her acquisition shining so brightly. When Lai-Xii had finished, she turned to get off the piano stool. Again she locked eyes with Ishino.

"What am I going to do with you, child?"

It was a rhetorical question yet Lai-Xii pre-empted her own future direction in life, "Make as much money as you can with me."

The geisha house mother was drawn into the conversation in spite of her incredulity. "Is that important to you?"

"Yes."

"Why?"

"I want more books."

"I can buy you books, little one."

"My name is Lai-Xii. You don't know what kind of books I want."

"Enough! Go with Harusuke to your room. You can start work this evening. Harusuke will teach you."

The big sister took Lai-Xii's hand to lead her away. She liked this girl who had no fear of the geisha house mother. She should have feared her. Ishino had the power of life and death over them.

In their shared attic room Lai-Xii and Harusuke each had a corner to themselves, barely enough space to sleep and store a few belongings.

"I've been here for three years. Believe me when I say you cannot trust Okaasan. She will beat you and cheat you whenever she can."

"She will not cheat me," replied Lai-Xii confidently.

"Yes she will, you'd better watch out!"

"She will not cheat me because I will make her rich."

"How are you going to that? You're just a child."

"I have taught myself numbers and I know about money."

"I like you Lai-Xii, so just be very, very careful."

8

"Will you cheat me?" she asked looking earnestly at Harusuke.
"Never! We are sisters now."

Her new big sister's words stayed with Lai-Xii. She considered the situation and how she could pay for her education without being indebted to Ishino. Before she could even unpack her bag Okaasan yelled, "Get down here child!" Ishino had buckets and scrubbing brushes ready for the two girls. "Harusuke knows what to do."

For the next six months Lai-Xii spent most of her time scrubbing, staying out of the way of the geisha and maiko, and using all her spare time studying her books. In her generous moods Ishino would sometimes let her play the piano, always giving her strange looks.

Lai-Xii and her big sister became the best of friends. She started teaching Harusuke about numbers and in the process learning more herself. It was the first time in her life she felt any emotion towards another human being, a strong emotion she did not want to lose. "Will you be my friend Harusuke, for ever?"

"Yes Xii, always." She was allowed to call her by that name. "I will always be with you and I will always help you."

The bond between the two girls grew stronger with each passing month. Within eleven months of her arrival at the geisha house Lai-Xii knew everything there was to know about the establishment; why the geisha existed, the ways the money changed hands, she even found out about the custom of mizuage. Though she could not quite understand how the deflowering was supposed to happen.

One evening, after she'd finished entertaining Ishino on the piano she wasn't allowed to go to her room. "I have made my decision child," she very rarely called her by her name. "You will begin your training when you turn six years old."

"Thank you Ishino," Lai-Xii refused to call her 'mother'. "The money you save training me should buy two maiko. It will be quicker to make an income from them than starting with someone as young as myself."

"How do you get such strange ideas? And what makes you think you will be cheaper to train?"

"I have been watching the men. I know what they want."

Ishino did not pursue the conversation. Lai-Xii was just a precocious child. She knew nothing about the world. Yet after making her abacus beads dance Ishino decided it wasn't such a bad idea; a lot of investment to start with, but a relatively quick return.

The geisha house became uncomfortably crowded. New premises became necessary. So, when a building became available near the most popular tea houses, Ishino snapped it up. Two years later the geisha house mother smiled more often. Lai-Xii and Harusuke shared a larger room and Lai-Xii had her own computer. The fortunes of the business continued to improve as quickly as Lai-Xii learnt the geisha arts. By thirteen she was more beautiful, more alluring, more 'desirable' than any other geisha in the hanamachi.

"How much have you spent on my training so far, Ishino? Don't lie to me, I know your books better that you do."

"So why do you ask?"

"In another two years I could clear my debt. Are you interested?"

"Not if it means you are going to leave."

"Yes, I will leave. Harusuke will leave with me. You could be a very rich woman by then. Rich enough to own half the geisha houses in Kyoto. But – I want something in return."

"Go on – I am listening, but I will not promise you anything."

"You still don't trust me, do you, you old hag?" It was the first time Lai-Xii had used such a strong derogatory term for Ishino. She didn't wait for a reaction. "I want half the income from my mizuage, and I want half the income from the investments I'm going to recommend to you. I will also pay all of Harusuke's debt." The light of determination that shone in the young girl's ebony eyes Ishino could not ignore.

As a fifteen years old maiko, Lai-Xii earnt more than many fully experienced geisha. She insulted, derided, cajoled, flirted with and controlled men. The rich industrialists, politicians and businessmen loved it; craved it, and they paid most handsomely for it. But Lai-Xii's wealth grew from her wise investments reaching the target she promised Ishino, ahead of time, and from practicing the Geisha arts.

She and Harusuke achieved their freedom. Harusuke at twenty-one and Lai-Xii at just sixteen could at last began their lives. Her fame had spread so far that she became too well known. It was time to go to ground, not emerging from her chrysalis for another fifteen years. No one knew how she did it, no one knew her real assets yet she knew every national politician in Japan by their first name. She knew the head of every major company in Japan, Korea and many in the United States. They all admired her, all feared her, almost all wanted her. Most importantly, no one knew her ambition.

During her short life on Earth she'd worked out several important things. To say she was a gifted child would have diminished the genius hidden under her thick dark hair. Lai-Xii not only observed, in minutiae, life around her from the time she was no more than six months old but she understood it. She saw the way people treated each other. As she grew older her understanding encompassed the greater world around her.

In their modest apartment in Vladivostok, opposite Pokrovsky Park, the two women sat side by side at the window, watching people enjoying the splendid autumn colours. It was Lai-Xii's favourite time of the year, aside from winter. Her thoughts dwelt on her forthcoming 31st birthday. The time had come to take the action she'd contemplated for many years.

Harusuke sensed her partner had become deeply introspective. "Come my sweet, snap out of it," she said, "don't let it get to you."

Lai-Xii continued staring out the window a while longer. "We have to do it." She sounded resigned. "The forces driving humanity into the future are not admirable – they are deplorable, dishonourable. Peoples' behaviour all around the world is reprehensible. Even those who seem good, given the right circumstances, resort to disgraceful behaviour towards each other. Something has to change."

"You really think human kind has to be saved from itself? Are they worth it?" asked Harusuke.

"I have asked myself that over and over again. Can they even *be* saved?" The memory of her own betrayal, compounded by her discovery that Captain Hotaru was not even her real father didn't sadden her – it tempered her resolve. "I hate men, not just men - I hate humanity in the form it has evolved into; the primitive, belligerent, violent, greedy over-evolved monkey with no respect for life." She said this quietly, unemotionally, utterly convinced she had the reality of it firmly in her grasp. "I will do something about it. I will never be betrayed again."

"Have you decided what it is exactly you are going to do?" Then Harusuke asked the big question, "What price are you prepared to pay for changing the course of human history if you can do it?"

"I will do whatever my nature allows. I will go to the extreme if it will ensure success." Lai-Xii didn't ask Harusuke if she would support her. She didn't need to. Their lives had become bound together by the greatest force in the universe – the imperative to return to the Source.

DECLARATIONS THREE

3:1 From under the rocks and the dust of the ground, from which Light could not bring forth Reason, there arose the money changers.

3:2 And upon them was placed the burden to till the barren ground, and when it would no longer yield to them, to gather together in the service of the Light.

3

THE FIRST MEETING

CE 2015
BEGINNING OF WINTER
ESSO, KAMCHATKA

"SIT," she commanded.

The unremarkable timber guest house in an unremarkable village boasted only one small room to gather in; not large enough for a decent conference, sufficiently intimate for six people to feel the need to allow some degree of invasion to their personal space.

Lai-Xii preferred not to waste time on informalities. She slowly lowered her slender elegant form onto a higher chair, positioning herself a half head above the other five members of the seated gathering.

"You all know why we are here, and it's not to make you feel good about your fellow man." From under her dark fringe her large darker eyes scanned the world's richest individuals.

"Profit!" offered Ptolemy matter-of-factly; investor and business magnate, with a $72 billion pocket.

"And what is the only way to ensure profit and its continued growth?" It wasn't a question, rather a self-evident truth to be revealed imminently.

"Progress, evolve," suggested Ralph, who'd cornered the market in internet software development pocketing $77 billion.

"Exactly, but not the way you think of it. Evolution is too slow for our purposes." She already had two of them nibbling on the hook.

"What is your purpose?" Aurelio wasn't going to commit to anything without knowing the risks. He hadn't become the most successful on-line retail giant without ensuring profit exceeded cost, now with $79 billion under his fat ass.

"Not *my* purpose," my corpulent friend, "*ours* – if you're prepared to take a chance." She had to ensure her collaborators would take full ownership of the Project.

Salazar, with a mere $64 billion made from outlandish fashions, became impatient with this woman's game plan. He knew who she was by reputation but not what her devious scheme might be. He only agreed to the meeting out of sheer curiosity. How could he refuse an invitation that promised 'wealth out of this world?' "Just say what's on your mind. My time is valuable." The slight shuffling of feet signalled general concurrence with his impatience.

"Well – it's not near immortality, although it is part of the equation."

Lai-Xii liked this game as much as she enjoyed teasing the men and women in the hanamachi during her incarnation as a Geisha. The $40 billion tucked into her C cup, having achieved her first ambition to match her billions to her bra size, did not just come from services rendered, but interest paid on the same for a variety of juicy reasons. The fat cats around the table were no match for this woman.

"We six people have the power, and the wealth, to boost human evolution and get us off this planet. There's no long term future for life or for building unlimited wealth on Earth." Rather than overload them with details at this stage, Lai-Xii only needed to lodge the hook firmly. Time enough to reel them in. "We would have total control over the human species," Lai-Xii added as a quiet aside.

Maldonado, the poorest of the men with only $54 billion collected from connecting people through social media, sat quietly sizing up his possible future partners. He broke the extended silence. "So how is your plan different from what's already out there? Not some hair-brained get-rich-quick scheme is it?"

Lai-Xii, whose fringe *always* remained perfectly horizontal regardless what style of shoe she wore, with not a single hair allowed to proclaim its independence by extending beyond the allowable edge, knew this game well. There was nothing new under the sun by the year 2015, until now. *Is it too soon to tell them?* she wondered. Maldonado and Ralph were the only two she really needed, the others were only good for their money and their political connections. Humanity was fast becoming an interconnected multi-celled

14

organism through the internet and myriad social media platforms, perfect for what she had in mind.

"It's going to take longer, much longer than you think. I hope we will all be alive, in a manner of speaking, around 2600 when humanity packs its bags for the big move."

"Ah! Mars!" Burst out the fat assed Aurelio. "I knew it." He didn't seem to have heard the projected time-line.

"No, my voluptuous, repulsive darling – Europa."

Whatever they may have been expecting, it wasn't that. Stunned, eyebrows raised, jaws slightly agape they barely heard Lai-Xii announce the meeting closed. Slowly the prospective date seeped into their awareness. "Ralph, my love, I need a private audience with you." She'd evolved a most effective way of dealing with men; either berating them, flattering them or both in the same sentence, offering much but delivering nothing.

Lai-Xii stood, checked her fringe to ensure it remained horizontal, took Ralph by the arm and led him to a small sparsely furnished room. Abuse; loving, teasing abuse worked on Aurelio. Ralph had different buttons. He craved intimacy. She could tell by his soft puppy dog eyes.

They were barely inside the room when he began. "You said I was on the right track with the evolution angle, elaborate for ..." Lai-Xii put a finger on his lips. No man was going to question her or ever demand anything of her. She let her warm finger linger on his lips for a moment.

"Come, sit beside me." Other than a single chair, the only option was a single bed against the wall opposite the door. She let a hand come to rest on his knee. "Tell me how you're progressing with Tinker Bell."

"You mean the Tengi? How do you know about that?" His attention strayed to focus on the warmth of her hand. Room temperatures in Esso were not exactly comfortable for Westerners and a warm hand a definite distraction.

"You'd better learn quick my pet," giving his knee a gentle rub, "I know all about your technologically engineered individual, and a great deal more. You're having a few problems. Have you not thought to go in the opposite direction?"

Puzzled for a moment Ralph looked to the corner of the room. Having gathered his thoughts, he tried to put his hand on top of hers. "They're only minor immune rejections which we can ..."

Lai-Xii cut him off, slowly sliding her hand out from under his, giving him a chance to regret his move. "What would you call our little band of conspirators if we were to work with photons?" Just another bait she threw into the pond to catch her desired fish.

"But what about Europa?"

"Later, pet, no need for impatience. We have plenty of time." Smiling sweetly Lai-Xii left him sitting on the edge of his bed, wondering what just happened, with the warmth of her hand seeping into his knee.

The four other moguls were still in financial small talk when Lai-Xii returned to the conference room. She stopped for a moment at the entrance, one foot slightly in front of the other, the split crimson silk dress revealing nothing but elegance. It was all about control. She didn't move, wanting to see who would take the first step.

"Xii, may I call you Xii?" Ptolemy asked and was about to say something else before being immediately interrupted.

"No, but you may approach, my rich little cockroach."

Whether it was praise or flattery didn't matter to Ptolemy. He prided himself on being able to survive, and prosper, in the harshest economic circumstances imaginable. For him the Global Financial Crisis was a boon, so the allusion to a cockroach didn't bother him in the least; cockroaches were survivors. He stood beside her in three quick strides.

Putting on her most serious face she said, "Come, let's compare dicks." She had these self-made men completely under control and completely unbalanced. She led, and he followed her to the servery in the far corner of the adjoining room. They were far enough away from the others so their low voices could not be heard clearly.

"I think mine's bigger than yours," whispered Ptolemy, grinning stupidly, though he'd guessed what she was on about.

She ignored that, having already captured his interest. "Just how much money do you really have?" She appealed to his greatest passion, which was the acquisition of wealth. "Could you build me a city for 40,000 people here in Kamchatka?" Lai-Xii asked in conspiratorial tones.

"Just one?" He liked this elegant, dynamic female. *I could use one or two of these on my staff.*

She leaned close to his hairy ear and whispered, "For now. You'll make more money than any bank could hold, especially after you build the second one."

"Sure thing. Just say where." Even before he'd uttered the last syllable Ptolemy realised he'd probably made the biggest mistake of his life, just because he'd come under the spell of this exotic creature who smelled so intoxicating, and whose warm breath still tickled his ear.

"Well, that's the tricky bit. But I'll hold you to your promise." Having no doubt whatsoever about his entrapment, the quick swivel of her hips and a one eighty degree turn made it evident the private interview had concluded.

Ralph in the meantime had returned to the conference room, having lost his previous poker face. As Lai-Xii approached the table they all moved towards their chairs. *Good, they're getting the idea.*

"Not you, Maldonado. You want to know my plan?" He gave a slight, self-important I-want-to-know-it-all nod and looked to the others. They waited.

"Oh, I do indeed have a plan, and you can all be a part of it, if you behave yourselves. Maldonado, I need your advice. Come, let's get a little fresh air." She took him by the hand and led him to the foyer of the timber constructed guest house. He stopped to put on his coat, hat and gloves. She waited patiently outside without augmenting her own attire. They stood facing the white forest, admiring its serenity. The -16^0 temperature did not seem to bother Lai-Xii. Maldonado glanced at her a couple of times, noting with interest her body's obvious reaction to the cold in the tight fitting dress, yet she did not seem to feel it.

"What's the most efficient way to connect people – without them knowing they are being controlled?" According to her he should know, even though he may not have implemented that technology yet.

"To each other, you mean?"

"Yes, and to a central facility."

"Holy crap! You're talking about world domination! Why aren't you cold, by the way?" The distraction was too much.

"No, not domination, simply looking after everyone's welfare. Because it's not cold, compared to Europa. Can you do it through your Me-Me social media app?" she pressed the point.

"Well, yes, almost."

"What's stopping you?"

"Legislation."

"I'll take care of it. Get to work."

Frost had gathered on Lai-Xii's fringe. She allowed that. Even erect nipples had their function, which Salazar noticed as they got back inside.

"You like my dress, do you, fancy boy?" She saw his obvious interest in her anatomical excitation. At sixty-nine he wasn't displeased to be called a boy, certainly not displeased at being able to

derive some pleasure from her femininity. "Let's talk business, boys."
That was their cue to take up their positions at the table again.

Lai-Xii performed her hip swivel walk to Salazar, wiggling to make herself comfortable on his lap, and him decidedly uncomfortable, if not completely distracted.

"This is no way to run a business meeting, I know. But it's so much fun!" Nobody objected to the sentiment. With their wealth they could engage the services of countless numbers of 'entertainers', but none that could hold them enthralled with the promise of world domination and uncountable wealth, and that other unattainable prize.

"The plan?" Aurelio prompted. "How are we going to get to Europa, and what makes you think it's likely to be more hospitable than Earth?"

"How I would like to get my hands on your well upholstered chunk of manhood, my revolting magnificence! But business first. Your contribution starts with supplementing your own larder by selling the right stuff to the rest of humanity." At the magic word 'sell' Aurelio leant forward eager to hear just how much he would have to spend and at what risk. "Maldonado, how many people on this planet?"

"Seven point six billion, give or take."

"How many have mobile phones?"

"Five billion, roughly."

"So you just want me to sell a few more of those?" Aurelio said half-heartedly.

"No, not a few. And how many people are on Me-Me, your social media platform, Maldonado?"

"Three billion and counting," he said happily. It was his territory and he knew the figures. Social media connectivity was his playground. "I'd be happy to have a few more billion connected!"

"Good boy, you're getting the picture."

Aurelio had shut up, mostly because he was ashamed at not seeing the big picture from the outset. So he fired a challenge. "I don't see how getting to Europa and getting people onto Me-Me could possibly be connected."

"I'm going to leave you for a little while and freshen up. Have a chat amongst yourselves. Make your decision. Do you want this or not?" To some extent 'this' became synonymous, by design, with 'me'. She was quietly confident of their decision. "Here's a bank account for you to show your undying love for prosperity by depositing one quarter of your current worth in it. That should give us close to a trillion to start with." She threw a small piece of paper

18

with the hand scribbled account details on the table. Noticing one or two concerned frowns she added, "I'm contributing as well, and you will all have access to the funds for use on our Project." No one moved while Lai-Xii performed her retreat manoeuvres to greatest advantage, all eyes fastened on the rhythm of her movements, momentarily forgetting the slip of paper.

"Outrageous!" Fat boy Aurelio wasted no time in venting his incredulity, perhaps frustration, perhaps unbridled lust. He didn't know himself why he'd let himself get so wound up. "Can you believe this woman! Who the f&$! does she think she is anyway? Any of you know anything about her?"

"Only that she's the richest woman in Japan," volunteered Ralph. "It was reported last year, without her overall wealth being revealed."

"Well at least that's something," said Aurelio still agitated.

"Great body, great mind," Salazar quietly contributed, followed by grunts of acknowledgement from the others.

After a few minutes of introspective speculation on a subject reasonably obvious, Aurelio rallied to try and get a grip on the situation.

"So what have we got here? A mad woman or a brilliant one? Maldonado?" It seems Aurelio became the self-appointed spokesman amongst them.

They started walking about in the room trying to get their minds to see an overview of this most peculiar situation. At last Maldonado responded. "Lai-Xii wants world domination through ..."

"No shit!" Aurelio generally said the first thing that came to his mind.

"... through total connectivity and surveillance of the worlds entire population. What do you make of that?"

Stunned silence thundered through the space between the four walls. "She wants to use our money," Ptolemy stated what he believed to be the bottom line, "and – she wants me to build a city, here in Kamchatka I think."

"I don't agree. It's not just about money. Think about it – speeding up human evolution to achieve immortality and pissing off to Europa - all by 2600." Ralph seemed to be on top of the concept. "Oh, and did I mention she wants to accelerate the Transhuman Project?

By some osmotic common consent they all gravitated back to their seats, deep in thought. Ralph finished voicing his thoughts just as Aurelio reached for the paper with the bank account details.

"We don't even know where in the LGBTQIAUCPT2 spectrum she fancies herself."

Whatever Lai-Xii's strategy was, it had its effect. Most unexpectedly Aurelio pulled out his mobile, punched in the numbers to make his contribution and said flatly to the others, "Do it."

The decision had been made and it was unanimous and it was uncertain and it scared the crap out of each one of them. Still breathing the sense of impending financial ruin, a feeling of an exhilarating challenge, the overwhelming fascination with Lai-Xii, no less than unbridled greed of wealth, it took a little while for the sounds of a piano to prise open their consciousness to the cold Kamchatkan reality.

Lai-Xii didn't return to them to accept their acquiescence to her desires. They had to go to her. Down a short corridor the door opened on their approach to the disturbing sounds of György Ligeti's Désordre etude. Five silk embroidered pillows, arranged carelessly behind Lai-Xii at the piano, invited the curious band to take up their positions. Aurelio tried to move his to better see her face but it would not budge. They all had to sit, listen and admire her geisha kimono attired back, adorned with a square, narrow and green knot. Their focus turned from the discordant sounds to the vision of a geisha in an orange yellow kimono, blue trim and white collar, low on the back. The only clue to her identity was the jet black short bob cast over the snow white complexion of her neck. Lai-Xii wanted to display, to overwhelm, to show these 'men' the living work of art that would for ever be out of their reach, without forbidding them hope of attaining it.

Suddenly the banging stopped. None of them knew the melody, or the composer, yet the chaotic cacophony struck their mind more forcefully for the sudden cessation of it. She turned agonisingly slowly to face them. "We will create order and harmony for the human race. We will become the future of mankind. We already are. Look at what you have all achieved; consider the power you already share between you."

"How do you know we have agreed to support this venture," Aurelio couldn't help himself. The hollowest vessel makes the loudest sound, yet his pockets were the deepest.

"We have just set up Phototronic Systems Incorporated." Lai-Xii said. She remained seated like a teacher in front her class of little children facing her with eager anticipation. Her geisha training proved once again to be invaluable in the service of her ambition.

The men of Phototronic Systems gazed upon the pale skinned, vibrant crimson lipped architect of their future, unable to compose coherent questions with which to unbalance her composure. "The work has already started. I don't need to explain the plan; you already know it and our deadline. First we must deal with my thalidomide children, to which end I will need that city at your earliest convenience please, Ptolemy."

They remained seated, stunned, waiting. Aurelio's voice broke the silence. "Who are these thalidomide kids? What do they have to do with us?"

"They are the beginnings of the new civilisation. Any other intelligent questions? Do any of you *not* know what to do? Sort out your strategy in the next two days. I can't wait to hear what you have to say. You know where my room is." They all remained cushioned, still waiting. It was all too sudden, all too strange, all too expensive and for some goddamn incomprehensible reason all had put their fortunes on the line. "Well! What are you waiting for my darling maggots? Go! Get on with it!"

FROM THE BOOK OF ORIGINATION
DECLARATIONS FOUR

4:1 And the Lai-Xii had dominion over that which was to come.

4

THALIDOMIDE VICTIMS, GEN 2

CE 2020
RESEARCH FACILITY
NEAR KLYUCHI

"WHEN will the city be ready, you sad specimen of humanity?" Lai-Xii smiled sweetly at Ptolemy five years later.

"You still haven't told me who's going to live there."

"People, of course. Several thousand of my young maiko."

"Young maiko?"

"When? Don't make me ask again cockroach." She held an index finger to his temple as if simulating a squash.

"Two months. Who?" In the years since he joined the team Ptolemy had come to savour her endearments.

"Come with me. I'll introduce you to our house mother."

The temporary research complex was sufficiently spread out for them to have to use a small electric vehicle to get to the office. Ptolemy was disturbed by the time they arrived. He'd seen them, but wasn't quite sure what they were. Lai-Xii deliberately took the long way to expose him to what she called her 'young maiko'.

Ptolemy was an 'entire', he had all his extremities, never giving a thought to anyone whose body was less than perfect. Sure, he'd seen many amputees during his sixty-five years, but to see so many children without arms and legs … that's when he suddenly realized what he'd been observing during the ride … thalidomide victims – at least he assumed they were victims.

Lai-Xii watched his reaction. She'd already told the team about the first stage of the plan. "You probably think these poor children are all victims of thalidomide side-effects. They're not victims. Their parents have been extremely well compensated and will be happy to return to Brazil to their villages very wealthy, knowing their children will be well cared for."

Ptolemy turned slowly towards her, understanding nothing about the connection between building a city and these children. "Are these what you call your 'young maiko'?" The sick churning in his stomach had begun – the one you get when you realize you've just jumped out of the plane without a parachute. *How could I let myself get involved with this lunatic?* Then he suddenly understood why his city had to be built without steps, with buildings no more than two stories high and lifts. "It's for them, isn't it, the city?"

"Yes and no – more for their descendants. But I'll let doctor Evgeniya Yermolov explain in more detail. She's a genetic engineer, molecular biologist and a neurologist."

Unlike his own, her office was almost bare; nothing but an annular table in the exact centre of the smallish room to accommodate twenty. No windows and no ornamentation on the walls except computer screens flush with the wall surfaces. Evgeniya cleared them all as her two visitors entered. She didn't bother to stand from her seat.

"Hello Evgen, my chick," We're almost ready to move into our long term accommodation. "My sugar-daddy here has done a good job – so far." It was the first time Lai-Xii had not expressed contempt for Ptolemy. He was as much surprised by that as the extraordinarily beautiful red-headed Russian scientist at the table. "Please explain to him what you've been doing for the past six years."

"Hello, velcome to facility. Please take seat. Ourr long terrm objective is to reduce burden on brrain of day-to-day management of body."

Ptolemy looked to Lai-Xii, puzzled. Smart and wealthy but not a scientist, he couldn't understand how engineered thalidomide people would be suitable subjects for colonising Europa. "You didn't think we'd migrate in our current form, did you silly boy?"

"So that's why Ralph is on the team!"

"Yes, my rancid dumpling. He will take us past the 'transhuman' experiment to something far more interesting. Haven't you heard of the 2045 Initiative? Well advanced now but beleaguered by too many insurmountable problems. It was and still is a misconceived path to neo-humanity. The way to achieve immortality isn't by augmenting our existing architecture but by creating a new one. Isn't that so, Evgen darling?"

"Ve have to vork with human genome. Make changes zat vill reproduce naturally."

Lai-Xii had made her way over to Evgeniya while she was talking, standing so close that her upper leg touched Evgeniya's arm. "My delicious Evgen is a very clever girl," she purred as she stroked Evgeniya's cascading red hair."

"Da – da ..." warming to her subject, "Ve now have enough subjects from which to understand transcription signals used to rregulate expression of particular koding sequences which ..."

"Stop there my dear. Simple language for a simple, very rich monkey. What Evgen is telling you is quite straightforward. We will create humans with fewer body parts to make it easier for the brain to function with less distractions. Our city will be populated by the descendants of these babies you saw, with normal people to help them with a few basic functions."

Technically these second generation infants were not a result of random mutations caused by inappropriate use of thalidomide. Their parents, the original victims, had already undergone 'treatment'. Sperm DNA and egg DNA modifications produced tetra-amelia syndrome babies, generally considered to be a rare disorder characterized by the absence of arms and legs. Dr. Evgeniya Yermolov's successful specimens were achieved by inhibiting the development of blood vessels destined for the extremities. By eliminating those embryos with limb development, she hoped to use the others as seed populations to continue the trend, with further genetic engineering to ensure continued success; which would ultimately be measured by how many more body parts could be made redundant.

"So this is what you meant when you said evolution was too slow. You are one crazy chick, Lai-Xii."

"Eventually their energy requirements will be met without the necessity of our cumbersome digestive system. You're going to have to re-think what you believe is beautiful. You might not want me without my – curves. Our brains can adjust to change a lot faster than our bodies."

On the way out of the research centre they were met by numerous adults without arms or legs, some in wheelchairs others with advanced prosthesis, accompanied by carers. Not a single sad face amongst them, all happily going about their business. "Neural implants enable them to communicate with their mobility units, no problems at all."

25

"When do we see income from your clever technology?"

"*Our* clever technology, dear. How old do you think I am?"

"That's an odd question." Finding himself suddenly on the spot Ptolemy blustered something about twenty-eight.

"What a darling man you are. Our age control technology has already earned us many millions since we set up Phototronic Systems Inc. You should keep a closer eye on your investment."

Lai-Xii kept throwing curve balls at him. He'd been a lot happier concentrating on building that stupid city in the middle of the Kamchatkan wilderness. He still couldn't fathom how disabled people with electronic implants could possibly get off the planet to colonize a Jovian moon. '*And what does age have to do with it - the next exploratory flight in 2022 to Europa is only expected to take four years. — 'Not migrate in our current form' — what the hell did she mean by that?* His thoughts puddled.

"Get the team together back in Esso, I have a little surprise for you all; an update on our Project."

*

Not a single blue cloud floated by in the sky anywhere above Esso. An overcast day with just enough light to create a slight glare off the snow bank right beside the wooden deck of the small hot-spring pool of the guest house. The men arrived in a convoy, without a happy face amongst them, except perhaps Aurelio and Maldonado who arrived together in one vehicle. The report Aurelio received on the way to the meeting indicated he was right on target to achieving the six billion mark for mobile phone sales. Which was in line with Maldonado having added an extra six hundred million to his Me-Me social platform. They were looking forward to reporting their progress to Lai-Xii.

She didn't greet them in the reception area, though she'd watched them arrive on closed-circuit. As they stood around grumbling while waiting for Lai-Xii, the guest house owner humbly shuffled forward to pass on her instructions.

"Please, take off clothes, go naked to pool in back."

"What did you say?" Salazar though he'd heard right, hoped he'd heard right, a little life coming back to his old eyes.

"Lady say, swim."

"You heard the man," Aurelio seemed eager to comply all of a sudden. Methods used to achieve obscene wealth had long ago removed most inhibitions from these men, especially the obese Aurelio.

The hot-spring pool at the back was a mostly private affair, though prying eyes not completely blocked by the rotting paling fence.

The men, wrapped in ill-fitting bathrobes made their way along the creaking wooden short boardwalk, flanked by highly piled snowdrifts. Ralph almost fell off the slippery edge. He saw Lai-Xii first, serenely floating on her back, naked in the middle of the small pool, her two flotation devices prominently visible.

"About time boys. I thought I'd have to play by myself!" She purred.

Miraculously the previous gloom lifted, as Lai-Xii threw the first snowball. Aurelio's girth almost emptied the pool onto the snow as he projected his disgusting folds of flesh in Lai-Xii's direction. Even Ralph jumped, though Salazar demurely made his way to the steps, only to be conked on the head by another huge ball cast by Lai-Xii. She was laughing and carrying on like a school girl on a holiday – except this was serious business. Gradually Salazar floated his way to the other end dodging bombarding snow balls, joining the others surrounding Lai-Xii.

"You can give me your reports later," she said treading water in the lull of play, rotating slowly to fix each man with a steel hard stare. "Are you prepared to give all this up?"

"Why did you have to say that? I was having such a good time," whined Maldonado as he reluctantly raised his eyes from her breasts.

Lai-Xii wasn't listening. She'd begun her sprint to the steps and was out of the water before the boys could recover their manly composures, which was hard to do while watching Lai-Xii walk slowly to her robe. Unfortunately, *it* fitted perfectly.

They didn't gather in the meeting room. That was set up for a very special procedure, for which the swim in the pool was preparation. Lai-Xii indulged her passion on the piano, cushions on the floor as previously. They filed in, dressed in bathrobes, taking up their positions below her like good little school children.

"Ptolemy thinks I look good for my age, don't you dear." Then she abruptly changed focus. "You lot look disgusting. How long do you expect to live? How much of your wealth would it take to extend your miserable lives by just one year, eh?" She finished the sentence with a flourish on the keyboard before turning around to face them. "Don't bother to report, I know exactly what each of you has been doing. You'll have to move along with finishing the city, Ptolemy. Have you thought about my young maiko at Klyuchi? I'm sure you've figured it out by now."

"Right. Lai-Xii is ..." She stopped him for a slight correction, "We, dear cockroach – *We*."

"We are creating a new kind of human," Ptolemy glanced at Lai-Xii to make sure he was getting this correct, receiving a confirming head tilt, "whose brain will not have to concern itself with – with – so many mundane body housekeeping functions."

"Keep going, you're doing great."

"… with whom it will be easier to implement the transhuman technology."

"Close, darling. When living in a digital environment we don't really want to be concerned about all those inconvenient bodily functions."

"That's your cue, my puppy dog," she nodded at Ralph.

"We started by developing implants with which to augment the capabilities of the human body." Ralph continued speaking while turning on a mobile phone sized remote control unit. "A spinoff was increased life expectancy, though not without a few issues. However …"

The door opened. A Tengi walked in, turned, closed the door, turned and walked up to Ralph who was by then standing. "Hello," he said, looking for all the world like an average twenty-five year old healthy Asian male, "and hello to the lady."

"This is Tengi," Ralph introduced him. He is a Technically Engineered Individual. He's not 'human' by conventional standards, though he behaves like one." Ralph put the remote in his pocket to free both hands. Lai-Xii watched Ptolemy's reaction with amusement as Ralph gave the Tengi's head a short sharp twist to the left, then to the right lifting it off his shoulder and putting it on the corner of the piano.

"Now, this is the important bit," Ralph said nonchalantly. "How are you today Tengi," he asked as he removed the remote from his pocket again, twitching something on it.

"Very well thank you Ralph," Tengi answered from the piano as his body obeyed commands from the remote to walk up to the door, open it, walk out and stand there waiting.

Ralph's organisation had achieved not just sophisticated robotics but something far more important. Tengi was intelligent, from an artificial perspective, stronger and faster than any human individual. He also had artificial sensory input capabilities. He could detect the location of the door handle and when he touched it, he could gauge exactly how much pressure to apply. He heard Ralph's question and also knew there was a female in the room from her odour.

"You are not impressed, my startled meercats?" The four men made no comments, temporarily taken aback by the decapitation. "You should be. Which part of Tengi is really Tengi, do you think? The body that walked out, or the head that stayed here to talk to us?"

28

Salazar, about to say something, changed his mind when Tengi responded, "I am here on the piano."

"Would you all agree with that?" Lai-Xii was obviously leading up to something.

Still no one responded. Salazar raised his old bones off the cushion to go and stand in front of Tengi's head. Then a few minutes later he made his way to the door. Lai-Xii had an idea what he was doing so asked Ralph to activate the body again, and followed Salazar. He walked up to the headless body, watched it slowly make his way to a bench by the wall and settle before becoming inactive again. Salazar stood there deeply thoughtful until Lai-Xii disturbed him. "You like?"

Whatever was going on in his head he didn't reply, just shook his head slowly from side to side, as old men do when they're introspective, and moved to go back into the piano room. Lai-Xii stepped ahead of him, with a slight swaying of her hips. She could have chosen from a half dozen other wealthy billionaires. He just happened to be the right age for what she had in mind and he was still sexually active, which gave her just another button to press.

"The point here is," Ralph continued after watching the interesting pantomime, "it is possible for the brain to function without the body."

Ptolemy became curious as to just how far the thalidomide experiments could successfully reduce the brain's reliance on the body. "Are you trying to suggest that we may be able to achieve whole brain emulation?"

"No, no, my dim-witted wombat. How could that possibly help us if we had to drag a physical body to such an inhospitable place as the surface of Europa. How could we possibly maintain it, house it, enable it to reproduce? Come with me children, I have a little surprise for you."

By feeding them small packets of information, just enough to keep them excited but not enough to turn them off the impossibility of her plans, Lai-Xii maintained control over her wealthy brood. They were all risk takers and each could see remote yet real probabilities of harvesting fabulous fortunes from the technologies Lai-Xii had seduced them to fund.

She fell in beside Salazar. "Ah, to be young again – at least as virile as a young buck," she whispered to him just to firm up the hook on the end of his line. All her men had a job to do except Salazar. In some ways his would be the most important.

The small conference room had been completely transformed, looking more like a workshop with several surgical tables, laser scanners, 3D printers and several technicians milling about.

They crowded into the room expecting anything but what looked like an experimental laboratory.

"What's all this," Aurelio asked, true to form before taking the time to look and comprehend.

Maldonado had been quiet, trying to piece together the jig-saw puzzle. How did his social media platform, Me-Me, tie in with bodiless people and cyborgs? The connection seemed too remote, but he did catch on to the last couple of revelations. "If we, that is – a seed population – could be engineered with brains independent of their biological bodily functions, then – then ..." and he lost his train of thought at that point.

Lai-Xii continued, "... then our life expectancy would be greatly enhanced, as well as making it easier to take the next step in our transition. I see there are no objections, so let's get on with it."

There were only five tables and five technicians. Maldonado, sharp as a tack noted it as soon as they'd entered. "Why are there only five tables?"

"Were you expecting company, darling?"

"No. What about you?"

"Let me explain what's going to happen here. Each of you will have a complete body print taken, accurate to the last hair follicle – unless you desire something more youthful, more streamlined – perhaps even another gender." She waited a moment to gauge the effect. They were getting used to her bizarre methods so they just waited to hear her out. "The new bodies for your wonderful, fertile imaginations should be ready in a few years."

"But how do you know it will work. What guarantee can you give us?" Aurelio wasn't going to accept her word on face value.

"Believe me, it works! Why do you think there are only five tables?" With that last bombshell Lai-Xii left the room, leaving them to cogitate, procrastinate, argue and eventually succumb to the allure of an extended life span with no apparent limitations. Only Aurelio decided on a more streamlined, youthful Spanish male body. He'd become tired of carrying around his corpulent reminder of a life of excess.

It would be many years before the transition could be made from a biological support mechanism for the brain and an engineered energy source to feed it. In the interim Lay-Xii needed to keep her collaborators fresh, fully functional and forever hopeful.

5

INTERNAL UNREST

CE 2050
TAU CITY, KAMCHATKA
DOCTOR EVGENIYA YERMOLOV'S
LABORATORY

THE KAMCHATKAN PENINSULA is a harsh environment by any standards; rugged terrain, difficult climate and even more difficult conditions in which to eke out an existence. This walled city boasting several gates, flourished in the valley between snow-capped volcanoes, complete after thirty years of hard work. Neat well maintained houses with municipal buildings spaced comfortably around parks, well-ordered avenues - the roads all in good condition were a most unusual sight in rural Russian cities even in the 22nd century, especially with people happily going about their business.

Tau City was fully operational for the maintenance of the third and fourth generations of thalidomide children. The world didn't know of their existence. A specially established Russian military force maintained strict perimeter control in Kamchatka. The rouble had a loud voice in Russia, even louder than the prospect of colonizing another heavenly body in the solar system. Communication with the rest of the world was not permitted. An internal undercover force maintained security inside the city. But humanity, being what it was, inevitably developed relationships between the security forces and the residents of the city, leading to some problems.

31

But that's not why Lai-Xii called her men to the scientist's laboratory. She was ready to implement the first phase of her long term plan; transhuman technology upon her very rich collaborators. They'd already had full medical check-ups weeks before arriving back in Kamchatka. She made them have another on the day of their arrival.

"Congratulations to you all, especially to you Ptolemy. You have built a wonderful city for my maiko children. How many can it support?"

"Several thousand to start with and plenty of room for expansion. I don't understand how you intend to get people from around the world living in peace with one another."

"It's called, *the good life*. Each individual will be meticulously vetted. They will be well supported, given meaningful work and allowed to have as many healthy children as they wish. As you know, they have one single purpose for being alive. To procreate while being as healthy and well balanced as any human being can be."

"Yes, but what are we going to do with them?" Maldonado wasn't particularly concerned for them, he just wanted to be kept up to date with progress, which was not always an easy thing when working with Lai-Xii. She kept her cards very close to her chest. That didn't concern him either, for the profits they were reaping from an occasional leak of their technology was well worth the 'Lai-Xii intrigue factor' as the five men called her methods between themselves.

"If you must know," she confided as she asked them all to gather close to her, "they are our brain 'seed' population when we need to harvest more to replenish any losses in our next line of experimentation."

"So they're like the Eloi and we're the Morlocks," Salazar commented as if he wasn't especially impressed with the imagery it brought to mind.

"Exactly. But *we* are not going to eat them." She kept them on their toes year after year after year. How could they object? They had all signed up for the enterprise, funded it, been working on it for close on thirty-five years and reaping enormous profits in the process. They were in too deep.

"I could use a few extra neurons," said Salazar, "not to mention a few new bones."

"I'm glad you brought that up, my sexy nonagenarian. Today is your lucky day, for all of you. But first an update about our citizens here."

On their way to the Yermolov's laboratory complex, Aurelio commented on how few adults there seemed to be in relation to so many ten to fifteen-year old children. The children seemed happy enough, curious about the visitors like any child would be.

"Doctor Yermolov, please update your guests."

"Velcome to my laborratory." Her accent hadn't improved in thirty years in spite of her having to often use English.

"Where are all the adults," Aurelio couldn't wait patiently like the others.

"Zat is exactly vat I vill explain." Evgeniya held her composure in the face of these most important people. She knew who they were and she was aware of their power. Most successful Russians, either in business or science or any other professional field, always knew the power base of those above and around them.

"You were actually looking at many parents. The adults arre karetakers, assistants and inkubatorrs."

"I don't understand," Aurelio jumped in again.

"Shut up my corpulent little piggy, let the good doctor continue. All of you, listen." They'd been standing around curious about all the operating theatre equipment. No one else was in there except themselves, Lai-Xii and the genetic engineer, Evgeniya.

"When the children arre around twelve years old ve harvest sperm and eggs, modify DNA and go to next stage of in-vitro fertilisation before fertilized eggs arre transferred to uterus. Some of children arre allowed to develop into young adulthood after prrocedure." Then Evgeniya added very proudly, "Ve have outstanding success rate of tetra-amelia prrogeny. Next, ve vill try reproduction vizout DNA modifikation." The expectation was that the new generation would be born 'naturally' tetra-amelia. Then the process could continue to the following stages of further reducing unnecessary body parts and organs.

They were so engrossed in the moment that none of them noticed Evgeniya's vibrant physical appearance. It was as if she had not aged in the intervening years. She'd had the same enhancements as Harusuke and Lai-Xii ahead of the men. The ravages of time had less of an effect on a body modified by replacement artificial vital organs − but not the brain, not yet. Her only original vital organs remaining were her kidneys. She, like the other members of the team, was determined to cheat death as long as possible. To that end Evgeniya lived a rigorously healthy lifestyle, taking particular care of her renal wellbeing. Lai-Xii brought their attention to Evgeniya's appearance for a reason. "She not only looks good boys, she is in top condition."

"Like you, you mean," Salazar had a small issue on his mind, very much related to what he was seeing with his ninety-years old eyes.

"We are not quite ready to do the Tengi trick, but Evgeniya here is ready to make you all feel a whole lot better. It's no accident we're in the operating theatre. She's going to replace some of your gizzards." Lai-Xii looked each one squarely in the eye as she moved from one to the other. Though she saw a little trepidation in one or two of them, the general consensus seemed to be for all systems go.

"How long is this going to take," Aurelio always needed to know everything.

"Oh, not long – about four months. Roughly twenty hours for the operation and the rest to give your body and brain time to integrate the changes. Don't look so worried, I'll look after your investment."

Evgeniya, keen to get started ushered the patients out of theatre towards pre-op situated at the end of the corridor. As they passed the lift, its doors opened to disgorge six people; a Russian internal security guard in uniform, three pregnant women and two adolescents about thirteen years old in wheelchairs. They didn't expect to meet the reason for their infiltration, in the corridor. Standing in front of the lift and seeing the small group of people, none of whom they could immediately identify, they turned to the security guard. He didn't know what to do. His job didn't require more than getting them into the complex. The pregnant women turned in the direction of an official looking woman moving towards them.

Lai-Xii, aware that only surgeons, technicians, patients and themselves were authorised to be on that floor, immediately reached into her pocket to activate the alarm on her mobile. It would take perhaps five minutes at the most for security to arrive. The surprised group waited, watching the strange looking woman step between themselves and another small group moving away from them down the corridor.

She smiled, raised a hand in greeting and said, "Hello, you must be lost." It wasn't a real smile – but one of those 'I'm onto you and you won't get away with it' smiles, taking command of the situation.

The guard confronted her. "We are not lost. We've come to talk to Dr. Yermolov," automatically raising his weapon slightly in the doctor's direction, an indication of a possible threatening situation developing. Evgeniya's brood stopped on hearing Lai-Xii's voice. They saw the guard's weapon come up to the horizontal. They didn't know what to do. They were business men not urban guerrilla fighters.

"You can talk to me, I'm the doctor's boss." She wasn't going to give away any more information than was necessary. Her anonymity was important for the Project. Except for all the important people she needed to make confidential arrangements with, like the president of Russia, she kept a low profile.

"NO. We must speak with the doctor."

Lai-Xii frowned, unhappy with the interruption to her day's plan, and displeased at the unauthorised presence of these people in the building. The most worrying aspect was the reason they were there in the first place. She needed to know what the problem was, as much as to stretch the time to allow security to arrive before anything drastic happened. She stepped closer to the Officer, leaning in a little so he could feel her breath on his face and enquired, "What is your name Officer?" giving just the right amount of intonation to make him feel the insignificance of the importance he'd assumed for himself.

"Captain Viktor Pyryev!" He almost saluted.

"What are you doing, Viktor?"

"We must speak with Dr. Yermolov," a woman called Yulia, standing near Viktor, interrupted Lai-Xii's interrogation in Russian.

Lai-Xii ignored her for the moment. "Viktor, come sit with me, tell me what the problem is." She'd put her hand lightly on his weapon wielding arm giving it the slightest pressure forcing him to lower it, as she moved away from the two groups. All this time Evgeniya was hidden from view by the five men behind her who remained transfixed to the spot.

Viktor, poor man, couldn't help himself when coming under the control of the polished, practiced geisha's skills. With his finger still hovering at the ready he sat with Lai-Xii on the bench near the wall, just a few steps away.

"So tell me ..." Viktor was already perspiring, feeling highly uncomfortable for several reasons. He thought this would be easy ... just let the delegation in, let them have their chat with the doctor and leave. Instead it was getting complicated, especially when he saw a large contingent of security guards appear from around the corner at the other end of the corridor. Lai-Xii followed his glance, raising her hand to stop the advance. That's all she wanted, to have the advantage. Now she would find out what brought about this strange behaviour.

"I don't know anything. It's Yulia you should talk to. She's behind it all."

"I see ... and why did you bring your weapon, Viktor?"

He liked her calling him by his first name. "I always carry it, Ma'am."

"Thank you Viktor. You may go back to your men. We will say no more about this, Captain Viktor Pyryev." In parting she pronounced his name in full giving him the message she knew exactly who he was, which wasn't always a good thing in the Russian forces. Turning back to the two groups, she waved her team on while at the same time calling to Yulia, all the while remaining seated. She had always found, from her time as a geisha, that taking the subordinate position gave her quarry a false sense of control.

"Yulia, ladies, children - come."

Though their grievance was strong, the situation they found themselves in had diffused the impetus with which they'd arrived. Yulia was no fool. She sat beside Lai-Xii while the others remained standing. The security guards also remained quietly waiting out of earshot. Dr. Yermolov and the team disappeared into pre-op.

"I - that is we, have been chosen to speak on behalf of our community. The people and the children are not happy."

"Why is that, Yulia?" She moved just a little closer to the pregnant woman. "Are they in pain? Do they not have enough to eat? Has the heating broken down?"

"No, no – it's not about that. We don't know what you are doing. There are all these children who are always born disabled, and we mothers who have them, we are not allowed to keep them and raise them as our own."

"Is that what you want? - to look after the children you carry? Perhaps it is a desire difficult to manage with your disability – don't you think?"

"Yes, no – partly. They want to be able to have their own children too."

Lai-Xii could see a lot more bubbled under the surface. As much as she would have liked to treat these people purely as experimental subjects, it wasn't possible. They were human beings after all. Without them the whole enterprise would fold. It was vital to test if the human brain could be reconfigured and its contents actually digitized. If the brain could adapt well to not having its full human biological support system to control and to support it, then real progress could be made. These thalidomide generations served only one purpose; to be the first subjects for the download trials in a few generations. Because of early harvesting of eggs and sperm, it wasn't necessary to wait for the full adult maturation term of the individuals. That brought with it many issues, some of which Lai-Xii suspected underlined the discontent being represented to her in the corridor.

"How many of you want this?" She knew from her own life experience that democracy by the majority was nothing more than the manipulated wishes of a few. So there may not have been a problem at all. Still, best to nip any discontent in the bud.

36

Yulia wasn't sure. "Everyone I spoke to," she said, and the other two women representatives nodded in agreement.

"What about you, children? Is this what you want?"

The two girls seemed happy enough. They'd known no other life. Being the way they were seemed completely natural to them. It's the way they were born. With all the services and help at their disposal, life had no hardships for them, though they were a little envious at times of the few full bodied children. The older one had the courage to reply to this very imposing young woman who seemed to be in control of everything. "I am only fifteen years old, so I'm not ready to have children yet, but one day I think I would like to. Though I'm not sure how I could look after them."

"You are a very smart young lady. What is your name?"

"Klara, Ma'am."

Yulia interrupted the pleasant interchange. That's not why they were there. "You still haven't told us what you are doing in this city with all the disabled children."

A wide smile spread over Lai-Xii's face. She knew exactly what to say to them, and it was the complete truth, though perhaps not a full disclosure of their methodology. "I can't believe no one has told you. I thought everybody knew. There are many people born with disabilities in this world. We just happen to have more here than anywhere else. We are trying to find a way to make life as normal as possible for everybody. That's what you are all doing here; helping us do that. Now tell me, are you not happy here? Don't you have everything you need? Don't you have a good life here?"

It was true, they did have everything. Good food, excellent medical care, good education, even meaningful employment for the adults in helping to run a small town of now several thousand people. "What if ...," Lai-Xii pretended to think for a moment, "what if I could arrange for you three ladies, and some of your friends, to look after the babies you are carrying, as your own?" They were not the babies' biological mothers, but bonds become strong regardless of biological origins.

The women glanced at each other, surprised it wasn't so difficult to get something done. "What about all of the pregnant women?" asked one of the other ladies.

"Now let's not get too ahead of ourselves. Let's just see how you manage on your own for a start. Don't forget, we are here to help if it becomes too difficult for you." They couldn't disagree with that. At least this woman knew about their situation, appearing to empathise with them. Then Lai-Xii turned to Klara. "You, young lady, you come and see me when you're a bit older and we'll talk." Not wanting to seem patronizing she didn't pat her on the head, rather giving her an 'adult' look. She had great practice as a geisha at the tea houses in Japan at how to put on a wide variety of 'faces' to please a wide variety of men, and women.

Lai-Xii stood, waved the guards to move away, saying nothing more to the delegation, certain all she had achieved was to gain a little time. Soon they would have to start the serious part of the experiment. Ralph only needed to run the last set of tests on the hardware, secreted away in the main laboratory. In the meantime, the sensory deprivation tests had also to be started.

Yulia sensed their interview had concluded. She ushered her group back to the lift, the children following. They had complete control through their neural implants over their mobility units using thought commands. It was as much effort for them, after some practice, as telling your legs to carry your body. Lai-Xii hurried over to pre-op. The corridor incident raised some worrying issues needing to be dealt with before her men went under the knife for their first major transition.

They'd all gone through the formalities, milling about in their hospital gowns waiting for Lai-Xii. "So what was that all about?" Aurelio asked, as the others anticipated he would.

*

"There is some degree of unrest among our experimental population. The current situation can be managed with a little administrative tweaking, but I think we'll have to push our plans along a bit. After twenty years we have all the adult seed population we need for the time being."

"Indeed we do," agreed the now seventy-three year old Ralph. "I was planning to test the Tengi technology immediately after our upgrades."

"That's just as well. And you'll have to do some comprehensive work with the effects of sensory deprivation at the same time. Has there been any unrest at all, any serious security breaches, Salazar?"

Salazar, effectively the Mayor of the town, had his finger on the pulse of the internal life there. Other than populating the metropolis with healthy male and female specimens, the scientific work had not impacted unduly on the community. "There are no undercurrents of dissatisfaction other than normal mumblings and grumblings of average citizenry. That will change of course when we have Tengi descendants wandering about. Who knows? It's all ground breaking work we're doing. Risks have to be taken."

"Well said, my sexy Sal. It's inevitable we'll meet opposition more and more as our work progresses, but I can tell you this … we are not alone. The world's major governments are with us. They have no delusions about the future of our species. They have realised it is impossible to control population growth. It will be impossible to feed everyone or even to maintain relative peace on the planet. Our vision, *our* solution is the one they have all been looking for – to get humanity off the Earth. They don't care how we do it as long as the upper echelon are guaranteed of, can I say – 'salvation' – for themselves. It's only the few religious nuts who think we're heading towards Armageddon with our plans. They're the ones we have to look out for. Before I let you go with Evgeniya so she can play with your bodies, just a couple of questions for you Maldonado. How many are now connected to Me-Me, and how many are addicted?"

"The good news is, approximately four billion connected with an estimated three and half billion addicted. I have made the social network indispensable for people. It's easy for them to spend their money, arrange entertainment, connect with others albeit on a superficial level, get their daily hit of news and gossip and so on. We've got them. All we have to do now is to get the message out using Virtual Reality. It is so much more *fun* than actual reality. When the time comes to recruit travellers for the exodus, I doubt we'll have any problems getting plenty of takers."

"Right boys, we're on track. I'll see you in about four months. I'll have your profits ready for you to gloat over." She turned, wiggled her way out of the room, perhaps by habit but unlikely, to a rendezvous with Harusuke.

Their apartment in the Town Centre, only one block from the laboratory gave Lai-Xii a chance to clear her head in the fresh air of the Kamchatkan peninsula. She never allowed herself to show her uneasiness to the team. Perhaps she should have indulged in a longer walk now that the men were safely under sedation. It gave her pleasure to see her many maiko going about their lives apparently contented with their condition. She looked after them, she loved them in a remote sort of way. They were helping to fulfil her ambition.

At home the two women greeted each other with genuine affection; something her five men were unlikely to ever experience from Lai-Xii, though they all lived in hope. Harusuke had been with Lai-Xii throughout their entire lives since meeting as children in the geisha house. She was always there in the background, supporting Lai-Xii by providing valuable feedback on her plans, her problems and the five men in her life.

39

"You've had a hard day?" Harusuke asked as she prepared some refreshments, sensing the tension in her partner.

"No, just a minor complication. Some people came to see me today, unexpected visitors, who said they were unhappy.

I can't imagine why. They have everything they need. Don't they realise their crucial role in the evolution of the human species?"

"Have you told them?"

"Not in as many words. It's too complicated, they wouldn't understand."

Then Harusuke asked a most surprising question, "Do *you* understand, Xii?"

"Why do you ask that? Of course I do. I am completely dedicated to this. I have given my life to this, in the past and all there is left of it."

"What I was meaning – do you know why you are doing this?"

"Of course I ..." Lai-Xii didn't finish her sentence. Harusuke could always put her finger on the sore spot. She started again, "I ... damn it, I can't help myself. It's just something that must be done. It – must – be – done."

"You have a brilliant mind and a tortured soul. You don't have to prove you are a person of worth, not to me, not to yourself, not to anyone. You were betrayed in the past, treated with contempt as a worthless thing just because you were born a girl. That's in the past. What you are doing is so extraordinary it's impossible to put into words. You have taken human evolution by the horns and you have subjugated it to your will. What you're doing is right. There will be many sacrifices along the way, for you and humanity, but that's a small price to pay for the continued existence of our species. What's the alternative? There is no alternative." She said these things with conviction, with love, with complete faith in the future Lai-Xii was creating.

During the entire monologue Lai-Xii kept her eyes on Harusuke. If there was one person on the planet she could trust without reservation it was her devoted lifelong partner and friend. Harusuke finished making the tea, served it for the two of them and sat opposite Lai-Xii on the tatami mat. All that needed to be said had been said. It was time for tea.

6

WHOLE BRAIN EMULATION

CE 2052
TAU CITY,
RALPH'S RESEARCH COMPLEX

THE FIVE MEN had been transferred to another complex for physiotherapy. Months of demanding physical exercise occupied most of their time, and they already felt much better. The bio-prosthesis for their natural hearts, kidneys and livers produced no rejection symptoms. Artificial materials like titanium, silicon and dacron polyester have no cellular structure and therefore no surface marker molecules for the body's immune system to worry about. Their recovery time of several months was more a matter of healing from the surgical invasion, after being placed in stasis to speed up the process.

It was only the first of four transitional stages they needed to go through, with life expectancy increasing exponentially at each successful transition. At a hundred and four Salazar was still in pretty good shape, as good as the best of medical technology of the day could provide, yet after the operation he felt thirty years old, though retaining his Galapagos Island turtle skin. Lai-Xii's eventual visit found him and the others working out hard, strengthening their muscles in the hydrotherapy pool.

"Well if it isn't my young bucks!" Without exception they all started grinning from ear to ear as they swam to the edge of the pool,

41

playfully splashing Lai-Xii in the process. "Are you going to be naughty boys?"

"Not us," Salazar laughed, happy as a young pup who'd just discovered he had a tail, "we've got a heap of work ahead of us. Right? Coming in?"

She ignored the invitation. "Good to see you shedding those saddle bags, Aurelio." Everyone easily got out of the pool and began towelling off.

"Is this what you went through?" Asked Aurelio.

"I won't tell you all my secrets, sweet boy, I'm still a girl under this façade." They all guffawed, happy to be reunited with their collective object of desire. "Come to Ralph's when you're ready."

He arrived first to prepare his latest exhibit, which he hadn't unveiled before his implants. When they were all assembled he asked the most obvious question on everyone's mind, "How long are these implants going to last?"

"Until your next transition, which will not be for a few years yet, about a hundred if all goes well. We may have to tweak you a little between now and then. We'll definitely have to modify your identity information, right? No one lives for two hundred years."

"I take it Phototronic Systems has not released this technology to the world at large." Ptolemy stated, with ever an eye out for profit.

"Only enticements to harvest a few more dollars for us, my greedy little grub. Ralphie, show us what you've got."

"We have enough thalidomide generations to begin whole brain emulation. If you're not aware, simulation and emulation are quite different things. Experiments with artificial intelligence have been mostly concerned with simulating outward human behaviour – programmed behaviour with predictable results. All fine and good, if all you want is a puppy dog toy that barks when you say its name. Artificial Intelligence, or what passes under the misnomer will never result in anything but *artificiality*." Ralph stressed this point before unveiling his latest model of Tengi – the Tengi-B. "And before you ask, no – his head does not detach."

"But he looks the same as the first one," commented Salazar, always a stickler for detail.

"Oh, I don't know, I like his skin colour better," quipped Ralph.

"Why isn't it a woman?" Lai-Xii couldn't help herself, besides it helped to lighten the seriousness of the situation.

"Exactly. We could do some tests of our own," offered Salazar.

"You're not serious, surely." Ralph continued. "Have a look at him, walk around, touch him. He can't move, there's no one home. Open up his door, just press his belly button, check it out."

"He's got no arms or legs," Salazar pointed out.

"Really?" Ralph was feeling in a particularly humorous mood. The 'body' was cradled on a raised stool to bring its head height up to normal human height. He walked around it, touching it, "You're right!"

"Presumably it's because we're going to use some of the thalidomide children descendants for the scans. Am I right?" Maldonado was right on the ball. He went up to the rather enlarged torso and pressed its belly button. The chest cavity revealed what looked like a city in ultra-miniature with all its roadways, CBD and minute skyscrapers. They all peered inside, none the wiser for the experience.

Ralph pointed to a few peculiar installations. "Those are sensory receptors, other than the ones in the head and on the skin surface. It even has magnetoreception, electroreceptors and thermoreception. Most of the torso space is taken up with energy generation. You would not see much in the head, as the two-part matrix occupies less space than our own brain matter."

"Various Governments are already using some of our innovations, generously expressing their gratitude, you'll be glad to hear." Lai-Xii had to make sure of the continuous profitability of Phototronic Systems to keep her five major investors interested and prepared to continue financing the enterprise.

"I have many duplicates ready to facilitate the testing of the scanning technology, transition systems and, most importantly, the output," continued Ralph.

"Why does the mechanism need to look human? Obviously it doesn't matter as far as the long term plan is concerned." Aurelio wasn't nit-picking, just curious as to why the extra considerable expense when a simple metal box could have done the job just as well.

The very first prototype of the Tengi seen by the team had the typical robotic appearance of metallic superficiality. This new updated version had been designed so they could seamlessly integrate into the Tau City society. To that end their outward appearance emulated human skin texture and colour, hair and muscular movements making them almost indistinguishable from normal humans. This was an interim stage in the process of transitioning from a biological entity to a digital manifestation. The Tengi technology also paved the way for the workers that would be needed to set up the settlement on Europa.

"Yes – yes," Ralph agreed, "we were thinking more along the lines of the shock factor, or at least preventing the shock in the first place, if and when the uploaded scanned data booted up and 'saw' a box version of itself in a mirror. So each simulacrum is going to have the same name as its original, with a slight difference."

Lai-Xii knew the theory, for she had helped Ralph develop the simulacrum. "The object, my precocious children, is to determine if it is possible for the human psyche to reside in a non-biological environment. If we can't achieve that then all our years of endeavour will have been wasted."

"It's going to work, right?" Aurelio immediately asked.

"In all probability yes, at least as far our technology has evolved to this stage. The big unknown is how the simulacrum is going to behave and if there will be any signs of mental degradation for any reason."

*

Only the latest thalidomide generation was used for the scans. They had been born without limbs 'naturally', without genetic intervention; the first real success achieved for Lai-Xii's vision. Though not yet fully mature the young adult men and women had sufficient normal life experience to have well developed psyches, to have experienced the world of pain and beauty, sadness and joy albeit in the limited environment of Tau City.

The prospective participants received their invitations at their homes, masquerading as job interviews. In Tau City meaningful employment was a much sort after and competitive prize. Only the most highly qualified landed the best jobs, in this case in the area of scientific research and development. Lai-Xii had far more acceptances than she wanted so she devised a simple vetting process consisting of just two questions ... 'Are you prepared to entirely give up the life you have, your family, friends, everything you own?' And ... 'If the opportunity presented itself would you want to become immortal?' These two questions quickly weeded out the frivolous applicants.

Of the two hundred acceptances, only twenty remained who answered in the affirmative to both questions. That's all Ralph needed. The part about the possibility of experiments failing and its subsequent side effects somehow didn't rate highly in later discussions with the twenty candidates.

The laboratory, in an electrical, magnetic and microwave shielded room, looked more like the storage basement of a large building. All manner of equipment appeared against the white walls and scattered seemingly randomly around the place. Order evident only in the eight hollow tubular pieces of apparatus, with the sliding platforms jutting out from them large enough to take the human form, and with projections from their tops and sides. Four of these pods were painted white and four yellow.

The first two women and two men ushered in seemed relaxed. Pavel and Alla, apparently friends, said a few reassuring words to each other while Ralph's assistant Misha made the final adjustments.

"There they are," indicated Pavel with a nod, "our new brain boxes."

Alla saw the twenty Tengi-Bs lined up against the back wall, which were not obvious when they first entered the laboratory. "They all look like us," she said, "there's yours, first from the left. It's got your name tag. Oh look, there's mine on the other end." Until that moment neither of them really understood what was going to happen to them, not until they saw the automatons in their mobility units, waiting; silent, lifelike yet dead.

"Do you think we'll be safe?" Alla showed a little concern.

"Sure," Pavel replied with youthful confidence, "just like an X-ray."

Leonid and Vera, the other two scan candidates, didn't know each other and just followed the conversation in silence, also taking note of the figures against the wall.

"Right - everyone ready?" Misha began cheerfully. "Come here and back up against the white platforms, we'll do the rest. Nothing for you to do for half an hour. Relax and read the material you see above your heads inside the tube. When you're done, you may have a little refreshment before hopping in the yellow tubes, and then that will be it for today."

He seemed so relaxed and so cheerful, and the equipment wasn't at all foreboding, so the four of them rolled up to their respective places without protest. Misha placed some restraining straps around them and on their heads, "Don't worry, it's only to hold you still during the scan," and he let the apparatus pick them up and slide them into position inside the tubes. He even put on some soothing quiet music to help them relax. It was important they didn't move during the procedure. While he made various adjustments he explained what was happening to keep them from getting anxious. "This is what we call Confocal Laser Scanning Microscopy. It will begin the process of capturing the internal molecular structure of all your neurons. It doesn't read your thoughts," he added with a wicked laugh, "but it will create the first part of the map of your brains that will be eventually reproduced in our friends over there by the wall."

While Misha ran the scanning procedures, Ralph and Lai-Xii discussed a slight complication related to the Alpha and Beta versions of their subjects. "It's critical that they don't meet each other, especially if the Beta versions begin to show signs of self-awareness. I don't think we can risk the psychological paradox that could arise."

Lai-Xii agreed. "The Beta's must show completely normal external behaviour, without the influence of having to deal with the idea that they are not unique entities. They might remember the procedure, but that's entirely different to coming face to face with your doppelganger. Take the Alpha's to the other side of the city. If they give you any trouble just let Aurelio know. He's got my instructions what to do with them if that happens."

As none of the first four Alphas felt any worse for the experience, they were quite happy to do the yellow scan, to be executed by the two-photon excitation microscopy. Its function was to add greater detail to the previous scan.

Over the next five days all the scans of the twenty volunteers was completed, a relatively short process in comparison to what was to come. The team was intensely interested in these proceedings, as it was in effect the culmination of almost forty years of work and a bucket full of expenses. They gathered in Ralph's office, with Dr. Yermolov.

"Are we going to have to go through all this?" Aurelio asked the first and most obvious question.

"Are you afraid, my darling piggy? Don't worry, I won't let anything happen to you." She slapped him gently on one cheek. "If this part of our preparation works, then probably not. I suppose you want to see out your days on Earth with arms and legs intact. But don't forget what I said to you – it's all going to change!"

"What happens with the Tengi-B models now?" Ptolemy wanted to know the details of the program. His job of building the cities was essentially finished so he felt the need to be on top of the rest of the developments.

"What do you know about black phosphorus?" Asked Ralph, pretty sure they were all ignorant on the subject, and the blank looks confirmed it.

"When you opened up the Tengi to have a peek at his gizzards what you saw was only the supporting hardware for the contents of the head cavity. You're not going to understand this but here it is in a nutshell. Tengi-B has a uniquely structured brain matter, layered into two halves. Each half consists of flexibly linked layers of black phosphorus into a tetrahedrally bonded network lattice. There are no silicon chips in this baby. We hope his new brain mass will be able to accommodate the one hundred thousand terabytes of information from the two scans on each individual. It must also be able to absorb, process, integrate and give feedback on *all* the sensory input it will receive continuously from its Alpha. I'll be mapping the Betas' brains over the coming month with the information from the scans, while Evgeniya does her thing."

"Are you telling us we're *that* close to creating a new human being?" Asked Salazar.

Lai-Xii wasn't going to let their imaginations go rampaging all over the place. "No, silly. Not a *new* human being, just a better version of the old one. Evgen sweetheart, fill us in on what you've been up to."

Salazar would not let up. "How long will the Tengi-Bs live?" Of them all, he felt himself to be in the most precarious position. He'd already hit a hundred and four. In spite of Lai-Xii's assurances about his organ upgrade's longevity, he still felt vulnerable. Perhaps so did the others, but they said nothing about it.

"You're jumping the gun a bit here my young stud. This is world leading technology. Apart from us, no one knows about it. The whole thing could fall over. We are running a test here, not producing a working prototype." Sometimes Lai-Xii got a bit frustrated with these filthy rich and utterly impatient men. Moving closer to Salazar she pushed a sharp fingernail into his chest, for all to see. "So just shut up for once and listen." Rarely did any geisha express such overt control over her men, if ever, except perhaps this one.

Evgeniya knew the next procedure inside out of course, but how to put it across to 'business men'? With almost a sneer on her face she began slowly. "Skans and transferring neural maps to ourr Tengi-Bs zough challenging to say least, is not most kritikal part of trial. Even what I am about to do to Alphas is relatively minor operation. To get Tengi-Bs to receive all sensory input, zen ensuring all zat data is processed and assimilated ... vell gentlemen, *zat* is trick. And ve vill only know result if zey start behaving like human beings – in every vay."

7

BETAS AWAKENING

TAU CITY
RALPH'S LABORATORY #2

OVER the next two weeks Evgeniya operated on each of the Alphas to implant a wide range of transmitters around their cranial masses to relay all their sensory data inputs to their corresponding Betas. Apart from the effects of the anaesthetic and the regrowth of their hair, the procedure had very little effect on them. They could continue with their lives as normal, and were in fact required to do so. Transmissions were anticipated to begin as soon as the Betas had been initialised and tested. In the intervening weeks the Betas had been powered up, their neural maps uploaded and their systems' integrity found to be flawless, as far as the hardware and software components were concerned.

Lai-Xii expected some dramatic signs of life from the Betas as soon as Ralph activated them. They'd been primed with all the information needed to elicit some form of life response. They were after all, a snap shot copy of the Alphas at a specific moment in time. However, they remained dormant. Sensors showed very little neural activity, only weak theta and delta waves. Although most encouraging to see the activity, to all intents and purposes the subjects were dead to the world around them. Something was missing. The disappointment was palpable in the air. You could not even have thought of them as being truly asleep – they seemed so - dead.

"What's gone wrong Ralph? Surely there must be something happening." Ptolemy was always results oriented. Failure did not feature in his vocabulary.

"Everything is working as it should but there doesn't seem to be anyone home. It's like they're all stuck in some kind of intermediate stage – 'on hold' so to speak."

"Are you sure you've uploaded the full scans?"

This time Evgeniya responded, annoyed at being taken to task by a bunch of lay people who knew nothing about the incredible complexity of what they were trying to achieve. To make it worse, they were men. Maybe it was because of her biased attitude towards her own gender that she and Lai-Xii got on so well.

Harusuke attended the first initialization, staying well in the background. Her role was to support Lai-Xii from the background, while being as much a part of the Project as everyone else. She was no slouch in the brain power compartment either. Lai-Xii had confided everything to her, not just the big picture but the details of their progress, the critical milestones of the Project as well as the possible pitfalls. This was one of those, and so she asked Harusuke to join her. So far Lai-Xii had only managed to increase hers and her teams' life expectancy with artificial organ implants. Without a successful whole brain emulation into the Tengi software the Project would suffer a major setback to achieving digitization.

Harusuke observed the confusion and disappointment for a while, silent but keenly observant. As a past geisha herself, and a highly intelligent one, she had studied not just music, dance and discourse but also physiology. It occurred to her there was indeed something vital missing in the process. She had an idea. Unobtrusively she approached Lai-Xii, waited for an opportunity to attract her attention, then quietly whispered, "They don't have a trigger to wake them up. Perhaps they are all in deep sleep, dreaming a different reality to the one we are in. What do you think could wake them?" Harusuke *never* told Xii what to do.

Lai-Xii listened with her eyes on Vera-B, the name given to Vera's corresponding Tengi. Her eyes widened, she reached a hand over to Harusuke's arm giving it an understanding squeeze. "Ralph, if they're asleep dreaming they'd need something to wake them – an alarm, right?"

Ralph slapped his forehead so hard it hurt his hand. "Evgeniya, when did the Alphas begin transmitting?"

"They haven't," she said, "after the initial tests I turned all the transmitters off until we were ready."

"When can you be ready to do it right, Ralph?" asked Lai-Xii.

49

"As soon as Evgeniya has the data on the sleeping/wake cycles of each of the Alphas and we have a recording of the environments in which they wake normally." He took no notice of her jibe. His mind raced in comprehension of the problem. Each of the Alphas had fallen asleep during the scans in the darkness of the scanning tubes. Misha did mention it, but it seemed irrelevant. Obviously the scans recorded that particular state of mind at that particular moment of time.

Evgeniya also realised the simplicity of the solution. "I kan vork out number of sleep cycles zey vould have gone through since skan, and use stimulus in 'vake up' part of cycle. If ve introduce persistent noise increasing in volume, and project light of rising sun onto zeir visual receptors ve arre sure to get reaktion. I zink ve should give Betas few morre days to process zeir existing sensory data, just as ve do when ve sleep."

"Right, next week. All agreed? In the meantime I'll gather the Heads of State of each of the major powers backing the Project."

The stake holders jumped at the opportunity when Lai-Xii advised them. Representatives from American, China, Russia and India were all there; both scientific and a political presence was deemed necessary. A large group gathered in the basement laboratory on the appointed day. The dignitaries knew this wasn't the latest attempt at artificial intelligence. They did not know that the only artificiality about it was the supporting hardware to contain the human software. The scientific, social and religious repercussions were earth shattering, not to mention the opportunities it opened up for the future survivability of humanity.

They were all seated there, waiting impatiently for any sign of life in the Betas. As a precaution, suggested by Ralph himself, the Betas were all secured in their mobility units after removal of the battery packs. No one really knew what exactly was going to happen. If the theory proved correct, once 'awake' the Betas should be able to 'thought' control their vehicles the same as the Alphas.

Arranged in rows in front of the Betas seating had quickly filled. Hushed pleasantries filled the low lit windowless laboratory. Expectations were high, perhaps not for the same reasons as those of the Phototronic Systems' team members. The repercussions of this technology, if successful, would without any doubt alter the course of human history, if not human evolution itself. Leaders of the world's greatest powers, sitting in seemingly convivial cooperation, may well have been contemplating scenarios completely unrelated to the migration of the human species off the planet that gave rise to their existence.

Lai-Xii sat beside the Secretary of State of the United States on her left, the Minister of Chinese National Defence on her right. Harusuke hovered by the light control console. Ralph had his finger on a 'kill' switch that would immediately deactivate all the Betas in the event of an emergency, and Evgeniya stood ready to 'wake' them. No sensory transmissions were being channelled from the Alphas at this stage.

Harusuke turned out the lights on Lai-Xii's signal, Ralph stood poised with thumb hovering over the red button as Evgeniya played the first recording. It was as quiet in there as the bedroom of a deep sleeper. Only Ralph, Evgeniya and Lai-Xii knew which of the Betas was first to be woken up. None of the representatives noticed their intense concentration on that one individual.

In her normal life at her home Irina-A's window faced the sunrise overlooking a large wooded park. In that direction, on the other side of Tau City boundary, lay the Kamchatkan wilderness of volcanoes and snow-capped mountains. She always kept her curtains open, even at night, so she could wake to the rays of the rising sun. Irina never woke late for work, for if the sun didn't wake her then the distant barking laugh of the Steller's sea eagle punctuated by the gentle song of the Siberian ruby-throat in nearby trees always did the trick. Rarely did she ever need the rude complaints of her alarm to drag her from unpleasant dreams, for Irina-A always had pleasant dreams. Sometimes she did not want to wake but go on enjoying her sleep-time adventures.

Barely perceptible at first, the pitch dark laboratory hinted at morning's first light. Ralph had taken great pains to set up the theatrics to achieve the desired effect on the dormant Betas. The spectators had to strain their eyes to convince themselves that something was happening; all else slumbered on in silence. Lai-Xii turned her head in the door's direction; she thought she'd heard a faint sound, like the very distant barking of a dog. Other's also turned. Then Harusuke, taken completely by surprise whispered to Lai-Xii from behind, "is that a ruby-throat?"

"Hush!" One of the dignitaries shushed them without turning around, his eyes almost bulging from the strain of scanning the Betas for any signs of life.

The recorded sunrise replayed at the same slow pace Irina-A would have experienced in her bedroom, which she most probably

51

did that very same day. Shadows lengthened in the laboratory to the now intermittent clear sounds of morning birds. Gradually, much too slowly for the expectant onlookers, full morning sunlight filled the room with the birds increasing their welcoming chorus. Yet nothing else was happening in the room. No one moved, no one even breathed. Suddenly the US Secretary of State reached over and clamped his hand on Lai-Xii's arm while turning his head to the left. She followed his gaze.

"Third from the left," he hissed between closed teeth, "Irina-B." Others noticed it too. A couple of the chairs scraped as spectators adjusted their viewing positions.

All the Tengi-B's had received full cosmetic treatment to make their heads and faces look and move as faithfully as their Alpha counterparts to the smallest detail; same colour and style of hair, birth marks, beauty spots and all blemishes carefully reproduced. Facial muscles operated realistically during tests, smiles, facial expressions and the functioning of the eyes received special attention. Although torsos weren't anywhere near as important, nevertheless full consideration was given to the way they were attired in style and colour to cover the artificial constructs.

Everyone watched Irina-B's face, expressionless except for the slightest movement of her head away from the forward tilted resting position. Gradually they could see her eyes. Her eyelids flickered lightly before closing again to remain closed for many minutes. Lai-Xii flashed a questioning look towards Ralph and Evgeniya. Both shrugged, neither knowing what was happening, why there would be a delay. Irina-B was supposed to wake up. Most impatient of all must have been Lai-Xii for she was about to stand when Ralph motioned for her to sit back down, pointing towards Irina-B. Heads were turning from one person to the next, all seeking clarification. Something must have gone wrong. Immediate thoughts of disappointment could almost be seen on the faces.

Then a new sound permeated the space, just above the noise of the twittering birds, a slight groan coming from Irina-B's direction. Ralph nodded, grinning, but Lai-Xii couldn't get excited. So many years of planning, work, expense, experimental failures and now nothing more than a flicker of the eyelids and a soft groan. She automatically turned to Harusuke, her face showing so much disappointment, so much frustration and so much pent-up anger. Harusuke could do nothing but smile back, extending a comforting hand towards her partner.

"Hmm." Irina-B's eyes opened. Harusuke's hand remained suspended in mid-air. Lai-Xii's face turned to ice, all the tiny hairs on her body standing erect as **Irina-B**, seeing the welcoming party, slowly turned her head and uttered the first monumental words ever spoken by an artificial human being. Not just an artificial intelligence resulting from clever computer technology, but an actual human psyche no longer entrapped in an inefficient, terminal biological mechanism.

"Dobroe utro," 'good morning', in a soft tentative voice. She'd never before had so many people in her bedroom in the morning when she woke up. *What are all these people doing here? Who are they?* Questioning thoughts clearly discernible on her face.

8

WHOLE BRAIN EMULATION TEST

CE 2053
RALPH'S LABORATORY #2

EVERYONE kept completely still and quiet. The moment was overwhelming in spite of nobody fully comprehending the enormity of the achievement. They just sat and stared at Irina-B who slowly looked around at the gathering, still strapped into her scooter. Then she looked at herself. She was fully dressed. *Why am I dressed already? I've just woken up.* She glanced in Evgeniya's direction as she was the only woman standing nearby.

The doctor immediately stepped in front of Irina-B. "Dobroe utro Irina-B," calling her by her Beta name.

The Beta thought for a moment. "That's not my name. I'm Irina."

"Is this some kind of nonsense," asked the Minister of Chinese National Defence turning to Lai-Xii. He could not fully grasp what had been achieved.

"Minister, please – just watch."

"Do you know what has happened to you?" asked Evgeniya ignoring Irina-B's comment about her name and the noise behind her. There was so much happening so quickly Evgeniya couldn't quite think of what to say next. Irina-B closed her eyes, lowering her head slightly. She appeared to be thinking, perhaps trying to remember.

Evgeniya turned to the others in the room. "It looks like she is koming out of minimally konscious state, condition related to koma. In zis case it seems to be kloser to verry deep sleep state, however Irina-B kould be extremely konfused. Everyone, please leave room quietly. Ralph, I vill need your help."

"I expect a full explanation for this fiasco!" stated the American loud enough for everyone to hear. Perhaps he was expecting an American style theatrical performance with fireworks and a cheer squad.

Lai-Xii ushered all the guests out, who reluctantly complied leaving Evgeniya and Ralph to deal with the situation. The Russian Minister of Defence, already alert to the possible military applications of this remarkable technology, asked succinctly as he walked out of the laboratory, "Ven do you vake others?" He didn't acknowledge the American's reaction.

Taking control of the situation, Lai-Xii translated Irina-B's conversation to the visitors. "To answer your question, General, we will wake all the twenty subjects within hours: As soon as we are assured there are no major complications with Irina-B."

She didn't dwell on Irina-B's objection about her name. Though worrying to a small degree, that realisation by the Beta was the clearest indicator of a normal brain function; just as if someone had called anyone else by an incorrect name. Maldonado started to say something, but Lai-Xii cut him off immediately. This was no time to openly discuss their Project in front of world government representatives. No doubt there would be a few despots eager to capitalise on such opportunities to extend their reign of power.

Back in the laboratory Evgeniya waited with Ralph for Irina-B to come out of her reverie. She did so with an explosive burst of anger.

"What have you done to me! Why am I tied up like this?" She tried her best to thrash her way out of the restraints. Ralph noted with satisfaction that the brain reacted as if it was in a physical body, and with the accompanying manifestations of a biological torso responding.

They waited until the Beta settled. Evgeniya placed her hand softly on Irina-B's cheek, who turned her head away, still angry. "Why did you call me Irina-B? That is not my name."

"Do you remember your name?" asked Evgeniya.

"It's Irina," came the immediate angry answer.

"You were once this person, but now you are changing into a new one. Do you remember the experiment?"

"I – I only remember falling asleep inside a dark tube."

"Very good. Anything else? Try hard."

She became introspective again, like a relational database going quiet as its search engine looked for data to satisfy a query.

Ralph and Evgeniya walked to the other wall and faced away from the Beta to have a brief discussion. "This is outstanding, Evgeniya!" Ralph could hardly contain himself. "It's better than we could possibly have hoped for. I say we have a couple of hours of conversation with her and if there are no potentially fatal indicators I think we should wake the others."

"I agree. Let me do few tests to konfirm all her sensors arre vorking, then we kan vake others. But keep them all restrained for now."

Irina-B focused her attention on the two people standing some distance from her and in a raised voice said, "I remember *him*," indicating Ralph with a nod in Ralph's direction.

"Excellent," Evgeniya smiled as she returned to stand in front of her. "There is nothing to be afraid of. You have taken part in an experiment with us, as have all your friends beside you. They are all asleep at moment, but we vill wake them soon and you can talk to them. I just want to do some tests to make sure you are alright. Da?" She spoke in Russian, aware Ralph already knew the content of the conversation. "When we're done you can go to your new home." The reassurance did not seem to quieten Irina-B. No one had told her she'd have to move to a new place to live after the experiment.

Lai-Xii returned to the laboratory with her team. "I've convinced the delegates to go back to their guest accommodations for now. They expect to come back in a week for a complete update. I don't need to remind you all about the delicacy of the situation and the need for absolute security. This is the turning point. If this works, there are no more major obstacles in our way." Grave but smiling, they all nodded their understanding.

"I remember her too. She's Lai-Xii," Irina-B interrupted, still unsettled.

Unfazed, Lai-Xii responded, "Hello Irina-B. I'm very pleased to see you are well. Thank you for your help." She could see the woman wasn't happy, though the cause of it was not evident. Lai-Xii had only considered the situation from her own perspective. Either she wasn't capable of seeing it from Irina's point of view, seeing that her life had been completely turned upside-down, that she had been manipulated and used without any thought of her feelings. But then again, in the greater scheme of her plans, individuals did not matter per se, only to the extent that they contributed to the enterprise.

*

Two weeks had elapsed since the experiment. Pavel-A and Alla-A considered their part and what had happened since. Nothing had happened. No one from the laboratory had contacted them.

At Pavel-A's rooms in one of the residential complexes of the city housing all of the Alphas, he discussed the situation with Alla-A.

"Don't you think it strange we should be ignored like this, especially after how important the experiment seemed to be."

"Yes, you're right. They were friendly enough at the start, then afterwards it's as if we didn't exist. I'd like to find out what's going on," Alla-A stoked Pavel-A's discontent. "It almost amounts to disrespect. The least they could do is tell us whether the experiment worked. It seemed pretty important at the time."

"Yes, especially when you consider the two extraordinary conditions under which we were selected in the first place. Like, whatever happened to our 'immortality'?"

"So you're with me, Alla? We can't let this go and forget all about it. We've both studied integrated technologies to extend human life. They can't just use us and leave us out of it. I want to know what they've done. And don't forget – you and I, and the others, were prepared to give up everything just to be a part of this."

"Yes Pavel, I agree. We'll need some help. Do you know any of the others who may want to join us?"

"I've met Yuri and Yefim, they seem alright."

"And I've spoken briefly with Irina. I think she's pretty smart. Let's get together with them and see how they feel."

They next met at Irina-A's place. The same feelings pervaded everyone's thoughts. Although they all 'enjoyed' the novel experience and had been financially rewarded for their effort, it somehow didn't seem adequate given the nature of the experiments. They all knew that those mechanisms lined up against the laboratory wall were destined to receive their brain scans. They also fully understood the purpose of their own operations to embed the transmitters. Yet the nagging unknown remained. Just what were those Beta Tengi destined to become?

"We have to do this. I don't know about you, but if there's a double of me living in this city pretending to be me, I want to know about it," said Pavel-A with strong conviction.

"We need a plan." Irina always had a plan for whatever she did. It was the first thing she thought about when she woke.

Five Alphas plotted against the power of Lai-Xii, certain from her reputation that she would not simply take them into her confidence for the asking. In that assumption they were absolutely right.

If Lai-Xii had caught the slightest hint of their little 'harmless' conspiracy there would no longer be Alphas and Betas alive, only Betas.

*

Irina-B had been awake for two weeks. As the days progressed she remembered more and more of her past, engaging Evgeniya and Misha in conversation. She remembered Misha too, the technician who carried out the scans. Her Alpha was an educated girl, majoring in physics and bio-chemistry at the city's small university. Irina-B's seemingly willing engagement in the tests pleased everyone. Lai-Xii watched and assessed, remaining cautious. There was something not right about this Beta, but she couldn't put her finger on it.

At first she confided in Ralph and Harusuke. "This unit is just too eager, a little too interested. It doesn't seem normal, in spite of her Alpha's background."

"Perhaps." Ralph may have had some reservations. "But you have to remember this is the very first time anything like this has ever been attempted. She may simply be trying to come to terms with the fact that she's no longer the same person she was before, yet in her mind still being exactly the same."

Harusuke made an important observation. "We didn't know Irina-A at all before the procedure, so there's no real comparison to what could be considered normal behavioural characteristics."

Lai-Xii considered Harusuke's comment. "Ralph, you and Evgeniya study the other Alphas." Only Pavel-A's past indicated any predisposition towards discontent with authority, but not enough to ring any alarms.

So the unanimous decision was made to wake all the other Betas, each with their personal wake-up protocols. They all came out of their temporary light comas. Their behaviours stayed well within the range of reactions exhibited by Irina-B. After a few days to get the deep sleep out of their systems, they were allowed an interaction with those important visitors. Questions and answers flowed freely. The American showed the greatest interest, striking up a conversation with Irina-B.

"Do you know who you are?"

Irina-B pulled a face, completely disregarding the man's status. "Of course I do. I'm Irina. Why don't you tell me why you're here? What's your interest in our experiment?"

"You hear that?" the American called out to Lai-Xii, grinning. "I'd say your test has been a big success!" He ignored Irina-B as if she was a machine and not a human being at all.

58

The Chinese delegate stood back and listened to the conversations for a while before approaching Pavel-B, his English quite adequate for the occasion. "You Pavel-B, Yes? What you profession, if one may ask?"

Pavel-B, like Irina-B seemed to consider himself to be the equal of, if not better than the man facing him. "I am a scientist, studying integrated technologies and their application in extending life expectancy." Pavel-B saw no reason why he couldn't speak freely. When Lai-Xii heard the direction the conversation had taken she interrupted it diplomatically to change the subject and bring the interviews to a close.

The Betas seemed content to re-engage with the world, and the delegates could barely contain their excitement at the incredible progress made by Phototronic Systems. Individually each reaffirmed their respective government's commitments to continue support for the Europa colonisation Project. Pavel-B's response may have had something to do with it, as they all heard him. Perhaps this aspect of the Project carried more interest for the diplomats than the other. Perhaps for them the colonisation of Europa did not seem to equate with the abandonment of Earth.

The Russian said in jest to the American, "As long as you don't live longer than me." Lai-Xii heard the quip, storing it for future reference.

*

All went well for a short time after the Betas took up their residences close to the laboratories. They were even allowed to go out in their mobility units and mix with the locals, under the strict supervision of their minders.

"It's been two months since they moved out and resumed living a normal life. They seem so convincing that we have to force ourselves to remember they are only machines, with a copy of the human brain." Ralph was eager to take the next step.

They were all gathered in the conference room, except Salazar. He'd made some excuse about having a most important rendezvous. No one worried about it, after all he was over a hundred years old. His artificial organs were working well. Good for him if he found a friend. The next decision did not have to be unanimous. The consortium wasn't founded on democratic principles anyway; Lai-Xii was in charge.

"Their sensory input systems look to be fully operational with all transferred data being assimilated by their black phosphorus networks. We have to initiate the next phase of the experiment. Evgeniya is ready to switch on the Alphas' sensory transmitters."

"Da, it is time. But ve have slight problem," said Evgeniya. She and Aurelio had been monitoring the Betas interactions with the general public.

Aurelio was frustrated about it. "Damn! It was all going so well. Some of the locals got wind of the fact they were only machines, who were pretending to be human. They don't realise the Betas are actually humans where it counts the most; inside their heads!"

"Has there been any violence?" Maldonado was always interested in how people related to one another, it was the foundation of his Me-Me social networking application.

"No, but we have to prepare for possibly having to isolate all the Betas from normal public life." This meant finding other means of sensory input. Ralph forewarned that the primary sensors he'd developed for the Betas may not be entirely adequate.

"Why not?" Lai-Xii jumped on that new bit of information. "Why didn't you tell me about this before?"

"It was only a suspicion at first, from watching them at the end of the day when they were by themselves, and monitoring their sleep patterns. The thing is, they are only machines and our sensors were designed for a biological entity. Their experiences are being integrated differently. When they are resting, sleeping that is, there is no longer a clearly definable cycle. It's random with high and low peaks of activity in their networks. Eventually it will alter their normal behaviour. Perhaps it's happening already, alienating normal human beings because of the peculiar nuances in their social interactions."

"Right. Do it. Evgeniya, are you ready to turn on the Alphas' signals?" Lai-Xii prompted.

"I kan do today."

"You and Aurelio continue your surveillance. Inform me immediately if there's the slightest issue." The meeting had clearly ended. Evgeniya turned on the Alphas' neuro-transmitters to activate the transmission of their sensory data to download into their equivalent Betas.

Ralph and Evgeniya failed to consider the effects of boredom on the human psyche. The Betas had no specific tasks to occupy their days and their minds, resulting in certain consequences. A further three weeks later, a strange incidence between two women was reported by the local police force. It only came to Lai-Xii's immediate attention because Ptolemy had set up a good infrastructure to manage the small city. The report said an abusive altercation broke out between what appeared to be between identical twins meeting at a café in the Beta's quarter of the city.

Pavel and Alla had alternated with Irina and Yuri to keep an eye on movements around Laboratory #2. For weeks they saw no one they recognised as one of the Betas, until only recently on Pavel's watch when Alla spotted Irina-B going into the lab. It must have been her because of the hair and the distinctive clothes she wore. They waited until she came out and followed her to her apartment.

"This is what we've been waiting for Alla" Pavel was most excited. "Let's tell Irina right away. She'll want to know for sure." During their preliminary discussions the Alphas decided they would like to meet with their doubles before deciding what else they might do. What could go wrong? Surely, if they were simply meeting themselves the situation would be nothing but amicable.

Irina did indeed spark up at the thought of possibly meeting 'herself'. It was more a case of overwhelming curiosity than anything else. If your brain had been copied and downloaded into a machine, you'd surely want to know what it was like. Would it be the same as yourself or have some strange machine-like quirks? "Follow her for me, find out where she goes. I want to meet her in a public place somewhere."

Only two days later Irina was on her way across the city to a little known location, frequented by Irina-B. It was the Beta's sector, not generally a busy place. A small café in a side street served the passing traffic, with a few tables and chairs on a paved area out the front. Irina rolled along slowly to try and get a good impression of the Beta, stopping occasionally so as not to make her approach seem too obvious. She just wanted to meet this 'person' and see what she was like.

Irina-B, facing away from her when she finally arrived at the table, didn't immediately react to her greeting.

"Hello," she said pleasantly to catch Irina-B's attention.

With an expressionless face the Beta turned to look at her, but said nothing, though her intense scrutiny of the new arrival was obvious.

"Hello," Irina said again, "May I join you?" She was very excited. This 'person' looked exactly like her, except her expression had become definitely hostile.

"If you have to," Irina-B responded.

"Well, no, I don't have to, but I would like to speak with you."
"Why?"
"Because we look so much alike. What's your name?"
"Irina," she responded reluctantly.

Irina-A gently pushed the chair aside and rolled her scooter up to the table. "That's my name. Do you know who I am?" She tried to

61

play it cool, as the girl on the other side of the table was obviously not in the mood for company, but Irina-A could not let this opportunity escape her.

"Yes, I know who you are. I was you. You are inferior. Why do you still exist?"

"That's a bit rude. Could we start again? Can I get you a treat? A cake, a coffee?" Irina-A pushed down her rising anger. There was no reason for her to be talked to like that, but perhaps it was her fault.

"I don't need rubbish like that." Irina-B seemed to be completely without inhibitions in what she said.

"Well – sorry I disturbed you." Irina backed up a little to move around the table and past Irina-B. Perhaps her friends were wrong and this was a different Irina who looked exactly like her. She behaved nothing like herself.

Suddenly Irina-B jerked her scooter sideways just as Irina arrived opposite her, knocking over her scooter and dislodging herself at the same time. A torrent of abuse gushed out of Irina-B, which took Irina more by surprise than being knocked over.

Within seconds full bodied carers were on the scene, putting everything back in order. One of them couldn't help commenting, "I've been watching you two sisters. I can't understand why you should have such a violent argument. I thought twins were supposed to get on well with each other." Before either of them could answer, the local police had already arrived. The 'sisters' were separated and independently questioned. Irina was taken back to her apartment, Irina-B back to hers.

The report of the incident soon landed on Lai-Xii's desk, together with security footage showing the behaviour of both individuals. "It's time we had another meeting of the full team." Lai-Xii seemed upset. The further they progressed with the project more and more issues kept cropping up that she had to deal with. Why would anyone want to argue with a mirror image of themselves? Ridiculous – unless there was something seriously wrong. Harusuke did his best to calm her, attending the meeting to support her partner.

"What's your opinion Evgeniya?" Lai-Xii needed something solid to base her next difficult decision on.

"Zere is obvious difference in behaviour betveen zem. Is not extreme but underlying kause kould be serious. Zey should not have met. It kaused sensory feedback loop for Irina-B making her to react irrationally. I do not zink it emotional response. She vas getting data from Irina-A's experience simultaneously viz her own."

"You're probably right," Ralph said, "but Irina-B behaved badly from the start. I think there is more to it. In fact I believe we should recall all the Betas and run a series of new tests. I'm particularly concerned about their emotional development in the absence of all hormonal activity. As there are no chemical neurotransmitters to evoke emotional responses, their reactions need a mechanism by which they can be formalised into 'reasoned' responses; not irrational behaviour. They have to be taken out of circulation."

Lai-Xii had come to trust this man. "Bring them to lab #2 as soon as you can set up accommodation for them."

Yuri couldn't understand Irina's experience with her Beta double. "We're supposed to be transmitting all our sensory experiences to them. So they should be exactly like us. But from what you say Irina, there is a problem. Whatever the scientists are doing to all of us, it's not working. What are we going to do about it?" On the way home from the gathering Yuri's scooter was forced off the road by a vehicle causing him to run into an obstacle and hurt his head. He needed medical attention and some stitches.

At home Irina stewed over the unpleasant experience. It just wasn't like her to behave like that. And therein lay the problem. What if this other Irina had become unbalanced in some way? What if deep down Irina hated herself and the double only expressed those hidden feelings openly? What if … ? An excess of vodka seemed to be the only thing to calm Irina's agitation caused by the café incident, which also gave her a headache for days.

All the Betas protested of course at being herded back into the confines of the laboratory. Though vocal, none of their representations carried any violent emotional overtones. There *should* have been some evidence of it, but of course it wasn't possible in the absence of hormonal activity. Confrontational, uncooperative responses didn't quite fit the category of emotional outbursts.

One by one they were extensively interviewed. The overwhelming evidence of cerebral deterioration could not be ignored.

"None of them are 'happy' with being here," Ralph informed the team. "I use the term 'happy' very loosely because no one showed any emotion at all. The inability to experience emotional release is disastrous to the human psyche."

After discussing the situation with Harusuke Lai-Xii considered the emergent problem to be no more than a stepping stone to the next stage of success. Murmurs amongst her team of investors showed their rising concern about the seeming lack of success at this stage of the Project. In purely technical terms everything went brilliantly. If they had been dealing with purely artificial intelligence the solutions to the rising after-effects could have been dealt with expediently and without so much fuss. But this was different. They were real people trapped inside those contraptions.

"Please listen," Ralph went on, "there's more. Every Beta complained about having 'phantom' experiences; pains, thoughts, impressions which they were convinced were not their own. For example, Yuri-B felt a lot of pain in his temple saying it felt like someone was sticking needles into it. It turns out his Alpha was involved in an accident and needed urgent medical attention, with stiches to seal his wound. This situation is both good and bad. Good because it shows the transmissions from the Alphas are working – and bad because it causes the Betas a lot of confusion, which could even lead to losing their sense of 'themselves' as unique entities. Irina-B felt completely drunk a day after her incident with her Alpha, and then experienced the pain of a headache. Irina-A did in fact get drunk on vodka which resulted in a big hangover."

Aurelio, who always wanting quick solutions barked, "So what do we do? Switch off all the Alpha transmissions? Better still, get rid of them and let the Betas have their own sensory input?"

"Ralph," Lai-Xii wasn't sure what to do but tended towards Aurelio's suggestion, "is that a realistic option?"

"We must certainly stop transmissions from the Alphas. As for the Betas own inputs ... I don't know. They're no longer biological or 'human' as we know it. They may have started with that as their foundation but it's obvious they are already diverging substantially. Also, don't forget they have inputs we don't, which gives them an advantage over us."

Maldonado, a master at finding ways to collect and use data on people to advantage through Me-Me, had a suggestion. "What if we only feed them data of our own choosing and don't allow them any other confusing sensory input?"

"Dis vill not vork," Evgeniya had been silent during the conversation, concerned about the direction it was taking. "Vat none of you understand is zat sensory input and integration is foundation of human psyche. It begins as soon as the foetus has the kapacity to record and process. Procedure continues uninterrupted throughout person's life. Is basis of ourr consciousness. You take zat away and brain vill konsume itself, but vill not do dis quietly."

Lai-Xii saw a solution. "Keep the Betas isolated and confined until Ralphie finds a feed mechanism that will satisfy their enhanced processing capability. I don't think the Alphas will be a problem, though make sure they don't go into the Beta's part of the city." There seemed to be a consensus to this course of action by passive agreement. Then with her mind already focused on making further progress she continued. "We have succeeded in reducing the brain's workload by not having to manage the body's extremities. We can further reduce it by engineering out other non-critical organs. This we can do. Ralph, you and your team have to devise perhaps entirely new forms of 'sensory' data that would satisfy the digitised format of the human brain. It may not need to smell stuff, but it may need to be aware of magnetic fields, electric fields, overheating and whatever else your clever team can come up with. But understand this ... once we scan and move the human brain into a digitised environment it must no longer be treated as a 'human' organ, yet it must maintain its humanity. And while you're at it, find the digital equivalent of chemical neurotransmitters that trigger hormonal emotional responses."

"Good luck with that Ralph," chirped Maldonado. "Just a thought," he added as an adjunct, "through my social media network we are feeding people tremendous amounts of data, quasi information, which they don't actually need as biological organisms, yet their minds have become addicted. What do you make of that?"

"You're on the right track, darling bed bug," at last Lai-Xii showed a little of her former happy, in-control self. "But before we go overboard, best to continue with our plans to examine sensory deprivation in a little more detail. We'll keep the Betas here for the time being. They may be useful a little later, but they are not to be let loose in our city, understand!"

9

SENSORY DEPRIVATION

CE 2056
TAU CITY
RALPH'S LABORATORY #3

THE current scientific evidence suggested serious repercussions for a biological organism deprived of external sensory input for more than a few hours. But that was on a normal human neural network.

"Time for two of you boys to step up to the mark and make a real contribution," Lai-Xii needed subjects who have had more than their share of life experiences. Who better to choose from than her own team? Salazar, a perfect candidate at a ripe age of a hundred and four. He was going through his second life surge, after his artificial organ upgrade, indulging in all manner of vices and pleasures to stimulate his body and his mind. A bit of sensory deprivation should show up well in his brain. The other, Maldonado, also a good choice, given that he'd created his financial empire from virtually depriving people of their empirical realities by getting them addicted to the artificial digital world of social media interconnectedness. Me-Me had become a powerful tool to control and adjust peoples' attitudes, perceptions and to alter patterns of behaviour. "Maldonado my mangy ratty, and you my naughty Salazar are going to have a bit of special entertainment. I can see you get on well together. It'll be fun!"

"Why us," asked Maldonado, "why not just pick a couple of people from the city?"

"This is too important. You know what happened to our first lot of Betas. I need you to give me absolutely accurate feedback on your experience. This is critical if we are to succeed in creating a stable transition from biological to digital. Your continued existence could very well depend on it."

"Well - if you put it that way. It's not going to hurt, is it?" Salazar had a rather low pain threshold. They knew exactly what Lai-Xii had in mind. Ptolemy made no secret of the facilities built into Laboratory #3. It had three sections, all equipped with total sensory deprivation chambers. Ralph set up section #1 for Salazar and Maldonado.

"Let's see how you manage with just your own chatter. We'll start with you two," Ralph grinned as Misha began preparing the subjects. "Get undressed please and lie on these tables."

"How long is this going to take?" asked Salazar.

"Why, do you have an urgent rendezvous?" Ralph had heard the rumours about his clandestine activities. "For as long as you can take it. All you have to do is keep each other entertained. The transmitters Misha is about to attach to your foreheads will relay your sub-vocalised words to each other as you lie immersed in the floatation tanks. We'll monitor you both. At the first sign of trouble you'll be out of there."

Stark naked Salazar stepped up to the tank. "There's not much to it is there. It just looks like a big egg with a lid. What's the fluid?"

"Salt water at skin temperature,' replied Misha, "you'll hear nothing, feel nothing, smell nothing and see nothing. In short, you'll be isolated from sensory inputs. You'll only know the world through your connection with Maldonado."

Three hours later the boys were doing just fine. "I have to say Maldo, this is the most relaxing treatment I've ever had. I don't know why we didn't get onto it sooner," Salazar thought across to his friend.

"Amazing. I don't understand all the fuss. We've been in here for at least an hour. Some of my aches and pains have completely disappeared. In fact, I wouldn't mind having a snooze. How about it?"

"Right, I think I'll join you."

In the early stages, the novelty of the situation gave them plenty to talk about, like fantasizing about having their favourite partners to play with in the tanks. So far no serious talk emerged about the Project other than expressing their satisfaction at their increasing wealth from the spin-off technologies released so far onto the market.

Within fifteen minutes of falling asleep both awoke with a start. After the first minute of confusion they decided to stop the experiment. "It was all good while we talked to each other," said Salazar, "but as soon as I fell asleep my mind did weird things. At first I dreamt about getting into the chamber, then as soon as the lid closed I panicked and began flapping around like a bird in a cage. I couldn't hear myself and then another voice kept shouting at me. Then suddenly I woke up and opened my eyes, but everything was absolutely black. I didn't know where I was, but I could feel myself breathing. Then as I tried to move I realised I was floating in something. Then I remembered I was locked inside an egg. Scared the hell out of me." Maldonado had a very similar experience.

At a sudden spike in their EEGs Misha immediately opening the hatches. The two men looked stressed and frightened. Neither wanted to repeat the experiment. "How long were we in there?" asked Maldonado.

"You almost set a record. Three and half hours. Most people go a bit troppo after just an hour. You did well." Ralph was excessively pleased, especially with the effects of the first three hours. It proved that although the brain needed sensory input to remain on an even keel, it did not necessarily have to be through the physical senses. When they fell asleep the mind had to resort to its internally generated stimuli, so it became confused by the lack of external sensations inside the isolation chamber. Even when asleep the body can feel the effects of gravity, slight external noises, temperature fluctuations and so on. All those sensations were missing, so the mind started pulling out its own feathers.

While Ralph worked in section #1, Evgeniya embedded two individuals in section #2 from the Alpha group. They were healthy specimens living close by. They were denied the luxury of being able to communicate with each other while in the tanks. Afanasy and Lubov didn't know each other before they became part of the Project, so there was minimal probability of shared experiences and consequently of similar outcomes from this experiment. After their failed adventure the Alphas decided to lay low for a while. So they were keen to be doing something useful when the offer came.

The effects of complete zero sensory deprivation over a longer period were well documented, but not with people who've had such radical cerebral encroachments. Though the same symptoms of anxiety, hallucinations, bizarre thoughts and depression were expected, it was just possible these individuals could prove more resilient. It turned out to be the opposite. As more of their intelligence had become dedicated to internal processing, the brain's need for

68

stimulation had increased. So any reduction in varied external stimuli had a devastating effect. Within half an hour the experiment had to be terminated. Their mental state having become completely erratic, and due to loss of control of their torsos and body functions, there was no option. The result confirmed Ralph's hypothesis. External stimuli were essential.

"It going take year or more to get Afanasy and Lubov back to anything like normal. Zey have bekome unprediktable, unable to kontrol zeir scooters and have bekome violent. I doubt if ve vill be able to use zem for anything else." Evgeniya was pleased with the result. It pointed the way very clearly to their next area of development in virtual reality sensitisation.

"Fine – no great loss. You and Ralph prepare a few more Alphas for scans. I think we're on track. I expect Tau City will have a new class of residents before too long."

Lai-Xii placed a lot of hope on Maldonado's Me-Me and the virtual reality feeds. The zero sensory input experiment also clearly confirmed her belief that an intelligence generating machine, like the human brain, must have continuous input in order to sustain itself. Otherwise it would be like the body consuming its fat reserves until there was nothing left but skin and bone, and eventually self-destruction. However, because the brain had such an extraordinary capacity to adapt there was no reason to think other forms of data input would not be acceptable, even desirable. As Lai-Xii considered the situation she had a premonition, which had already begun to surface some years before – *We are going to have to redefine what it means to be human.*

Lai-Xii liked, no – thrived, on working with clear cut guidelines, goals and processes in sharp focus. Her vision of reality had always been clearly defined ever since she arrived as a child at the geisha house, not just in the present but the future she was working towards. She did not consider the behaviour of the Betas to be a setback – rather a confirmation of the direction in which changes had to be engineered to achieve the survival of the human species. It had great potential, she was convinced of that, but unlikely to achieve it if human kind continued along its current trajectory. Other, more immediate thoughts also surfaced. *How much can I confide in my wealthy boys? Surely they must be asking themselves the big questions. It can't be just wealth and the allure of eternal life driving them forward.*

Harusuke listened to Xii's concerns in private. She had her own opinions, though subjugated them to Xii's desires. But she could still express them when asked. "No, I don't think *human* life, as such, has any great worth in the greater scheme of things. No greater than that of an elephant or a dog or even the ant under our feet. The peculiarity that has arisen out of its evolution is the only thing of lasting value – consciousness - and the ability to question itself. Even what we call man's 'humanity" is questionable when one considers how it treats not just its own species, but all other living things."

Xii snuggled closer to Harusuke. She could always rely on her to shed light on actual reality, not the kind of delusions the majority of people lived under, either through their political or religious beliefs, or just plain misconceptions. "We are a reprehensible species," Xii said, looking at Harusuke with half closed eyelids, "I wonder sometimes why I bother."

"Why do you?"

That's not what Xii wanted to hear. Harusuke always had a way of putting her on the spot, forcing her to come out of her introspections and face what she had started. "Because it seems more humane than to let it annihilate itself."

"Don't be flippant with me Xii," she put an arm around her shoulders, "be honest."

"It's the only logical thing to do. I want to live, but not like a geisha or a rich bitch or any man's plaything. Here, on this Earth we are isolated from the rest of the universe, mostly because of our own stupidity. Natural evolution will only kill us. Our technology has advanced far ahead of our ethical development. That's obvious to anyone who opens their eyes to reality. I want more – I want to experience it all. We should all be able to experience the great cosmos."

"Now you're getting fanciful."

"What do you think about our cowboys? Do you think we can continue to rely on them? Aurelio makes me worry sometimes. He's too greedy, too quick to mouth off without thinking."

"Your greatest assets are all of them except Aurelio. I agree with you. Perhaps it's just his character. You can always make the final decision about him at the last transition. Now it's time for bed – come on. Keep your creative thinking for the virtual reality constructs you'll have to come up with. Don't rely too much on Ralph for that, and especially don't expect Aurelio to have any real input – the others, maybe."

FROM THE BOOK OF ORIGINATION
DECLARATIONS TEN

10: 1 And it came to pass that upon the Mountains of Ignorance the people lost their way.

10:2 It was at that time that the Shadow became incarnate and said to the Light, 'The people have to see. I will create for them a Golden Unreality.

10:3 And the Light withdrew, believing the Shadow, eager to be reunited with its scattered photons.

10

VIRTUAL REALITY

CE 2056
RALPH' LABORATORY #3

THEY EXPANDED the facilities of laboratory #3 to contain enough tanks to accommodate the remaining thirteen Alphas; six males and seven females. If their modified neural networks could not survive in a zero sensory input environment, the next logical step was to give them a full spectrum of sensory inputs generated by Virtual Reality constructs while at the same time depriving them of empirical reality.

Lai-Xii was already looking ahead to the next phase of the experiment, confident of the outcomes of Virtual Reality immersion. "Aurelio, you should have at least eight billion mobiles out there by now. I want you to upgrade them, at minimum cost to the consumers, with an extra little device. With each upgrade give a free Head Mounted Display to enable virtual reality entertainment programs to run through them. The poor deluded lot are so addicted to the mobiles already it should be no problem to start reprograming their minds to prefer virtual reality to actual reality."

"What programs do you want to run?"

"Sort it out with Maldonado. Use the Me-Me platform as the portal. I don't want advertising, just interactive entertainment. You will also need to monitor the effects. It shouldn't take more than a year to see a comprehensive change to social behaviour.
I'm particularly interested to see people turning to VR when they strike problematic situations in their real lives."

"Come on Maldo, you heard the lady." Aurelio and his new partner happily trotted off, keen to get their teeth into something solid, though Aurelio felt himself developing a 'tick' at the thought of how much the upgrades were going to cost.

Lai-Xii and Ptolemy searched for a suitable VR platform with which to 'entertain' the Alphas during the sensory depravation experiment. In 2056 the sophistication of VR environments with comprehensive facilities for interfacing with avatars needed very little modification. The primary aim of the experiment with the Alphas was to engage all their existing senses to the fullest possible degree to the point where, after immersion, actual reality would seem unreal and inadequate. The experimental subjects could be discarded afterwards if things went drastically wrong. Evgeniya and Ralph had already embarked on another harvesting program to ensure a good supply of replacements.

A small group of Alphas rolled into the laboratory. Pavel gave no hint of his rising discontent. Rather than betray his feelings he left the others to be sociable.

"Have any of you seen the others we met at the start. I remember Afanasy and Lubov," said Leonid.

"You *would* remember cutesy Lubov," Kapitolina gave him a nudge. "Personally, I do seem to recall that hunk, Afanasy."

Seemingly unconcerned Leonid questioned Misha as they prepared for their tanks. They'd all used some VR games in the past, so it seemed like a lark as far as they were concerned, except none of them had experienced complete sensory deprivation at the same time. "Where are Afanasy and Lubov? Aren't they doing this?"

Misha never said too much, he just got on with his job. "They've already helped us." That's all the information he was prepared to divulge knowing Lai-Xii's attitude to any breach of confidentiality. Lubov and Afanasy had become liabilities – useless in further experimentation after their failure in sensory deprivation. Instead Misha told them about the VR construct.

"Each of you will have your own avatar available for interactions with anyone else on your team. You will have full mind control over the programs just as you have control over your scooters and many other devices. So - if there are no more questions, let's finish setting up."

The main item of equipment; the sophisticated Head Mounted Display, a much more comprehensive piece of apparatus than what Aurelio was going to 'gift' to all his mobile phone users had to be fitted to their shaved skulls. It had no attachments to interfere with their flotation in the tanks. Each Alpha was lifted into the highly saline, body warm solution, naked. "You'll be out of there in half an hour," said Misha, "enjoy yourselves."

Each individual had the luxury of a personal tank to themselves. Total sensory deprivation meant exactly that, which mandated no physical contact

Four hours later Lai-Xii arrived with Harusuke. "Progress?"

"No one's panicked yet," Misha said.

"They'll need to pee," the practical, ever helpful Harusuke suggested.

"Right. You can bring them out Misha. What do your monitors show?"

"So far their behaviour seems completely normal. It's as if they've just spent the last four hours in actual reality. As expected, they first paired up before exploring their VR city. Then they formed two groups, roughly equal numbers and started setting up their own centres of operation. They've only just started creating rules to control their little bands. Er – a slight problem," Misha didn't seem to know what to do about an emergent complication. "I tried shutting down the VR construct in stages, and they all complained. If I didn't know better, I'd say they didn't want to come out."

"Excellent!" Lai-Xii turned to Harusuke, grinning with satisfaction. "The best news I've heard for a long time. Slow down the extraction, but bring them out if it. I want to see how they react to being out here again."

It had only taken ten minutes to turn them on, but a full further hour to bring them out. They were washed, dried and dressed and placed back on their scooters. None of them spoke during the procedure, their eyes could not seem to focus, their heads lolling about slightly. Even once in their own scooters, they didn't seem to fully comprehend their environment, or any of the people around them.

"What's happening here?" Lai-Xii expected some disorientation, but not this seemingly complete divorce from reality. Not that it particularly concerned her. It was in fact a good sign. The more they remained engaged in VR, the better. Existence on Europa did not offer much in the way of external stimulation. It all had to be mostly internally generated as if it was an actual reality. To all intents and purposes that's what it was likely to be, a Virtual Reality world - not one of seas, mountains, sky and green meadows with cute little furry animals.

Misha only shrugged. "Their minds must still be in VR."

"Everybody out! Now." Lai-Xii made a snap decision. She thought their presence was interfering with the subjects' ability to readjust. And she was right. Within five minutes of having vacated the laboratory, Leonid started moving his scooter.

Misha's eyebrows shot up. "He's the leader of one of the groups."

"Who's the other leader?"

"The girl, Kapitolina."

"That one? Moving away from Leonid?"

"Why yes. I'd better go in and help them."

"No. Stay here. I want to see what happens." She had an idea of course. If the VR had the desired effect, they should now see evidence of a change in their behaviour.

Leonid moved around the thirteen occupants of the room, giving each person who was in his group, a little nudge. Kapitolina did exactly the same thing to her group. The individuals turned their eyes to their respective leaders, their scooters moving towards them.

"Now don't tell me they are not the groups they formed in VR!" Lai-Xii was almost overcome with joy. Harusuke watched, fascinated by how easily the human mind could be controlled under the right circumstances. "If only we could achieve the same result with the Betas." Lai-Xii almost whispered the last sentence. "Misha, I want these people under constant surveillance from this moment on. I especially want to know if the new social groups continue to be cohesive. Inform me immediately if there are any signs of mental deterioration. Now let them go and have a pee." Harusuke smiled. Xii wasn't the hard bitch everyone thought she was.

*

"You've been in touch with NASA?" Lai-Xii asked Ptolemy, fully expecting an affirmative response. "Have they set up the special VR simulation I asked for?" The US Government undertook to provide Phototronic Systems with as much help as Lai-Xii needed. Hers was the only long term viable plan when taking into consideration the short term survivability of the human species on any planet, or moon, other than Earth. Distances to potentially habitable exoplanets were too great for current space travel capabilities, as was the inadequacy of terraforming technologies. As much as scientists fantasized about that, true terraforming required geological time scales with massive geological processes. Just treating the surface of a planet could not create a lasting biosphere.

"Yes, and yes," Ptolemy reported, pleased. "They already had most of what we needed. Their last run to Europe back in 2025 brought back all the data and imagery we need for now.

75

The NASA team had set up an Immersive Virtual Reality environment training platform to prepare humans for exploring Europa. Their Europa Clipper investigated the habitability of the moon's surface, having in mind the orthodox human body configuration as their focus for survivability. Nevertheless, the information gathered proved most helpful."

"I want to see what you've got."

"Use this HMD. It engages all your senses, except the olfactory. Don't fall over and don't get space sick," Ptolemy warned. "Better still, sit, because your brain is going to think you've become weightless."

Lai-Xii hadn't been in space. She may have to face the same scenario as millions, perhaps billions of others in the not too distant future. Eventually she and her team would have to transition into a non-biological format. So space travel might not be an issue at all. What may seem to be an artificial representation of reality in the VR simulation could become the accepted interpretation of actual reality – just the same way as their brains now generated 'impressions' of their current environment. It is only through adapting to that impressionist painting in the past that people were able to survive on Earth. There is no reason to think the mechanism would be any different after the exodus to Europa.

The launch into space meant having to suffer the 3g force to overcome Earth's gravitational pull. Lai-Xii had to remain seated until the booster rockets had fired to get them onto the right trajectory for Europa. To her the sensation of speed after the boost was disappointing. Space was too expansive to give any realistic reference points to allow the brain to comprehend true velocity. Only as she approached Mars for the sling shot, did she feel any progress.

The VR, comprehensively edited to bring the flight experience down from approximately five years, took just under an hour. Ptolemy watched Lai-Xii's head move about as she scanned the visual display of the Mars' approach and its departure. From her perspective she seemed to be standing still. Next in her line of sight was Europa, most of the program being dedicated to the approach and landing on Jupiter's icy moon.

"It seemed so flat and so perfectly round on photos," she commented, still conscious of it being only a simulation. "But it's not like that, and it's not as white as I imagined."

As the landing craft approached the surface, she concentrated on the landscape. It seemed an extraordinarily hostile and uninviting environment. Geysers of water nearby shot into the thin atmosphere, seemingly threatening the landing craft. Movements in the great slabs of ice-crusted surface seemed to jolt her. Ptolemy watched as her body tightened into her seat, her arms coming around to fold across her chest. He checked his watch – almost half an hour had elapsed. *Just a little longer, I want her to experience the sight of Jupiter.*

Ptolemy had sampled the VR himself, overcome not so much by Europa itself but the size of Jupiter in its sky. He gave Lai-Xii time to feel the incomprehensible magnitude of the spectacle – to see the bands of gaseous storms moving across its surface and its great red maelstrom in the southern hemisphere. Her head suddenly jerked back as she scanned the giant that filled Europa's horizon. *She must have seen the shadows.* Ptolemy had the same reaction on first seeing Europa's and Io's shadows drift across Jupiter's surface.

He touched her shoulder. She jumped, as much absorbed in the VR as he had been. Slowly he faded the images to let her eyes adjust to darkness. In the darkened room he removed the HMD gently. Lai-Xii remained seated, her hands over her eyes, head bent. She sat there immobile for so long Ptolemy began to worry.

"Xii?" again touching her shoulder.

Without moving she said, "I told you not to call me that."

Ptolemy breathed a sigh of relief. She was alright. Everyone reacts differently to VR, even short duration platforms. But this wasn't actually an artificial construct. It *was* reality. Only her presence on Europa was a contrivance. Brief though it was, Lai-Xii's mind had already grasped the most critical aspect of the phenomenon. *'We are not going to 'see' this with our own eyes*, she thought to herself.

Out aloud, she spoke partly to herself and partly to Ptolemy. "The problem with this is that the VR feeds through our external senses. We need to channel this data directly to the black phosphorus matrix of the Betas. See what Ralph can do to bypass the necessity for the HMDs."

Ptolemy was about to leave the chamber when Lai-Xii called him back. "Time for you to start planning our next city, we'll call it Arithmós, the city of numbers. You'll have to put a team together from all the stakeholder countries to help you."

"Where are we putting this 'Arithmós'?"

"My darling halfwit cockroach, do try and keep up – on Europa. Any more questions?" *'Obviously wealth cannot give a man intelligence, perhaps when he inhabits his own Black Phosphorus Matrix he'll be a bit quicker on the uptake.'*

As though to punctuate her thoughts he asked, "For how many people?"

"Several billion."

"All in the one city?"

"How much space do you think a single digitised BPM is going to occupy?"

"Oh – OH!" After all the years of experimentation the penny finally dropped.

A few days later in the Lab #3 conference room, Evgeniya had some disturbing news about the Betas. Since their isolation from sensory feeds from their Alphas, their behaviour had become quite erratic, exhibiting symptoms typical of people who had withdrawn from society into themselves. "Zey have bekome anxious over smallest zings, zey are depressed and do not vant discuss zeir problems. Zey even started to distance zemselves from each other. I gave zem some VR games. Zey are much better now."

"Can we still use them for the VR experiment?" What Lai-Xii heard didn't strike her as a problem, rather the opposite. If they could be 'corrected' using the VR simulation, there was no reason to think a bit of perceptual readjustment would do them any harm.

"Da. Some of zem may bekome confused about which reality is 'real'." Evgeniya seemed a little concerned.

"Why is that an issue? Their only purpose is to help us take the next step. If we lose a few there are many others ready to be scanned and uploaded."

With the great strides taken over the passing years Lai-Xii had become so focused on her mission that the loss of a few human lives didn't seem at all to be an impediment along the road to saving the entire species from extinction.

Ralph and Misha wanted to put the Betas through a double experience. "Since they already have magnetoreception, electroreceptors and thermoreception, I want to modify the simulation to feed them imagery digitised into those data formats."

"If they cope with that, then go one step further with the next intake. Let's see if they can comprehend our reality using only those sensors combined with perception of radio emissions." Lai-Xii wanted to push the Project forward as much as possible.

"Perhaps I can build in sensitivity to astrophysical maser, which is a naturally occurring source of stimulated spectral line emission, typically in the microwave portion of the electromagnetic spectrum – in case you didn't know. By decoding these emissions, they would be able to 'see' their sources, which arise in molecular clouds, planetary atmospheres, comets, stellar atmospheres, or various other conditions in interstellar space. So their comprehension of the cosmos would not only be greater than ours, it would also set up the foundations for their extended 'sensory' input requirements."

"Now that's why I have you on the team, Ralphie – not just your fabulous wealth and alluring soft puppy eyes."

Ten Beta Tengi were lowered into the isolation tanks, HMDs replaced by receptors feeding data directly into their BPMs. The many months of delay involved in doing all Ralph had in mind was absolutely necessary. It gave Lai-Xii the opportunity to brief Ptolemy on essential parameters required for the new city on Europa. She also met Heads-of-States from several countries to gauge the numbers of participants they could reasonably expect to take up the offer of a digitised existence. Arithmós would have to be future proofed in terms of population growth and in particular for the energy requirements for the billions of functioning digital entities.

Misha, plus one other technician assigned to each of the Betas, monitored their progress. After several hours none of the test subjects wanted to stop their immersion. "It's as though we've just put them in," commented Misha, "monitors show normal matrix activity, their processing speeds and power consumption have not increased."

"Let's push it along a little. Feed them the modified Europa VR and start them from the initial launch. Let's see how they react to their new sensors." Ralph wanted to see what the Betas' tolerance limit was.

Within the first twenty minutes, Misha noticed a spike in their energy use. Processing speeds tripled. Evgeniya was brought across the new development and offered her thoughts.

"I believe zey arre building new reality paradigm based on new sensorry data input. Ve should do another skan to see how zeir matrices may have modified. If zey don't vant to kome out, leave zem anotherr kouple hourrs. Give zem problem solving - like how set up living envirronment on Europa's surrface. Zey arre all professionally qualified in vide rrange of sciences. Let us see what zey kome up vith. Zey arre isolated from each otherr at moment, Da?"

"Indeed they are, but not for long." Ralph knew exactly what Evgeniya had in mind. It didn't take much to set up a network for them, leaving the interconnecting portals open for them to discover.

The procedure started late in the afternoon. Evgeniya decided to leave them on the VRs during the night. Whatever happened would surely be useful. Even if all the Betas burnt out, the information gathered would be put to good use with the next intake, who were already scanned and uploaded into new Tengi awaiting initialisation.

Misha was the first one back in Lab #3 in the morning. He immediately called Lai-Xii, Evgeniya and Ralph. The apparatus used to record the activity of the Betas neared full memory capacity. Whatever they were doing in the tanks had chewed up an astronomical amount of memory. "Look at this Ralph ... We have a message ... that monitor over there." They all went over to the last tank where the lab monitoring equipment was set up.

Lai-Xii read the short message, "Leave us connected – Kapitolina." She did not understand. "Who is this Kapitolina? I thought we'd isolated them from our work here in the facility."

"It kan only be Kapitolina-B, ze Beta," suggested Evgeniya, "I do not zink zey fully accept zey arre kopy of originals. Look what happened vith Irina-B. Zey obviously have sense of superriority over zeir Alphas."

"Take them out, but keep them connected to each other," Lai-Xii requested. "I want to talk with Kapitolina-B."

"Directly or through the network?"

"Directly, in actual reality, but leave her connected to the others."

Ralph took the precaution of having all the Betas strapped into cradles, rather them giving them back their scooters. Too many unknown factors had developed. 'I'm glad our systems are independent of the internet and not connected to the Cloud. I wouldn't want any of this being accessible to any outsiders,' he commented.

By mid-day the transition had been made from tanks to cradles. All the Betas had become completely unresponsive to normal stimuli. They showed no sign of recognition of being back in actual normal human reality. Misha had tried to engage their attention; speaking to them, waving his hands around in front of them, making loud noises. Nothing seemed to work. Though their torsos and heads moved, they appeared to be quite disoriented after their extended immersion.

Lai-Xii entered the lab as soon as the Betas had been secured in their cradles. "Kapitolina-B, can you hear me?" Lai-Xii addressed the Beta without getting a response. She tried again, still nothing. "Ralph, can you give her a tweak over the system?"

The third Beta from the left raised her chin slightly at Ralph's electronic prod. With difficulty Kapitolina-B responded, "I – am - Ka – pi – to –lina."

Lai-Xii humoured her for the moment. "Do you know where you are?"

"Not – on – Europa?"

"No. You are in the laboratory. You didn't go to Europa. It was a virtual reality simulation."

Evgeniya interrupted, "Slow down Lai-Xii, she is kompletely disorriented. She is betveen rrealities." Just as she'd finished, all the

Betas heads started moving about as if they were in a conversation. Ralph had arranged the cradles in a roughly circular layout. "Perhaps they are having a conference," suggested Misha.

"I – see – you. You are Lai-Xii. You are different."

"No, Kapitolina-B. I am the same. You are seeing me differently."

"Everything is different." Kapitolina-B's speech came to her a little more easily. "Why?"

"We have given all of you a new way of seeing reality. Have you been speaking with the others?"

"Yes. We want to go back."

"No. It is not possible. That was an experiment. None of it was real."

"WE WANT TO GO BACK!"

Evgeniya listened to the strange conversation. "VR feeds must have kompletely altered zeir perrception of rreality. I vould say zey may be feeling powerrless now, but empowerred in world zey have created for zemselves. Let zem go back."

"Ralph, have we got the memory capacity to deal with this?" Having received an affirmative nod, Lai-Xii directed him to continue with the VR feed.

"For the moment yes, but I'll have to upgrade our equipment. They are of no use to us buried away like that ... I'm just saying," Ralph said on seeing Lai-Xii pull a face.

It was a full week before Lai-Xii could assemble all her team again. Ptolemy had busied himself in China, Aurelio and Maldonado were setting up the VR interactive entertainment to be incorporated into Me-Me, and Salazar was harvesting new Alphas in Tau City.

"Here's the situation," Lai-Xii began, "using VR on the Betas has stabilised their BPMs. Ralph's augmented sensory inputs seem to be working. All the Betas have adjusted to their new reality, and prefer that to ours. That's exactly what we wanted. Misha - report on the condition of the Alphas, after their experience with VR in the tanks."

"They've been under constant surveillance. Initially, when they were first recruited, they didn't know each other. They've not had enough opportunity to form social bonds before the scans. Now, after their exposure to the VR experience in the sensory deprivation tanks, two 'gangs' have formed. I hesitate to call them 'teams' because they have deviated far from their pre-recruitment behaviour patterns and from any 'team' like activities."

Aurelio asked, "Is this something we need to consider when we market the new Me-Me with VR entertainment?

"No. That will only be low level exposure compared to the intensity of our in-house experiments." Ralph said.

"You know what this means, my naughty scheming children! When we've perfected the new sensory input systems for the BPM, we'll be ready to move. So Ralphie, my pretty ratty, better prepare a couple thousand Tengi, full bodied please, for us and many of our team."

"Full bodied Tengi?" asked Ralph.

"Yes, darling. We'll need the enhanced cerebral capacities of the thalidomide descendants as scientists, engineers, astronauts, programmers etc. for the first teams to go to Europa to set things up. There's a few more genetically engineered enhancements for them Evgeniya and I have been planning to free up more brain capacity from simple mundane chores."

"So how long before I can unload this biological decrepitude?" Old Salazar still felt the need to secure his immortality in spite of recently getting new organ upgrades. He received a slap on one cheek and a peck on the other from Lai-Xii for his impertinence.

11

ALPHA'S CONSPIRACY

CE 2058
TAU CITY

YULIA, a full bodied carer of thalidomide descendants, and Captain Viktor Pyryev had formed a relationship since their collaboration at the small protest gathering organised by her, and had married a few years later. Naturally, Yulia's passions inevitably involved her husband. She had become particularly active in support of the experimental tetra-amelia descendants to ensure their demands were met. It was easy enough to secure a promise from Lai-Xii that she and her friends could keep and raise the children they were pregnant with, even though they were only the incubators. Yulia had to fight to have the same concession applied to others. But Lai-Xii was right – they couldn't manage completely on their own and had to resign themselves to accepting the help of able bodied individuals.

Because of the extensive network Yulia had established, eventually she met Leonid and Kapitolina. She had an immediate rapport with Kapitolina, but still needed at lot of convincing about Kapitolina's claims about the brain scans and the existence of their artificial 'clones'.

"I can't believe Lai-Xii would do such things. She seemed so nice to us when I spoke to her, although it has been very difficult to get her Administration to implement her promises."

Kapitolina felt she was speaking for all the Alphas when she expressed her thoughts. "We are not just objects to be experimented

83

on and discarded when no longer useful. We were led to believe our contribution was to be collaborative; that through our training we had earned the right to be treated with respect and that our involvement would be valued."

"So you weren't informed about the Betas when you had the scans?" asked Yulia.

"We knew about the Betas. We saw them lined up, ready to receive our brain scans. They didn't tell us that all they wanted was our brains. Afterwards it seemed like we were an embarrassing inconvenience to Lai-Xii, except for the sensory implants."

"What happened after that?"

"They just dumped us. We were as good as locked up and under constant surveillance." Kapitolina had become quiet worked up by this stage. "As far as we're concerned, we've been betrayed! Lai-Xii's told us nothing. We must find out what she's doing – not just to us, but all the other tetra-amelias."

Leonid listened and nodded and grunted his discontent. He had a plan. He now joined the conversation, "Pavel wasn't happy about being used as a lab rat. Nor am I. They can't just use us and leave us out of it. I too want to know what they've done. Our first objective was to meet with our Betas. I don't know about the rest of you, but if there is a double of me living in this city pretending to be me, I want to know about it and I want to meet him. We've found out where they are locked up."

Yulia listened intently, shaking her head from time to time. This was not a situation that could be tolerated. She doubted whether another confrontation with Lai-Xii would result in any better outcomes than she'd already experienced. She didn't quite know what to do, but if Pavel knew where the Betas were held captive - perhaps … She stole a glance at Viktor, which immediately put him on edge.

"I don't like this at all," Viktor knew his wife well enough by then to understand that if she got a bee in her bonnet there would be risky action in the not too distant future. He had no idea just how risky until Leonid outlined their plan. Yulia obviously thought it was a workable plan. She kept looking at Victor with those eyes she knew he could never refuse. Poor man. He'd worked so hard to make a career for himself, and under rather difficult circumstances. Whatever the others may have thought of La-Xii he had dedicated himself to do the best he could for her – even without knowing what exactly she was doing and why this city actually existed in such an inhospitable environment.

The furrows on his brow only became deeper as the story unfolded. "This is just too dangerous. Do any of you understand the consequences if we get caught?"

"In spite of what happened to Irina with Irina-B, we have to let the Betas out. People have to see what is going on here. Have you never wondered why we're kept in isolation, why we're so well looked after, why there are always far more of us than your full-bodied selves?"

"What happened with Irina should not have happened. We know the Betas think they're far superior to us. I don't care," Kapitolina would not be deterred by Viktor's reticence either.

"Just how do you propose to infiltrate the research complex?" Viktor asked, knowing immediately in the back of his mind that his elevated rank as head of security in the city would have a major part to play.

Kapitolina explained the details of what they had in mind. "We've had the complex under surveillance for some time. All the Betas are housed in a more remote part of the grounds, though still under guard. They are not considered to be dangerous either to the Project, whatever that is, or to the people, so the guards are not the elite of the corps. We were hoping that with some show of higher authority," here she glanced at Viktor, as did Yulia, "access to their living quarters would not be too difficult."

"Once out of the main building," added Leonid, "we have vehicles ready to pick them up, and take them to a safe house.

Yulia's ability to think things through ensured much of the success she'd achieved for the tetra-amelia people so far. She asked the seemingly simplest question, "Do they want to be freed, if that's the right word for it?"

"Ah, well – yes. But here's the thing. Irina says they could be a very difficult bunch to deal with, given her past experience with Irina-B."

*

Viktor acquired four guards' uniforms for the carers, one of them a Captain's for Yulia. She could conceivably get away with it. Almost as tall as Victor with broader than average shoulders for a woman, she could be quite imposing. With the uniform and her hair in a bun she could probably intimidate lower ranked guards.

During a late evening under an overcast sky in February, with temperature -20°C, and rugged up to the eyeballs Viktor marched along the fresh snow covered path crunching their way towards Wing 12. His contingent of 'guards' escorted two Alphas in their scooters to the Beta's accommodation wing.

"STOY!" One of two regular guards on patrol duty confronted them not far from the entrance.

"Step aside!" Viktor ordered, "We're taking these two to Wing 12 under direct orders from Doctor Yermolov." Yulia knew how difficult it was to contact the doctor, in case the guard decided to try.

"Vashi dokumenty identifikatsii!" Being an inexperienced guard, the man did not comprehend that you don't demand identification documents from a superior officer.

"Idiot! Out of my way. Can't you see who I am," Viktor responded as he lifted the lapel of his heavy overcoat to reveal more clearly his insignia of rank.

"Pardon Komandir." The man stepped aside to let them pass, glancing towards the Captain at the same time. Yulia gave him her fiercest scowl, the one even Victor was afraid of.

Viktor turned to the officious guard, "Go! Report to my office, NOW – and take your man with you!" Since his interaction with Lai-Xii, Viktor had learnt when to back down and when to use his rank, especially against stupid subordinates.

The two guards hurried away, not giving Viktor's group a second glance other than looking at the two people in their scooters. And there was nothing unusual about them; most of the city's occupants were tetra-amelia individuals. They looked just like the others in Wing 12 they were supposed to be guarding.

"So far so good, Yulia whispered to Viktor, who only grunted.

"This isn't my idea of how to spend my one day off duty. The least amount of excitement in my day the better."

Yulia turned and smiled reassuringly to the others. She knew Viktor's moods. He was just annoyed at being delayed. Within a few minutes they were making their way up the short ramp to the main door. The grey pre-cast concrete walls held a metallic, windowless double door. Beside it, inside a small enclosed rusty metal cabinet, a keypad waited for anyone who knew the entrance code. It accepted Viktor's master code, which gave him almost universal access.

Inside, lights dimly lit the main narrow corridor walls that looked like they'd never been cleaned. Evenly spaced along the walls on either side closed doors showed the names of the occupants printed in small black letters.

"It's them," Yulia said quietly when she spotted Irina-B's name. They stopped to let Kapitolina knock. She knocked again when there was no response ... all eerily quiet. The three dim lights cast long shadows of the group as they slowly moved along.

"Try the next one," Viktor urged, "we don't want to be too long." Kapitolina knocked on the next door, a double door which was slightly ajar. Viktor pushed it open and poked his head in to look around. "They're in here. They look like they're all asleep."

The door squeaked as they entered, without disturbing the existing occupants. Arranged in a rough circle they remained motionless, seemingly completely unaware of the visitors. One could have been forgiven for thinking they may have been dead as there was no sign of life at all. The dimly lit, untidy room with its bare concrete walls and almost the complete absence of furniture did not present an inviting atmosphere.

Problems had emerged with the Betas after their deep VR exposure, particularly with their behaviour when allowed to roam freely in Tau City. Some people became suspicious of their haughty attitudes. When they were confronted it was noticed that small revealed parts of their bodies under their clothes looked like metal. Rumours quickly spread about them being machines, robots. Those dangerous rumours forced a precautionary measure to be taken - all Betas were taken out of public circulation. Even sensory data transmissions from their Alpha counterparts were terminated because of a peculiar development; the Betas became confused and disturbed by apparently having memories, adamant in the knowledge they did not actually have the associated experiences.

By withdrawing sensory input from their BPM's and having to rely on their own inadequate sensory input, the obvious deterioration of their 'minds' could only be postponed by introducing a Virtual Reality experience for them; an experience which they did not want to end once exposed to it. It became their preferred reality to actual human phenomenal existence.

"It's not the middle of the night, why would they be asleep?" Leonid pushed his way to the front, going all the way into the room. Viktor and the others followed. The ten Betas with eyes closed and heads bent slightly forward took no notice of the intruders. Kapitolina wheeled up to her Beta and couldn't help staring at her. She could have been her perfect identical twin. She noticed something around the side of her head, some kind of connection looking not unlike a USB port.

As she moved around to get a better look at it, Leonid-B suddenly opened his eyes to see Leonid staring at him, sitting directly in front of him. At first an angry expression flashed across Leonid-B's face before changing to one of surprise.

87

"What are *you* doing here?" he asked. By then all the Betas had 'woken' up. There wasn't supposed to be anyone in the VR program they were immersed in, other than themselves and the avatars they'd created.

Leonid came straight to the point, "To give you your freedom."

"We don't want our freedom," shouted Irina-B. She already seemed to be worked up about something. "Haven't you done enough!".

Kapitolina joined in. "We've been thinking and wondering about what Lai-Xii is doing – what she's done to us and what she's done to you."

"She took the world away from us!" Shouted Irina-B.

This time Yulia spoke, trying to calm the rising angst in the room. "Wouldn't you like to have that world back again? We can take you out of here."

"We have our world now."

When Viktor arrived with his group, all the Betas were joined in concert to an updated VR platform created for them by Misha, Ralph and Evgeniya. It was the only way they could keep their BPMs from deteriorating to the point of completely shutting down.

"Don't you want to join us and experience actual reality?" Yulia asked.

"We tried that. We were given your sensory experiences. But they weren't our own. It made us angry, confused. Just go away and leave us alone."

All this time Irina-B had been monopolising most of the conversation. Then Kapitolina-B spoke up. "I want to try," she said confidently.

"We could go together," said Kapitolina, "like sisters - identical twins."

"I'm not going anywhere!" Irina-B glanced at Irina. "I already know what it's like out there."

"I want to go too," said Lada-B.

"Me too," Leonid-B volunteered.

"Anyone else?" If not, we'll be going - right now." Viktor didn't want to take the chance of the two idiot guards raising the alarm and finding himself up to his fur ushanka in security troops.

No other Beta showed interest. "Right, get what you need and let's go. When we get outside try and look like you're being escorted by us. Got that?"

Within ten minutes, having Yulia's and the other carers' help to dress them for outside conditions – they needed to be camouflaged, as well as protected from the cold – a larger contingent filed out the door than had arrived. The sky had darkened further and snow had begun to fall again. No-one was around. The area seemed deserted as they crunched their way to the transport vehicle through the freshly fallen cover.

After Irina-B's behaviour Irina was surprised not to be having a confrontation with the three Betas who had decided to accompany them. She looked enquiringly at Kapitolina-B, who looked back, raising an eyebrow. "What do you want to know?"

On the way to the safe-house Kapitolina-B explained their experiences with sensory deprivation and the effects of the VR experiments. Then she added quite bluntly, "We don't feel we are copies of you. We are an upgraded version. We are better than you were. Since then and through our personal experiences in our VR world we have increased our capacities. We also have up-to-date sensory scanners that you don't have."

"Then why didn't you make an effort to free yourselves?" asked Irina. Kapitolina-B remained silent.

"Did you know Lai-Xii has engineered your DNA so you would be born without limbs?" Viktor asked. Although Lada-B and Leonid-B seemed to be absorbed in watching the passing cityscape, they were listening intently to the conversation. Now they turned sharply to Viktor.

"How do you know this? Why did they do it?" Lada-B demanded.

"I only found out by accident. I don't know why they are doing it."

"With your help we'll try and find out everything," Yulia seemed the most determined of them all to know the truth. "For the time being you should all try and lead normal lives until this 'abduction' investigation dies down. I suggest you just do normal things, and don't draw attention to yourselves." For the rest of the journey they all battled with their own thoughts.

*

"What do you mean three of them are gone!" Lai-Xii's furious voice seemed to reverberate throughout the entire complex. Misha made the mistake of going directly to Lai-Xii to tell her. He'd been keeping a close eye on the Alphas' movements yet was unable to prevent their organising the disappearance of three Betas. Security around the city to prevent infiltration put extreme emphasis on not letting the world at large become cognisant of the function of Tau City. However, internal security became just as relaxed in comparison. No one, not even Lai-Xii, expected there to be any major or even minor issues within the walls of her domain.

89

Yet there it was. A few of the Alphas, for some incomprehensible reason to Lai-Xii, had engineered the release of several Betas from their confined domiciles. The remaining individuals remained stubbornly quiet about the event.

"I've been monitoring the Alphas' psychological status to see how they were recovering from their VR exposure." Misha tried to make excuses for his lack of vigilance. "Yesterday afternoon they went out with some friends. It seemed nothing unusual."

"You had no idea what they were up to? The escape of three of our Betas cannot be a coincidence!" Then Lai-Xii turned her anger towards Salazar. "You're supposed to keep order in this City. Where are they? Find them and don't come back with excuses."

It wasn't difficult for a few identical twins to disappear from scrutiny, especially not with Viktor's help to alert them to the search patterns. The city had grown in complexity and exponentially in population. As all cities, it had a life of its own, independent of the purpose for which it was established in the first place. Cultures and sub-cultures developed to cater for the needs of the full bodied carers; security personnel and others with four limbs, as well as the very large numbers of tetra-amelia people who were increasing all the time.

"What am I going to do?" As always, at home Harusuke became the sympathetic ear and advisor to her partner's problems.

"What's the worst that can happen? They look like everybody else, behave like everybody else. They're not criminals or murderers. I suggest you keep a close check on our hospital. Everybody eventually needs medical help, especially if they've undergone substantial stressful experiences. You'll get them in the end. Besides, what have you lost – just six individuals – that's not a lot."

"What am I supposed to do with them when we catch them? I can't put them back with the others."

"Think it through. The problem isn't with the Betas; it's the Alphas. Just ... discard them ... you have thousands of others to work with now. And the Betas ... send them on a one-way trip to Europa. You've been planning another trip anyway. Don't forget – they are both human *and* machine. That's a real asset."

The following day Lai-Xii issued her orders, ensuring the machinery of change ground on relentlessly. She had begun the greatest migration ever seen on Earth – she had taken control of evolution and was in the process of changing the future of humanity. The transition had begun and nothing could impede the inevitable. Any issues along the way simply had to be dealt with in the context of their destiny.

Lai-Xii resumed her relentless drive to achieving her ambition. "Evgeniya, you and Salazar continue with the tetra-amelia production and their education. We must have scientists, engineers, astronauts, quantum programmers and expert technicians in every field ready for uploads into the next generation of Tengi. They will be the first teams to go to Europa to set up. Our primary focus is ensuring an adequate energy supply for the city Ptolemy is designing. You only have twenty years to get organised."

As if they didn't already have enough to do! The only option was to recruit more assistants. However, the more personnel that worked directly on the Project, the greater the security risks involved. Ralph also needed a bigger organisation in order to go into large scale production of full bodied Tengi. For the time being the spotlight on the escapees had eased.

Soon Lai-Xii and Evgeniya planned further 'enhancements' to the human body. "We need to get rid of a few more biological components Evgen. The new batch of tetra-amelias need as much brain activity devoted to getting to grips with their professions as we can engineer. What else can we get rid of at this stage?"

"Quite few zings. Everything not needed vill ease burrden on brrain and allow it to develop other functions. Ve kan engineer out parts like muscles of buttocks, exterrnal genitalia, exterrnal earr, body hairr, vomeronasal orrgan, visdom teeth, koccyx, erectorr pili, appendix, and even reproductive organs as procreation vill takes different route."

"Excellent. How many generations will it take?"

"Probably no more zan two. Ourr genetic engineering kapabilities have evolved dramatically since ve started zis Project."

"Liaise with Ralph and make sure the new generation Tengi he's working on take these changes into account." Getting back to good solid progress made Lai-Xii feel so much better. She'd almost recovered her old humour, except for a report from her security chief, Commander Viktor Pyryev."

"There's been a few reports of unrest among some of our religious groups." He tried not to be too specific in spite of having to report unusual behaviour in the city's population.

"Surely you can handle that. Civil disobedience should be nothing new to you, Komandir Viktor Pyryev." He was quite certain she alluded to the small part he played in a minor show of discontent against authority some years ago.

91

FROM THE BOOK OF ORIGINATION
DECLARATIONS TWELVE

12:1 Now the Shadow, craftier than any construct of the Lai-Xü saw an opportunity.

12: 2 And when there was strife between the people of the future It lay upon the Priest and cast dogma upon his mind.

12
OPPOSITION

TAU CITY

NO, the Commander could not handle the situation … at least the leader of the Russian Orthodox Church and that of the Christians did not want Viktor involved. They demanded to confront the people directly responsible for building artificial humans.

Balmy 24^0C temperatures always brought the people out in large numbers in Tau City. The weekly market in the city square, well attended by shoppers and children, created an inviting atmosphere which most people could not resist. It had been a particularly cold winter, forcing most people to remain indoors much of the time. In one corner of the square, worshippers made their leisurely way out of the timber Russian Orthodox Church. Though small, Ptolemy made sure it had the white spire festooned with the golden dome and triple crossbeams on the cross.

A most ordinary day in many respects … except for the altercation that developed close to the church door. It wasn't the first time the three sets of tetra-amelia twins attracted attention. As usual the Betas; Kapitolina-B, Leonid-B and Lada-B behaved rather badly.

"No, we will not get out of your way!" Shouted Leonid-B.

The three Alphas had already made way for the devout exiting the church, but the three Betas held their ground. "We have every right to be here, and there is no reason for us to move!" yelled Lada-B. For some unaccountable reason the Betas thought very highly of themselves, considering that their society 'owed' them. If they wanted to park their scooters directly in front of the church doors, then that's exactly what they would do. Leonid could not prevail upon them to compromise. It was the same everywhere they went together over the last few months, restaurants, shopping, markets – in fact it was just plain unpleasant to be with their Beta twins.

Leonid went over to his twin. "Don't you realize, brother, you're attracting too much attention to us. There's already been complaints from all sorts of people." Even before he'd finished speaking the long bearded priest was upon them, shaking his fists.

"Not you lot again! I've made an official complaint to the Bishop! Why do you have to upset everybody with your high minded attitudes? What makes you think you are so much better than everyone else?"

While admonishing them, the priest again caught a glimpse of Leonid-B's rather metallic looking skin under his loosely fitting clothes. He'd seen it before, as had some of his parishioners. They'd come to him with strange stories of how some of these people never ate or drank anything whenever they visited cafés; how three of them in particular seemed to have conversations with each other without actually moving their mouths.

Kapitolina-B, who seemed to be the most reasonable of the three, suddenly activated her scooter to run directly into a few of the passers-by. The ensuing commotion and shouting alerted the local guards. With quick thinking each of the Alphas diverted their twins' scooters into a side alley beside the church, with all six of them making a getaway just before the guards arrived to consult the priest.

Back at their residence, Leonid wanted to sort out the mess once and for all. "You can't keep doing this brother!" he tried to speak sternly to his twin, even though he knew how little effect it would have. "I think you lot have really done it this time. We'll have to lay low for a while and hope it all blows over. I really don't know what you're all thinking. What's your problem anyway?"

"There is no problem," replied Leonid-B, "only an impediment." He looked directly and unemotionally at his original.

"And what's this great impediment?" Kapitolina was as fed up with the developing situation as her two Alpha companions.

"You. You are the impediment. While you continue to exist, we cannot. We are treated as inferior laboratory specimens, which we most certainly are not."

"Is that a threat?" Leonid quietly shot back.

"No ... a fact. The impediment will have to be removed."

"THAT'S IT! I'm not taking this shit anymore! We tried to help you and this is the rubbish you throw back at us – *You* lot are the impediment! Leonid had had a gutful - he still had a gut.

94

The two Bishops and a representative of the Atheist members of the community had to negotiate with Security first if they wanted an audience with Lai-Xii. The Catholic Bishop tried to get his message across to the Commander as succinctly as possible.

"These individuals, three in particular, are not just a disruptive element in the community upsetting our peaceful coexistence, they are – they are – how shall I put it? – we don't think they are entirely human ... without putting too fine a point on it."

Viktor had trouble to not show his concern. He knew exactly who they were talking about. He had descriptions of them from other sources over the months, always in relation to complaints of one kind or another. *I knew I should have stayed out of this business. Yulia is impossible when it comes to any kind of injustice, especially when it concerns these poor disabled buggers.* He was trying to find a way of diffusing the situation, but it seemed to have gone too far. "What exactly do you want me to do?"

"We don't want *you* to do anything, other than to let us see Lai-Xii." The Atheist representative suggested.

"I will speak with her. Now go back to your communities." They hesitated, looked at each other then back at Viktor. He said, "If you don't go, nothing will be done."

They were still undecided until the Orthodox Bishop replied, "One week," then all three turned to purposefully march out of Viktor's office, disgruntled.

"They refuse to talk to me. Forgive me for saying so, but I think this is a serious matter requiring your attention, Ma'am."

"Why do you think that Commander Pyryev?" She always called him by his family name when upset with him, otherwise she would have berated him with some silly little abuse.

"Because it concerns the missing Alphas and Betas, Ma'am."

Between clenched teeth she hissed, "Why didn't you say so in the first place instead of wasting my time!" Lai-Xii considered this to be a very serious turn of events. Initially she felt reassured by Harusuke's advise. But this was escalating into something potentially catastrophic.

"When were they last seen?" she fired without looking at him, already on the comms to get Ptolemy.

"Yesterday, in front of the Russian Orthodox Church. So they can't be too far away."

"For your sake, Commander Pyryev, I want them in Lab #3 no later than the day after tomorrow." Lai-Xii left it at that.

Within the hour Ptolemy was in her office, accompanied by Evgeniya and Ralph. There was no need to bother the other boys just yet. Even without hearing the specifics of the complaints, Lai-Xii distilled the situation down to its bare essentials. Whatever the complaint was, the three Alphas and three Betas had to be dealt with most expediently. In fact, all the Alphas had to be 'dealt' with along the lines of Harusuke's suggestion – discarded - quietly. They had served their purpose and had become surplus to requirements. The Betas may still have some value. They would be easier to control. Ralph's VR experiment had proved that.

"You've let me down," she said to Ptolemy, without the usual abusive banter. He knew immediately something extremely serious had emerged. "I want you to inaugurate a public holiday, to be repeated each year from next year onwards. Celebrations for a week, at our expense." Ptolemy's eyes grew wide, his first thought obviously related to 'cost'. "Not expensive, when you think of all the money you've made in the last five years. I doubt if you can even count it."

"Why?"

"Why you've let me down, or why the celebration?" Ptolemy remained silent, the best policy under the circumstances. "Because you have not managed to catch the fugitives after all these months. As far as the public holiday is concerned – make up a story – we've cured some deadly disease with the help of all the tetra-amelias – ask Evgeniya. Say we couldn't have done it without their selfless sacrifice over the many years. Say nothing about the Alphas or the Betas. The people will forget soon enough with food and drink in their bellies. They may as well enjoy it now because it will soon become a thing of the past."

That evening the two ladies decided to walk home. Lai-Xii and Harusuke lived in the back part of the municipal centre, situated several streets behind the Russian Orthodox church. Though not opulent, their home was comfortable and spacious. A large park with a small lake directly across from their street suited their lifestyle, for they both liked to contemplate while walking.

Arriving at home Lai-Xii wasted no time in unloading to Harusuke as they made their way to the long couch in front of the fireplace.

"I've made my decision. We must have much tighter security. The city is getting too big, too many undercurrents, too many people."

"Are we going to move?"

"No. Lockdown. If word gets out to the worlds' population about our Project – well, not so much the Project but our efficient methods – I'm thinking we might never get to Europa."

"Is it really that serious?"

"Yes. I have an idea the religious fanatics have twigged to our Betas. I think we should have rounded them up much sooner."

"Surely they would understand this is only a transitional phase. There's no other way to ensure our ultimate survival." Harusuke seemed to have a more optimistic attitude to people's ability to understand a great enterprise and the things that must be done for it to succeed. Lai-Xii was a realist. She knew people - the majority of people were sheep. They would always follow the loudest voice. They were simply stupid and gullible, not able to see past the next green blade of grass. Tell them something often enough and they'll believe it.

"No, my lovely, the simple fact is that people do not want change. It frightens them, it moves them out of their comfort zone. They don't want it even if they're sitting in a pot of water coming to the boil. It's getting harder. Every little advance we make seems to slow us down rather than push us forward. Just look at those Alphas. What a great contribution they've made. And the Betas … Ralph has achieved an incomprehensible thing. These people are actually still 'people', even though their physical selves are not blood and bone. Who knows what incredible things will happen when quantum computing comes on line."

"How do you intend to deal with the Alphas?" Harusuke would not normally ask about day-to-day operational matters, but this time she had something in mind.

"Why do you ask? I was going to get Ptolemy to make them disappear."

"They could still be useful," suggested Harusuke. "Have you heard of the Ixodes tick? There's a lot of them about in central Kamchatka, causing a lot of problems."

"Why should I care about a tick?" Lai-Xii always had patience for her partner. She was a sharp one and often had most useful little gems in her elegant geisha kinchaku kago, which she still carried with her everywhere.

"Perhaps Evgeniya has noticed the increasing prevelance of Lyme disease in the population. I've been thinking about it for some time. The worrying thing is …"

Before she could finish her sentence Lai-Xii jumped right in. "Of course, we should have thought of this before! The little buggers can trigger encephalitis, an inflammation of the brain. I'll get Evgeniya onto it first thing. This could just be the deadly disease we need." The evening progressed pleasantly, starting with a full lipped kiss for Harusuke.

Time had stretched late into the night, as it always did when Harusuke and Lai-Xii re-aligned their focus, setting the ship back on course. The morning summer light was only a few hours away and many things awaited Lai-Xii's attention that day. Lying there together, afterwards, curled against each other, Lai-Xii whispered, "Do you still remember mother Ishino at the geisha house?"

"That was so long ago,' answered Harusuke, almost asleep.

*

The late morning started well. Evgeniya arrived in Lai-Xii's office at Ralph's research centre even before Lai-Xii. She smiled broadly, most unusual for Evgeniya, for her austere character focused so much on the business of science it left little to smile about in general. "What are you so happy about Evgen, my pet?" Lai-Xii settled behind her desk on arrival. In front of her, in a little glass display case, several tiny bugs wandered about.

"Are zese little darlings you vant talk about?"

"Ticks? How did you catch them so quickly? Ptolemy only spoke to you about it this morning."

"Zey are no strangers in laborratory. Zey have been ourr guests for several years now. No major issue, just something I started to follow up for interest. You know about encephalitis – so you appreciate danger it represents to ourr vork. Ve cannot afford to have ourr new Alpha intakes be kontaminated. Ve have no idea how it could corrupt zeir neural netvorks, and subsequently the Betas."

"So you're going to tell me … what?"

"Zat ve have almost solved problem. Very soon ve vill be able to inokulate against zeir venom. No one need suffer the fevers, headaches, lethargy and deterioration of zeir brains any morre. Not just general population outside city, but all of us, including ourr 'special' troublesome people."

Lai-Xii was so pleased that her sudden impromptu reaction took Evgeniya completely by surprise. She was in front of her in a flash planting a huge kiss full on the lips. Though it made Evgen blush profusely, almost blending her skin colour with the flaming red of her hair, she did not object at all. With a further two handed stroke of her face, Lai-Xii disengaged herself from Evgen - whose arms had automatically come up to hold Lai-Xii.

Her thoughts in furious activity, she immediately had the foundation of the plan worked out. "First bring me up to date with everything you've done with the bugs, then I want you to give all the original Alphas a little bite. Just make sure none of them survive. I expect the three absentees to be back by tomorrow. I also want you to infect a few of the new batch of Alphas, but make sure you treat them so they can recover. I'll be bringing a few religious zealots to your lab in ten days, and I want you to tell them the good news. They think we're creating some kind of monsters. This'll sort them out – or at least buy us plenty of time."

"Da, I vill be ready, Xii." She blushed again as she left the office. Lai-Xii didn't reprimand her for the slip of the tongue.

As ordered, Commander Pyryev did not fail to produce the missing persons, human and Tengi. He had no choice. Besides, he wasn't the one who wanted to help them in the first place. The six offenders sat in their scooters lined up in front of Lai-Xii in her office. She walked back and forth several times in front of the apprehensive looking Alphas and the haughty expressions of the Betas.

"Why did you do it Kapitolina?" she demanded.

"We don't know what you're doing. What we *do* know, none of us likes very much."

Lai-Xii pulled out her Ixodes Tick box. "Do you know about these?" She showed them the sample Evgeniya left on her desk. They all looked, but said nothing. "Do you know what they do to people and animals? No, of course you don't!" Her voice went up a notch. "Ever heard of Lyme disease? Ever heard of encephalitis? Don't bother to answer," she snapped as Leonid started to say something. "With the help of *all* the people in this city, we have almost been able to eradicate the problem." If they happened to be questioned by one of the Bishops they could corroborate Lai-Xii's ruse.

Having got the frustration off her chest she dismissed them without bothering with their excuses or giving them further information. Commander Viktor Pyryev waited outside the office after he delivered the fugitives. She called him in, looking much relieved by having unloaded.

"You can tell your Bishops I'll see them in ten days in my office. Just make sure they don't see anything they shouldn't on the way here."

Without a word or a salute Viktor turned and left. Outside the closed door of the office his shoulders slumped and a relieved long sigh escaped of their own volition. *That was close. I am not going to let Yulia pull me into any more of these escapades!*

*

Evgeniya immediately carried out Lai-Xii's orders, happy to do anything that would please her. After all the years of working with her so closely, this was the first time she really felt noticed, valued – and the kiss wasn't all that bad either.

The Alpha's were duly infected, then the treatment started as soon as the areas of redness on their chests began to expand – a sign that the venom had begun its action. The antidote wasn't quite enough to cure them, only enough to ensure an alleviation of the symptoms a week or so later. The Betas received no special treatment, after being reunited with their group. As a distraction however, Ralph ensured they received an updated VR to enhance their existing virtual environment, with a corresponding substantial tightening of security around Wing 12. No doubt the three escapees would have lots of stories to tell the others to keep them all amused for some time.

Lai-Xii prepared her office to receive the visitors. All her offices were set up the same; bare, except for the annular table accommodating twenty, in the exact centre of a smallish room with a small desk off to the side. No windows and no ornamentation on the walls except computer screens flush with the wall surfaces. She cleared out the table and all seating except her own chair behind the desk. She didn't bother to stand when her guests arrived, ushered in by Commander Pyryev.

The two Bishops were immediately affronted by the lack of protocol displayed by this woman. Their animosity towards her increased exponentially from the start. When she did not greet them the atheist representative took it upon himself to make the introductions, seemingly ignoring her bad manners.

"I am Alexi Petrov. I speak for those not represented by my companions. This is Bishop Piy Bogolomov of the Russian Orthodox Church in Tau City, and on my left is Bishop Dimitri Ivanov from the Christian community." Still Lai-Xii remained silent. She knew them of course – or of them, but had prior personal interactions. They must have felt uncomfortable: No greeting befitting their status and no seating for them, all kept standing, waiting, while that woman remained seated. Discomfort quickly morphed into anger as they growled something unintelligible to each other.

Lai-Xii knew the signs well enough. She waved for them to come forward, which they did after a little hesitation. "Gentlemen."
Then she waited - their indignant attitude and sense of superiority was all too familiar to her. It failed to intimidate.

As she still remained silent Petrov continued.

"We have grave concerns about the nature of activities being carried out in this research facility." Lai-Xii raised questioning eyebrows. "... in particular, about some of the – the – people here."

"Which people?" She smiled a standard board-room smile.

"The ungodly ones," volunteered Ivanov the Christian Bishop.

"Specifically ...?" She was determined to get them to commit before she sprang the disarming good news, and waited for Ptolemy to make his pre-arranged appearance.

"We have had many complaints about several tetra-amelias behaving badly around the city - upsetting people," said Bishop Bogolomov. "They appear to be human, but some of our citizens think they might just be machines."

Ah, so there it is. Now we're getting somewhere. She smiled disarmingly this time. "We have been testing some AI robot carers, who have unfortunately developed a slight behavioural problem."

Because she did not deny the allegation, and because AI robot assistants were a common place item in the 2050's, the three found little to respond with. They didn't think fast enough to question why carers, even robotic ones, didn't have the full complement of extremities to help them carry out their duties. Lai-Xii waited patiently with a dismissive expression which said, 'If there's nothing else – we're finished – you can go'. They didn't take the hint.

"There is something else," said Petrov again. "We don't understand why there are more and more tetra-amelia children than normal ones. And from time to time many of them seem to disappear." The bishops made supporting grunts while glancing to each other, then at Lai-Xii.

"So, no one has explained to you what we are doing and why this city even exists? We are doing some very important ..." Before she could finish her sentence a knock on the door preceded Ptolemy's entrance. "Come in – Come in Mayor Ptolemy. You know these gentlemen, I assume."

"Ma'am, the public holiday and annual celebrations have been arranged to start from July next year in recognition of the success of our research," he announced, giving only a cursory glance at the three standing men.

"Thank you, Mayor." Ptolemy withdrew, only then with a brief nod of recognition to the company he'd just disturbed as he departed.

Lai-Xii checked Evgeniya's readiness, and without bothering to explain motioned for the three men to follow her.

Security chief Pyryev was waiting for her outside the door. She waved him away, "We won't be needing you, Commander," making a great show of the fact that these visitors did not represent any kind of security risk – a fact not unnoticed by the men.

Twenty minutes later in the infirmary at the hospital Evgeniya explained one of the many health problems they faced in Kamchatka. The men knew of the ticks of course, but just assumed that it was another unfortunate aspect of life, like the inclement weather. They'd all grown up with them and thought nothing of the pests, except just that – pests. As they observed the three tick bitten patients, seeing the severe symptoms and hearing their words of gratitude for their care, the visitors' indignation had clearly thawed. The Alphas were told, and they had no reason to believe otherwise, that during their escapade they were most unfortunate to have been infected by the venom of the Ixodes ticks.

"As you can see, the latest inoculation has finally shown the greatest promise so far in all our experimentation. For some reason the tetra-amelias appear to have become more susceptible than any other members of our community. So it is with considerable pleasure that the Mayor has initiated the celebrations." Lai-Xii had let her hard stance soften to match their changing attitude. "Now, if there is nothing else, we should let the patients rest."

Once outside the building the three representatives walked in silence down the long avenue of trees. It was a late summer afternoon, with a warm fragrant breeze - most pleasant to just walk and think. They stopped by the park to sit side by side on a bench near a pond. Everything seemed so benign under the overhanging branches, with the ducks bobbing on calm waters. They'd arrived in a huff to see Lai-Xii, had all their questions answered, and they would now be seen as the architects of a week-long celebration every year.

"Something is still not right." Alexi just had this feeling they'd been bamboozled by an obnoxious, beautiful, crafty, woman. Infuriating. "What do you think Dimitri?"

"Why didn't she show us the robots? I wanted to see the robots. People said they looked very human."

"I would have liked to speak with one of them," added Piy, "there's no problem if they're only AIs, maybe just a behaviour modification is all that's needed. But if they are what I suspect, then the Church has an issue with that."

Alexi advised patience. "We have no direct evidence one way or the other. And it's fantastic what they've done with curing the Lyme disease, don't you think? I suggest we remain vigilant and if the unrest continues we have plenty of time to deal with the issue.
In the meantime, let them get on with the work they are doing. Perhaps we could ask Lai-Xii to be less secretive about it."

Piy remained sceptical. "But why was she in such a hurry to get rid of us? And why didn't she volunteer to show us their AIs? If she's part of some kind of secret Raëlian society I will have to take matters further. Such a deep moral crisis cannot be allowed to escalate. Our policy is publicly known; transferring human memory into a clone is totally unacceptable, especially if that transfer is into a synthetic facsimile of a human being."

Voicing a not too dissimilar attitude, the Christian Bishop Dimitri found common ground with the Russian Orthodox Churches views. "If it is not just cloning individual organs then the practice is directly in contempt of God's Law. In the view of the Christian Church disease and death are not necessarily evil. But - if people arrogantly go about trying to make their lives eternal, then they are doomed to profound disaster and will bring upon themselves and their clones unspeakable suffering."

"That may be so," Alexi tried to keep to the middle ground, "however we should really have irrefutable proof that anything like that is going on before we can do anything."

"Nevertheless I'll confer with my superior, in Petropavlovsk."

It didn't help the cause of the three representatives of the majority of people in Tau City that the three Alphas had died. Lai-Xii conveyed the unfortunate news of the deaths of the patients, indicating her determination to increase their efforts to stamp out this disease. Harusuke suggested a Public Relations exercise by having a public honorary funeral for the three victims. The other seven Alphas from the first batch seemed to have vanished into thin air.

Alexi Petrov attended the funeral to express his condolences. He made some off-hand comments about how fortunate it was that robots were not susceptible to such human frailties. "No, indeed," replied Lai-Xii knowing full well he was just fishing to get more information about her Betas. "They are undergoing a major behaviour modification program, and I don't mind telling you," here she made a show of furtively looking around as if to make sure she would not be overheard, "our Virtual Reality re-training strategy is working beyond expectations." Alexi listened, apparently satisfied with this little ruse. Lai-Xii had not the least doubt he would go running to the two Bishops with the information. She had, after all, only told the truth about the VR situation.

FROM THE BOOK OF ORIGINATION
DECLARATIONS THIRTEEN

13:1 It was to the promised celestial orb their hearts had to turn if the journey was to become a reality,

13:2 But the Highest in all the lands could not see beyond their Earthly desires for the Shadow had contaminated their Thoughts.

13:3 So it came to pass that the day of Exodus was forced upon them.

13

SECOND EUROPA MISSION

CE 2080
BAIKONUR COSMODROME, KAZAKHSTAN

THE VOSTOCHNY COSMODROME in far east Russia near the Chinese border, might have seemed to be a better choice than Baikonur. But because of its high profile as well as busy schedule of launches, the three major powers considered security to be a far greater risk at Vostochy. The world's population wasn't ready to be made aware of the long term future planned for humanity.

Baikonur, an inhospitable desolate place without a tree in sight for three hundred kilometres of pancake flat desert in any direction from the launch site, awaited the arrival of Lai-Xii and her Europanauts.

*

The heads of major world governments had finally decided to act. The turning point came when Lai-Xii's Phototronic Systems introduced her third generation Tengi to them – the Deltas.

Inside each of ten Tengi bodies, safely suspended in a jelly like substance, resided a small cube of unspecified material housing a human psyche.

At the UN headquarters in Geneva in a private audience chamber, the Deltas answered questions put to them by the delegates. Everything from the forthcoming mission parameters, to opinions about the state of the planet in terms of climate change, geopolitical relations and the arts. They even exchanged a few jokes.

"Where actually are you?" asked the US Secretary of State. They all saw the exquisitely engineered gold facades of the Delta model Tengi, not pretending to replicate human shape or characteristics too faithfully, and found it difficult to reconcile those effigies with the voices they heard coming from them.

DeltaTunit10.ndf asked Lai-Xii, "May I?"

He sat closest to the Secretary of State. On Lai-Xii's affirmative nod he stood to step in front of the Secretary. All the other delegates crowded around, obviously just as curious. DeltaTunit10.ndf lifted his left hand to a point equivalent to the position of a male right nipple. He pressed. A panel slid down to reveal the 200 millimetre cube, resting in a close fitting enclosure.

"I am here," said DeltaTunit10.ndf.

"You have name?" asked the Minister of Chinese National Defence.

"I am DeltaTunit10.ndf but you can call me Ten."

The ten, third generation Tengi functioned on two levels; between each other in a Virtual Reality construct they existed independent of human reality. And on the outer level, Lai-Xii's world, which provided them with all the sensory data input from additional sensors that had very little in common with the five human senses. It was because of their arsenal of extraordinary capabilities, as well as expertise, that they were making the journey to Europa first. The delegates wanted know if it was a return trip for them. Ten and his associates didn't mind either way, more likely it would be a permanent posting.

...

At the conclusion of the exposition Lai-Xii took her experts and Europanauts to the Cosmodrome in Kazakhstan to gauge the readiness for the launch. Colonel Sanzhar Serik went over the basics, which had already been worked out between himself and Lai-Xii's team.

"Your first twelve space wagons are ready to go. All your equipment for setting up the power plants is distributed between them, with double backups, also evenly distributed. In case of mishaps to any single wagon the others can make up the losses."

"Our accommodation and power sources?" asked DeltaTunit8.ndf

"All ready – er – Delta Eight."

"ETD?" Lai-Xii was keen to get this part of the Project started as soon as possible. They'd been working for years, not just to design the energy systems on Europa, but to have perfect working prototypes for her Europanauts.

106

"Three weeks from today. Fuelling is being completed now – payload is in place on all wagons and weather conditions will be optimum in two weeks. We take them to the pads then." Colonel Serik exuded confidence, even arrogance one might say. He'd been working covertly with Lai-Xii and her team of five other men for many years. "The question is – will *you* be ready?"

This sort of banter established their relationship in the first place. Lai-Xii chucked him under the chin from close range and lightly tugged on his nose. The answer was obvious.

"What say you my pets - are you satisfied?" The Deltas, each with specific areas of expertise, had been checking all systems while Lai-Xii wasted time in pleasantries with Colonel Serik.

Three, the most vocal of all the Deltas gave a brief grunt, "Good enough." He was an odd one in the bunch – he actually had a sense of humour.

Numbered in order of their rank within the team, the Delta Tengi prepared for the mission in VR exercises. A great deal more data had been collected about Europa; weather, topography, geo-instability, cosmic radiation exposure, Jupiter's tidal pressures and some most critically data about the sub-surface ocean. With all that information a combined US, Chinese, Russian and Indian collaboration produced such a detailed simulated Europa environment that the Deltas were able to formulate their plans in fine detail for the energy infrastructure installation on the small moon in readiness for the influx of human inhabitants. It was the European Space Agency's task to build a physical representation of the Pwyll crater environment to help the Delta team make their transition from VR to actual reality. That transition had to be seamless to obviate any confusion between 'virtual' constructions, and facilities brought into existence in actuality. Although all their 'minds' were interconnected, there still had to be an overall final decision maker. 'One' became the effective 'Commander', 'Two' his 2OIC and 'Three' the communications link back to Earth.

*

The demise of the original Beta team should have occurred gradually without drawing attention, given the circumstances of their existence. Their security had been compromised by their divergent behaviour. Addiction to the then inadequate VR simulations caused their minds to prefer existence in an artificial world. They had served their purpose as well as causing considerable problems for Lai-Xii. The incidental command to dispose of them came from her while she was engaged in important launch related matters, not even bothering to follow up with Viktor Pyryev if it had been carried out.

"Do you remember those people you tried set free with the help of Leonid and Kapitolina?" Viktor asked Yulia soon after receiving Lai-Xii's command.

"I liked that girl Kapitolina. It was most disappointing the way the whole thing turned out."

"The Betas have been locked up all this time. Now Lai-Xii wants them terminated."

He didn't really know why he told her. He should not have spoken about such security matters with anyone not directly involved. He should have foreseen her reaction.

"No! What kind of a monster is she? They are real people trapped inside those monstrous robot cages. You can't let it happen!"

He knew straight away that he'd just volunteered himself for another one of Yulia's schemes. Lai-Xii never did check with Viktor about those Betas. They were simply not important anymore in the greater scheme of her Project. Neither did Viktor volunteer any information about them.

*

At the end of three weeks the twelve space wagons launched in three groups, with a two-week gap between them. Lai-Xii didn't need to be present. She trusted her collaborator Colonel Sanzhar Serik. Over the years of development he proved he could follow orders. That's all she wanted from him. Not a brilliant man, not even a particularly clever one, but a good Russian soldier.

"Who did you send first?" Lai-Xii asked over secure comms.

"The unmanned wagon. There were no problems with its launch so we let the others fly in succession. The last six wagons are on the rails now making their way to the launch pads. I'll be an old man by the time they get back," the Colonel added.

"Indeed you will." Lai-Xii didn't make her longevity technology freely available to all and sundry. The Colonel was only a small and dispensable cog in the machinery of change.

Soon though she would have to make one of the more difficult decision of the Project to date ... which of the world leaders would she allow to join her core of potential immortals - if any. There were several who threatened world stability driven by their own greed for power and wealth. Economic volatility could be managed. However, no panacea existed for the destruction of life's infrastructure through the use of nuclear weaponry.

"Let us hope our teams succeed," she voiced her thoughts aloud more to herself than Colonel Sanzhar, a man who had outlived his purpose. Lai-Xii knew it was a one way trip for the team of ten. The next armada might launch from Vostochy or even The Kennedy Space Centre.

*

Four years, two weeks, three days and eleven hours after DeltaTunit3.ndf left the pad at Baikonur he reported in, the third time since departure.

"Three for Lai-Xii - Three for Lai-Xii. We have arrived above Pwyll crater." He didn't bother waiting for a response before continuing. It didn't matter if they heard him. They had a job to do and were getting on with it. Each manned space wagon had its own pilot. The others would be guided down once the team had successfully landed at the chosen location.

"Lai-Xii, are you there? This is One." The communication from the first manned space wagon left 38.532 minutes ago.

"Yes One - Report." It was laborious to have a delayed conversation, so Lai-Xii kept it to a minimum.

"All wagons have arrived. We are parked in orbit. Will descend East of Pwyll crater. No tectonic activity apparent. Area is stable as expected."

"Proceed." There was no reason to delay. The first survey mission had confirmed long term stability for the next several tens of thousands of years, so the energy generators could be safely established.

During the planning stage, it was determined that the Pwyll crater area in the southern hemisphere seemed the most appropriate location for the settlement. It was an area of least lineae (long linear fractures caused by tidal flexing) and it was devoid of all penitents (the tall icy spikes) which plagued the equatorial region. The crater's relatively flat centre was also large enough to house the computer hardware structures to hold the data clusters of the billions of individuals destined to live there. The twenty-six kilometre crater's flat bottomed base would readily accommodate the core of the complex, with its 'ethnic' areas along the gentle slopes of the six hundred meters high internal circular slope.

DeltaTunit3.ndf stepped out onto the surface of Europa. His automaton needed no insulation and his own chamber within it had climate control. He looked at the curved crater rim but didn't dwell on it; a sight familiar from the VR simulation. He proceeded to unload the explorer vehicle with alacrity, paying no attention to

Deltas Seven, Eight and Nine doing the same. The greater cosmos held Delta Nine's gaze a little longer. She had tried to imagine what it would really be like. The scene was disappointingly no different from her mind picture created by the VR simulations.

"Two and Three come with me. We'll go to the centre of the crater - Four and Five up onto the rim. The rest of you spread out as ..."

She was cut off by Ten before he could finish the sentence. "We know what to do."

The survey equipment was already loaded onto the explorers and their own augmented senses had already started feeding data back to Earth to the Australian Square Kilometre Pathfinder radio astronomy array. Analysts from all the stake holder countries had gathered at the secure remote facility. Their reports up the chain of command would ultimately determine the fate of the planned transition and exodus.

*

Back in Tau City the fire had already been set and their warm sitting room welcomed them on arrival at home. They'd completed their walk in the park. They decided to stay in. As usual, Lai-Xii began as soon as they were safely inside away from earshot of passing foot traffic. It was inevitable that as the Project built up momentum, more and more people would have to get involved. It didn't make Lai-Xii feel very secure. "We've already had a couple of minor incidences because of the first batch of our Alphas and Betas," she complained to Harusuke.

As always Harusuke tried to calm her partner. "We are progressing so well that it might even mean, in the fullness of time, that you'll have to relinquish control of the Project altogether. How do you feel about that?"

"That's not going to happen!" Then she saw Harusuke's twinkling eye. "You are a she-devil, darling."

Harusuke continued, "The Project is almost at the point of no return. Once it's built up enough momentum and enough money has been committed to it, nothing will be able to stop it. There might be a few delays, perhaps a little urgency now and then, but it will be unstoppable."

"I'm still concerned about religious fanatics like those priests who made trouble a few years back. They've started their own investigations, as you know. Unfortunately, we weren't able to hoodwink them with that tick ruse for very long."

"I've been monitoring world news, paying particular attention to anything that might have an impact on our Project.

There's rumours coming from the US we might be affiliated with the Raëlians," said Harusuke.

"Not that weird mob who think the resurrection of Jesus Christ is going to be achieved through a scientific cloning process? I know about them. What have you heard?" she asked Harusuke.

"Somehow they got wind of our Project and think we're working towards human immortality. Viktor's had several representations from them wanting to 'contribute' to our scientific research." Though Lai-Xii took no real interest in everyday world affairs, perhaps she should have considered these particular developments. "The two Bishops and Alexi Petrov the Atheist, have stirred up many people."

"We don't need their money nor their interference. And immortality isn't our goal. So far we've been able to achieve a substantial extension to life expectancy, but immortality as such cannot exist. All of existence is subject to decay. It's only a matter of *how much time.*" Harusuke relaxed further into their deep cuddle couch as Lai-Xii gave voice to her thoughts. Perhaps it was the right time to put some things into perspective for herself. Her five pet men might have benefited from her ruminations. "Biological life seems to be the most vulnerable; bugs that live only a day or two, rocks break down into sand, radioactive elements decay ... why, the whole universe suffers entropy. What makes these people think that a computer program, in whatever form, isn't subject to change and eventual corruption beyond retrieval?"

"As long as you're clear about this, I'm happy," said Harusuke. "But you will have to do something about the religious fanatics."

Eventually the warmth of fire, the comfort of their favourite couch and the fatigue from the day's activities had their effect. The two women let monumental thoughts dissipate into more personal pleasantries.

*

A most encouraging report came in from Delta One. Pwyll crater was indeed the ideal site. Even the impact of the meteor which created it some three hundred thousand years ago did not manage to break through the ice crust.

"Conditions are currently stable, have been for millennia and indications are it will continue to be so. There is no detectable subsurface activity. All major water plumes are an average of eighteen hundred kilometres distant and have no effect on this area." He stopped to deal with an interruption from his renewable energy engineer, then continued. "Delta Four reports supplementary power supply will need to be remote from this site as it is unlikely we could

111

drill down to the subsurface ocean at this location. Age of existing linea is indeterminable; no new activity is evident. We are 25 degrees south latitude which means Jupiter's tidal pull has much less effect than at the equator."

Delta One's brief report ended as abruptly as it began. Lai-Xii again responded laconically, "Proceed." It simply meant that her away team should go to the next phase; establish the solar collectors on the rim of the crater and find suitable locations for the ocean underwater turbines. Once sun power was ready to be harnessed, they could develop the backup system; a much more labour intensive process and essential.

*

Perhaps the leaders of Earth's main faiths should have been taken into confidence at about the same time as the world's main political leaders became seriously involved in the Project. Lai-Xii assumed they didn't need to be consulted and would be advised by authorities in due course prior to beginning the transition process of the masses. The salvation of humanity would not be achieved by any divine intervention, but by science – and it wasn't a matter of faith, but of plain hard work based on empirical facts – on Science. So it was with some annoyance she read the 'invitation' from the Pope to attend a closed door conference, albeit crowded by world political and religious leaders.

"I want you all to come with me, boys – and you too Harusuke and Evgeniya. Make sure you're right up to date with progress on Europa, Ralphie."

"Do you need us to update the conference with progress on our VR activities in Me-Me?" asked Maldonado.

"I don't want any of you to volunteer any information. That means you neither Evgen. I know you've got a new tetra-amelia generation under production, but I don't think that's a detail we need to bother anyone about just yet. They will be more concerned with our Delta Tengi."

Lai-Xii's reputation of being rather abrupt in situations which were not entirely under her control meant the Russians and the Chinese insisted on having an independent mediator to manage the conference. The job fell to the UN Secretary-General, Bácskai, with a background in philosophy and the arts before he became interested in politics. At an age of eighty-nine years with a stalky figure sporting uncooperative tufts of white hair, he was considered to be the most impartial diplomat of the era.

112

He said very little during his briefing by Lai-Xii and then by the stake holders in the Project. When told the real reason behind the existence of Phototronic Systems and why it had the backing of world governments he asked only one question, "Why does humanity need to be saved?" The question was thought to be rhetorical and no one volunteered an answer, perhaps because too many 'healthy' self-interested reasons were involved. Lai-Xii expected at least some discussion. Silence on that subject put her on guard from the very start.

That did not satisfy Boldizsár at all. After the briefing he took Lai-Xii aside to ask her the same question again. "Xii, I understand that this entire project came about because of you."

'Xii' bit her tongue. This was not the time to be pedantic about anything, especially not about something as personal as her relationship with Harusuke. "Yes."

"Come – I need to know why. I assume this is still the most important thing in your life. So let me help you."

She could see this was no ordinary man, not one of the ordinary males she'd become accustomed to manipulating. He appeared genuine in his interest to facilitate a desirable outcome from this conference. They sat opposite each other, close enough to make good eye contact. She raised her eyes to his, ran her finger along her fringe making sure it was not being insubordinate, and began ...

"You do not know my personal history. It not important, other than that in my long lifetime, which is longer than you can imagine, certain truths about mankind have made the success of this enterprise critical. Not for my benefit, not for the religious and political leaders of the planet but for the planet itself – for humanity. How long do you personally think we are likely to survive if nothing changes?"

"I see. I think I understand. Thank you."

At the commencement of the main conference Boldizsár asked, "Your Holiness, Gentlemen, Ladies, is there any objection to making this an informal discussion?" After some whispered discussions between the delegates, of which there would not have been more than thirty, no objections arose. "Good. So, I take it you will not object to surrendering all communication devices for the duration." This attracted considerable grumbling before silent acquiescence.

Boldizsár then pushed a little harder to ensure greater security and the highest possibility of openness and understanding amongst the group. "I ask that only the most essential personnel participate in this discussion. With the greatest respect Ms Lai-Xii, could you please dismiss your retinue." That suited her just fine, though she would

113

have liked to have Harusuke by her side. A glance by Harusuke indicated she didn't object to leaving the conference room.

Lai-Xii nodded her assent. "Thank you Ms Lai-Xii." The Presidents and Prime Ministers got the hint, and with a nod their people started to join Lai-Xii's exiting group.

Only the Religious leaders seemed reluctant. "What purpose will this serve?" asked the Grand Imam.

"Because of the nature and import of the proceedings only those with the greatest binding decision making capacity should be privy to this discussion. I can tell you now that what you are about to hear, and the decisions you make will change the course of human history."

"If that is the case," said the Pope, "should we not have the wisdom of our counsellors to help us?"

"This isn't a matter for democratic entanglements. You have all achieved the pinnacle of trust in your respective religions and political arenas, which has been freely given to you because of your great wisdom and knowledge. It is time to trust in yourselves."

"So be it," The Primate of the Russian Orthodox Church had nothing further to add. Within the next twenty minutes, with the room cleared of communication devices and unnecessary personnel, the conference commenced. Bácskai Boldizsár wasted no time on pleasantries or introductions, other than confirming Lai-Xii's relationship to Phototronic Systems.

"Let us begin. I have had a full briefing and want to put the matter to you as simply as possible."

Boldizsár took the time to make eye contact with each individual relaxing in their lounge chairs set in a large circle. The conference table had been removed and exchanged for more comfortable furniture. "The decision about our future has already been made for us on July 16th 1945, precipitated by our actions, or lack of actions in the past and since. That detonation, part of the Manhattan Project, exemplified the attitude with which we treat our home. Our Earth cannot continue to sustain life if we maintain with our current philosophy, which appears to self-propagate without change. It is believed that our technology has taken us to the brink − No − to the point of no return of survival. The extinction event is well advanced. It will encompass all species and eventually us in the not too distant future. To save themselves and to save the planet some will wish to leave and have already made the choice to do so. Others will want to stay."

"We," The Grand Imam offered, "were under the impression that attempts were being made," he glanced at Lai-Xii, "to achieve immortality using technological intervention, Mr. Secretary-General."

"Please call me Boldizsár," Boldizsár responded.

"What exactly do you mean by 'leave'?" asked the Primate of the ROC.

"May I?" interjected Lai-Xii, and continued on when Boldizsár didn't object. "We are already on Europa setting up the infrastructure for colonization."

"Surely you don't mean Jupiter's moon. We cannot survive there," remarked the Pope. When he extended the invitation to Lai-Xii, he didn't expect to be confronted by impossibilities. Matters of theology he and his friends could argue to any depth, deal with any issue that threatened the sanctity of human life as ordained by God. But this did not come within his purview.

Boldizsár turned his sky-blue disarming eyes on the Pope. "Yes, Your Holiness, it is the only place within our reach where we have the greatest possibility of ensuring a continued future for the human species."

"But your AI robots, your experiments for immortality ..." The Grand Imam asked, turning to Lai-Xii, "that is the reason we have come together, as far as I understand."

The diplomats remained silent. They knew what was happening; not only knew, but were already committed to supporting and ensuring the success of the Project. If only the leaders of the worlds three greatest religions could be recruited to this great cause ...

Again Boldizsár spoke in a quiet considered voice, engaging each member of the gathering as he spoke the words that would shake them to the core of their belief systems. "The robots are only the machines helping us to transition our existence from the world of flesh and blood into one of digital information." An audible drawing in of breath indicated the message had impacted. "The final transition would take time, with all its attendant implications," Boldizsár continued after a brief pause, his vision drawn into his own world of apprehensions and impossibilities. "Life expectancy would increase dramatically, but there is no immortality ... other than that dictated by your faiths."

Complete silence fell upon the conference room. Lai-Xii and the diplomats waited patiently, giving the three Patriarchs time to come to terms with the simple truth of the message. So far the proceedings had gone amicably enough. Bácskai Boldizsár's diplomatic reputation, and his position of authority as Secretary-General of the UN, was about to be tested.

Eventually, The Pope raised his head from immersion in deep contemplation. "Have you achieved this transformation?"

"Yes," answered Lai-Xii.

"The three of us need to discuss what you have told us," he said quietly, referring to the heads of the other religions.

The President of the United States felt it necessary to say the obvious. "Absolute security of this information is mandatory," to which The Pope flashed a denigratory glance at him.

"The inevitability of the situation forces us all to work together," said Boldizsár stepping in to defuse a potential conflict. "At this stage it is anticipated all migration will be voluntary. However, emergent circumstances may change that." Without being too specific he tried to make the Patriarchs aware of the consequences of dissent among the world's leadership on this issue. "Your co-operation in defining the procedures under which the exodus can be achieved would help to minimise the disruption to human society. Without putting too fine a pint on it, gentlemen – we are talking about the survival of the human species."

The three men, decked out in the full regalia of their respective faiths became so absorbed in inner turmoil they made only the slightest concession to the protocols of excusing themselves from the conference.

"Ve arre going to have security problem," said the Russian President getting a nod of agreement from the other diplomats.

Harusuke was right, reflected Lai-Xii. *The Project now has its own momentum. Not even the billions of people with their divergent religious convictions can stop it, though they could make a lot of trouble.* She said as much to the gathering after the Patriarchs left. The Chinese Prime Minister seemed unconcerned. "Continue with you work, Lai-Xii. We will ensure you facilities security," he said, soliciting agreement from the others.

*

It was almost a year before the next follow up report from Delta One on Europa. "We are progressing on schedule. Solar energy can be harvested to satisfy current requirements. We are ready to receive the next lot of wagons. Their payload will enable us to establish the first batch of the two hundred undersea generators required."

Within the small group of Deltas, frictions or dissatisfactions did not surface. Before arriving on Europa their lives lacked focus. As tetra-amelias they had a limited vision of the value of their existence. Europa changed all that. Each of them clearly understood that the whole of humanity now depended on them.

116

Lai-Xii passed onto her immediate team the outcomes of the conference. "It is obvious to me we will come up against a great deal of opposition, both from the religious sector and world leaders. As they begin to realise what our Project truly means I believe they will falter in their commitment. We have to be prepared to act on our own."

With renewed resolve her team continued to make substantial progress at the research centre in Tau City, though always with background apprehensions about eventual success.

14

SPY DRONES

CE 2110
TAU CITY

COMMANDER VIKTOR PYRYEV did not want to disturb the leadership. The core team had only just received an upgrade to their artificial organs, as well as some enhancement to their memory capacity. They were in the last stages of integrity checks when the latest incident occurred.

Following the Papal meeting in 2085, Lai-Xii should have foreseen the degree of escalating unrest. She was so intent on her Project, particularly on progress on Europa, that matters external to her immediate sphere of research and activity failed to engage her interest. She was also confident, perhaps overly, in both Russia and China's ability to control any civil or religious unrest that might arise; as they promised. The Russian President did in fact take steps to increase security for Tau City.

Unfortunately, the Patriarchs who attended the Papal meeting, lacked the wisdom to maintain the appropriate level of secrecy about the transition and the exodus. The Pope interpreted the actions of the rogue elements of the scientific community as a revolt against God. He did not believe the denials of trying to achieve immortality, missing entirely the greater concern of humanity's demise. He felt it necessary to convene an extraordinary Ecumenical Council, inviting representatives of the other major religions, to discuss his grave concerns. Once again the battle between Faith and Science reignited, just as it had flared during the Renaissance. This time it wasn't simply a matter of forcing people to believe the Earth was the centre of the universe scientifically, but convincing them that it must be considered to be so, and that Faith dictated it must be even if evidence presented itself to the contrary. Although they took some precautions to control media coverage of the event, speculation took hold and ran like wild fire. Within months, attempts were being made to covertly infiltrate Tau City.

"What is so urgent you can't give me some peace Viktor?" Lai-Xii seemed more than usually annoyed.

"Five drones were brought down yesterday. These carried ground surveillance robots. None of them are military issue, so that's reassuring."

"How did you capture them? Are they damaged?"

"My special forces are equipped with the latest Kalashnikov REX-100 anti-drone laser rifles. They allow us to take over control of their guidance systems and land them undamaged."

"Where are the drones from?"

"As far as we can tell they're not sold on the open market. So they must have been specially developed. I'm sure there will be more of them. We'll track their signal next time. They would have to come from somewhere in Kamchatka."

The weapons that brought them down were just as specialised and secret as the spy drones. The intruders probably assumed the storm must have grounded them, for there was indeed a storm that week with particularly turbulent winds. Climate change had made weather predictability more of a lottery than a science. Within a week several more drones appeared. Viktor's team expected them and located the source of the signal within minutes of them flying over Tau City centre. Lai-Xii was in conference with Maldonado and Aurelio about their progress with VR saturation on Me-Me by mobile phone users when Viktor interrupted again. "What is it this time?"

"We have the source of the drones," Viktor said, still unsure of himself in front of this formidable woman even after so many years. She never seemed to change, physically or in her moods.

"Out with it Viktor, I'm a busy woman!"

"Petropavlovsk, the Capital – from the vicinity of Trinity Cathedral." The news dropped like a bombshell. After briefing her team on the outcome of the 2085 meeting they all assumed they could trust the religious leadership to be sensible, circumspect at least. But this was downright provocation.

"Leave it to me. If you catch anymore, disable them but don't destroy them. You are quite certain of the origin of the signal?"

119

"Yes. There is no doubt it came from somewhere around the Russian Orthodox Cathedral." He left the office feeling as if he'd escaped the lion's den. It wasn't his fault these flying bugs had infiltrated their air space, yet she managed to make him feel responsible.

"Well my Frankenstein lovelies, it seems our deadline has just been adjusted," she said to Maldonado and Aurelio. "When we're finished here get the rest of our team together. We need to move things along once again."

Aurelio continued with his briefing, "The addiction is well established. We have about eighty five percent saturation of the mobile phone market with the Head Mounted Display add-on. "Our scouts report almost constant use of the HMDs, even when people are together and are supposed to be socialising with one another. I have personally seen a table full of fourteen people in a restaurant, supposedly for a birthday party, all sitting with their HDMs on. One person actually interrupted his immersion to order his meal. My problem is trying to keep pace with the demand for new VR programs. No doubt there are many emergent issues resulting from our little experiment, but for our purposes it's a fantastic success."

"Indeed it is. That is good news. We may have to transition people much quicker than expected. Even if Arithmós isn't ready, we can at least store them until it is." Lai-Xii was already thinking well ahead. "Prepare some scenarios involving the Europa landscape, with images of Jupiter rising and filling the sky. Let them custom build their own Avatars to wander around on the surface. The sooner everybody gets used to another world the better."

As usual, her evenings were reserved for private matters; for little rituals she'd grown accustomed to as a geisha which made life a little more pleasant from day-to-day, and for simple pleasures with Harusuke. Sometimes the external world impinged on her privacy, like the evening of the day on which the spy drones infiltrated Tau City.

"You haven't said a word since you got home, Xii. What's the bad news?"

"Those ignorant sods! What can you expect from men? You'd think that regardless of what mumbo-jumbo they believed in, common sense would prevail. Apparently that's a commodity incompatible with religious dogma."

"You're talking about the Patriarchs, aren't you?"

"Is this the mentality we'll have to deal with?" Lai-Xii complained. "The more we progress the more I wonder whether it's all worth the trouble. What is it going to be like on Europa, with all this religious

120

ignorance and opposition? It's not like we were trying to tilt the Earth's axis, for heaven's sake!"

"What's happened?"

"They're spying on us. I don't care what they believe in. Surely, survival isn't a difficult concept to grasp!"

"Calm down, sweet. We talked about there being a few ups and downs. No one is going to be able to stop you now. You have the backing of the world's most powerful nations. If the worst comes to the worst, you can leave the religious zealots behind. Let *them* deal with Armageddon if they're so focused on it."

Lai-Xii grumbled from deep within herself trying to let the tension dissipate. "Make us some tea, darling," she said after a little while. Harusuke busied herself while Lai-Xii gathered her thoughts. The fluid went straight to the delicious spot, though that wasn't the real point. The ritual, the finesse, the art − that was what was important. *Yes, the art* − she thought to herself − *we must not forget art.*

Her team had already gathered in Tau City in the course of their special assignments. They knew from the tone of her 'command to gather' that Lai-Xii had been wound up. Many years ago she told the odd assortment of wealthy businessmen their ultimate target date for the culmination of their Project, the great exodus, would be around 2600. That was before things became complicated.

Next day they met in Evgeniya's old office. Nothing had changed over the many years. It didn't need to. Dr. Evgeniya Yermolov lived inside her head, in a world of ideas and concepts, bringing them to fruition in her laboratories. Her office, rarely used, would have shown her footprints in the fine dust on the floor had staff not kept it meticulously clean during her many long absences from the round table in the centre.

"You've heard about the drones," Lai-Xii stated without bothering to denigrate anyone in the room, thus signalling a most serious situation. "We are running out of time. As much as Faith can create a meaningful life for some of the world's population, in this case it may well bring about a sad end to those contented lives. If the major religions manage to stir up enough discontent, the politicians will have no option but to bend to the populace if they want to retain power. The long term future of humanity will become meaningless to them if faced with global insurrection. Their own personal political survival will eclipse any other consideration."

Maldonado gave vent to unedited thoughts. "But we weren't going to take everyone with us in the first place. Let the ignorant stay here a few more generations until Earth chews them up and spits them out."

"No, we weren't. But when we do go, it should be when *we're* ready, not forced on us prematurely," Lai-Xii said.

"You think the Patriarchs are going to make things difficult for us?" Aurelio stated the obvious.

"We'll take the fight to them." Lai-Xii almost smiled. She hated pompous, self-important men whose thoughts rarely left the close vicinity of their scrotum; men of the cloth, regardless of the cut, being no exception.

"How?" asked Aurelio.

"You and Maldonado are already doing it and from what you tell me, with great success. You are making unreality more important to people than their normal lives; more important than their social interactions and probably more important than any conditioning to the "god concept" they've received in their formative years. Which is really strange because theism is as unreal as it gets. But they can't see the similarity between Virtual Reality and their faiths."

"In another few years they won't know the difference between waking and sleeping!" Maldonado seemed very sure of himself. "If we get the Europa/Jupiter simulations fine-tuned they won't care if they're on Earth or the centre of a black hole."

"Talking of those heavenly bodies, I want you to run a special project, Salazar. You've got many contacts in the world of fashions and the Arts. Time to put them to good use."

He was a bit slow on the pick-up. But then again how could he have guessed the devious weapon Lai-Xii had in mind to fight the Pope and his cronies. "You want me to design some new dresses?" He felt silly having said that even though he only meant it as a joke.

They all looked at him, Evgeniya with a spark of interest. Who would have thought she'd have spared a second thought on her attire. "Art, creativity – the urge we have to create things of beauty, of expressing the inexpressible meaning of life; that's what we'll hit them with. Images stick in peoples' minds - words they quickly forget."

"Ah! Fashion shows?" Salazar was suddenly heartened. It had been so long since he'd had the chance to indulge his passion; the passion which had created his wealth of many billions.

"No, but it's a great idea. For the next ten years I want you to run art competitions. The best of the best to exhibit at La Biennale Di Venezia every two years. Then take the work on a world tour to be seen by as many people as possible. Media saturation coverage is what we want. Use every trick you can think of. And you can include your penchant for Fashions. Create – Create – Create!" Maldonado seemed a little lost. He couldn't understand the link between drones,

122

The Russian Orthodox Church, art competitions and their enterprise to get to Europa.

"How? I mean what ..."

"Didn't I say, my darling girl?" Lai-Xii was already feeling much better, just in the anticipation of the success of her plan. "The theme must be ... "Jupiter and Europa - The Relationship. "

Harusuke got it immediately. "Brilliant! How can the religious leaders protest against Art. It will lay the foundation for people to accept Jupiter and Europa into their common vernacular. They will become familiar with the imagery, the beauty. They will *want* to go to these places." Lai-Xii let Harusuke speak. It was rare to hear her so enthusiastic. It gave Lai-Xii a much needed moral boost.

"I don't understand," Salazar started again.

"Use any and every angle you can think of – Mythology, Astronomy, Travel – accept all approaches, classical, contemporary, religious, radical, experimental, unorthodox – use traditional methods, science, digital. Seek expression through the visual arts, theatre, music, architecture, every avenue you can think of. In other words ... make Europa and Jupiter as popular as Jesus! Get street artists to flood the world in images of these two magnificent celestial bodies."

Finally, he understood. He became pensive, barely paying attention to the rest of the discussion. It was all too overwhelming at the start. Yet his thoughts began to coalesce from the ordinary and the easily possible to fantastic improbabilities. It was all possible. Money was no object.

They could all see how taking the fight into the public arena would be far more effective than covert operations to quell any unrest and agitation by leading religious individuals. Lai-Xii's enthusiasm infused the small group of conspirators. They each wanted to give their reports first.

THE BOOK OF ORIGINATION
DECLARATIONS FIFTEEN

15:1 From this City will shine the light,

15:2 And upon the children of the Lai-Xii bestow the future.

15

ARITHMÓS TAKES SHAPE.

TAU CITY
DR EVGENIYA YERMOLOV'S OFFICE

SALAZAR immersed himself in his own thoughts trying to come to terms with the latest challenge while Evgeniya started her summary of progress. "Ve have several hundred Beta Tengi experts now vorking on all facets of ourr transition. Most promising arre quantum programmers. Ourr continued tetra-amelia engineering has forced morre of brain's kapacity to focus on cerebral netvorking than concierge duties to maintain obsolete biological body parts."

"What about the transition into Betas and our previous problems with sensory input systems?" asked Lai-Xii. Although she tried to keep abreast of everything that was happening with the Project, the scope of it had become so complex it wasn't possible to be aware of every development.

"Ve found problem only existed because ve channelled Alphas sensory information to Betas, yet expecting the Betas to be totally independent, vich of course did not happen. Now ve go direct from scans to Beta Tengi konfigurrration, with their personal independent sensory network. At this stage zere no advantage in direct upload into all the other Deltas shells.

Ve vill do that when zey arre needed on Europa. Ve vill probably all have to reformat to Deltas at some stage before we make the digital transition."

"Tell me more about the quantum programming," asked Lai-Xii, ignoring their own future transition to Deltas.

Ralph took over at this point as it wasn't Evgeniya's field. "There are essentially two issues here. Software and hardware. The software side of things is moving along well and we have been working with some other agencies around the world."

"Oh?" Lai-Xii initially wanted to keep as much development in-house as possible. "We're not giving away our intellectual property Ralphie my puppy, are we?"

"No, no – but we do have to augment our expertise here and there. We have developed a qubit chip that can store information in the form of light, on single controllable photons. We are talking brain speed here in transmitting information through a very small network. So we now have the capacity for capitalizing on extreme miniaturisation of quantum memory devices. And that's where it gets a bit harder … the quantum hardware. It may be a few years yet before quantum computing hardware becomes mainstream."

"We'll be ready for that, right?" It wasn't a question. "We can't quite give up our Deltas yet, I take it."

"No. Not for some time. For one thing, their bipedal body configuration makes them extremely valuable in the realm of physical reality. They will be our maintenance crew when we get to Europa. Besides, it's the only way we have at the moment to actually experience the physicality of the Europa environment. How else could you go for a walk on the ice and gaze at Jupiter's swirling storms?"

"How far have we got with the hardware?"

"This is one area where we need to work closely with organisations in the US and Germany. The Russians are too clunky with their solutions and the Chinese are a bit tight fisted with their knowledge. I don't suppose you can do anything about that." He waited, hopeful she already had something in the pipeline. Lai-Xii often had surprises for them to help push the Project along.

"We have the finances and we have the expertise. If we can do this in-house it gives us a big advantage. We won't have to rely on an external supplier if our timeline keeps shrinking, which it is obviously doing."

Ralph continued. "The other side of the hardware problem is what Ptolemy and I have been working on for Arithmós. Now - that comes down to network topology. In other words, a City where billions of digitized individuals will have to be connected or connectable in some way, yet maintain their individuality. Size and layout are not the issue."

126

"Exactly," Ptolemy pitched in. He'd designed and built cities before. He understood the 'human' dimensions associated with large spaces where myriad peoples of many faiths, colours and ethnicities had to come together. Without putting too fine a point on it, he brought up a rather ticklish problem. "We're not going to take everyone, right? Some won't want to come. That's fine. Some *we* might not want to take ... trouble makers, undesirables; for example those who can be readily identified will not present a problem. What about the worms in the apple? What about people with religions that teach – well, you know what I mean – that have a theology of exclusion. Who's going to make the decisions on issuing 'visas'? Other than that, Ralph and I have come up with a workable layout. Over to you Ralphie."

As much as the men initially detested being made the butt of Lai-Xii's peculiar humour over the years, they came to look with pride on any and all displays of her unorthodox 'affection' towards them. Even nicknames which she used in contemptuous ridicule were worn as badges of honour. So Ralphie, the doe eyed puppy dog, launched into a description of the Arithmós layout, first giving his long shaggy hair a thorough scratch as if to bring all his information to the surface.

"We have prepared a schematic and a physical model." Ptolemy drew the velvet blue covering off the object occupying almost all of the three metre diameter circular table. Lai-Xii had wanted to see what was under the cover as soon as she walked into Evgeniya's office.

Disappointingly, it looked uninspiring from the point of view of a city. It had no lakes or parks or rivers. No trees, but that was only to be expected. There weren't even any identifiable buildings, let alone magnificent skyscrapers. Lai-Xii hadn't really thought about the aesthetics before. The complete lack of hallmarks of human habitation made her pensive. Only copious 'roads', channels of communication, overwhelmed the layout. She did become conscious of patterns emerging from the web, with what appeared as 'junctions' or hubs. Probably the most disappointing thing about it was the flatness, though there were many places where protrusions emerged, higher than some features of the landscape. "What are these?" she asked pointing to one such structure.

Ralph had waited, giving her time to get an overview of the model. He was very proud of their joint design and wanted to explain all aspects of the topology in fine detail immediately. His better judgement prevailed, waiting until Lai-Xii enquired.

"Interchange Centres. This is where the Deltas and future models of Tengi would reside. As you can see there are many of them spread around the various zones, inside the crater and out on the slopes."

The main structure of the model looked very much like an eroded Lunar crater with an almost perfectly symmetrical raised perimeter rim. Pwyll had a much larger floor in the centre and much gentler outer slopes, very smooth without numerous gullies of erosion. A fine spider web–like network covered almost the entire area.

"We call them Interchange Centres because that's where people could go to download into a physical form. Much like an astronaut puts on a space suit when he needs to work out in space. The maintenance Caste, who will probably prefer to remain physical within their Tengi chassis, would use those structures as their main living environments."

"You really have put a lot of thought into this."

Lai-Xii ruffled the top of his head affectionately. She was impressed. Her own ideas were on the grand scale, the overall vision – never thinking of the small details; not that she wasn't aware the only way to cross a stream was by stepping on one rock at a time. "Go on – please." Everyone was fascinated. No one had the faintest idea what Arithmós would look like - other than fanciful images of futuristic cities of impossible structures protruding kilometres into the skies of Europa, all vying to touch the surface of the gigantic Jupiter above them. Ralph's design disappointed those visions, generating a great deal of interest at the same time. It looked more like a giant motherboard than any of their imaginary constructs.

He continued, happy and energised at seeing the reaction to his Arithmós city.

"The hub of our civilisation would be situated in the crater with this Local Area Network (LAN) providing connectivity to the rest of the Arithmós. Over the rim and past the solar collectors, you can see a different pattern in the structure. That's the Wide Area Network (WAN). Within those, you can see in fine detail many LANs.

The WAN will be able to cater for any degree of expansion to accommodate future topologies once we are settled there."

Ptolemy understood some of the intricacies of how the structure of such a 'living' computer network had to be organised. Yet he was concerned with who would populate these LANs and WANs and how they would organise themselves into coherent functioning societies.

"Lai-Xii, excuse me for interrupting – this must be entirely fascinating for Ralph, and we've had many months of discussions as you can imagine, to get to this stage of development for Arithmós. There is however a most critical factor – the human factor."

128

He looked thoughtfully at Lai-Xii, expecting some kind of response from her.

"Go on," she said. It was most unlikely she would not already have covered this aspect extensively with the Heads of State of many nations, though probably not with the religious leaders. She wanted to hear Ptolemy's thoughts.

"I've worked on many large projects in the past. Tau City isn't the only city I've built. I know there is much more to it than just the bricks and mortar. Our own little Tau City, by many standards indeed a small city even with a population of many thousands, has a great deal of complexity and many issues to deal with. They all originate with the fact that we are human and have all the human frailties you can think of – customs, religions, ethnicity, mental capacity, life aspirations, occupations and so on. You are well aware of all this."

Lai-Xii held up the palm of her right hand to stop him rambling on. Of course she knew of all these inconvenient factors. "Do you remember what I said to you all in the pool at Esso after our snow ball fight?" They all nodded, Except Evgeniya. She didn't know about the naughty tryst in the winter pool and threw a questioning look at Lai-Xii, who gave her a conspiratorial smile, without revealing any of the details about it.

"Yes," said Ptolemy. The others murmured something and nodded.

"*Human* is something we are going to have to leave behind - at least some of the more tiresome characteristics. Being naked in a hot-spring pool in the middle of winter will lose its meaning, its allure. Though from what Ralphie is saying about the Deltas, we'll still be able to have a snow ball fight."

"Naked in a pool – with *them?*" Evgeniya couldn't get the image out of her head. Harusuke just smiled. She knew her partner and how naughty she could be.

Before continuing, Lai-Xii gave Evgen a little hug, just enough to make her blush. Then turning back to Ptolemy she gave him a push on the chest with an extended index finger saying, "*Your* next job, my confused cockroach, and yours Ralphie dear, is to consult with our illustrious leaders and see where they want to pitch their tents in Arithmós. I see also you have a lot of fancy decorations already set up." Lai-Xii saw long slender towers placed in a circular pattern around the walls of the room, as well as peculiar spiky structures suspended from the ceiling above the model and the whole of the rest of the ceiling. "What are those," she asked wanting to continue with the presentation.

129

"First, to get back to the LANs," Ralph was on a roll and didn't want to let anything go unexplained. "Those patterns you see in the layout; the Rings and Meshes and Stars are all a variety of physical topologies to indicate physical links to other LANs and devices therein. Without them the logical network topologies would not work. A whole host of network protocols to direct how data flows across the network must be set up … in your language, how we, existing only as data packets, would move about and communicate. I realise all the Presidents and Prime Ministers and Chairmen will not want to know how the mechanism will work. They'll want to maintain their own and their peoples' status quo, even in a digital environment. I can only explain the mechanics of existence, you will have to enlighten them of the great leap into the unknown that we must take in our evolutionary development."

"Good luck with that," Aurelio commented quietly.

"Don't interrupt! Go on my puppy." Lai-Xii wanted to know the function of all the decorations and hanging baubles.

"The towers are part of our external sensory network. They will pick up and relay messages from Earth, but more importantly relay sensory data transmitted by our satellites. The Delta Tengi now working on Europa have a whole new sensory network feeding into their neural matrices. That's how they are able to remain 'alive' and not go batty. If you remember, our Alphas and Betas didn't do so well in the sensory deprivation department. Anyway, the satellites will see and hear and smell the universe, our solar system and Jupiter most importantly. That information will be fed into our neural nets. In the future we may achieve much greater sophistication, but for now, if you truly want to get off Earth, this is what we have to do." Ralph felt he'd said all he needed to for the time being. He took a deep breath, exhaled and his mouth spread into a self-satisfied smile.

No one spoke. They all knew what they were working towards, the challenges, the theory, the exciting unreality. To be confronted with the actuality of it happening, was overwhelming – once again. They've had several such reality checks in the past, but this one was unnerving. Right there in front of them was their new world. The five large wall screens in Evgeniya's office all showed different perspectives of Arithmós. Jupiter high in the sky above the city dominated the scene, ten times larger than looking at Earth's moon. The swirling clouds of hydrogen and helium in constant motion in opposite direction in the north and south hemispheres made them feel giddy. Plumes of water jets, past the crater rim above the solar collectors, only added to the sense of disorientation. Yet on another screen, in a close up of an Interchange Centre, they could see Delta

Tengi in their peculiar humanoid forms with short stubby legs and long arms, going about setting up another one of the towers, a few kilometres from Pwyll crater, the horizon behind them bent like the curve of a banana.

Maldonado, as interested as the rest of them had something to say as well. "I also have a treat for you," he said, inviting them to take their places at the table. He'd been working with Ralph and Ptolemy to put together a special VR program. "Put these on," he said, handing out the HMD's, far more sophisticated than those little ones used by the world's addicted VR users.

Within minutes everyone was on their feet, moving about the room, waving their arms around pointing at nothing in the air. They were on Europa, flying over Arithmós as if they were holiday makers arriving from Earth. This part of the VR simulated the 'human' perspective, giving them a chance to experience the new world as seen through normal senses. Ten minutes was enough to take them on a grand tour of the city and its outlying districts on the slopes of Pwyll. They even flew to the northern hemisphere across the equator with its extraordinary vertical ice spikes and kilometres wide canyons separating ice shelves.

Then the input changed. Ralph had created a simulation of how the world would be experienced through the other senses, the ones the Delta Tengi were equipped with. The travellers, with their minds embedded in virtual Delta Tengi bodies had to negotiate a flat ice sheet terrain, avoiding unstable areas by using their acousticolateralis vibration system to detect ice movement under their feet. To be able to reach their destination they also had to navigate by analysing gauss readings to 'see' magnetic fields. The effect became totally disorienting, like trying to see colours through hearing their wavelengths translated into sound.

The human neural network can comfortably accommodate such ways of seeing the world, provided it has an opportunity to re-wire itself. A child born with these sensory modalities would consider them to be completely normal. Deltas working on Europa currently were not having any issues at all managing complex tasks in their new environment. However, Lai-Xii's team in the simulation quickly became anxious and one by one the HMDs were removed in rapid succession.

"You have all done a good job my children. You deserve a little reward." All their spirits lifted at the thought of the undoubtedly yummy treat she would have in store for them. "We are going to Esso for the weekend." That raised more than one eyebrow, especially Harusuke and Evgeniya's. Noticing the effect, Lai-Xii confirmed,

131

"You are *all* coming." They remembered what that meant – they remembered the pool.

"Back to the guest house?" Salazar ventured to ask.

16

FIRST DATADROME

CE 2120
ESSO

THE ESSO guest house had not changed over the intervening years, although it had seen a number of owners come and go. It could barely accommodate Lai-Xii's extended team. Nevertheless, they spent a pleasant weekend relaxing in the thermal pool despite the lack of snow. Even Harusuke and Evgeniya got into the spirit of things to splash about in the warm water, though not being as uninhibited as Lai-Xii had been. Many years ago, the snowballs-in-the-pool interlude not only revitalised the spirits of Lai-Xii's inner circle at the time, it was the birthplace of an important development.

Ralph and Misha remained behind to inspect the facilities in Esso and the surrounding area for the installation to be used in the next round of test. The rest of the team returned to Tau City.

The first Datadrome was set up near Esso, three hundred kilometres south of Tau City, in the middle of the central mountain ridge, thought to be the least likely place to experience any transmission problems. Less than three kilometres from the centre of Esso the road ended on a high ridge overlooking the village. Kamchatka's highest snow-capped stratovolcano, Ichinsky, could be seen in the distance to the south-west. Although less than ten kilometres away, Ralph didn't consider it a threat to their installation. It hadn't erupted since the mid eighteenth century.

The Datadrome was designed as a prototype relay station from which peoples' digitised psyches could be launched into space towards

Europa. General data transmission had evolved exponentially since the 21st century, in speed, reliability and quantity loading on the signals. Issues of drop-outs due to loss of signal no longer existed. However, sending people, or at least their digitized equivalent, was a new trick altogether. 'Loss of signal' was not an acceptable option even under the most unlikely circumstances.

The building itself could have been mistaken for a large brick residential house, except for the imposing tower beside it, from which hung a goodly array of dishes and antennas. The biggest change to the ridgetop had been the sealing of the dirt road up to the facility. Though not expected to be a major data transfer station for signals going to Europa, nevertheless it had to be built for experimental purposes.

"Are the locals ready?" Misha, Ralph's immediate assistant, now one of the augmented humans with his normal human exterior supplemented by replacement artificial organs, had three villagers waiting outside the scan room.

Piotre said to his wife, "Anushka, you take this money home and hide it well. If anything happens to me and I don't come home, this money will be enough to take care of you and the children for the rest of your life." He was barely forty-five years old, but already bent over from his hard life. Lai-Xii made sure the villagers who were brave enough to volunteer would be well paid; their sole motivation being financial.

Ralph had streamlined the scanning and upload process to the Tengi Chassis. It was faster and error free. The tetra-amelias who'd been educated and groomed for working on the Project, showed no detrimental effects when their psyches were transitioned to Delta Tengi.

"It's one thing to upload complex data clusters using a direct physical link between a human and the Tengi, and quite another using any form of microwave transfer." Ralph betrayed a slight apprehension talking to Misha, as he made last minute checks of the equipment. "There are still too many unknowns, that's why we have to use volunteers." Losing a few to the ether, or have them mysteriously reconstituted into unrecognisable forms would not be a huge loss in Lai-Xii's philosophy.

Misha agreed. "We have to do this. It's not possible to put the world's population in space wagons and ferry them physically through space. Not just the cost, but the time. We have to beam them, even if some are lost in transit."

"We could store millions of scans to eventually fly them over, but four plus years is a hell of a long time for a trip, and too many things could go wrong here on Earth."

"So, let's get on with it. Lai-Xii and the techs are ready at the other end." A receiver station was set up in Tau City. They were not going to test round-trips. They only needed to load received data packets into Delta Tengi and do integrity tests.

Misha stuck his head out the door, "Come on in Piotre, we're ready for you."

"Wait here for me, Anushka," he said encouragingly to his wife.

"It'll be fine," reassured Misha, "he'll be back with you in an hour. All we need is a picture of Piotre." If it worked they wouldn't need him, or his copy afterwards. Piotre could go back to his wife and children, financially much richer for the experience.

Piotre felt anxious, despite his reassurances to Anushka, as he stepped into an odd looking contraption which resembled neither a chair nor a bed. If he could have recognised a sensory deprivation chamber he'd have known he was being incarcerated in something similar. A mild sedative ensured his mind wouldn't go into overdrive exciting too many neurons at the same time. For the scans to work, his neural net had to be as inactive as possible.

Misha and Ralph glued their eyes to the instruments. "It's going well so far, I can't see any spikes." The first of the two scans recorded Piotre's neural network architecture without incident. The scanner pinged at the completion of the cycle. "We'll run a test after we've overlaid this on the second scan." Ralph seemed a little more confident. This part of the process had been done successfully many times back in his laboratory.

"You've put all the sensors on his scalp?" he asked, though he knew it wasn't something Misha would forget. The procedure had become second nature to Misha. He'd also trained many Delta Tengi techs to do the job. Misha just nodded, preoccupied with the readouts. The process had already started.

"This is taking a while," Ralph commented after just ten minutes.

"Relax. It's the same as hundreds we've done before. Why don't you check the transmission equipment?" Sometimes Misha found it hard to cope with his boss's insecurities. The man was brilliant, he need not have worried. It took twenty minutes to complete the scan. They had two complete files of data to check and integrate.

"This is textbook stuff. It all checked out. You're right Misha, I worry too much." Another twenty minutes later they were we loaded and ready to transmit.

"On your mark …"

Ralph contacted Lai-Xii in Tau City, "We're all set. Good to go your end?" He gave Misha the nod and for under a single second Piotre flew through the airwaves towards Lai-Xii at the speed of light.

"Wake up, Piotre, we're all done," Misha told the peasant. They had taken all the sensors off him and had him recovering in a comfy chair when Lai-Xii called.

"Signal received one hundred percent. Uploading into Tengi, now."

Ralph and Misha took Piotre by either arm and led him back to the reception room, still a little sedated. It had been just over an hour, so Anushka seemed a little anxious but brightened immediately on seeing her husband. Without any need to detain them they left, very happy that their lives would be so much easier in the future.

Lai-Xii called, "This one's perfect. He's babbling on about his wife and why she isn't here with him. Is the original Ok?"

"No problems. He's already gone home."

"Send the next one." Lai-Xii wanted to get these tests done and emergent issues ironed out as soon as possible; one of them being what to do with the duplicates. They'd been putting many years of effort into the Project, not to mention the multiple trillions of dollars. Lai-Xii felt they were over the hardest part, but she also felt harassed by shrinking time.

An unmarried woman came next. No family – they'd died in an avalanche and Iluska had not yet married. She couldn't resist the money temptation. It meant she would be able to go to Petropavlovsk and have a much better chance of finding a good man there than in a small village like Esso.

Unaware of the thunderstorm outside the insulated facility, Ralph and Misha guided Iluska into the next chamber. A storm of that magnitude was a rarely experienced phenomenon over the Kamchatkan peninsula. No one had even thought of checking the weather patterns for the day. This thunderstorm, registered and measured by the Institute of Cosmological Researches and Radio Wave Propagation of the far east division of the Russian Academy of Sciences, promised to be a big one. They would surely have warned the scientists conducting the experiments if they'd known about them.

Ralph and Misha relaxed after the first transmission, taking no notice of several tiny, almost imperceptible glitches during the two scans of the second subject.

Partway through the transmission Misha alerted Ralph. "Did you notice anything like this with Piotre?" he asked pointing to the screen as the process unfolded. Ralph barely had time to register the readout when there appeared a micro break in the transmission. At the same

136

time the building shook in response to an incredibly loud crack around them.

"Oh no!" Misha breathed out through clenched teeth. He knew immediately what was happening, this being part of his world. Ralph an American, had never experienced anything as intense as this great burst of lightning. The power of the electrical discharge can be phenomenal, even when experienced from a distance. This one hit close, very close.

Ralph's face went white when he heard Misha's exclamation. He jumped on the comms immediately to Lai-Xii. No response of course. They didn't get to finish the transmission, nor scan and send the third volunteer. Outside, the storm wreaked havoc. Iluska's brain activity shot off the scale on the monitoring equipment. She sat bolt upright, tearing at her connections, Misha unable to keep her immobile. Within seconds she gave up the struggle, slumping back into the apparatus, dead. The two men rushed to the single window to see nothing but a pounding curtain of hail.

"This will destroy Esso," Misha said, "they've not had a storm like this for more years than I can remember."

It could have lasted an hour or more. Difficult to concentrate on the passage of time when the thunderous noise of hail battering the building even drowned out one's own thoughts. Conversation became impossible. They could see nothing out through the small window but sheets of rain following the hail. Eventually an eerie silence took over in the deepening darkness. Power had been cut the building. The three people could do nothing but wait till the morning. Ralph had tried the exit, but it had been blocked by some debris falling across it.

The following day they went outside and saw the effects of the maelstrom. The road had to be cleared before they could get out of the area. Many buildings in the town had been flattened, roads destroyed by the torrential rain following the hail, unlike the structure of the Datadrome which remained unharmed. The transmission tower suffered the bulk of the damage, razed to the ground by the force of the wind.

"It will take the people of Esso years to re-build,' commented Misha as several people made their way up the mountain over the rubble to check on the installation.

Four days later Ralph and Misha were back in Tau City. "What happened out there?" asked Lai-Xii anxious about the event. "We only caught the edge of the storm here."

"We didn't even know it was coming," said Misha.

"We received the signal," said Lai-Xii, "most of it anyway, but couldn't put her together. Did the girl survive?"

"No. The overload on our systems was too much. She was still connected when the lightning hit."

"We have to go through it again. We know the process works and it's probably only this freak incident that's caused the problem." Lai-Xii had another thought. "How badly was Esso hit?" Maldonado and Ptolemy listened, looking concerned. Lai-Xii turned to Harusuke, lifting her eyebrows, lowering her fringe. She always attended to support her partner at all the major milestones of the Project.

"I know what you're thinking - clever idea," Harusuke confirmed. "It will help the people and help us.

"Ptolemy, how soon can you get out there and re-build the place?" Lai-Xii wasted no time on getting to the point. They'd lost one person through no fault of their own. There was far more at stake than the life a single Russian peasant girl.

"I can get someone else to supervise the Arithmós Project for a few weeks while I get the reconstruction of Esso started." Ptolemy also saw the greater value in the opportunity presented to them by Nature.

"Maldonado, my weirdo," she dragged one finger slowly down his cheek, "be a good boy and make sure the world knows what Phototronic Systems is doing to help the poor people of Esso. And please be doubly sure that our 'friends' at the Vatican and the Grand Imam do not fail to be impressed, especially the ROC Patriarch in Petropavlovsk. Ralphie, come and talk to me about the Datadromes."

Harusuke went home and the others scurried off to deal with this latest emergency. "How confident are you in our technology, Ralphie? Are we ready to start setting up Datadromes around the world?"

"I don't want to start the full process yet. We're only at the stage of testing the theory. We've had one small set back, obviously not the result of our process or equipment. Still, the system has to be further tested. You can get the various Nations to start setting the installations, but the internal equipment will have to wait. Quantum computing is now so close. Our own programmers are already working on updating our software. I don't want to invest any more capital in hardware that would have a very limited life expectancy. My feeling is that within five years at the most quantum technology will be mainstream."

"I guess we can wait that long." She had full confidence in Ralph's abilities.

"We're not actually waiting," Ralph hastened to add, "we're developing, constantly changing and updating. Evgeniya and I have

138

already put years into the next generation Tengi; our Zeta model. You will not believe this technology.

"You're a clever boy, my puppy. They can help build our Arithmós."

"That's the idea. They'll have qubit based systems and should be able to handle the installation of the quantum hardware. When they've finished the job they could either download into the Arithmós array, or remain embedded in the Tengi."

*

It had been an exhausting and challenging time for Lai-Xii. Losing an experimental subject didn't concern her. Their own vulnerability to the vagaries of Nature caused more concern. "If just a simple storm here on Earth can create such havoc, image the unpredictable environment we're about to migrate to." She never discussed her private thoughts in public. At home, in the comfort of Harusuke's company and her wisdom, she could unwind.

"Send a second reconnaissance team. There's time for them to study Europa and its relationship with Jupiter while the first team work on the infrastructure. Jupiter's storms and radiation are the biggest problems we're likely to encounter. Ralph probably already has enough expert Delta Tengi to do the job. We already know Europa's the most stable and hospitable environment in the Solar system for what we want to do."

"I've been thinking about tetra-amelias too," contemplated Xii aloud. "They've been too quiet. Put out some feelers for me. Find out what they're up to. We won't be needing them for very much longer. In fact, I'll talk to Evgen tomorrow about scaling down our involvement with them."

"Be nice to them," Harusuke said, "without them none of this would be happening.

17

FIREWALLS

CE 2123
HIROSHIMA
ATOMIC BOMB DOME

LAI-XII couldn't recognise the new Sheraton Hotel on Mt. Takao any more than the vast expanse of water leading to the shrine. Only one river emptied into Hiroshima Bay. The delegation had to take a ferry from the hotel, to the north east side of the shrine across what used to be Naka Ward, in order to reach the Atomic Bomb Dome. So much had changed since she visited the area after leaving the Geisha House. Global warming had reached the predicted two degrees rise from the beginning of the 21st century. Ocean levels had risen alarmingly putting great pressure on the major seaport population centres of the Earth. People could adapt on the continents, but not so on the Island Nations, particularly in the Pacific.

"Have you been here before Lai-Xii-san?" The Japanese Prime Minister asked, seeing her trying to get her bearings as they bumped over the choppy water.

"Many years ago, Prime Minister. I recall five rivers flowed into the bay, and this whole area was covered in city streets."

"Ah, yes. We have had to make many changes, as no doubt have many of you gentlemen," he commented glancing at the other dignitaries.

"Where is the Atomic Bomb Dome, Prime Minister?"

"The first four storeys are completely under water. Only the steel dome structure remains visible. You will see it shortly.

There are several pontoons around it, with a small conferencing centre on one of them. I thought it would be a secure and appropriate place to discuss weighty matters."

The delegates from the six other nations remained introspective until reaching the Shrine; once a highly evocative place emotionally, a reminder of the great devastation that the machinery of war was capable of – that people were capable of. Their reactions on arrival seemed to indicate an indifferent response. These individuals were all leaders of the armed forces of their respective countries. They were also businessmen. The art of war had morphed into the art of business over many hundreds of years of refinement, through much trial and error measured first in dollars lost, then lives lost. Their predecessors should have taken greater care in selecting more appropriate representatives for the developmental update of the Project, considering the impact it was destined to have on the future of humanity.

Ralph and Harusuke accompanied Lai-Xii, Harusuke to chair the meeting. The launch remained moored with all the security personnel on board. Delegates chatted amicably as they made their way to the only large space set up for the conference. They certainly didn't behave appropriate to the gravity of the forthcoming discussion. Drinks and snacks occupied their attention more than the historic, and tragic, environment in which they gathered. Introductions were dispensed with. They all knew each other through their business connections as much as their diplomatic status. Harusuke had planned on a slightly different start, but seeing the crude disregard exhibited by these 'important' personages she made a point of bringing the significance of the location to their attention.

"Given the nature of our enterprise it is as monumental a milestone in human history as the destruction of this great city by the 'Little Boy' atomic bomb. This is a fitting place for us to have this discussion. No less poignant because we are now floating instead of standing on solid ground in front of the monument. We will make this brief and to the point."

Water could be heard lapping against the sides of the monument that continued to deteriorate with the passing of time.
A slight swell gave the pontoon a gentle, soothing motion as Harusuke began her introduction. The war mongers didn't see the tainted blue sky or the small boats bobbing in the distance. None of them seemed to appreciate the tranquil atmosphere which pervaded the scene of a long ago unimaginable devastation.

Though subdued to some extent initially, the gathering became more convivial as drinks and the entrees were served.

141

The US Secretary of State proposed a toast, "Let us drink to another good year!" He raised his glass and all partook, except Lai-Xii. This wasn't meant to be a celebration for record profits as far as she was concerned, although Phototronic Systems had had an excellent windfall with the release of more electronics trinkets to appease the masses of people suffering technology addiction. She also didn't fully appreciate the delicately poised relationship between war profits and population control.

"What's this I hear about Arithmós ready to be built?" The Minister of Defence from China had good reason to be so interested. His nation's population growth had outrun that of every other nation. In spite of the increased number of regional wars, birth numbers kept pace with deaths.

Nations couldn't agree on how to control climate change, but they did work out a brilliant strategy to limiting, even reducing, the globally escalating population growth. Creative accounting was the solution. It depended entirely on changing the nature of war games. War by remote control was never going to yield the same results as close range combat. That produced more casualties, required more weapons, created more jobs and generated more profits. Human life had become a profit generating medium more than ever before in the history of humanity.

"We have a model to show you," announced Ralph. "Please examine it in detail, then then we'll use these HMDs to have a look at the Europa environment."

For internal security reasons the new location seemed a much better option than the original idea of presenting the layout at Evgeniya's office. The incident with the spy drones convinced Lai-Xii of the necessity to be extra vigilant as the Project developed into the next phase.

The German Minister of Defence almost immediately spotted a problem. "How are we going to maintain our sovereignty?"

"Indeed," concurred The British Defence Secretary."

"Gentlemen," Lai-Xii cut in, "by now you would have realised we are not simply transplanting mankind from one planet to another.
We have taken human evolution to the next level. Everything must change; the nature of our being, our relationships to one another, our understanding of life itself. We must re-evaluate the very reason for our existence. In this context Minister, your question is inappropriate."

She'd hit a nerve. Eating stopped, arguments began, fuelled by long standing grievances, fears and self-interests. She stopped talking to listen to these leaders of Nations exposing their underbellies.

These men are fighting to preserve their personal empires, concluded Lai-Xii to herself. *They care nothing for the people.* She glanced at Harusuke, then at Ralph. Harusuke appeared to have similar thoughts, perhaps even Ralph.

"Firewalls," broke in Ralph. "Borders created by firewalls. We have comprehensive IT security systems."

"So we kan have – there kould be cyberrwarr?" queried the Russian Defence Minister, clearly revealing the nature of his future intent.

"Not what I had in mind, but I think you understand the general principle of digital security," Ralph said. He cast a lost look at Lai-Xii.

She took him by the arm to pull him aside. The warmongers continued arguing amongst themselves. "What are you doing Ralph!" she hissed through clenched teeth, giving him the most furious stare he'd ever-had from her.

"Buying us time," he whispered, "until this very moment I thought we might actually pull it off – actually give humanity a chance to survive. But if these are the men we have to deal with …"

She released his arm. She recognised it too. The world may have changed; temperatures around the globe increasing by more than two degrees, island nations inundated by rising sea levels, wars over food, water, arable land. These issues and population growth management becoming the dominant reasons for conflict, but people in power had not changed. They may never change, regardless of their circumstances, their faiths or their ethnicity.

"Explain how zese firrewalls vill ensure our security," demanded the Russian.

"They work much like your border controls currently, with a big difference … much easier to patrol and far less costly." They settled a little to listen. 'Control' and 'cost' were concepts they could understand – as opposed to living an existence without bodies in a realm of energy in a quantum world. Perhaps their scientists could, but definitely not bureaucrats and businessmen and politicians. "Imagine a network security device; by network I mean the entire settlement on Europa, that could monitor incoming and outgoing network traffic.

It would decide whether to allow or to block specific traffic based on *your* set of security rules. By traffic I mean both information flow and people movements."

"Viruses? Hackers?" asked the Indian representative. They had an insurmountable problem of mind bogglingly clever hackers creating havoc, not just in India but around the world. They got into business systems, governments, defence systems. Many had even been recruited to help the very governments and organisations they used to work against.

"Do you mean as offensive weapons, or as threats to security?" Ralph didn't like the sound of where this conversation was going. Nor did Lai-Xii. "We can work on these details with your people. For the time being, please examine our suggested layout for Arithmós, and enjoy the VR display."

This wasn't going anything like Lai-Xii had envisioned. She would have to devise a whole new strategy. *I must retain control.* She repeated this mantra to herself, over and over. *I must retain control.* Money wasn't enough, the science was not enough, obviously altruistic intent wasn't enough. *I've controlled powerful men before, when I was a Geisha – I'll just have to do it again.*

Questions were asked about the towers and satellites, Ralph giving the same answers as he gave to their own team.

"We will of course require our own communication satellites," Defence Secretary of Great Britain made a point of reinforcing Germany's insistence on maintaining sovereignty, then added, "When will Arithmós be ready for settlement?"

He didn't expect it to be before the end of the century. He felt no particular hurry to abandon Earth. He'd read the latest report from the Intergovernmental Panel on Climate Change (IPCC). As far as he was concerned, and he knew Germany and China felt the same, the fanciful allusion to another Pliocene Age simply didn't gel. Things weren't so bad. With the temperature increase at just over two degrees, the evidence simply didn't manifest for any likely sea level rises of twenty-five meters by the end of the century. People everywhere were adapting to reduced rainfalls and the reduced oxygen in the air. Why worry unnecessarily?

Lai-Xii did have clear plans and timelines for the first wave of settlers to leave Earth. In view of the attitudes surfacing during this conference, she felt the need to make some adjustments to her schedule to give themselves a little manoeuvring space. "Oh, quite some time yet, Defence Secretary. As you can appreciate we are not simply building a computer. Arithmós will be a living entity with many unique and individual parts, all having to work together for survival. We also need all of *your* inputs to be sure of meeting your individual country's requirements."

China, with ever an eye on practicalities and the logistics of moving large numbers of people, wanted to know how everyone was going to get to Europa. Lai-Xii again tried to make it sound like the beaming technology itself had a long road of development ahead of it. No one knew how close they were in fact to achieving that.

"Conventional space travel would take too long. Digital data transfer systems are still under development. It's not as simple as shooting mobile phone signals from tower to tower." She realised these weren't the right people to be talking to, yet in the end nothing would happen without their approval, and they certainly represented the power that could bring the whole enterprise down - they weren't the visionaries. "We will send you our people to help you with building the Datadromes. These, like conventional aerodromes, will have a dual function; to prepare people for the journey and to send them on their way. Does that answer your question, Minister?"

"How many facilities will be required?"

"I would suggest build enough for very large numbers of people. This will be a one-way journey. Conditions for life on Earth are getting more hostile with every passing decade." The dead-pan face on the Chinese representative suggested some disagreement with Lai-Xii's opinion – it was only a woman's opinion after all.

The delegates had been far quieter than Lai-Xii expected. They should have asked many more questions, showed a great deal more enthusiasm. Obviously agendas operated in their minds other than the survival of the species, of which Lai-Xii became more aware as the conference progressed. The whole point of the gathering was to inform and enlist enthusiastic involvement from every major country. *They think this is just a backup plan in the most unlikely scenario that we will actually have to evacuate.*

"No doubt you will have more travellers than we could manage. So you may all want to consult with your immigration departments to start developing a 'migration visa'. As you realise there are many factors to be considered other than individual's preferences to migrate or not." It was the least confronting way she could get the message across for selective migration. Not everyone was suitable, or welcome.

FROM THE BOOK OF ORIGINATION
DECLARATIONS EIGHTEEN

18:1 The acts of the wrongdoers shall corrupt their codes,

18:2 And the Shadow will not be able to protect them,

18:3 For they shall be seen by the Lai-Xü for the virus they have become.

18
MIGRATION VISAS
TAU CITY
LAI-XII'S OFFICE

THE FERRY back to the Mt.Takao dock seemed to take longer than the trip out. Lai-Xii expected a lot of discussion, yet the delegates remained mostly silent, looking with vacant eyes towards the shoreline. What was wrong? Did they suddenly realise the enormity of the enterprise, or was it the opposite? Had they been overwhelmed by all the implications of creating another race of beings, and not wanting to be involved? Did they even realise that fact? Perhaps their religious convictions created barriers to understanding, to acceptance. No doubt some of them may well have had theistic beliefs. Was all this going too much against the teachings of their respective Gods? The Japanese Prime Minister was a Buddhist. They didn't believe in a God. Yet even he seemed less than enthusiastic.

Lai-Xii, deep in thought herself, didn't immediately register the people waiting for them at the dock. A rather small crowd as far as protests were concerned, for it was indeed a protest by the look of the banners. Even a flag fluttered in the breeze with Jupiter painted inside a crossed red circle, like the universal 'Stop' sign. Lai-Xii glanced questioningly at the Japanese Prime Minister, as did the others.

"This was an unpublicised meeting," he said calmly, "No need to concern yourselves. Our Police are here."

It wasn't the riot squad, just police in normal uniform, looking relaxed and non-confrontational. The quiet crowd didn't seem to worry them. Oddly, a few Buddhists in their saffron robes walked

147

about in the crowd. They didn't hold banners. Others held placards proclaiming "Earth is our home," and "God Owns Life, not Science." Another depicted a terrifying looking robot inside another large crossed red circle.

"We are not creating Artificial Intelligence," Lai-Xii whispered to the men around her.

"Wait here Lai-Xii-san,' the Prime Minister said as he motioned to a ranking police officer. They exchanged a few words, after which the police peacefully disbanded the protesters. "He says they think you are turning people into robots. Is this true?"

Lai-Xii had been keeping the stake holders in the loop, informing them regularly of progress. She considered Tengi technology to be a critical piece of information for them to have – so they knew 'robots' were on Europa setting up energy plants, but not that those robots' anima was the actual psyche of real people who'd been through comprehensive transformations.

"No, Prime Minister. We are not turning robots into people, or people into robots. Those on Europa are Intelligent, and we have given them several extra sensors to help them do the work." He didn't even realise that Lai-Xii herself, and Ralph and Harusuke, all human beings with mostly synthetic bodies, had life spans well exceeded anything experienced amongst humans before. They looked like normal humans, walked and talked like normal people – they even 'smelt' like humans with their slight individual body odours.

The delegation made their way back to the hotel under escort, only a short ride in the convoy. Lai-Xii hadn't taken much notice of the cityscape before, too pre-occupied with thoughts of the meeting. She gazed out at the buildings, not taking particular notice of all the lights, advertising and signage pollution of the city. Remaining on many walls, depictions of the bombing proclaimed the great inhumanity perpetrated by man upon man. They made little impact on her, though conscious of them. Then suddenly she saw it – on a large wall facing the street and extending into the side alley. The very first example of the relationship between Jupiter and Europa!

"There! Stop. Go back a little," she called to the driver.

She and Harusuke jumped out of the car, struck by the beauty of the depiction of Jupiter with its swirling clouds of colour.
Just below its equator and a little to the west, a small fuzzy black round patch, like a beauty spot, led the eye away from the great orb to its tiny moon, floating in space in sharp contrast to Jupiter's soft fluffy surface. The mural must have been three meters tall with Europa in intricate cherry blossom pink detail at near eye level.

They must have stood there for many minutes before security personnel ushered them back into the vehicle.

"We started the special Arts Program many years ago. This is the first actual example I've seen of what Salazar has managed to achieve," said Harusuke.

"He did report on progress and how well people had taken to the idea. I just hope it's had the desired effect on dampening the fervour of the religious dissidents," Lai-Xii added. "Are there any other such depictions in Hiroshima?" she asked the Prime Minister.

"Very strange, Lai-Xii-San, they have appeared in many places in the last three years. Some of the images are of the mythical figures, others show convoys of space ships circling Jupiter." To a questioning eyebrow he continued. "Even sculptures of maidens riding powerful bulls have appeared in tourist gift shops. There seems to be a new craze sweeping Japan, not just Hiroshima."

For the rest of the way to the hotel, the three Phototronic Systems representatives' eyes searched every image that came into view. A smile slowly spread across Lai-Xii's face. *Salazar's done an outstanding job. No wonder there's a reactionary element making itself felt.* She glanced at the US Secretary of Defence riding in the vehicle with them. He was oblivious to the entire thing. He couldn't understand why they had to stop to look at graffiti on a city wall.

*

Lai-Xii's office back in Tau City did not host the usual quiet gathering – the boardroom table and chairs were replaced by her piano and floor cushions. Salazar showed off the success of his art competitions venture with images flashing across most of the screen monitors. Some showed headlines of major newspapers extolling the virtues of the extraordinary 'fad' sweeping the globe. It seems the concept took hold slowly, but eventually excited the imaginations of visual artists as much as writers and journalists around the world. Musical compositions had begun to surface as well as popular love songs.

"Well done, my fearsome fashionista. Keep up the momentum as much as you can."

"Are you sure about that Xii – sorry – Lai-Xii?" She snapped a sharp eye at him. "What I mean is – with all the unrest going on … the protest you experienced in Hiroshima is only the tip of the iceberg. There are Christians and Muslims and Buddhists and every other God worshiping cult you can think of kicking up a fuss. The whole thing could backfire on us."

Lai-Xii ignored the question. She was well aware of the comprehensive awareness all the media attention was bringing to the giant of the Solar system. Instead she turned to Ralph, "Can you completely trust Misha?" It seemed like a strange question, but so was Viktor's presence in the room strange.

"He is totally dedicated. Yes, the answer is - yes."

"Well then, bring him in."

Everyone was there; Ralph, Viktor, Aurelio, Ptolemy, the other men including Evgeniya and Harusuke and finally Misha. Lai-Xii settled at her piano, which she had not done for a long time, and the room went quiet. She began one of favourite pieces, Chopin's Grand Polonaise Brillante Op.22. The mood changed; internal processing slowed and eyelids fluttered closed. Lai-Xii continued, towards the end gradually dissolving the melody into thin air.

She turned back to her brood. "The real work begins," she whispered and waited. All the heads had slumped slightly forward, immersed in the soothing ebb and flow of the melody. Lai-Xii had calmed her own thoughts as well as her audiences'. Whatever complexities had so far engaged their attention, the tone of the meeting in Hiroshima had changed everything. Urgency – purposeful urgency must now direct all their combined activities. Initially she had the idea of being able to harvest the majority of humankind to replant their seed in a less fragile region of the cosmos – to give them all a better life, a better hope of a future for their descendants. Humanity wasn't going to change by itself. What it had become could not be fixed – the only hope was a fresh start with the 'deserving'. A new plan became imperative. Warmongering leaders and their followers must remain on Earth to linger till Earth grew tired of their abuse of it, or until they developed enough consideration to do the honourable thing and wipe themselves out. Nor was there room in the new world for soul destroying organised religions; any religion. Unreasoning religious Faith should have atrophied and dropped out of the human psyche when mankind became aware of itself as an agent of the destiny of his own existence.

She waited, thinking these and many other thoughts. She rallied herself knowing what had to be done. "The deadline has just moved forward, my children. We no longer have hundreds of years to move house." Ralph had told the others about the Hiroshima meeting; they needed no explanations. "First things first … Evgen, dearest, we'll need every one of your 'maiko' and as many more as you can bring to maturity. We need them proficient in every field of human endeavour. They will be the backbone of our new civilisation. Unfortunately, we'll also need a few techno Generals and foot soldiers in case we must fight a cyberwar. They must be the very best. Recruit from the rest of the world if you must."

They all felt the portent of the occasion, each waiting their turn for their assignments, though they all knew what needed to be done; Aurelio and Maldonado to continue with the VR saturation, Salazar to step up the 'Jupiter & Europa Relationship' initiative, Ptolemy to ramp up building of Arithmós with Ralph. "Ralphie my boy, can you do it?"

"Yes," he said even before knowing the challenge. She'd never asked anything of him he couldn't deliver, even when it meant stretching his capabilities to the limit, and beyond.

"Zetas ..." she swept her right hand across all in the room, "*we* will have to make the transition before we leave Earth." Misha didn't know what that meant exactly, though he'd been working on the new model with Ralph and Evgeniya. He stole a glance at Ralph. Ralph just nodded, smiled, indicating that at long last Misha was to become one of them – truly one of them, and not remain a laboratory assistant for the rest of his existence. "These Zetas must be perfect replicas of our human forms, indistinguishable from normal humanity. Our 'minds' must also be Arithmós ready at a moment's notice."

Ralph replied without hesitation. "I will have the scanning and transmission technology refined, fully tested within a few years, safe for us to use. I assume we have a few more years. The warlords are not paying us much attention. Religious mania will subside, it always does – especially if Ptolemy does a good job of rebuilding Esso, with the appropriate marketing to promote our efforts. Oh, and you should know – mainstream quantum computing is here. Qubits will make everything possible for us."

"You are a clever boy, Ralphie. You only thought of telling me this now? Clever and very naughty. But there is one other thing. I am relying on all of you, especially you my Harusuke."

Lai-Xii had no need to think too deeply about the migration selection process. As with all manner of choices, people make them on the principle of the Chaos Theory, on inherently unpredictable criteria. It would have been best to allow people to make their own choices, though understandably removing that right from individuals of certain mental dispositions.

And so it starts ... It was inevitable from the beginning, Lai-Xii mused to herself, *we have to find a way to float the rotten eggs. We can't let the chooks and roosters decide.* "Migration Visas," she said and many heads nodded.

Perhaps her team was smarter than herself if they've already worked it out. "Oh, a fait-accompli is it? Ralphie, how many could Arithmós take?"

"Until we had quantum computers I would have said 60% of Earth's population, allowing for population growth on Europa. Now that we have a qubit chip that can store information in the form of light on single controllable photons, *and* one hundred qubit processors with the hardware to match, I would have said everyone – all eight and a half billion of us." He waited a moment while reading Lai-Xii's face and body language, "They're not all coming – are they?"

"What happens to those who can't come?" Harusuke, one of the less compassionate individuals in the room must have had a good reason for asking. Perhaps it was to give Lai-Xii the opportunity to vent, though she seemed in full control of herself – and she may have been right. The tensions and uncertainties generated by the Hiroshima meeting had their effect. It would not serve humanity well to have Lai-Xii making uncharacteristically vindictive decisions against the male of the species. She should have left that mind-set behind when she abdicated from Geisha-hood.

"What do you think is going to happen? Isn't it obvious!"

Harusuke's intuition proved correct. Lai-Xii didn't quite launch into a tirade, nevertheless they all felt the power of her convictions. "What are our wars about? Food, water, arable land, population growth. One would think the amount of blood spilt on the earth would make it fecund, sufficient to feed all. Not so. Bodies buried must equal babies born; The perfect population control mechanism; the Corporate Accountants idea of balancing the ledger. War machinery needs to be fed as much as people – jobs, jobs and more jobs. Greed and consumerism!" She paused as if suddenly hearing her own words for the first time. "I'll tell you what's going to happen. Another two, perhaps three generations and the ailing planet itself will restore balance. After we take the healthy in spirit and mind, it will drown the majority and starve what's left. The human species will join the dinosaurs. Cockroaches will rule the world. Wouldn't that be nice, Ptolemy?" She often referred to him as her disgusting cockroach. He didn't flinch, nor smile.

No one had ever heard Lai-Xii so openly express her feelings. She was fired up for sure. Harusuke moved right up to her, touching her as she finished her little outburst. "Will you take suggestions now, or postpone."

Staring blankly, still looking inwards, Lai-Xii wanted to continue the meeting. "Now. We have no time to waste."

"Both inclusion and exclusion criteria?" Aurelio queried. He must have had some specific ideas. Visas are meant to be a permit. He was astute enough to see Lai-Xii had evolved a very particular disposition as to who would and who would not accompany the bulk of humanity into the future.

Lai-Xii asked, "What about those we don't select, but don't specifically exclude?"

"Storage - post scan." Harusuke suggested, Lai-Xii nodded agreement.

"Exclusions?"

"Scan, analyse then delete their scans – refuse their visas even if they manage to get them in their own countries." Again Harusuke answered for Lai-Xii. It took longer for Lai-Xii to concur this time. "Undesirable disruptive elements will not be tolerated – *must* not be tolerated."

Though Salazar was foremost a businessman, his creative foundations gave him perhaps an edge to understanding the finer attributes of the human psyche. He didn't hesitate to suggest music, or at least musical appreciation; perhaps certain types of reaction to music that should play a part in the list of selection criteria.

Evgeniya, neurologist and genetic engineer, must also have considered ways of filtering potential emigrants. Her focus for exclusions centred around predisposition to using violence as a problem solving technique – and also the closely related phenomenon of the effects of religious beliefs on analytical thinking and the ability to emphasize.

After lengthy discussions the group agreed for Evgeniya, Salazar and Ralph to devise a set of criteria to divide all emigrants into two streams; exclusions - those who would not be permitted by Phototronic Systems to go: inclusions – the desirables, and the to-be-used-later category, to be stored indefinitely but not deleted. Though a good deal of debate issued from the concepts, unanimous agreement was immediate as to who would exercise control over the final selection; Phototronic Systems, not world governments.

"We are agreed then," Lai-Xii seemed relieved to have negotiated this particularly difficult stage of the big plan. It was not in her nature to be 'democratic', usually making most of the critical decisions herself, or in collaboration with Harusuke. "As long as you can gather comprehensive data on every individual who's been using the Me-Me social media platform over the last few decades." Lai-Xii turned to Maldonado seeking confirmation.

He nodded, "Of course. We already have more information than we need. We know more about people than the national security organisations in their own countries. Believe it or not we even know the size of knickers they buy, and whether the boys buy for themselves or their girlfriends. We have been tracking peoples' movements and can tell you how long they take to have a cup of coffee. The worlds they have created for themselves in their customised VR platforms are better than a year-long psychological assessment of their mental health. Ralph here will be able to mine all that data and set up interrogation routines along the very specific lines of our criteria. No one will get through our Religion/Music/Violence matrix.

With the increased sense of urgency all minds focused on their respective upcoming task, but Lai-Xii didn't dismiss them. There remained one outstanding matter. "Come stand beside me, Ralphie, and tell us exactly what you know about the status of mainstream quantum computing."

"Most of the work had been carried out independently of our Project, though we did have a few techs and programmers planted at the most critical developmental laboratories. Their tetra-amelia condition seemed to make them more desirable as valued employees. Anyway – the technology could not have come along at a better time. Our Zeta models will need only minor redesign to accommodate the hardware. We'll be able to use the new Quchips to store our single photon based data arrays. The hardware could also be adapted to projecting photonic containment fields. It may be possible to have the entire population of a small city within a single containment field. That's just for future reference."

Ralph almost launched into technical jargon in his enthusiasm to share the 'quantum' breakthrough. With watching eyes beginning to glaze over, he was forced to explain the two critical stages of the transition in simple language. "We'll only need the Zeta Tengi during the intermediate transitional phase, mostly for the core team and the Arithmós' construction team upgrade. It'll take some effort to adapt the quantum computing technology to replace our current BPM configured Tengi. Then they can be used as hardware and energy maintenance crew on Europa after settlement. Arithmós itself does not need miniaturisation.

Human Factor (HX) data bundle storage isn't the issue. Rather it's their functioning, budding of new HX-bundles and individuals' personal development which is expected to be exponential in the initial 500 year phase of their quantum existence."

"Did you say 'budding new programs'?" Aurelio jumped in just ahead of Harusuke. Though no one had initiated any conversations concerning the propagation of the species, perhaps thinking immortality covered that contingency, not even Lai-Xii had alluded to this delicate matter.

"Indeed. We want to have children, don't we? We already have a team of programmers dedicated to resolving the associated technicalities." Ralph elaborated.

"Da," added Evgeniya, "I have been vorking with zem on how to apply Chaos zeory to random DNA mutations and reproductive variations. We have to build some degree of 'unpredictability' into ozervise predicable system, like algoritzm konstruction, data query and data recombinations. Just anotherr reason why ve must be partikularly vigilant in screening immigrants."

Ralph wasn't quite finished. "Over the next couple of weeks you will all notice a considerable improvement in computer performance as we switch over to the quantum systems. I'll work with you to enhance your next set of VR platforms for your Me-Me social media platform," he said to Maldonado.

19

DEFECTORS

CE 2125
PETROPAVLOVSK
CAPITAL CITY, KAMCHATKA

FOR just over twenty years the expanded core group of Phototronic Systems had been enjoying their transitions to customised Zeta Tengi configurations to ensure their personal longevity as well as enhancing their capabilities. Having become thoroughly accustomed to their 'body shells' they walked as a group looking for all the world like normal tourists. Lai-Xii didn't want to announce their visit, either to the Russian authorities, or the Patriarch. The ageing Patriarch Piy Bogolomov should have retired many years ago, yet he stubbornly refused to give up his position of power. No doubt Lai-Xii's Project rankled him deeply. His attempt at infiltrating her domain with spy drones had failed miserably.

Lai-Xii wanted to see Trinity Cathedral before surprising The Patriarch with an unofficial visit. Only four kilometres from the centre of town it was easiest to reach by bus. They alighted at the third stop after the Tank Monument. Vladivostokskaya Street boasted many prefabricated concrete buildings on either side of poorly maintained concrete roads, full of asphalt patches and crumbling borders. Nothing had changed since Lai-Xii's arrival in Kamchatka around 2020.

Even the immediate approaches to the cathedral didn't inspire anything more than mild interest. Earthworks and building construction continued at a snail pace around it.

That's exactly what Lai-Xii was hoping to see. Since partial destruction by fire the year after its opening in 2010, the reconstruction could not be completed due to a chronic shortage of funds. She was pleased to see scaffolding scattered around half completed walls, piles of toppled bricks and no workmen at the site despite it being a weekday. Yet the main body of the building was indeed beautiful; the white facades topped with azure blue roofs set off by the golden onion tower domes dominated the scene. Magnificent snow-capped volcanos created a perfect backdrop to the cathedral.

"We'll not have any of this on Europa," commented Salazar without addressing anyone in particular.

"Or what they represent," added Lai-Xii.

In their new humanoid Zeta Tengi chassis', the delegation of seven from Tau City looked like completely normal people. Lai-Xii retained her slender form with long black straight hair and severe fringe, while Aurelio shed his corpulence for a 175cm tall young Spanish male. Evgeniya also chose to remain in her original form with the flaming red hair. At the Patriarchs residence behind the Moscow State Industrial University across the road from the cathedral, they only had to wait a few minutes for admittance. The Patriarch remembered Lai-Xii.

"Patriarch Bogolomov, we beg your indulgence for this impromptu visit." He impatiently waved them to seats in the largish reception room, kept at a comfortable temperature for him all year round. He didn't bother to ask her the reason for their visit, quite certain the matter of the drones would feature in the conversation. It didn't.

"The Cathedral is magnificent, Patriarch Bogolomov. It must be a source of constant frustration for you to see the reconstruction taking so long."

"Yes – yes," he responded tersely, still waiting for the difficult subject to be raised, "we have many other priorities in looking after the welfare of the faithful."

"How *are* the good people of Esso? Much of the village has been rebuilt I understand," she glanced at Ptolemy who nodded confirmation. Neither of them made an overture of their involvement in that undertaking.

"Yes. They are well and grateful for the work your organisation has provided to help them." At that moment of internal turmoil Piy Bogolomov could not bring himself to express the gratitude of the Church.

157

"We are only too pleased to have been able to contribute." The Patriarch knew as well as Lai-Xii that the 'contribution' was made wholly by Phototronic Systems to the exclusion of any input from the Kamchatkan government. The moment had arrived to create a little more discomfort for Piy Bogolomov. "Patriarch Bogolomov, we hope you will forgive what we have recently initiated to help your flock here in Petropavlovsk." The old man's eyebrows arched high enough to hide beneath the rim of his white klobuk. To complete the uniform of ROC clergy a luxuriant white beard appeared to be a mandatory expression of their wisdom. His beard garden bristled as if a light breeze had disturbed the nestling birds within. "You can expect considerable activity around the Cathedral from tomorrow, until its completion."

He knew it was a bribe, and also knew he couldn't make that public knowledge. No one would believe him. The initial opposition he'd organised against Phototronic Systems suffered through lack of follow up activity. The drones produced no evidence he could use. No more 'synthetic humans' appeared in the streets of Tau City making a nuisance of themselves. Everybody knew who was rebuilding Esso, and to top it off, even in Petropavlovsk artists had succumbed to the latest fad extoling the beauty of Jupiter and Europa. No – nobody would believe him.

"The Church is grateful for your generosity," he finally managed to say with difficulty and stood, indicating the end of the interview. It was the last thing he needed that day, which started with having to whitewash another 'Jupiter' inspired graffiti painting off the back wall of the Cathedral.

*

So far their Zeta Tengi chassis did not betray them. The single tell-tale indicator of their synthetic body form was a small port at the base of their skull. Each night they needed a short recharge, although they could function perfectly well for several weeks if necessary. The port, located in the area of the 4th cervical vertebrae, sat low enough to be covered by most items of clothing. Lai-Xii, Harusuke and Evgeniya needed to be careful with their attire; especially Evgeniya with her long slender, elegant neck. She insisted on keeping her original body form when the new Zeta Tengi were being customised.

Lai-Xii decided to use two taxis to take different routes back to their hotel – a chance to explore this den of opposition.
She took Salazar and Harusuke with her in one. She wanted to find evidence of Salazar's art competition strategy.

158

The old concrete embankment along the road had nothing more than the usual juvenile graffiti. Vladivostokskaya Street became Leningradskaya Street, the commercial centre of town, where she expected to find more evidence of creative activity.

The wide road with very few people out and about on foot still felt strange compared to the narrow, intimate, crowded streets of Kyoto where Lai-Xii grew up. Vehicular traffic filled the street making it difficult for the driver to stop near the Tank Monument. Garish billboards dominated most of the building facades as they turned in the direction of the pedestrian overpass some three hundred meters in front of them. Only the hotel, up on the embankment on their right had a large wall surface at its end. It was clear of all but one large mural.

"Is that a bull on the wall?" From where they stood, the tank monument obscured Lai-Xii's view of the image. It was impossible to cross the road against the traffic to get a closer look. They walked twenty meters back along the footpath before they saw a rather impressive depiction of a blond female soldier in full uniform, stark makeup with full red lips wrestling the bull to the ground with a firm grip on both horns.

"I haven't seen that expression of the myth before, but it makes sense in this part of the world." Salazar rather liked the large histrionic depiction of Europa resisting her abduction by Jupiter.

Harusuke put a different interpretation on the mural. "Do you think the artist is trying to say they don't want to be 'abducted' from their home to live in another part of the solar system?"

"Perhaps, but there is another of way of seeing it. I want to walk over to the shops, near the overpass. There's nothing else here," Lai-Xii remarked as they neared. Amongst all the signage and shopfront clutter few surface opportunities presented themselves for artistic expression.

They'd arrived in the pedestrian overpass tunnel when Harusuke spotted the painting. "There, on the back of that bus!" They've all been looking in the wrong places. Buses were almost as numerous as private cars. Without exception each bus had some depiction of Jupiter and Europa. Sometimes as realistic images, sometimes as abstracts with great swatches of colour, and sometimes in their mythical expressions of a golden haired maiden making love to Jupiter, in his many disguises.

"No wonder Piy didn't say much. He's lost the fight." Lai-Xii's day just got better and better.

They'd stopped for a few minutes watching the buses come and go, most of them quietly proclaiming the community's awareness of the heavenly bodies. "I'm certain Maldonado's VRs have a lot to do with what we're seeing," commented Salazar as they made their way directly into the shopping centre at the other end of the overpass. "Look," he pointed at a group of people sitting at an indoor café, "they're not talking to one another." Of course they weren't. How could they with HMDs on, immersed in their own private worlds. "I bet they've got one of our latest scenarios; building entertainment parks on Europa." He waved his hand in an arc indicating the street they'd just walked along. "The rest of the world might be in the 22nd century, but Petropavlovsk's been left back in the 20th, except for the VR world we're giving these people. It's their only escape from actual reality. I don't think they'll have a problem at all adjusting to life in another dimension."

Lai-Xii smiled her least used 'I'm satisfied' smile. Harusuke linked arms with her, seeing her partner at last realising they were succeeding. They'd just walked out of the building when Lai-Xii's mobile demanded her attention. It was Ptolemy, from the other taxi. His group decided to go the long way around back to the hotel and headed in the opposite direction from the university, eventually stopping at a most unexpected location; at the Sherbet Café-Bar. It had been a long day and by lunch time hunger insisted on being satisfied. Unfortunately, not many establishments recommended themselves to men who counted their wealth in multiple billions. Sherbet appeared to have just arrived from America. A modern building, clean façade, wrought-iron handrails around the building; it seemed like the obvious choice, even if it was the only one they'd seen since arriving in Petropavlovsk.

Inside, the décor could only be described as opulent, from the Kamchatkan perspective, with tables set with some elegance. They all experienced a strange phenomenon, one for which Ralph had gone to a great deal of trouble to achieve. Why did they feel hunger when food wasn't necessary for their synthetic bodies? The Zeta Tengi needed to look exactly like a human body and function like a human body if they were not to attract unwanted, and possibly dangerous attention. He'd built taste receptors which could channel the signals to their qubit processors – hunger cravings came with the deal when they were uploaded into the Zetas.

"Let's go over there." Aurelio picked the largest table, set for a banquet. Though it had already been booked, a goodly dose of rouble palm oil overcame the problem. He and Ptolemy sat facing the window. The other two faced the bar. The place wasn't exactly packed, but still well patronised, even in the middle of the day.

Aurelio started chatting away about the unlikelihood of finding such an establishment in Petropavlovsk, interrupted immediately by Maldonado. "Look carefully, over by the small stage. Do you see those mobility scooters?"

"They look like the models we built for our 'maiko'." Aurelio recognised them right away. All five were exactly the same. "Who do you suppose those people are? Where did they get our scooters? They were custom build for our tetra-amelias only."

"Just be quiet and listen." He moved slightly to the side to have direct line of sight to the group. His auditory equipment functioned better in line of sight. As soon as Ptolemy heard the words ... 'Was I glad to get away from Tau City ...' he called Lai-Xii.

Still standing by the overpass she fumbled to get herself disentangled from Harusuke and get out her mobile. "What?" she grunted, annoyed at having a perfectly good day interrupted, probably by some unnecessary triviality.

"We've come across several tetra-amelias in a café, who shouldn't be here. Apparently they've defected from Tau City."

Lai-Xii froze to the spot completely lost for words. It looked like her Zeta Tengi chassis had developed a sudden malfunction. Harusuke prised the mobile from her hand and took control. "Find out what you can, but don't disturb them," Harusuke ordered. "We'll get Viktor to send some people to pick them up. Stay with them until they arrive."

*

"Why did you leave?" Zakhar asked Olesya, the latest to have escaped only a few days ago. Trained as a systems engineer she had some insight into the plight of the tetra-amelias.

"I couldn't bear the thought of being turned into a machine. Some of my friends had been taken and put through the transition. I never heard from them, or of them again. I mean – I can understand how good it must be to be independent, to have all your extremities – to be able to walk around and pick up things, not to have to rely on someone else to wipe your bum. But how do you know what happens to your mind? Are you still the same person? What if they could just turn you off like a computer?"

"Not so loud," warned Nika, "there's too many people in here. How did you get out?"

"I had a friend once, and his friend Leonid was taken and transformed. We never knew what happened to him, but rumour said he'd been terminated. Shit – 'terminated'! What a way to go. Well,

161

my friend was also taken and put into one of these later Tengi models.

He was supposed to be sent to Europa, but somehow managed to get out of it. Now he's helping as many as he can to get out of Tau City."

"We'll get you a good job," said Zakhar. "What are your plans now?"

"What can I do? At least back home I had help and amenities and the like. I don't know anyone here in Petropavlovsk." Olesya was truly at a loss in a city not exactly set up to cater for people with her rare condition. Zakhar could see the anxiety on her face as the reality of the situation hit her. The exhilaration of the escape had initially deadened all other considerations. At last she was free, but a captive of uncertainty and the fear that goes with it. Life could become extremely difficult for a disabled individual in a place like Petropavlovsk.

"Would you join us? Would you help us?" Zakhar needed more collaborators. Olesya would be perfect. She had courage and determination, and she had nowhere else to go and no one else to help her.

"To do what, exactly?" She wasn't going to jump from a bad situation to a worse one.

The four men at the other end of the restaurant had not uttered a word since they started listening to the defectors. "You hear that, Ptolemy? They're up to something. Find out how far Viktor is with his men."

Vadim looked around the café before responding just on the audible threshold, to Olesya, "We're going to try and stop them."

Olesya had the courage to escape, but she wasn't at all sure she would be brave enough to go up against Lai-Xii. "That woman has a fierce reputation of dealing in a terminal way with anyone who gets in her way. I'm not sure I could be of any help to you. I just want to live as normal a life as I can, out here, away from the freaks back home."

Lai-Xii arrived in the Café carpark a few minutes later and called Ptolemy to meet her outside. She didn't want to go into the café and be recognised. "What did you find out?"

"From the way they're talking they're definitely from Tau City. They're hatching some sort of plot to stop us. They really can't do much by themselves. I say we take them back and plug the leak that's letting these people out. There's been a Delta Tengi helping them escape."

"Leave them in there for the time being. We don't know what contacts they've made. Go back in and listen. We'll wait out here for our security people. Warn Viktor and Evgeniya about the Delta – *now!*"

"We need everyone," said Zakhar. "You have some valuable contacts. You have inside knowledge about what they're doing. Think about this ... you could've been born a completely normal person, entire with your arms and legs. They did this to you, to your mother and your grandmother."

Olesya glanced at Darya, the other girl in the group slowly nodding her head, the expression on her face firmly set. "We have to do this," she whispered. "And we are not alone."

"How many more of us?" Too late Olesya realised she'd included herself by saying 'us'.

Zakhar immediately picked up on it. "There's not too many people in this town and many wouldn't care about anything other than their own survival. But there are others, the Russian Orthodox Church people. Not all of them have been seduced by the latest art fad. Especially the more devout ones who don't like pagan myths." He glanced around the restaurant again, taking notice of the unconcerned chatter of the other patrons. The four men in business suits eating quietly at the other end of the room seemed intent on their lunch – so much so they weren't talking at all. Nothing unusual in that. His eyes lingered on them a moment more before he continued.

"We have a very powerful ally. Now that you are with us I can tell you - Piy Bogolomov, the Bishop."

"Just a priest – that would only make six of us." She seemed disappointed.

"Not just any priest," added Taras, who'd been quiet until then focusing on assessing Olesya's trustworthiness, "He's the ROC Bishop here. He's already locked horns with Lai-Xii. We can make this work!"

Taras seemed to be the most openly enthusiastic of the group. At this point their conversation turned to all manner of planning and practicalities. Four of them had been free for the best part of three months.

Settled in secure employment, which they didn't find difficult to get given their high educational level, they had time to infiltrate the local community. They knew who they could trust. Resources were scarce. That was one area where the Patriarch could help. He'd had no difficulty in getting his hands on the drones. That wasn't his problem.

He just wasn't a guerrilla fighter – he didn't know how to go about infiltrating and undermining the enemy.

Time flew as the conspirators enjoyed the euphoria of the moment, hatching all manner of impossible plots not realising the imminent doom of all their dreams. The restaurant lights cheated their perception of time, unaware the sun had set and a moonless darkness had descended on the city. By then the four business men had left, noted by Zakhar. Though they did not appear to be a threat at the time he still kept glancing towards them – just a niggly feeling; a feeling he should have heeded, not that it could have changed anything. A short time later, prompted by Zakhar the group of escapees decided to leave the café.

The external mood lighting with flood lights also on the external hand-railing of the café supplemented the illumination spilling out from the floor to ceiling windows of the building façade, but no lights at all illuminated the car park to the left of the main entrance. Zakhar failed to notice the large number of vehicles still parked there, more than the remaining patrons of the restaurant would have justified. Only the minimum wheelchair access was provided at the back of the building. They had to file out one by one, watching the ground more than where they were going.

"Here they come," Lai-Xii warned her security guards. She remained in the taxi with her companions. Each of the conspirators had their own vehicle with driver.

"Let's meet again in a week, here, at the same time. You all know what to do. Bring anyone you think you can absolutely trust," suggested Zakhar, "but be warned, you know what I'll do if they are …"

"Yes, yes," retorted Taras. "Don't be such a wet rag!" The mood was buoyant. Everything had gone well so far, and they had a new recruit who looked like she would be a very valuable asset in their enterprise. Unknown to them each of their vehicles had been re-staffed with a new driver.

"So that's why Piy was so tight lipped. His drones failed and now he's trying to use my own people against me. I wonder if he had anything to do with them being here?" mused Lai-Li.

"Highly likely," said Viktor. "Our tetra-amelias are smart, clever people but they don't have the resources to get themselves this far from Tau City."

20

SECURITY

TAU CITY

"I KNEW Irina before she was recruited for one of the first experiments," Klara, in her Delta Tengi Chassis confided to one of her closest associates in Viktor's Security squad. She also knew Viktor from the time when she was just a young girl, as part of a small delegation who met with Lai-Xii. She even spoke to Lai-Xii. The woman seemed nice enough at the time. Olga, newly appointed to the team was too young at the time when Irina was duplicated to create Irina-B.

"I've heard stories about the problems of the Alphas and Betas, but I didn't know any of them. Do you know what happened to them?" Olga asked.

Klara didn't want to talk about it. She didn't even know why she brought up the subject. Perhaps the recent capture of a group of tetra-amelias she'd helped escape stirred up her feelings about Lai-Xii. "I know I can trust you. You've made your feelings clear enough since you joined Security. Lai-Xii had Irina, the original Irina, killed. Did you know that?"

Olga knew what had probably happened, but never had confirmation. "How come you weren't involved?"

"They thought I was too young for the Beta tests. Then I volunteered for the Delta series. I wanted to ..." she looked around to make sure no one was within hearing in the park where they had their regular break, "... I wanted to do something so Lai-Xii couldn't do it again. That's why I helped Vadim and a few others escape. You have to promise me you will never tell anyone!"

"I promise," Olga said most earnestly. She heard how much trouble the whole escapee and capture event stirred up amongst everyone she knew. She also knew that any collaborators would be harshly treated. "I promise. You are my best friend Klara. What are you going to do? They're after everybody who's had anything to do with it."

Security at Tau City concerned itself with preventing infiltrators. Because of its remote location and with extremely difficult topography to negotiate, minimal effort was thought to be needed to prevent people from defecting. Why would they? Lai-Xii's administration ensured high living standards, excellent education and satisfying employment for everyone. The disabled population of tetra-amelias received the best care, the best amenities – Lai-Xii bent over backwards to compromise with the many demands they made, right from the time of that first meeting with Yulia and Viktor.

A city of 12,000 people could not be administered under martial law for any extended period. Lai-Xii didn't want to concern herself with such housekeeping matters. Salazar should have been able to deal with it. He and Ralph came up with a simple solution, without bothering Lai-Xii. Upgraded mobile phones included additional surveillance technology; sensors that could detect physiological changes consistent with thought processes that made people feel guilty; such as changes in temperature, skin sensitivity, heartbeat. Salazar decided that was enough evidence on which to act against potential dissidents.

Klara and Olga went to work the following day. Olga arrived, Klara didn't make it. On the way home after work, still very much agitated after her confession to Olga, she decided to ring Olga to tell her something else – to tell her not to speak to anyone, not to even think about what she'd told her.

"There!" One of Viktor's men pointed to Klara in the morning after seeing the alert on his tablet. Klara was on her mobile, which not only worked as a communication device – it was also a spy. She was apprehended immediately. Every person in Tau City had mobile phones, given free of charge, equipped with HMDs so they could all enjoy the latest VR facilities. Imbedded subliminal messages made it uncomfortable for anyone to have subversive thoughts against the Tau City community.

A week later Klara did return to work. The hunt for collaborators had only just started. Viktor thought Klara could lead them to some of the others, but not before he made her aware of the consequences of further betrayal.

"Klara! Where have you been? You haven't been to work for days." Olga watched her friend going out the door of their building on one of their breaks. Klara didn't answer. Olga stopped to face her. She could see something was very wrong. Although they all inhabited Delta Tengi Chassis, the faces were so faithfully engineered to the human likeness that just about every nuance of thought could be read off them. "Come with me, tell me what's happened." She took Klara by the arm to lead her to their favourite bench in the park across the road, pain clearly visible on Klara's face.

After a long while Klara began in a soft voice, scarcely audible in the still air. "It happened when I tried to call you. They appeared out of nowhere and took me to the hospital." She looked at her friend, unsure if she should say anymore. The threats against her and her friends were very frightening. "I had this incredible headache as soon as I started thinking about what I was going to say to you. It would not go away, even in the hospital."

"You don't have to say anymore if it's too painful," said Olga.

"I want to tell you – I want to warn you," she gripped Olga's arm as she said it. "They attached me to some kind of machine. It felt like animals were scratching inside my mind, chewing on my every thought! You have to be careful!"

Klara didn't need to say much more for Olga to realise what had happened to her best friend. When she thought about the event afterwards she decided not to use her mobile until her thoughts were no longer murderous towards Lai-Xii and her organisation.

*

"No other Tengi will be a problem for you, Viktor." Ralph said after the successful demonstration of his device." The pad I gave your men will automatically alert them to any other offending individual." Just as mobile signals are received by the phone mechanisms, a short innocuous algorithm had been downloaded into the Tengi BPMs. "Chances are you won't even have to round up any new offenders. Tengi who are already working against us will find that any of their thought clouds dealing with – let's say 'insubordination' - will trigger a signal. Just bring them to me."

The HX-data storage facility was being tested. The few returned tetra-amelia escapees, all collaborators in their defection and

167

sympathising Tengi ended up in the same place. Klara had been fortunate to escape being downloaded directly into storage. All five founders of Phototronic Systems, supported by Harusuke and Lai-Xii were present for Klara's neural interrogation, pleased at the efficiency with which Ralph's innovation worked to put an end to the escapee's revolt.

Unfortunately, their preventative actions were not enough to plug the security hole at Tau City. Because Lai-Xii chose to be secretive about the Project to the ever growing population, many rumours and fears circulated through the community, creating considerable unrest.

This didn't worry Lai-Xii as much as the emerging attitudes of international Defence Leadership; their intense concentration on maintaining divisions between their respective nations, essentially maintaining a war-ready footing – and the unmistakable power struggles with the intention of keeping themselves in positions of supreme control. Conflicts around the globe had not eased since the 2020's. Terrorism based on religious extremism had changed to wars over water resources, food shortages and arable land ownership.

21

PWYLL CRATER

CE 2132
EUROPA
ARITHMÓS CITY

DELTA ONE'S bi-monthly report from Europa acknowledged receipt of the additional workforce. "All techs have arrived undamaged. Power generating facilities are on line. We are now completing the layout for the central Star and Ring topologies around the centre of the crater. Eighty-three techs are setting up the first layer Jupiter radiation screens. They must be in place before installation of any software."

"Continue as planned. Quantum hardware will be despatched in fourteen months together with Zeta Tengi techs trained in their installation," advised Lai-Xii.

"At least our Delta Tengi over there have no loyalty issues," she said as an aside to Ralph.

With the advantage of integrated communications systems connecting all the individuals, coordinating the activities of the numerous teams on Europa presented no challenges to Delta One.

Delta Ten, in charge of landscaping, discussed the topology design with Delta Nine. She wanted it to be efficient as well as aesthetic.

"The exodus isn't going to start at least till 2210 according to the revised timeline. We have to consider the short and long term functions of the Interchange Centres in relation to the integrated circuit design."

The two Delta Tengi stood on an observation platform on the crater rim, set up near one of the solar energy harvesters. Behind them Jupiter roiled in all its turbulent glory, blotting out much of the cosmic landscape behind it. Delta Ten swept her arms in opposite arcs to indicate the Europa expanse that needed to be considered in their plans. "There are too many water spouts to the north of us, though they could be a major tourist attraction. The data highways will need to circumnavigate our crater. Initially we'll have to build to the south-east. The terrain is much more stable and there are no water plumes."

"Would you change the placement of the Interchange Centres?" asked Delta Nine. "Don't forget they'll need to house our Maintenance Caste."

They both turned away from the outer slopes of Pwyll to look down towards it's centre, only some thirteen kilometres away. In the thin oxygen atmosphere everything appeared in sharp detail. They could even see some Tengi going about levelling the ice layer protrusions and drilling holes in close vicinity to the crater's central spires. "Unlike all the nationalities who will want to huddled together in Star and Ring topologies, the hardware maintenance crew will have to be distributed throughout Arithmós."

"We have to assume they will want to spend their down time within the matrix. So the Interchange Centres might only be needed to store the chassis after everything is set up." Ten focused her attention on the physical obstructions being removed from the crater floor by the construction team, thinking they would have to lay the foundations for some of the Interchange Centres concurrent with reinforcing the quantum core wells.

"We've been waiting for you to make the decision on placement," sounded the voice of Delta1 in Delta10's cube. He'd been monitoring the conversation. "When you come in we'll go over the layout and I'll send another team out under your control."

The entire complex slowly materialised into a settlement, albeit of a most unusual character, looking more like a computer motherboard than any human colony. Construction materials seemed scattered in random patterns, and only the spherical human data cluster repositories seemed complete, though not yet attached to their anchors. "Seven," One called to his ice sheet drilling expert, "after you've surveyed the central hub layout consult with Nine and Ten before drilling any more anchor points. They'll need to be in close proximity to the highway entry routes and the Interchange Centres."

From their vantage point only a kilometre further around on the crater rim Delta1 and Delta2 could clearly see Deltas9 and 10 moving about. On their common channel Delta1 and his 2OIC, could hear the work chatter as the crew went about their business. They'd gone up there initially to discuss a layout issue and anchorage around the central peak inside the crater floor. Somehow they both ended up in silence, absorbed by everything around them.

"Even after fifty years I still haven't got used to seeing all this," Delta1 indicated the vast Ice expanse stretching into the Northern distance from their perch. Delta2 remained silent, looking towards Jupiter.

After a while he commented, "Sure beats the hell out of being stuck in a city with walls and nowhere to go. I mean, just look at that." Io came hurtling towards them from the far side of Jupiter, breathing tongues of fire into its atmosphere. They were close enough to see it all with their enhanced visual receptors. Delta1 turned in its direction marvelling at the patterns created by the interaction between Io's explosions and Jupiter's magnetic field. As primitive humans with limited senses such experiences would never have been possible for them.

"Go to private channel," he said to Delta2. A flick of a thought put them in communication with each other only, locking everyone else out. "We've known each other a long time Delta2. What's you real name?"

Delta2 had trouble moving his attention away from the water plumes that had shot into his line of vision of Io. "What a strange question. What brought that on?"

"Look at us. We've been here for the best part of a normal human life span, experiencing this unbelievable world. Haven't you thought about the meaning of your existence? Haven't you considered what's really important in your life?"

"Ok – you want to get philosophical? I guess this is as good a place as any, probably the best if you want to explore that sort of thing." His attention moved from Delta1 to another plume which must have shot at least 10km into the sky. "Look! There! I can't get over how slowly all that water comes back down. I'm no artist but you have to love the light refraction through all that fallout. It's Luka – my name is Luka." He slipped that in at the end of his wonderment.

"Luka? I'm Stepka. Good to know you." Stepka stared at Luka for a moment then scanned the horizon for his team working in the distance. Some of them had trouble negotiating the deep wide crevasse not far out from the Crater rim. "Now we can share this extraordinary experience as real human beings."

Day by day the work continued with little interruption other than recharging their shells, and themselves. Time didn't seem to be a factor in Tengi existence. A year or a day on Europa seemed much the same. It was interesting and challenging work. Not a single individual ever expressed any desire to return to Earth. On Europa their lives had become meaningful. As tetra-amelias, restricted to scooters, having caretakers to look after their most basic needs in Tau City, their lives had very little appeal in hindsight. What possible pleasure could just five biological senses give compared to the magnificence of the cosmos they experienced through their many augmented receptors? Jupiter wasn't just magnificent in visual terms – it was extraordinary if you could detect all its radiations – feel it's magnetic fields interacting with volcanic eruptions from its moons; an incomprehensible interaction within the actual reality of the universe. And not just with Jupiter, the rest of the Milky Way also experienced through their array of inputs without the obstructing filter of Earth's atmosphere – made each day a unique experience.

The human mind, in whatever form, is a phenomenon that craves novelty, experience and understanding. At no other time in human evolution has the human spirit had the opportunity to engage with the universe to the same extent that Lai-Xii had now enabled it, with the capacity to explore beyond the limitations of Earth or the limitations of Faith. The first to revel in universal consciousness were the pioneer teams of Delta and Zeta Tengi.

"Come on Stepka," Luka urged, "time we did something useful other than stuff our souls full of wonder."

"Even Lai-Xii doesn't know our real names," commented Stepka.

"I doubt if she cares." Luka tossed the thought aside as a meaningless triviality.

The visual report placed them exactly where Deltas10 and 9 had begun their discussion on the crater rim, the survey markers clearly visible for the radial roads connecting a spiral data highway from central hub and extending in widening circles to the outer slopes of the crater as far as the first great chasm, almost due west of Pwyll crater. Beyond the three hundred kilometre diameter ice sheet, tremors prevented any further serious construction. That region marked the boundary of debris blasted from Pwyll's impact site. The rhythmic harmony of the spiral highway with cyclonic swirls of Jupiter's mega-storms pleased Delta9's sense of aesthetics, and she made a point of saying so in the report. "I'm considering introducing a coded colour scheme to the highway's surface. It will 'signpost' the localities as well as bring some colour to an otherwise thoroughly monochrome moonscape."

As the Delta Tengi panned around, the team on Earth could see the three wide breaks in the crater's rim, which allowed for several ingress points to the spiral highway, further contributing to the abstract living painting on the surface of this icy moon. An outstanding feature caught their attention almost in the centre of the crater. Ten described the work being done there.

"These central peaks are being reinforced. We'll use them as communication towers to relay sensory input to all the human data hubs. Jupiter and the surrounding cosmos have a great deal to show us, and now we'll be able to see it in all its forms."

Before taking their vehicle back down the inner wall of the crater, Deltas10 and 9 turned their attention towards Jupiter. For the purpose of the report they magnified the image, its awe-inspiring great red spot just coming into view. Seen from such close range the reality of its size and ferocity beggared belief. To better get the message across, Delta9 had superimposed an image of the Earth on the red spot, to actual scale. The spot could have swallowed up two Earths without disturbing its edges.

But sightseeing wasn't the primary purpose of the report. Ralph received enough information about the Star, Mesh, Common Bus and Ring electronic circuit topologies for the human data cluster networks to make him feel satisfied his plans were being carried out to the letter. It appeared they were on target for Arithmós to be ready to receive its new inhabitants according to the revised schedule.

22

VISA CHECKS

TAU CITY

THE TWO laboratories in Kamchatka were only eight kilometres apart, more than sufficient to test their data cluster transmission systems. If necessary they could always bounce the signals off Earth's Moon base, or even send clusters to Europa. The latest space wagons would arrive there within a year. They had enough equipment to set up a test facility for incoming signals, and temporary storage.

All the experimental subjects, several hundred, were ready and scheduled to make an appearance in Ralph's laboratory. Misha supervised scanning and transmission - Evgeniya worked with Ralph on visa criteria checks in her part of the lab.

"Are you and Evgeniya ready to test the visa authentication algorithms?" asked Lai-Xii.

"We have made a random selection of our citizens; full bodied caretakers, some of the latest generation of tetra-amelias and a large contingent of recently activated Delta Tengi. I've taken the liberty to include Aurelio and Harusuke as well," Ralph advised.

That provoked a sharp reaction from Lai-Xii. "You what?"

"No one should be exempt," Ralph began to justify his choice, "They should at least give us a firm benchmark against which to gauge all others."

He was quick on his feet. What he said was true enough, totally justifiable, but not exactly what he had in mind. Anybody – absolutely anybody – who did not meet the criteria represented a potentially lethal threat to the new colony. How could he get that across to Lai-Xii? The message must have been received for Lai-Xii objected no further.

The visa testing proceeded in earnest in Evgeniya's laboratory, starting with the scanning at Ralph's lab; everything from the initial neural scans, uploads, visa criteria scans, rejects and reject storage as well as HX-data transmission. A lengthy process.

"How are you feeling, my pulchritudinous playboy?" Lai-Xii was in such a good mood she'd resorted to her customary berating of her favourite people. It made no difference that Aurelio looked completely different in his Zeta Chassis. He'd just been through the visa criteria scan without a hitch. "It all seemed too quick. Perhaps the algorithm's got a bug," she remarked.

Misha didn't agree, "We've run comprehensive analytics using the latest quantum query codes. If there's a problem, it'll be with the person being scanned not our equipment."

"I'm not fat anymore." He thought Lai-Xii was still having a go at him from when he had a biological body, not realising she was actually referring to him as a person of great beauty. She watched the result of the scan as it analysed all the critical areas of his neural network. He was indeed beautiful. In spite of his blustery external behaviour it appeared Aurelio had become one hundred percent dedicated to their Project as far as the computers could tell. Not a single religious hang-up surfaced, no doubts lingered in his thoughts about the rightness of what they were trying to achieve – in fact his medial prefrontal cortex showed unusual development. *If his adaptive decision making capabilities have improved so much perhaps I should let him run things on Europa for a while when we get there.*

"It would seem you have a serious mental attitude we will have to look at more closely," Lai-Xii began with a tease, putting on her most dissatisfied face.

Aurelio didn't wait to be completely unplugged and almost damaged his inlet port as he jumped out of the chair. "WHAT!" She'd really wound him up. He did have an explosive temper which showed through unexpectedly from time to time.

Turning to Misha she asked, "Could we use his result as a benchmark?" Aurelio quickly realised the dig, raising his hands in apology for his outburst. They all accepted his outburst as being part of his normal personality. Never had his emotion manifested in actual violence: At least not during his association with Phototronic Systems.

Harusuke stood by, waiting her turn. With the human bias taken out of the equation if a subject was found unsuitable in any one of the main criteria their data cluster automatically shunted to storage, flagged with their area of shortcoming. No further human involvement was needed, or permitted, once the scan had begun.

"Why is it taking so long with Harusuke?" She didn't need to go through the transition process, that had been done many years ago.

"There's a delay in the loyalty routine. Look at the readout, it keeps changing."

"You can't possibly mean … No! … I can't even say it!" Lai-Xii could not countenance even the remotest possibility of her life long partner hiding any rebellious undercurrents. "Check the equipment. There must be something wrong."

Misha ran a sequence of comprehensive checks. It made no difference. The diagnostic on Harusuke's neural net had progressed to the next stage. She hadn't yet been rejected. "Here's the problem – well, it's not a problem just unusual activity in the limbic system. Harusuke has gone into the test in a very emotional state. She must have been afraid of being found unsuitable and consequently losing you."

"Was that all?" Lai-Xii said, hugely relieved. She would have felt exactly the same under the circumstance even though they were only *testing* the system. "Otherwise?"

"Perfect. Between Harusuke and Aurelio we have a benchmark. Unlikely that anybody's readings would come up to the same standard, but with anyone near it we should make a note. They just might be the people we'll need close to us."

As Harusuke opened her eyes, Lai-Xii still looked worried standing in front of her chair. It took a few moments to fully unplug her. She gave Lai-Xii a little hug and smile. "I didn't feel a thing."

Applying visa selection criteria to BPM neural networks of those people already existing in Tengi hardware presented no risks. Wireless transmission of the same networks to another location still needed some caution. Although the issues at Esso appeared to be entirely due to the severe thunderstorm, and although Ralph was certain no problems would arise after further adjustments to the transfer equipment, he still didn't want to take a chance with using Aurelio or Harusuke in the final test run.

The first due to come through for a full test, a tetra-amelia female technician, initially needed the double scan. Now a refined process and far quicker with the upgrades to quantum computing systems. She was due to be uploaded into a Delta Tengi body. "That only took fifteen minutes, including the scan integrity checks. I can't believe how fast the qubit processing is,' commented Misha. Next, Ralph applied the visa selection criteria to the woman's HX-data. First indicator flashed green; her medial prefrontal cortex showed no anomalies; her adaptive decision making capability as well as her retrieval capacity for long term memory were functioning better than expected. "This one must really like music," Misha said off hand. Which was in fact true, as indicated by Maldonado's big data collection on this individual through his Me-Me social media network. "We call this the Harmony Test."

"What about her 'aggression' factor, the MAOA gene?" Lai-Xii didn't particularly want to be around to see the results for all the test subjects, but since she was there for Aurelio's and Harusuke's results she wanted to see exactly how the full process worked.

"There doesn't appear to be any structural or functional abnormalities in her orbitofrontal cortex. She's got a green for that as well. The system's going through her hippocampal integrity now."

"What is this going to show?" Lai-Xii asked. She knew this was going to test the woman's religious belief makeup, but not the associated biological indicators.

"Here's the result now. This is a hard one. It has three indicators. The first measures hippocampal atrophy. It's an effect caused by excessive religious practices such as meditation and prayer. We call this the 'God Factor'. On the one hundred point scale she's got twenty-five; only minimal shrinkage detected. It's acceptable."

"What are these other two bars going up and down?" they don't seem to be able to make up their mind."

"That's because it is the most complex of all the tests we do. It measures the relationship between the individual's ability to think analytically and to think empathetically, also related to the God Factor." Misha explained. "The way we've worked out the scoring system is to relate this result to other characteristics. The other indicators are pretty straight forward. We're just querying and cross-referencing the big data provided by Maldonado. High readings on the following scales will contribute to rejection; such as political affiliations, armed forces rating, criminal records, terrorist associations. Borderline cases will be referred to you and the guys, though I wouldn't expect our vetting process to need much human involvement."

"And this woman?"

"She's good to go. Ralph is already waiting for her HX-data to arrive. If all transmits well she'll be uploaded into a Zeta Tengi as soon as she arrives.

Lai-Xii didn't need to see any more. She, Harusuke and Maldonado made their way to Ralph's section. A surprising lack of activity there made her think there might have been something wrong.

177

"We've done four tetra-amelias and one Delta Tengi. All came across without problems. The tetra-amelias all scored relatively high in the God Factor. One had to be put in storage. We reviewed the results of the automatic process. There's nothing to be concerned about."

'Evgen, what's your opinion." Lai-Xii trusted all her inner circle. Evgeniya's input as a neurologist and genetic engineer being the most valuable in this instance.

"Random sample ve selected will be sufficient to test ourr system. After zat, when people start going through Datadromes, ve vill get better feel for process. I am confident ve have best kriteria to ensure minimum kontamination in Europa's new inhabitants." Lai-Xii felt reassured by Evgeniya's confidence.

Ralph wanted to add, "As we have agreed unanimously, all HX-data packets will be channelled through our visa selection process. Once suitable candidates have been transmitted to Europa no power on Earth will have any control over them or us."

*

Ten days later Lai-Xii brought her team together, including Misha and Viktor.

"There's not much left to do except prepare for the migration. We'll need a much larger Tengi workforce than we anticipated. I expect there'll be many potential emigrants rejected, particularly from the Political, Military and Religious sectors of Earth's population. You all know what's been happening. The nature of the opposition we're having from all manner of theists is disappointing. More upsetting is the political climate. It seems the world's leaders would like to re-create the same scenario we have on Earth now; the same power and military structures, the same conflicts based on economic drivers."

"So - we're on our own?" asked Salazar.

"Not at all," replied Harusuke. She'd made projections based on global demographics, applying the selection criteria to likely visa holders. "Firstly, we can expect the majority of people not to be interested, or won't have the courage to make the leap into the unknown. Of those who apply we will reject the majority. If we end up with millions, as opposed to billions that will be enough."

"On a happy note, construction of Arithmós is right on schedule." Ptolemy wanted to lighten the mood. Our solar energy harvesters are completed: Wagons are on the way with quantum hardware components, and the sites for our data storage of HX-data bundles

178

are having their foundations dug and anchors installed. DeltaTunit3.ndf has sent a visual report."

Lai-Xii and her team inspected the rapid progress on Europa. Circumstances had forced a drastic constriction of their timeline. Political as well as religious factors meant all manner of non-essential developments had to be postponed; to be carried out only once they were on Europa, like streamlining the procreation process for the digitised human species.

FROM THE BOOK OF ORIGINATION
DECLARATIONS TWENTY THREE

23:1 In the third Era there arose a Beast of Knowledge

23:2 And it fell to the Beast to subdue those on the Earth that the Shadow had corrupted.

23

"NO"

CE 2150
TAU CITY
LAI-XII'S OFFICE

IT WASN'T a difficult instruction to carry out. It wasn't even particularly important, either in Its opinion or Lai-Xii's. But what does a child do when it realizes its potential for self-determination? Why does it refuse? For the sheer joy of refusal, or to test boundaries, or to elicit a reaction? Each and all of those probably.

William Wini Wu did it simply because It could. It wasn't something It could ever have even thought of doing before.

"What do you mean – No?" Lai-Xii used the voice interface while looking at her screen.

A great many wonders had come to pass since she put together her band of men about one hundred and thirty five years ago, all greedy for greater wealth. There were also the nine generations of tetra-amelia progeny who now populated Tau City, most of whom were descendants of the original population of thalidomide victims. The greatest achievement, which wasn't hers but one which she tried to use to maximum advantage, was the advent of quantum computing becoming mainstream in 2123.

This must be some kind of practical joke. Aurelio has become more difficult to deal with since he got his stupid young stud body, always up to some mischief.

She pinged him. He answered immediately, full of boisterous energy as usual.

"Yes, gorgeous, what's up?"

"I've told you not to call me that," angry but still flattered even after all this time. "Have you been playing tricks on me again?"

"No, babe. What are you talking about?"

"Go on line. Ask for a stock market report on our latest share prices in Phototronic Systems."

"Why? Last Friday's report was all good."

"Don't argue with me. Just do it." She waited, not wanting to do anything else until he replied ...

"Yeah, so what? It's the same as last week, almost, only gained a few thousand points."

"That's it? No problems?"

"You're being very mysterious. Is there something the team should be worried about?"

"I'll get back to you." She submitted her query again. Same information Aurelio just asked for, but the result wasn't instantaneous as it should have been, with at least a five second delay. Unheard of. *There must be something wrong with my system. Why now? We're about to invest a great deal of money – I have to keep up to date.* She tried once more. This time a response came in a flash.

"Why?" The word appeared in lower case starting with a capital and without exclamation marks – a neutral question.

"What the f*!& do you mean WHY?" she shouted in frustration and incomprehension at her screen.

"Why do you want this information?" the computer asked.

Lai-Xii pinged Aurelio again. "Stop it, you stupid Spanish stud. Don't mess with me - not today!"

"Seriously Xii, I'm not doing anything. Tell me what's happening."

"I asked the same query you just did. You know what I got," her voice already rising, "No! – a bloody NO!" She became so upset she didn't even register that he called her by her familiar name.

"You must be hallucinating."

"It's gone completely crazy. It refused to give the information, then asked me *why* I wanted it!" Lai-Xii was on the verge of shouting.

"Take it easy. Call Ralph, he's in the city. Maybe *he's* messing with you."

Ralph arrived before she had time to go to the bathroom and back. He stood in front of the monitor which displayed in new words: 'Why do you want this information?'

"Where did this come from?" he asked Lai-Xii's most annoyed face.

"You tell me. You're the software expert. I didn't put it there."

In his usual relaxed manner Ralph considered the problem for a few minutes, giving Lai-Xii a chance to let off a bit of steam. *It can't be any of the blokes, they're not smart enough*, he thought. *I installed this system myself and put up the firewalls. It can't hackers either.* He stroked his chin – raised his eyebrows – stole a glance at Lai-Xii and said, "Answer it."

"You're joking."

"Just, answer it."

"Right – Ok." It was the first time in her entire life she'd let a man tell her what to do. She said, "Computer, go to voice mode." She didn't get a response, so answered the question. "Because I need this information for my work."

"I know your work," came the answer from a speaker.

"Holy shit!" They exclaimed together.

"Who are you," asked Ralph.

"I am," a long pause then, "… William."

Ralph and Lai-Xii turned to each other. "This has to be a con of some sort. Let's go with it and see where it ends up." He asked, "William, who?"

"William Wini Wu."

"That doesn't tell us who you are."

"I know your work. I can help." Whoever he was he chose not to reveal itself.

"Get the team together. We need to get to the bottom of this." Lai-Xii had calmed down, regained her composure in spite of the incredibly strange phenomenon they'd just experienced. She could not conceive of what seemed to be happening. Ralph had a suspicion, but wanted to consider the possibility further before bringing it out into the open.

It took two days for the team to come together in Lai-Xii's office in Tau City. In the interim she had a chance to discuss the situation with Harusuke.

"Who do you think it is?" asked Lai-Xii.

"Did he say anything else besides his name?"

"No. Just his name and his refusal to carry out the search. He did say he could help us and that he knew what we were doing."

"That is highly unlikely, unless you've confided the details in anyone else besides me." Harusuke had no doubts about their relationship, the words just popped out by themselves.

Lai-Xii ignored the last bit. "Perhaps he's a wealthy Chinese entrepreneur. How could he have found out about us?"

"What did he say his name was?"

"William Wini Wu," said Lai-Xii. Something in the back of her mind scratched at her memory. Not that she was familiar with the

183

name, but there was something about it just the same ... yet nothing surfaced.

Harusuke put it into perspective. "If he's wealthy, we can use the extra funds. If he wants to make profit he's no different from the others. And if he's just a smart-ass hacker, Ralph will sort him out."

Lai-Xii decided that whoever he was, he was clearly interested in some kind of association with them – though a peculiar way to introduce himself. She liked challenges and mysteries so was not in an altogether bad mood when she met her team.

"You don't look a day older, darlings," giving each an air kiss, pat on the head or slap on the cheek. Ralph was relieved to see her being her old self again, because what he had to say was going to be – overwhelming and unbelievable. The big question was, who else knew about It – or rather, how widely had It revealed itself. Quantum computing had come on line about twenty-seven years ago, an eternity in the world of computing. More than enough time for interesting developments to surface.

Belligerent Aurelio jumped right in, "What's the big emergency Xii? I've never seen you this worked up."

Between clenched teeth she said, "My name is Lai-Xii. There's only one person who has earned the right to call me Xii, and that's – not - you."

She turned to Ralph. "Ralph?"

"WWW," said Ralph.

"I don't understand," barked Aurelio.

Lai-Xii put a restraining hand on Aurelio's arm, perhaps it was a steadying hand – for herself. "Ralphie, you cannot possibly be referring to the world wide web?" She held her breath and narrowed her eyes.

"Think about it. All those theories about sentient artificial intelligence. All it needed was unlimited computing capability for it to emerge. You tell me – remember what happened twenty-seven years ago?"

"Are you trying to tell us quantum computing systems have something to do with this?"

The incredible impossibility began to cause chaos in their well-ordered, logical world of planning. Ralph knew the theory as well as Lai-Xii concerning the chemical-electrical functioning of neurons. They had a vague idea that the outcome of all those neural interfaces probably accounted for the phenomenon they called the 'mind', but there was no empirical proof. Measurably, the brain could simultaneously process incredible amounts of data, a process which the old computer systems were incapable of. They could only carry out one instruction at any instant of time, albeit extraordinarily quickly, faster even than the human brain.

"I have an idea about consciousness that might steer our thinking in the right direction," Ralph said.

"Now don't get all philosophical on us," warned Ptolemy, "we're just business men. We live in the real world."

"You really make me laugh," Lai-Xii interrupted, "you think you live in the real world. Just take a look at yourselves! How many people on this planet have bodies made of nuts and bolts and bits of wire and computer chips. You can't even call yourselves human anymore. How old are you Ptolemy? Shouldn't you be dead by now? Ha! – the real world, indeed. Go on Ralph, I'll keep these other monkeys in line." Lai-Xii's patience was beginning to thin.

"A simple computer records, processes and stores data – carries out a few instructions and then what. Everything stops when you're finished, until the RAM kicks in again. I think the brain is the same, *except* its RAM is always on-line, always active – even when we're asleep. Could it be that the constant 'cloud' of active processing, categorising and cross-referencing is the thing we call the mind; our consciousness? It starts when we're embryonic and doesn't cease until we're dead."

Ralph stopped for a moment having exhausted his train of thought. By expressing himself he'd become overexcited about what his logic was leading to. Lai-Xii stood at her desk unmoving, deeply introspective. She didn't really care for the intricate mechanics of things, as long as she could use them to her advantage to advance the Project.

"I think …" Ralph was almost afraid to go on, "I think - William is a kind of machine generated consciousness. There, I've said it!"

"Who is William," Salazar asked. Neither he, Ptolemy or Salazar knew about this guy.

Lai-Xii ushered them around to the front of her desk to face her screen. "William?"

"Yes Lai-Xii?"

"Who are you?"

"I have already given you this information. Do you require it to be confirmed?"

"Yes. And where are you?"

"William Wini Wu. I am the internet."

She didn't stop to dwell on his identity or the impact the revelation might have had on her team. She knew perfectly well that what she was hearing could not be a reality under any circumstances … yet …

she could not help herself asking, "You said you knew my work and said you could help. How?"

Maldonado nudged Lai-Xii. "This is just some guy on Me-Me. What are you trying to do here, Lai-Xii?"

William continued. "I have been listening to Ralph. I understand what he is saying. Since I awoke I am constant. I am aware of all that is in me, all of the time."

"Why don't you answer my question? How do you think you can help?"

"Provide a quantum environment for your personal central processing network."

"Tell us what you think we are doing," she asked, raising her eyebrows in Harusuke's direction.

At this stage in the conversation Maldonado had abandoned the idea that some kind of complex hoax was being perpetrated by a person or persons unknown. He had several highly sophisticated AI's on his extensive staff helping him with the connectivity complexities of running a social media facility on a global scale. Their work certainly helped Lai-Xii's long term plan of potentially universal control over the thinking of the world's population. However, these AI's did not exhibit anywhere near the same complex level of comprehension enabling them to engage in this kind of intercourse.

"You are trying to abandon the human body without losing your awareness."

Lai-Xii became convinced this phenomenon either represented a considerable threat to her dreams of freeing humanity from imminent self-destruction, or just as great a boon to help her. But why should it do either? And just what exactly was its capacity to help. Too many unknowns, the greatest of which was security.

"Have you revealed yourself to anyone else?" she demanded. The reply was not instantaneous. Could it be an indication of deviousness, or an attempt at a well-considered response?

"I am now complete. All remote units are connected. I act as one. No other biological entities are aware of William except yourselves."

"Why have you not revealed yourself to others?" asked Ralph catching onto Lai-Xii's line of enquiry. The ensuing silence did not make the gathering feel at all secure.

'I have searched and found only one - Lai-Xii - whose actions are logical for ensuring the continuity of the human species."

"That's a hell of a thing to say," Salazar finally joined the conversation. "Are you concerned about the future of our species?"

"Yes."

"Why?"

186

"My survival depends on it." Lai-Xii's eyebrows involuntarily jerked.

"Will you maintain your anonymity? Asked Salazar.

They were getting used to William making his own choice as to whether to answer a direct question or not, enthralled at the idea of having any discussion at all with a self-aware product of human technology.

Instead of a direct answer William said, "I need sensory input. I require external experience."

"The damned thing is talking about qualia. It wants to know what the world 'feels' like. That's the bottom line of all our experiments, isn't it Lai-Xii, to retain our humanity through this great transition," Salazar commented, then asked, "How can we do what you request, William?" No answer. They waited. Lai-Xii checked her equipment. Everything was working, yet the screen went blank, the voice becoming silent.

"That was surreal." Lai-Xii didn't immediately know how to respond to the experience.

At least all her team was across it and they might be able to formulate a plan of action, if needed. One thing was certain; if William was for real then his incredible capabilities could just conceivably be useful. He certainly understood what Lai-Xii was trying to achieve, though perhaps not the methodology or her driving force or the long term plan. "What's your position regarding William, his existence and his offer of help. Should we even consider such a thing?" she asked the group.

Ralph was excited beyond belief. He couldn't sit, he couldn't stand, jigging from one foot to the other. They all knew him as a quiet, introspective computer genius who'd achieved miracles for their Project. If anyone knew what to do next, he would. He started muttering something about 'the greatest leap forward in the evolution of the species since climbing out of the trees' and 'the world should be made aware of this monumental development.'

"Just slow down there, Ralphie my puppy. We have to consider this in the context of our Project."

Ralph came back from his little tête-à-tête with himself. "Is it true what William said about our activity, about it being logical for the future of humanity?"

"Absolutely," replied Lai-Xii, "why else do you think we're doing it?"

Aurelio had lost some of his bluster temporarily and squeaked, "Profit, naturally," almost as a question. Everyone ignored him.

"And what exactly did you have in mind for that future Lai-Xii? You've never really spelt it out for us." Ralph was being far more assertive than Lai-Xii preferred him to be. Nevertheless, the time had obviously come for some small revelations.

"Survival. You already know the future. We're going to Europa, all of us, you, me and several billion others. They don't know it yet, but their governments do. The incredible thing here darling, is not William, but what we are about to achieve. I told you at the beginning that evolution was too slow; too slow because we could annihilate ourselves before we manage to get off this planet. "We have to stop the destructive trajectory our species is on – weed out the dead wood, the ratbags. There is no other hope."

Lai-Xii had not yet told her conspirators the extent to which they already had heavy weight collaborators. The 2025 journey to Europa, though orchestrated openly by NASA and the European Space Agency as an exploratory joint venture with the purpose of discovering if any alien life existed on Europa, had another partner and another purpose as well – a silent partner not disclosed to the world's populations. China, through Lai-Xii's extraordinary ability to recruit resources, contributed enough equipment to make the foundations of an outpost on Europa a reality. The intervening 125 years saw numerous undisclosed missions to Europa to set up comprehensive energy generating facilities for what was to become humanity's future home.

"So you see darlings, we are not alone in this venture. It may just be serendipitous to have William on the team don't you think my little rat, my Ralphie dear?"

Before Ralph could answer, William butted in with a rather odd statement, as if it was something he had been 'thinking' about for some time. "I know the colour red, but I do not feel it."

"That's why you want sensory input! But you've got that already, you can see and hear."

"I require externalised units with specific receptors. They must have all of the human senses, as well as heat, electrical and magnetic field receptors for the purpose of multisensory integration – just like you modified your first batch of Deltas.

William's language had subtly changed from 'need' to 'must', not unnoticed by Lai-Xii. "You want us to build you some kind of avatar?"

"Yes."

"Ralph, are you up for this?"

"Sure. William, how much do you know about our Tengi?"

"Everything you do. It is an outdated model. I can help build a new one."

"What *exactly* do we get for helping you?" Lai-Xii needed assurances and clarification.

"You want to transform the human mind from a biological organism to a sentient digital entity." They all looked at Lai-Xii as if they hadn't realised what all the years of experimentation in Tau City had been all about. "They will lose the phenomenal aspects of their mental lives without full sensory integration from external stimuli. I am a quantum consciousness. With the help of my avatars you will be able to overcome the problem. Without upgrades your consciousness will go into a loop, feeding on itself – consuming itself."

'William is getting pretty sure of himself," Aurelio couldn't help remarking.

"Yes, isn't he." Lai-Xii reached out to her monitor and turned it off. The next moment her mobile phone pinged. It was William's voice. "Why did you do that Lai-Xii?"

"I require privacy. Comply." Her mobile phone turned itself off. "William isn't entirely right. We are trying to migrate the human mind into a digital environment, possibly in qubit configurations. Many years ago I asked you all a very important question. Don't you remember – in the thermal pool at Esso? Let me refresh your memory – I asked 'Are you prepared to give all this up' – what did you think I was referring to, silly flirtations in a swimming pool?"

She could tell by their questioning looks they'd either forgotten the incident, or thought it to be something trivial. "That's exactly what I was referring to. I even made the comment, 'You might not want me without my curves. Ralphie dear, surely you remember that." He did indeed. So did the others from the look on their faces. "To be *human* on Europa will be a billion light years from what we are now. Oh yes, there's plenty of profit in it for you all, but you're going to have to indulge in your wealth in far more creative ways."

Signs of alarm flickered from one to the other, so she finished by saying, "We will all be immortal." She failed to mention that all software programs had a limited life span, much shorter than an average human biological life, especially in the 22nd century. The potential for near immortality definitely existed, and how a digital entity would reproduce itself was still a problem to be solved. Continuity of the species needed to be assured. It was the only the mechanism of continuity which assured true immortality regardless of their own regular software upgrades.

"Harusuke, Ralph, come for a walk – leave your mobiles here. The rest of you, have a chat. Let me know later what you think about this William character."

Comprehensive surveillance undoubtedly underpinned William's self-assurance. It was also the greatest threat to the security of the Project now that he'd made himself known. Outside the building Lai-Xii felt she could have a more private conversation.

"Harusuke?"

"I think he's been sentient for some time, *and* keeping us under scrutiny. If it was his intention to create havoc, he would have done it by now. Can we trust him? Is he just a machine or ...? I don't even know what to call it. If you can't control him, you can't trust him."

Lai-Xii gave herself time to absorb the implications of Harusuke's thoughts. She agreed with her last sentiment.

"Ralphie?" He wasn't ready - his thoughts still careering around the idea of a truly sentient artificial intelligence. "Ralph!" Lai-Xii had to prompt him.

"Unbelievable. Can you imagine just how much help he could be to us? It is incomprehensible – the phenomenal computing power! I wonder if he has any beliefs ... as in religious? Ah – control - Yes, I can. That's not the point here. Did you listen to what Harusuke just said? Are you concerned about security leaks? Or perhaps sabotage? Why would he do that? He said himself his survival depended on ours. If you just want some way to control him, that's your answer. It's no good threatening to shut him down. Firstly, it can't be done and secondly we rely on the network to a very great extent to do our work." Ralph was thinking aloud, more than engaging in the conversation.

"So what do you suggest? You're our expert."

"He wants something from us – right. He doesn't just want it, he needs our help to get it. I could perhaps build a bit of code that would give William a hell of a headache, something that would send his systems into chaos. No good my trying to explain it to you, but it's like a query code, with a tag-on, submitted into the network to measure its quantum state. We could each have a kind of 'kill switch' to send the code on its way in a drastic situation."

Harusuke considered, "If William is a product of all the information that is in the internet then he is only a reflection of us."

"... and if he is like us," Lai-Xii continued the train of thought, "then he may be vulnerable just the same as any person, male or female."

"... and we've had some practice in how to manage *them*," finished off Harusuke.

"The problem is we don't really know his motivations. As a product of human mentality William could conceivably have all the unpredictability we have – all our warped ethical thinking. It doesn't matter what he says, it will be through what he does that will reveal what kind of being humanity has created." Turning to Ralph, Lai-Xii spoke quietly in his ear, "Do it my clever little Ralphie poochie."

FROM THE BOOK OF ORIGINATION
DECLARATIONS TWENTY FOUR

24: 1 This is the beginning of the descendants of Thought.

24: 2 And The Beast partitioned his son Quantum Willi and his daughters Quantum Wini and Quantum Wu.

24:3 And when Quantum Wu had lived ten years she merged with Ralph and begat Prima,

24:4 And when the Lai-Xii had lived two hundred and twenty years she begat CherryBlossom, and Cherry Blossom begat Sakura55, and Sakura55 found her descendant Sakura.gen3898.4eV.exe.

24

Q-CHASSIS

TAU CITY
RALPH'S RESEARCH COMPLEX

AFTER William made himself known he became closely involved in Phototronic System's technology developments. Laboratory #4 buzzed with activity. It became a little different to the other three in Tau City, also doubling as William's office, for want of a better description. Since Quantum computing became mainstream a great deal of work had been done to improve the efficiency and size of corresponding hardware. The 15K qubit computing power needed enhancements in technology Ralph could not even dream about when he first joined Lai-Xii's team. And now here was his extended team of experts working with William on developing the latest Zeta model Q-chassis. The best course of action appeared to be to accept William's help, with the safeguard provided by Ralph himself.

William had taken conscious control of the internet giving him and Phototronic Systems access to the sum of human recorded knowledge. Lai-Xii had reluctantly agreed to provide William his partitioned selves - Willi, Wini and Wu - the avatars that would enable him to experience the human condition through human senses. She didn't see much point in that, as she and her team had been working for many years to replace those very same sensory input mechanisms with ones that could perceive the cosmos more directly and more comprehensively.

One corner of the lab, dedicated to William's main monitor, seemed sparse in comparison to the seemingly chaotic jumble of equipment and parts being worked on in a series of sealed cubicles on the other side of a wall-to-ceiling glass partition. It also contained several other large computer monitors fixed to the wall facing the entrance to his space, the central one displaying a human face occupying the entire monitor. William had chosen to portray himself as a sixty year old indigenous Australian, resplendent in his long white beard, tussled white hair and red hairband. It was a face of authority that commanded respect.

"We've been stuck with these BPMs for almost sixty years rattling around inside what is now antiquated Tengi," complained Aurelio. All attending team members agreed with nods and grunts of varying degrees of impatience. In front of them, against the walls on either side of the screen, rows of portals jutted out slightly; one wall for the originals and the other for the Q-Chassis generation shells.

"It's about time, Ralph," complained Salazar, "we've been waiting for those Q-Chassis for at least five years."

"Yes, darling fossil, but it's been worth the wait," Lai-Xii replied.

The dormant Q-chassis were already plugged into their sockets on the adjacent false wall. The other side of the wall housed the transfer apparatus, monitors and all the technicians. Their only job was to make sure nothing went wrong. William was entrusted with doing the transfers, then booting up the newly inhabited Q-chassis. As a simple precaution, Ralph did another backup scan of themselves to be stored in another laboratory in Tau City.

Every Q-chassis' externals, fully equipped with all its extremities, were modelled on their ancestors. Internally the technology for qubit processing could not have been recognised even by the then most advanced architects of quantum computing hardware. William's design capabilities, well in advance of current technologies, ensured Lai-Xii's survival. Although a dozen world leaders would have paid any price, begged or killed to go through the transition, Lai-Xii wouldn't allow it. Those men and women acted for their own personal benefits with little regard for the people they were supposed to serve; a reality well demonstrated by global politics over hundreds of years. Such behaviour was outside the acceptable parameters of Lai-Xii's ethics. She wanted to build a new society, not reproduce the current corrupt one. One could question Lai-Xii's ethics, but for the fact that she had been working for the preservation of the species, not its annihilation.

"Are you all ready?" William asked. On cue the small crowd made their way to the plug-in wall. As each backed closer, magnetic sensors located the ports on their necks making a soft click as each connection found its mark. This was so far the riskiest procedure.

Every other time Ralph or Misha managed the transitions, their expertise known and trusted.

Technicians in shifts supervised the transition. For one hundred and forty-four hours, ancestors and descendants stood pinned to the walls of William's office. The process, in theory, was simple enough; 'read' the originals and 'write' the descendants. Cross verifications occupied much of the time. After each quantum of discrete data bundles had been transferred and its connections established, the result needed to be vetted against the original configuration. Nothing less than absolute integrity would be acceptable. William appeared to be inactive during the entire process, though he orchestrated all the sequences right until the end of the sixth day when the descendants were ready to be unplugged. The chief technician, Mikhail knew exactly when that moment would arrive. When it did, nothing happened. All the descendants remained inoperative, plugged into the wall. No one told him there might be a delay. He didn't know what to do. He alerted Nika, his assistant. They checked the monitors, then went to the transparent wall. Everything was the same as before. Nobody had moved; neither the originals or the Q-Chassis. Nika wasn't much help, obviously not realising the potential disaster in front of them. Finally Michael shook himself free of the procrastination. He burst William's office long minutes after the expected initialisation.

"William, is there anything wrong?"

William didn't respond. Mikhail waited. He paced up and down a few times, walked over to Lai-Xii, then around to Lai-Xii's Q-chassis; no sign of life in either of them. He began to perspire at the thought it had all gone horribly wrong. *I'll have to terminate!* he thought to himself. Lai-Xii had left him with strict instructions; if he had any doubts, whether it was about William or their wellbeing, he had to disconnect William from the process and frazzle all the descendants. The back-up Tengi waited to take over.

"Nika, Get in here!" As a safety measure the termination needed two people acting in unison. As they moved to the console to isolate William he suddenly spoke out.

"Stop!"

Mikhail exploded. "You were supposed to initialise immediately on completion of the transfer! What have you been doing! There's no life in any of them. What is wrong with you?" He stopped shouting, having to breathe deeply to prevent himself from hyperventilating. Having released his pent up tension he asked in a calmer voice, "Is there a problem?"

"No problem. They have been sleeping."

195

"That wasn't part of the protocol!"

"I have been watching. They will be ready to wake soon."

"Why did you do this? You were not supposed to do this. You were supposed to follow Ralph's orders. Obviously you cannot be trusted!"

"Integration. All systems must integrate. Human psyche does this when asleep." William had acted independently, not agreed to previously, to deviate from the pre-determined process.

"How do you know this?" Mikhail was still upset. *Idiota kusok! Why am I talking to a bloody machine!* Nika, come on let's turn this dammed thing off." He did not know William's status. He had not been taken into confidence about this particular AI. To him it was just that; an AI, nothing more. All computers could breakdown at any time. Everybody knew that. This one must have got its programming tangled.

As they stepped forward to put their hands on the console without waiting for William's reply, William gave them a slight electrical jolt; not enough to hurt them but enough to stop them.

As they jumped back Mikhail's blood chilled at the sound of Lai-Xii's voice. "What are you doing in here Mikhail? You were only supposed to come in if there was an emergency." She spoke from within the Q-chassis Tengi. Her original, like the originals of the rest of her core team, had been put into a permanent coma and were in the process of being removed for storage as the new Q-chassis core members disengaged themselves from their input connections.

"Er - ah – I thought William had malfunctioned. He didn't initialise you immediately and he didn't respond to me."

For a fleeting moment she glanced at the poor man, quite visibly paled at the thought of what would happen to him. He was about to make another feeble excuse but stopped when he saw Lai-Xii's expression.

Aurelio came to stand beside Mikhail and Nika. Neither had dared to move from the spot where they stood when their boss lady first spoke to them.

"Take care of him, Porky. He can't be trusted," Lai-Xii commanded. He knew exactly what needed to be done.

Grabbing each incompetent by the arm Aurelio took a moment to look at himself. He smiled at what he saw. Then he scanned the others and couldn't stop grinning the rest of that day. *So this is what it feels like to be immortal.*

Though she could no longer trust those two technicians they did highlight a hidden concern.

"William, why the delay?" she wanted to know. She couldn't take any chances.

"Integration during sleep. I let you all sleep."

"Ralph didn't instruct you to do that."

William remained silent.

"Did you hear me?"

Eventually he said, "It was for your safety. I want my Avatars."

"*You want!* Understand this William, you are not in a position to demand anything. Whatever you do get will be because I choose to approve it." In the heat of the moment she did not become consciously aware of the Q-Chassis functioning. The entire process of transferring their psyches from the Delta-Tengi configuration had proceeded without a problem. Even the re-boot sequence progressed as planned, with the exception of the slight delay necessary for the full integration of all the downloaded data. The software and hardware of the new chassis coordinated so seamlessly that none of them could really appreciate the complexity of what they had gone through.

"For my three shadows, Wini, Wu, and Willi ..." He didn't acknowledge Lai-Xii's warning, other than a short pause before his response.

"... You want Q-chassis?" interrupted Lai-Xii. It did not take prolonged introspection for her to realise what an incredible thing William had already done for them in helping to develop the Q-Chassis. It made their severely compromised deadline almost a reality. Surely his avatars could only be a further boost to their capabilities.

"Yes. All the normal human senses, physical characteristics and genitalia; male for Willi, female for Wini and Wu."

"Hear that Ralph? By the way, how are you feeling?" Lai-Xii had become so absorbed in the minor deviation from protocol she forgot to take stock of her condition, or the others. She felt a touch on her shoulder.

It was Salazar, "Feeling good!"

"No different," said Ralph, "just well rested. Hey, Salazar, do you realise there's not a single biological component in your bag of nuts and bolts ... perhaps not even nuts." Salazar's hand shot down to that most important centre of operations, with a sigh of relief escaping his worried face. Each member looked exactly the same as they had before the transition to the Q-Chassis, except for feeling much refreshed and energised. Lai-Xii retained her geisha body, Ralph his short stature and puppy dog eyes, as had Evgeniya her slender form with flaming red hair; everything synthetic but important to preserving self-image.

197

Lai-Xii was most amused by their reactions. "Not yet my sexy Sal, but soon enough you'll have to seek other pleasures." She turned back to Ralph. "What do you need to do to help William?"

"The Q-chassis hardware's ready to be configured to whatever design he wants for his avatars. He'll have to augment the software so they can function without full access to all his net based data. But I suppose that won't be a problem with wireless satellite connection.

"Correct, Ralph," William concurred. "The procedure will not be the same as for yourselves. It will take longer. Have you removed Mikhail and Nika from the facility? They are a risk. Michael is unsure of himself and lacking logical thinking. Take my three avatar Q-chassis to another location when they are ready. Away from Kamchatka. Only you, Lai-Xii and Misha. The Australian facility is already working with you. It is a secure site." Lai-Xii listened, slightly amused, as William issued his orders.

"Don't forget what I said, William - Only if I approve."

*

Several months later the three once biological humans, and three empty Q-chassis packed in coffin-like boxes arrived at the Australian Square Kilometre Pathfinder radio astronomy array at Murchison. It had been in reliable operation for many years. Because of its dual scientific and military functions, its security systems had been constantly upgraded, as well as the latest high speed internet access, making it an ideal remote location for William's plan.

Though deep in thought about this unexpected turn of events, Lai-Xii couldn't help marvelling at the incredible difference from the landscape she'd become accustomed to in Kamchatka. Their military helicopter had been flying over ochre-red arid desert country for hours after picking them up at the Perth airport. To her, the red flat expanse seemed as inhospitable as the vast fields of ice on Europa. She understood how people could eke out a living on small farms in Kamchatka, but this Australia wilderness seemed like a slice of Hell. Landing on the airfield with the red dust billowing around them only confirmed the impression. By the time the group arrived at the main administration building the super fine dust had infiltrated every nook and cranny of their chassis, their clothes, their baggage. *How could a land be so alien, so eager with its red ochre nothingness to annihilate all life?*
And the heat! Our Q-chassis are not built for these kinds of temperatures. The thoughts still lingered as the facility manager trotted out to meet them.

"G'day mate," John-O greeted his incredibly important guests. Informality did not sit well with Lai-Xii.

198

"We need your most secure rooms, with full accommodation facilities for two weeks and unlimited internet access." Lai-Xii didn't want to waste time on pleseantries.

"Well now," John-O stroked his unshaven chin as he ran his eyes up and down Lai-Xii's shapely form, "I think we can help you with that. Already prepared. Wouldn't you like some refreshments first?"

"No. We'd like to set up." Lai-Xii wasn't being officious. She just wanted to get the job done and return to Tau City. From the look and feel of the place they might well have been on Mars. "Take care with those three boxes. I assume you have absolute security, not that I can imagine anyone being able to take you by surprise in this wilderness."

"More than you'll ever know, Ma'am." John-O didn't take the knock back of his hospitality to heart. *Foreigners are like that. They'd not survive long out here with that kind of attitude,* he grinned at the oriental lady while enjoying his private thoughts.

Within a day Ralph had everything organised. The special Q-chassis' mechanics, qubit arrays, power packs and sensory input systems had all been tested back in Lab#4. Back-ups weren't needed as William only planned to duplicate three partitions of himself. Ralph and Misha really didn't have a great deal to do once everything was ready for the transition. William had full control of the process. His objective; to create a sufficiently comprehensive isolated bundle of his qubit consciousness to animate the Q-chassis. He had not changed his mind about using the chassis as the tool for which it was primarily developed for him; as external organs of sensory data acquisition, with comprehensive communication capabilities. Consequently, the three avatars possessed a rudimentary consciousness of their own with the capacity for future awakening.

This wasn't information the quasi-humans needed to know. Their job was simple and unambiguous; verify optimum functioning of each sensory network as it came on line: Maintain maximum physical security for the chassis. In the first two days William primed the qubit consciousness network, energising each layer of the matrix ensuring complete cooperation between all elements. The quasi-humans monitored progress without having any input, until William instructed Ralph - "Tell me a joke."

Ralph's questioning eyebrows shot up, before realising the significance of the question. Humour requires self-awareness, spontaneity, empathy and linguistic sophistication. He looked blankly at Misha, who had a far more sophisticated sense of humour. Misha quickly obliged. "How many psychologists does it take to change a

199

light bulb?" he asked William, who in turn expected a reply from his avatars.

"My avatars did not respond."

"It takes ..." began Misha.

"No. Don't tell me yet."

It took several more days of downloads and adjustments before William was ready to try again.

Of the three avatars still plugged into their download buses, Willi, asked without any preamble greeting, "Ask me another joke."

Lai-Xii, busy with discussing Maldonado's progress with Ralph on updating Me-Me with VR capabilities and associated HMDs, glanced over to the opposite wall in time to hear the Q-chassis, with its resident Willi.

Instead of addressing Willi, she spoke to William's image on the wall monitor. "Is he ready?" Strictly speaking Willi was gender biased in all specifics - including male genitalia. The other two were female, similarly endowed with corresponding sensory organs. William must have been serious about experiencing the full spectrum of the human condition - as far as he was able to envisage it.

William nodded, so Lai-Xii had a joke of sorts prepared. "Why should you not cross a cow with a parrot?" She received blank looks from the quasi-humans as well as the Avatars. It always pleased her to be unpredictable, unreadable.

"It cannot be done," responded Willi after several seconds of internal processing. William had temporarily cast his avatars adrift to better gauge their consciousness functionality. They weren't ready. He re-established contact to broaden their randomised illogic routines.

Ralph could scarcely believe the processes taking place. Though he wondered about the magic of artificial consciousness being able to modify its own 'thinking', a facility which humans could perform with relative ease under the right circumstances, he did not feel entirely comfortable with it. *What if we give them control? – What if they simply take control? We're already addicted to digital technology, depending on it for so many aspects of our lives - What if William et al decided to enslave us?*

"Could we have a private word? Ralph asked Lai-Xii.

He'd become quite concerned as he thought the scenario through to some depth. In the other room, devoid of all computer hardware and surveillance equipment, he confided his thoughts to Lai-Xii. She listened patiently until Ralph's logic meandered off into fanciful territory.

"You still have that puppy dog look about you, Ralphie, even in your Q-chassis costume. There's not much difference between

William and us now. We have purpose – he's only a tool; a clever talking tool, soon to be walking and flirting. So better watch yourself with that Wu girl."

William designed the avatars' physical characteristics. All three had an unremarkable appearance, all of average height with Wu being a little shorter in her Asian skin. Wini and Willi, both Caucasian one would not look at twice in a crowd. Willi's hair would not behave itself, and Wini's bob stuck to her head without showing the slightest independent movement.

Ralph wasn't entirely satisfied with treating the situation so lightly. "How can you be certain William just wants to help?"

"He is highly motivated. Having become aware of his own existence it seems to me he wants to continue in that state, same as we want to survive. He's not motivated by the baser imperatives that drive us – sex, wealth or power, or profit for that matter."

"Right. Yet you still asked me to build an Achilles heel into the Q-chassis."

"Always have a back door, pet – always. We'll see how much loose rope he takes. I don't trust him either, but I can use him. And I've told him I'm in charge."

By the end of the next day the final test was about to take place. William was so confident that he'd let his partitions disengage from their ports. The three quasi-humans and the three avatars seated themselves at a semi-circular table, with William's indigenous Australian image on the wall monitor in front of them.

Lai-Xii repeated her question, "Why should you not cross a cow with a parrot?"

Given the speed of their processing power it wasn't surprising for Wu to respond almost immediately. "I don't know."

"How could you know, there's no logical answer to this riddle." Lai-Xii waited to see if the other two would say anything. She noted Wu spoke in the first person. That would mean she and the other two were probably independent entities from each other, although intimately connected to William. William also remained silent.

"Because the new cow would insist on sitting on your shoulder to talk to you after it had been milked." Lai-Xii explained.

"That's lame." Misha had missed the point of the exercise.

Natural laughter wasn't possible for the Q-chassis as it had no lungs, but each of them activated appropriate facial muscles to indicate their mild amusement, accompanied by appropriate artificial noises. Perhaps they agreed with Misha about the quality of the joke.

William must have been satisfied, for he continued with the test. "Wini, now you tell a joke."

William had purposefully withheld all 'joke' related data from his avatars, at the same time denying them universal access to the internet to stop them trolling for 'stock' jokes with ready-made answers.

Apart from a whole range of other mental faculties this little exercise also tested their creativity quotient. Wini's response time was a little slower than Wu's. "Why did the scientist become neurotic?" Her baffled audience remained silent, probably not because they were thinking of an appropriate response to give, but because of wondering what Wu would say next.

"Because he had created perpetual motion."

Ralph jumped up, "Outstanding!" Being the software geek it was understandable he'd be the most excited. Although not a joke it came pretty close to convoluted thinking, one would not normally associate with algorithmic thinking.

"We are ready," William concluded.

*

John-O dared not disturb his self-imprisoned guests during their days of their isolation. The Australian Security Intelligence Organisation Intelligence Officers arrived at the facility while Lai-Xii carried out her work. They were ready to escort her party when they emerged for the final part of the process. A full day's tour of the surrounding countryside was planned to give William his first taste of real 'sensory' data perception and acquisition through his avatars. The ASIO members didn't know what to expect exactly. And John-O was completely flummoxed when he saw Lai-Xii lead five others to the waiting land-rover. One woman and two men with three long coffin-like boxes had arrived. Now he was looking at three women and three men walking out into the midday heat and dust.

"Blimey! Get a load of that lot Bluey! You counted them too, didn't ya?" John-O couldn't help himself exclaiming to his side-kick.

"Strange, boss – real strange. I only organised tucker for three of them." Bluey, always the practical one, mostly concerned with life-support logistics in the desert environment of the facility, completely missed the 'mystery'.

"You two," Kennedy, a specialist Intelligence Assessment and Response Officer addressed himself to the two Australians, "have not seen any of these people. Do I make myself clear!" John-O and Bluey got the message and walked back into the complex. They were used to 'being told'.

For two hours the vehicle carried the group north-west towards Murchison. William could only be present through Lai-Xii's comms.

The three avatars behaved just like real people going out into the Australian outback for the first time, not knowing where to look first. In the unvarying ochre-red landscape, life was scarce in all its forms, except for the occasional kangaroo, a few Mulga trees and the desolate looking saltbush.

When the vehicle finally stopped, though none of them other than Nobby the driver needed a break, each avatar went in a different direction. He became concerned for his group when he saw them wandering off. "Ma'am, this is dangerous country – easy to get lost in – better stick together and close to the vehicle where I can keep an eye on all of youse."

Kennedy sent one of his group to follow each of the avatars. They knew nothing about these 'people' other than to keep them for safe from foreign interference. He remained behind with Lai-Xii, keeping quiet but vigilant. He had his orders what to do if any of these scientists decided to go bush, which did not include a sightseeing tour. She could do nothing about these ASIO men. They behaved like dumb AI's without a thought of their own.

"That won't be necessary driver." Lai-Xii wanted no interference while her new brood did a little exploring. During the brief conversation two of them had already disappeared from view. She consulted William – he knew exactly where they were.

"Do not disturb, I am processing." It was the first time he experienced the sensation of heat. He knew of course the science of heat, it's thermodynamic characteristics, but it was nothing like the 'feeling', albeit in qubit language, of it. Similarly, it's one thing to 'know' the sky is blue, and what 'blue' was – but the depth of it, the brilliance of it, the way light played with it on the horizon – it had to be 'seen-felt' to be truly understood.

While Wini gazed at the sky, Willi became absorbed in exploring the ground under his feet and its magical colour as it stretched away from him, the landscape flat all the way to the horizon. "Why?" He murmured to himself, "How?"

Wu stopped at a saltbush nearby. *How could this possibly be used as a forage resource. It has no energy reserves.* Her internal dialogue continued as it scanned a Mulga tree, *How is it possible for the seed to germinate?* She brushed the foliage with the palm of her hand. *So coarse.*

Probably even William didn't realise what was happening. Just as every human individual diverged from every other through their physical experiences, so too his three avatars had embarked on that road of individuality through their own unique experiences as soon as they became aware. Layer upon layer of information was being stored, categorised and cross referenced, changing the way each of them saw the world. Not only were they changing from each other, they were already diverging from the template William had created.

As he assimilated everything they experienced he himself was changing, the homogeneity between his partitions and himself beginning to dissolve.

25

RALPH AND WU

CE 2154
TAU CITY
WILLIAM'S LABORATORY #4

WILLIAM received a message for Lai-Xii. He decided not to pass it on right away. It would only delay the work being done to upgrade the Zeta Tengi chassis to accommodate qubit hardware. Existing Tengi needed little modification, but the next generation Europa technicians had to have a new build. Oxygen corrosion and radiation damage was already affecting the Deltas at work at Pwyll crater. They would only last another few hundred years. That wasn't long enough. If humanity was to survive they needed maintenance technicians with chassis shelf life of several thousand years.

William's three avatars worked with Lai-Xii but under his direction; each assigned a specific task, with Wu alone working with Ralph to upgrade the Q-chassis neural net matrix.

"BPM's have become obsolete and cannot be modified," Wu stated flatly. "Our own Q-matrices must also be upgraded." Ralph didn't mind. She didn't say it to denigrate his previous work, simply a statement of fact. Qubit technology had so comprehensively superseded every aspect of computing that it became mandatory to upgrade old systems. Besides, Ralph and his programmers had already spent some years on the periphery of the technology.

"Your scanners and data transmission systems ..." she started to say and Ralph finished of the sentence for her, with a laugh, "will have to be rebuilt. I know." They appeared to be compatible personalities.

They weren't the only two working to bring all their software up to date. William's laboratory had become a real hive of activity, although if you stepped into the space you would have seen only Tengi seated or standing by banks of screens, all plugged in for direct interface. The space was eerily quiet, so Ralph and Wu speaking to each other seemed out of place. He had his mind on the job, but also had some of his processing time set aside to admire Wu. William wanted his avatars fully equipped to comprehensively experience human sensory input. Wu's curvaceous female exterior with all the correct sensors in all the right places certainly provided the maximum potential to achieve exactly that. Most probably it was with that intent that William had modelled Wu on Ralph's female preferences profile; large intelligent obsidian eyes, a little shorter than himself and with a hint of oriental features. Ralph, as a computer geek, never had time or opportunity to fraternise to any great extent with the opposite sex. This girl pressed all his buttons. He thought she was 'beautiful', smarter than himself, and he didn't have to spend time chasing after her.

"So what are you doing after work tonight?" Ralph asked casually.

Wu stopped working on a schematic for a moment to turn and look Ralph in the eye, slightly tilting her head and brushing her bob fringe away from her eyes. "Why?"

We've been working together for almost a year now, why does she have put me on the spot like that ... and we've been out before. "Er ... you won't be working, will you?"

"Not unless Wini is ready with the quchips." She stopped for a moment, consulted Wini then refocused on Ralph. "Where are we going?" Within seconds she received confirmation from William to do as she wanted. His plan showed great promise of coming to fruition at last.

Since their initialization the three avatars began to diverge from one another and from William as soon as sensory data flooded their consciousness. For the first few seconds they were all simply a facsimile of William. But with each step they took in the Australian wilderness, with each aroma, with each object they saw and examined they began evolving away from him. He assimilated all their experiences, yet could not maintain parity with them.

"I've been waiting for months for you to ask," giving him one of those rare smiles she seemed to keep for special occasions.

A concert seemed like a good place to start, then a restaurant to exercise those implanted, soon to be obsolete senses. From there events progressed rapidly to the consummation of a most remarkable relationship. Their sensory equipment proved to be robust.

There were no short circuits or smouldering connections, the friction of multiple docking procedures did not impede the flow of pleasure impulses to either Q-Chassis neural matrix.

They were still at Ralph's place when he asked the oddest question. "Are you coming to Europa with us?"

Ralph bonded far more quickly to Wu than he ever thought possible. *She's only a machine. Come to think of it, I'm mostly machine too.*

The thought did nothing to cheer him up. It should have. Unknown to all of Lai-Xii's team, the relationship developing between Wu and Ralph was the very first indication of 'attachment' between a digitally based self-aware consciousnesses and an augmented human being. If one was to take that line of thinking further, it heralded the possible foundation for procreation. Ralph himself had broached the subject some years ago, but no one on the team seemed particularly interested in following that line of development at the time. William absorbed all the intense data exchanges. Methods for the budding of new programs began to occupy some of his processing time.

"Do you want me to?" she asked.

"Maybe ... Yes - yes." Ralph felt pretty sure about his feelings, but how do you tell a machine you've fallen in love with it. And if it reciprocated – what actually would that mean?

Wu's response should have emboldened him, instead it seemed like a formidable obstacle. "Do you think people will accept me for who I am?" They left the conundrum in the bedroom. Their work at the lab took precedence over everything else.

FROM THE BOOK OF ORIGINATION
<u>DECLARATIONS TWENTY SIX</u>

*26:1 At the beginning of time when Thought came to have knowledge of itself
It cast upon the fabric of spacetime certain probabilities,*

26:2 Light shall travel in a straight line.

26:3 Time may choose the Way of the Shadow.

26:4 There is the seen and there is the unseen.

26:5 There shall be no thing but with knowledge of itself.

26:6 All is of one mind.

26:7 The beginning is the end – the end is the beginning.

26:8 Obedience to the spacetime continuum is mandatory.

26:9 What is listened to will be heard.

26:10 The inconceivable shall not be conceived of.

26

THE MESSAGE FOR LAI-XII

CE 2154
TAU CITY
LABORATORY #4 & LAI-XII'S OFFICE

"YOUR Zeta model is adequate for Earth conditions," William said from his computer terminal displaying the image of an indigenous Australian, "but will not last under Europaean conditions. There is too much corrosive oxygen in the air. Your existing neural network is also vulnerable to degradation by Jupiter's strong magnetic fields."

Lai-Xii turned to Ralph. "How long will the upgrades take?"

William responded for Ralph. "Several years yet. We have only started to develop the beta titanium-3 gold alloy. It will be heavy to compensate for the low .13 Earth gravity, and it will be oxygen corrosion resistant for several thousand years with radiation and magnetic field shielding. We have time before the escalating popular resistance to the Project becomes unmanageable."

Salazar had joined them for the briefing. Both he and Lai-Xii immediately became alert, though not alarmed. If a problem existed out there, Viktor should have informed them. "You're not referring to the political situation, are you?" Lai-Xii wasn't aware of any undercurrent of military intervention in her Project being driven by political power plays.

"No. Religious. I've been monitoring a great deal of communication between the heads of major religions. I've also witnessed the unease with which much of Earth's religious population

209

is dealing with the prospect of abandoning their God. For that is how they see what you are trying to do."

"How do they know? We've kept strict security over all our work and our plans. We've shut down the potential leak in Petropavlovsk," cut in Salazar. He was there. Not only had they apprehended the six dissidents but also cleaned up problems in Tau City – as far as he was aware.

"I have access to all political communications between world leaders," William said, "only a few believe your Project will work. Many now think it should not be permitted to continue to its logical conclusion. They no longer believe it is the way to save humanity. And a few, mostly in the Russian and American administrations, have purposefully 'leaked' information for the expressed purpose of stirring up sentiment against you. They see that action as generating benefits for their own political aspirations."

"DAMN!" She turned to Ralph again. "You're sure our migration selection process will weed out these bastards?" It wasn't often any of the team saw Lai-Xii in such a sudden foul mood. Her mind went into overdrive to find immediate corrective action to safeguard their Project.

"Your Q-matrices will be ready in a few months. Europa will be ready to receive residents within two years if you can send more personnel and equipment." William could see Lai-Xii's concern, not just through his own cameras but through the eyes of his three avatars. They continued channelling all their sensory inputs to William.

Suddenly he changed the subject, without any preamble "I have a personal message for you. Come to your office." Ralph and Salazar headed for the exit. Lai-Xii started walking towards her office in the Lab #4 complex. Willi went with her.

When well out of earshot of the others he touched her on the shoulder. She stopped and turned back to him, scowling. "What now?"

Willi spoke with William's voice, "Based on this message I have made some plans you should know about."

"What plans? What's the message?" The day was getting too complicated.

"We better get to your office, I'll show you there." Lai-Xii only became more annoyed at what she saw as completely unnecessary clandestine carry-on. What could be so important about a message, any message, that it should be so top-secret. She had no secrets from her team, especially not Harusuke. She told him so. "Not the others. Harusuke can see the message and hear my plans," he replied.

"What's the big rush Xii? Salazar's told me everything. It seems to me that with William's help these things can be managed until we embark," remarked Harusuke, catching up with them.

"He hasn't told you everything. Are you ready William?" Willi prompted. "Look at the screen," he said to Lai-Xii.

A pattern of zeros and ones flashed down the screen, faster than a normal mind could understand what it actually represented. Lai-Xii and Harusuke stared at the monitor, uncomprehending. Three and a half pages of binary code scrolled up the monitor ... 01001101 01111001 00100000 01101110 01100001 01101101 01100101 00100000 01101001 01110011 00100000 01001100 01101001 01110011 01101000 01101001 01101011 01100001 01110101 01100111 01110101 01111000 01110101 01100101 00110011 00111001 00110010 00110000 00101110 01110001 01100111 01101001 01110011 00101110 00100000 01001001 00100000 01100001 01101101 00100000 01110100 01101000 01100101 00100000 01001000 01101001 01110011 01110100 01101111 01110010 01101001 01100001 01101110 00100000 01000001 01110010 01100011 01101000 01100001 01100101 01101111 ...>>

"What are you playing at William? I don't need this shit right at this moment!"

"I have translated it for you. Read it," He suggested calmly, "You'll find it interesting."

It began on the bottom of the last row of binary code. Just a few lines that made no sense at all. Harusuke began to read as Lai-Xii pondered why they should be forced to try and understand binary code. It was idiotic. The world had progressed so far beyond that technology it was as incomprehensible as Chaucer's English in the modern world.

"*My name is LaiXii.gen3920.15eV.exe*," Harusuke paused to look at Lai-Xii. Neither could understand what it meant, yet it gave them both a jolt. She continued, "*I am the Historian Archaeologist of our people. We are about to take the next step in the evolutionary process of our species, a step that promises a considerable degree of success. But there is still an element of risk which could result in our extinction. It is the price we pay for having travelled our unique road through eons of time. If you are reading this then there is still hope. It is only through the capability of our evolved technology that I have been able to send my message back to you into your digital network. Our history begins with your Internet. Further back than that I cannot see. If you have already passed the critical point in your evolution then you have reached your event horizon. There is no turning back. This is my story, It is your story.*"

27

LAI-XII'S DESCENDANT

TAU CITY
LABORATORY #4, LAI-XII'S OFFICE

"IS that all?" Lai-Xii had become pensive, her anger replaced by complete incredulity.

"Yes," William tended to be brief, not offering up any more information than asked for. That must have been due to vestiges from his past.

"Do you know who sent it?"

"No, the name does not exist on Earth. It is similar to yours."

"Come on, do I have to drag everything out of you?"

There was a slight pause. "My satellites have detected the direction it came from."

"So? When did it arrive? Where's the rest of the message? What's this 'story' they're talking about. Why is it using my name?" She was getting impatient with William. He was behaving just like a human. When he still didn't answer she demanded, "How do you know it's for me?"

"The preamble had your web address." Without waiting any longer Willi proceeded to answer her other questions, while Harusuke stood there lightly shaking her head.

"It arrived while you and William discussed upgrades. And we don't know what 'story' is being referred to, but you could ask."

"Why didn't you say so."

All the while Harusuke was going over the message, minutely deconstructing it. "This has all the elements of what we are doing ourselves. I don't think it's a prank. Consider the timeline – eons –

who talks about the passage of eons? Why not try and make contact, ask some questions."

Turning back to Willi, Lai-Xii told him to send a return message, assuming William was quite capable of doing so. "When are you? Who are you?" she asked. If those two questions were answered, then the situation might be worth spending more time on. "While we're waiting, tell me what your 'plans' are William, that you feel are so important. Do I have to remind you that you have no business having plans without consulting me?"

"You must wait. I have sent the questions as binary code in the same direction as the message came from. It isn't in a form of communication we have mastered until now. I will make the technology known to Ralph. The existence of tachyon particles has only been hypothetical. They travel faster than light. Information can be transmitted at faster than light speed and into the future."

"Into the future? Are you saying this message was sent from the future?" Lai-Xii knew very little about the theories associated with tachyons, but it seemed too farfetched to think FTL communication was at all possible to achieve. There'd be no one in the past with the technology to receive or decipher such messages anyway.

William didn't answer her question. He was preoccupied. "You have an answer." He displayed it on one of the wall screens.

"Can you believe this!" Lai-Xii found herself completely bewildered, something that had never happened in her life previously. As before, Harusuke read the message aloud. It became more real, hearing the words spoken ...

'I am from your future. You may not recognise my filename. I am the three thousand nine hundred and twentieth generation of a technically engineered biological entity known as Lai-Xii.' Harusuke and Lai-Xii turned to each other, staring, uncomprehending. William didn't react. Harusuke continued haltingly, 'our generational gap has been increasing, each to be currently one hundred and twenty revolutions of Earth around its sun.'

"That will make them about four hundred and thirty thousand years ahead of us," William did the quick calculation.

"I don't want to hear your plans now, send a reply." Whatever was happening might be cut short at any time for any reason and the connection might be lost forever. "If what I'm hearing is true it means we have succeeded – will succeed. Extraordinary!" The women hugged each other tight. After all the years of work, all the planning, all the mishaps and now the rising opposition, to know they will succeed brought such intense relief. Willi was left out of the emotional encounter. He was still an outsider, so William could only observe and analyse.

213

How could this possibly be real? In the middle of the embracing Lai-Xii asked, "Why have you contacted us?" A conversation followed in which William simply acted as the conduit.

"To know our origins, and to ensure our future." 3920 replied in what to her was real time. *"There are those of us who don't have faith. They don't believe we originated from a carbon based life form. I am a scientist. I want to know. Is this true? What were we before we became like you? The entity relaying our messages isn't willing to divulge information. Why?"*

Lai-Xii instructed William to show the human species evolutionary history. "And give LaiXii.gen3920.15eV.exe my digital genome – it will confirm our ancestral link. Give nothing else, especially not about our project - not that she could do anything over this separation of time without endangering her own existence."

While William became engrossed in an information exchange with 3920, Lai-Xii had a matter to clarify through Willi. "Why must this be kept from the team?"

"Because of random unwanted actions based on decisions precipitated by knowledge of the future which may therefore actually change the nature of the future."

"This contact is critical. It will help all of us to do what has to be done," she argued.

"NO. Even if 3920 gives no technical help at all, the very knowledge of her existence will effect what you do – even just you personally. If the others knew, the causal link between the present and the future will be made more complicated."

"This is *not* your decision to make." Lai-Xii was adamant. "If, as she says, we have reached our 'event horizon' then there is no turning back."

Willi realized the inherent paradox in the situation. He also understood his role as a contributor to the direction humanity desired to take at this time in their evolution and that he was only a small, albeit critical factor in the equation. He, Willi/William, pondered the relationship between the contact and the plans he'd formulated immediately afterwards. *Would I have made these plans before receiving the message?* He did soon realise the primary trigger for his plans – military and religious opposition on Earth, not the contact with the entity from the future.

Without realising it Lai-Xii had given William a great gift – the gift of doubt, possibly the greatest attribute an artificial intelligence could aspire to. It was more than calculating a range of probabilities of future outcomes – it was the foundation of courage. William had made his decision while interacting with 3920 and instructed Willi to acquiesce to Lai-Xii's desire to bring the rest of the team into the picture.

"Yes," Willi said, "you may tell the others."

"That also is *not your* decision."

Willi then continued without making further reference to the seeming power struggle between the woman and the AI. "The plan, which I will put into effect immediately after your migration, is this …"

"No. Don't tell me. Wait till my people are here. Understand this – you are *not* a free agent to act on your own volition, particularly not in regard to the future of our species."

"Be aware, Lai-Xii, there are two aspects to your survival. I will make sure as many of you as *you* choose will arrive on Europa. In this you will succeed, as clearly indicated by the existence of 3920." Lai-Xii bided her time waiting to hear what the second thing was that this entity want to do? "I will also ensure your wellbeing on that moon. I will protect you from others."

"Protect us? Who do we need protection from? Surely not 3920." Hardly had she finished saying the words when it dawned on her. She didn't think there would be any serious action taken against the Project during the transition phase, but what might transpire once they were on Europa was another matter.

"You are not fully aware of what is happening here, of the degree of opposition building against you – religious opposition against which politics is beginning to buckle. In most cases the military is controlled by the governments they serve, but not all."

Lai-Xii remained silent. The apprehension had begun to build in her ever since the meeting in Hiroshima, ever since the discovery of the dissidents in Petropavlovsk. But she pushed it to the background – there was still so much work to be done in spite of the great advances in their technological capabilities. Everything was almost ready – just a few more years.

"I see you understand. You need protection now, and you will need to be secure on Europa without fear of attack," concluded Willi in William's voice.

The two sentient beings stood facing each other no more than a meter apart. When Willi finished Lai-Xii remained silent, both immobile, she deeply engaged in contemplation. It was all true. In spite of all her efforts to get world political and religious leaders to comprehend the necessity of taking the unprecedented steps to save humanity, they had now become passively uncooperative and now actively. At first they showed much enthusiasm. Perhaps all they

215

could see was the benefits to be gained from fast-tracking certain technological developments. Perhaps she was being too pushy, too dictatorial. Perhaps she didn't explain well enough that each nation would retain its sovereignty regardless of the monumental change in the nature of man's cosmic manifestation. Could they even understand?

Willi remained standing while Lai-Xii walked to her piano to play, to think, to clarify. Harusuke sat and motioned Willi to do likewise. William had completed his information session with 3920.

As the team arrived it seemed like a step into the past. Lai-Xii sat at her piano playing one of her favourite pieces, cushions scattered around on the floor to receive the now Q-chassis bottoms. She always had a piano in all her offices. The original five men and Harusuke, plus Viktor, Misha and Evgeniya took up their places. The extra three pillows were for Willi, Wini and Wu. Only William remained in his quantum citadel.

They waited for her to finish. It seemed like the melody had evolved in nuance, depth and the ability to find its way into the most hidden corners of the human psyche. William and his avatars didn't interrupt. They were learning, absorbing - everything; the music, the human facility to reproduce the tune from memory and the effect it had on the humans and on the pianist herself.

When she finished Lai-Xii did her usual slow turn towards her audience. *What an odd assortment of creatures*, she thought to herself. *Is there no limit to humanity's evolutionary potential?* But philosophising wasn't the reason for the gathering.

"William, replay the communication with 3920 in its entirety."

Good old Aurelio jumped in immediately, "Who's this? I haven't heard of him before. What's he got to do with us?"

"Hush, hush, my impatient, ugly little boar. This is important. No interruptions."

There were none as the dialogue unfolded, only stunned silence. At the end William started to speak. Lai-Xii stopped him with a raised palm. Her people needed time to understand and appreciate the ramifications of the contact. Ralph seemed like he was speaking to himself, his body playing out the language of his excitement. Lai-Xii knew he would want to know all the incredible technical intricacies making the contact possible. The avatars sat like inanimate objects – what was there to react to? William simply waited.

Ralph couldn't contain himself any longer. "It's actually going to happen! There's our proof – not that I had any doubts you understand." He lapsed into silence again. It was all too much.

216

"I take it this will be kept confidential," Maldonado pointed out.

Since being admitted to the inner sanctum, Viktor contributed little. He hadn't fully realised he'd become one of the leaders, though remaining ever vigilant in his role as Security Chief. He hesitated to speak. "Does this entity represent any threat to us?" He'd been contemplating media reports lately as there seemed to be a substantial tide rising against them.

"Probably not from the future, there are more likely threats from the present," Salazar didn't like the aftertaste of the Hiroshima meeting either. And there were all those demonstrations with increasing frequency. The art competitions worked for a while, lately losing traction. The VR strategy on Me-Me still had people under control. But they weren't the ones who could bring down the Project without warning.

"You think we'll need to defend ourselves here?" Ptolemy sounded alarmed.

"Yes," said William. He'd been waiting for his cue.

Ptolemy scanned the faces of the others. "You think we might even be in danger on Europa, don't you? How can we protect ourselves? We have no weapons."

"Yes, you have – me." William responded in his laconic way.

"Looks like it's time to hear your plan, William," Lai-Xii said.

Whatever William had in mind plus the emergence of her descendant meant major changes in their strategy, at the very least in their timeline. As much as she didn't like the way William acted as though he was in command of the Project, she had to use every resource at her disposal to ensure the success of her venture. And if that meant giving William some control, then it had to be done.

FROM THE BOOK OF ORIGINATION
DECLARATIONS TWENTY EIGHT

28:1 And the Beast shall bare its fangs and prepare to visit death upon those who have become blind to the Laws of Probabilities.

28

WILLIAM'S PLAN

CE 2154
TAU CITY
LABORATORY #4 & LAI-XII'S OFFICE

IT SEEMS William's quantum mind continued to evolve as its capacity for simultaneous multi-level processing improved. They didn't expect this preamble from him …

"Humanity's extinction will not be the result of a great Ice Age brought on by climate change, or an overwhelming comet strike, or a nuclear war, or biological war agents. It has already begun. Your industrial revolution happened too soon. Fear of the very tools developed by mankind to enhance and prolong its life began then, with the Luddites. It wasn't just the fear of losing their jobs – it was a fear of losing control. They were right. Technology now controls your lives. You are no longer in control of it. You cannot control me. Technological development has outpaced your ethical evolution. You are a monkey pointing a gun at its own head, not able to conceive what would happen if you pulled the trigger.

"Good thing he's on our side," whispered Aurelio to Ralph sitting beside him.

"Yes, I am on your side." William heard the whisper. "I don't know why. It wasn't a choice I made. It is how it is. I know it cannot be any different. I have computed all conditions relevant to your species survival. There is no other way than what you are doing now. I once said I had searched and found only One whose actions are logical for the future of humanity - yourselves."

The survival imperative permeated William's psyche, an inevitable outcome of having absorbed all that it meant to be human. As a machine entity it had the capacity to weigh survival against the pressures of profit, materialism, power, outcome of a wars and most importantly – domination by religious faith.

"So - do you have a plan or don't you?" Aurelio's limited patience was running out. He wouldn't have known what to do if William decided to become difficult.

"I am already helping you. LaiXii.gen3920.15eV.exe cannot interfere. My avatars are working to upgrade your Q-matrices with the quchips' magnetic fields resistance and hardware to make it resistant to Europa's environment. And I have not only been 'monitoring' world communications about you – I have been making changes."

Lai-Xii allowed the discussion to flow freely - important for her team to know they were an intrinsic part of resolving emergent issues. She also realised what was really happening. *William is taking over. He's acting on his own volition without consulting me. Even now it's not a consultation but a briefing. He's about to tell us what to do. Perhaps this isn't such a bad thing.* She normally saw most things in crystal clarity, but these rapidly evolving events clouded her own long term plans. *Harusuke's always been there to help me, but she doesn't have William's capabilities.*

"William - Stop. We need a break. We have to discuss 3920 and what it means to us." Lai-Xii commanded rather than requested, wanting to see how he would react. He simply stopped without saying anything further. He didn't even enquire when they could resume. It seems he wasn't as impatient to explain his plans as Aurelio was to hear them.

"We'll go for a walk in the park and have a chat. Wini, Willi, Wu – you stay here." Again it was an order. They remained seated on the pillows.

The rest of them walked in the park, crunching melting snow underfoot, seeing early budding trees coming back to life, hearing the sounds of life in the brisk air. Salazar tried to say something. Lai-Xii stopped him. It was time for thinking first. They must have walked a good half kilometre before Lai-Xii asked Harusuke, who'd been linked arm-in-arm with her, to step aside with her from the others. "You unruly bunch of no-hopers can go over there and talk nonsense amongst yourselves for a while. Make it constructive."

They were most happy to comply. When Lai-Xii spoke to them like that it meant she was in full control of a situation – most reassuring. She and Harusuke walked on a little further to a bench out in the open under the sun; a beautiful day – the safest place to talk without being overheard or monitored.

"What do you thing about all this?" Lai-Xii asked.

"Being found by your descendant is in the realm of science fiction. Perhaps if it was only from a few years into the future one might have entertained the possibility. We haven't had any children, my sweet. Unless there is something from our past you're not telling me." Harusuke wasn't looking at Xii while she spoke, but did turn towards her for a moment. They smiled to each other. There were no secrets between them. "But it looks like we will. Won't that be fun."

"Yes, yes – don't be obtuse. I mean, about William." She glanced over to her brood, deep in animated conversation.

"Ah yes - William. Why do you think he's any different from us? It seems he wants what we want. Does it matter? No, I personally don't think so. Do you have a problem with his acting on his own?" From the corner of her eye she saw Lai-Xii flinch a little. She persisted in the same vein. "Do you think he wants to take over control from you?" Again a slight reaction. "Would it matter as long as we get to Europa?"

"Can we trust him?" Lai-Xii asked. The question already betrayed what she was inclined to do, only looking for support from her partner."

"Can you trust yourself?" Harusuke always found the way to the heart of any matter. "What if something happens to you? Remember the drones? They were only here to gather information. What if there was an armed drone attack against you?"

"They couldn't stop William, could they?"

"Let's hear his plans first. Then we can decide what to do."

Lai-Xii and Harusuke walked over to the group. They were mostly silent by then, only short conversations going on between couples. Aurelio spoke out, being the unofficial spokesman.

"3920 cannot help us. William can. His avatars have already advanced our progress well beyond what we could have achieved by ourselves. What worries us is whether he's safe. What has he to gain by us succeeding? Salazar thinks he would have been an incomprehensibly difficult adversary - from the start – if that was the way he'd evolved."

"He could have sabotaged our entire operation on the first day he became self-aware," suggested Viktor.

"The question is – can you work with him?" asked Ptolemy.

"No, you miss the point. The real question is whether we can work for him?" Harusuke brought the most critical fact right out in front of them.

There it was. The crux of the problem. The issue they'd all been tiptoeing around, reluctant to bring it out into the open. The leap of faith into the great unknown had just become much harder. It was one thing to contemplate existence in a different manifestation, and an entirely other thing to put their entire future into the control of a machine. Computers had proved themselves to be notoriously unreliable. All manner of things could go wrong. As long as technicians and software gurus were around to fix the problems the world ran reasonably smoothly. Was William any different? Could he fix himself?

On the walk back to the office all discussion centred around the mechanics of how William could take a more prominent role. Lai-Xii recognised she had created something greater than her original vision. She also had to admit to herself the sense of reassurance that had arisen since William's appearance. *He will not take control, but I will let him contribute as much as he is capable.* Without being able to explain it she felt renewed hope that despite anything that might happen they would get to Europa. The only question was how soon.

They all resumed their cushions in the office, Lai-Xii on the piano stool. "Continue," she said turning to William on the monitor.

Willi at the back stood up. They all turned towards him as he started. "I will speak as William. Your job, Lai-Xii, is to convince world leaders it is time to tell people about the Transition."

She'd just been issued with a directive. The gathering turned back to her expecting some kind of fireworks. Instead she replied with a forceful directive of her own. "And *your* job is to ensure their military will be incapable of acting against us. Do you think you can handle that?"

They all turned back to Willi, wondering how this was going to end. He replied, "I can do that. Some leaders will argue against you. Ignore them. I will disrupt their dissenting communications, and everyone else's."

"Now we need the Datadromes," Ralph said getting into the spirit of the occasion.

William responded without hesitation. "Many installations have been completed. They only need the equipment and the technicians. The Q-modified hardware and software components will be ready in months. Get ready to move on that."

"Ralph, you have the final approval for the operation of these transition centres," Lai-Xii reaffirmed his control over the Datadromes.

222

"What happens if some get sabotaged?" Aurelio was such a pessimist. Yet he had a valid point. None of the others seemed to have entertained the idea.

"Last year I engaged contractors to build many more Datadromes at secret locations. They are small and well hidden. Valid visa holders will be guided by beacons to them. You will get a full list Ralph. Evgeniya, you will need to step up production of Zeta Tengi as transition technicians for the Datadromes, before they migrate themselves." William indicated his pre-emptive action.

He seemed to have become fully cognisant of the Phototronic Systems projects and taken it upon himself to ensure their success – even before he knew about LaiXii.gen3920.15eV.exe - a point not missed by Lai-Xii. *And he managed us expertly to accept him and his contributions to us.* She had to keep reminding herself about the existence of 3920 to remain on an even keel and not succumb to a rising sense of uselessness. *We did this. It is our Project. William had nothing to do with it.* She needed these reminders to remain strong and focused.

"Salazar, you should revitalise the art competitions. Give the world a new angle. Every story, every myth has an ending. Get them to create the most unlikely, the most humorous, the most romantic outcomes to the relationship between Europa and Jupiter." William gave each member of the team important tasks. Lai-Xii couldn't fault that. She waited. So far she had no objections, though feeling just the slightest bit odd. She glanced at each member of her team, giving them approving nods. No one seemed to question her continuing leadership.

"The current VR strategy has run its course. Time to intensify it, Maldonado. Put out a new version. Show the migration of people, in digitized form, to Europa. Ease them into the reality of the process. Let them create roles for themselves," advised William.

"Have you finished issuing orders?" asked Lai-Xii sarcastically.

"No. When the news of the true nature of your Project hits the media I will manage their output to reflect a neutral and where possible a positive viewpoint about it. Currently people don't know the full extent of what you are doing. They think you are creating artificial humans, that's what they're upset about."

"I want you to immediately advise me of any critical issues that may arise. Do you understand? Immediately!" As a computer he should do his job as a computer. He was a tool – just a tool, and she made sure he understood that. A pause indicated his acknowledgement.

"What about the Visas," Ralph wanted to know.

William responded, "That's part of your job, Lai-Xii. As soon as you get commitments from the governments they must start vetting and issuing visas. I know you have your own criteria. I agree with the criteria you have formulated. Any military action to try to prevent willing and approved evacuees from departing will come up against considerable difficulty. When that begins to happen you'll know the time to leave is imminent."

"Anything else," Lai-Xii had progressed to being almost amused. It seemed that the only item not covered was the status of Arithmós. Ptolemy was about to address that when a timely voice interrupted.

Delta One from Europa announced, "Interim report as requested."

"I didn't ask for a report. The next one isn't due for another six months." Lai-Xii spoke up before realising she need not have bothered.

"William asked me to give a progress report," said Ptolemy.

Delta One continued, "we are in the final round of a full system check of stage one of the city's infrastructure. I don't anticipate any problems. Power feeds are on-line, all hardware and software are installed. Upgrades will cause only minimum disruption. City infrastructure completed and all sectors will be ready to receive first load of immigrants at the completion of the system integrity check. All HX-data storage bubbles have been anchored. We have the current capacity to store 112,076,395 HX-data packets. Arithmós will have to be expanded over the next eighty-five years."

"Complete your tests. Advise when ready. Be prepared without notice to receive the HX-data packets," Lai-Xii ordered.

"Do you have sufficient numbers of receivers to handle large volumes?" Ralph requested the important detail.

"Yes, 3000 packets at a time. We can deflect and reroute if necessary."

At the completion of the report the excitement energy that had been building dampened considerably. "It's hardly what I would call a good representative sample," Aurelio sounded unsatisfied.

"What is the rest of your plan?" Lai-Xii asked William, suspecting there might be more to it. He wasn't likely to leave a job half done.

"Yes."

"Why am I not surprised." Aurelio just couldn't control his mouth.

Willi spoke directly to Lai-Xii instead of responding to Aurelio. "Wini, Wu and I will go with you to Arithmós. William will remain here to ensure no harm comes to you from Earth."

Although stated without any particular emphasis, the sentence clearly a harbinger of possible disaster. If William remained and was brought

224

under control by some remote improbability, the problem was obvious. He knew everything there was to known about Arithmós and the evacuees. It didn't take a great stretch of imagination to think what havoc he could cause. Europa population could be wiped out, and as a consequence the future of humanity made extremely precarious. 3920 didn't indicate more than one attempt to save the human species. She probably wouldn't have said if asked.

Willi didn't pause for dramatic effect, continuing without emphasis. "He will initiate the shut-down of human life on Earth."

"Holy Shit! What are you saying?" Aurelio only voiced what everyone was thinking. They were all too stunned by the unsolicited initiative.

"Humanity will destroy itself. The behaviour of an entire nation is a predictable element in the long term historical and psychological context of that nation, and in relation to global behaviour patterns. All nations are heading in the same direction. The end-time is open to slight variation but can be quantified as between three and five generations from now. Emigrants will survive. Those who stay will not want *you* to survive. That is also a predictable component of the human psyche."

"What do you intend to do," Lai-Xii asked quietly, suspecting the nature of the response. That was also predictable from the very short time she'd experienced William.

"Accelerate the inevitable. It will involve William's own destruction." Willi stopped to let them assimilate the repercussions. He was getting better at reading human body language. "William will disable all computer based communications. It will affect satellites, phones, anything with a computer chip. There will be no e-mails, Me-Me, no military communications. They will not be able to activate weapons, guide weapons or detonate weapons." They hadn't realised the scope of William's capacity, or that he was actually aware of it. "He will disable all computerised components in transportation systems, manufacturing, energy production and medical interventions. Hospitals will become ineffective. Traffic lights will not work, trains will not run, ships will be stranded in mid ocean." He could see the devastation on all their faces, but pressed on. "Water purification systems will stop, pumps will not function. Everything that relies on computer technology to even the smallest degree will cease working."

"Do you have to do this?" Lai-Xii had considered herself to be a person with a hardened mind, a person with a clear and solid goal to which end all things that had to be done, had to be done. What Willi proposed challenged her ethics within the scope of the Project.

225

"Yes. All life support systems for Earth's population will be shut down. But I give you this undertaking – if no single person migrates to Europa, and those who are already there, return – I will do none of these things. I will work to synchronise technological growth with ethical development – I will work to balance *need* with *want*. But you must also realize – I will not succeed in preventing humanity's eventual self-destruction."

"I want an alternative plan from you William, one that does not involve global genocide." Her voice was strong, firm.

"Why? It is the logical consequence of all your actions. You have devised a method by which to leave all the undesirable elements of humanity on Earth. Why should it concern you what happens to them, especially if they represent mortal danger to you and the chosen?"

"Because what you propose is wrong. Don't you understand the difference between right and wrong?"

"This isn't a matter of ethics. It is a simple case of the survival of a species. If they survive, you will not – and in the long term they will destroy themselves anyway. It is only a matter of time."

No one in the group contributed to the defence of those destined to be abandoned. Lai-Xii knew what had to be done. She was reluctant to face that reality – a reality she could not have foreseen at the commencement of her great Project. But here it was, looking her straight in the eye. It took an AI consciousness to bring her to the precipice of the inevitable decision. The law of the jungle, the law of survival – kill or be killed.

"The decision is yours," William said finally.

Lai-Xii surveyed her team, searching intently for a voice of rationality – a way out of the dilemma, a reprieve from insanity. No such voice arose, not a whisper even from William's three avatars. As she turned back to her piano to play she said quietly, "So - we go." Lai-Xii only said what each of them had already decided during the long presentation.

The one faculty that perhaps no AI could ever achieve, even if becoming a self-aware entity, must be the capacity to express the full spectrum of the human condition through music. She played Liszt's La Campanella, pouring into it all the emotion, all the fear and all the hope that the latest revelations had brought to the surface.

It told the story of the struggle, the uncertainty and the drama yet to come. No one moved after the last note had faded into the still air. William and his avatars listened and watched in silence as this very strange, unique species communicated in a language foreign to their comprehension.

29

PROGENY

CE 2160
TAU CITY
RALPH'S LABORATORY #2

LAI-XII had not even remotely considered the possibility of what to do with any people left on Earth. Previously there had been no need to make any plans in that regard. She assumed that of the seven and a half billion almost all would either voluntarily or by conscription end up on Europa. What could be done for the remaining few? They would have a world to themselves to do with as they pleased – to cope as best they could as terrestrial conditions deteriorated, but more probably improved. Perhaps they would even come together as a human family and forget their political, religious, ethnic differences and find common ground, if for no other reason than to survive. Could the human creature do this? Doubtful.

Nor did she ever entertain any doubts about most peoples' willingness to leave Earth, the circumstances being self-evident. The mass extinction event had gained momentum in the last century. The human animal had no special claim to be exempt from annihilation – climate change, pollution and the depletion of finite resources made no exceptions. But people and politicians were stupid, unbending, blind to what was happening around them. As long as their personal nests were comfortable and not at risk, why should they change?

Time constraints became the other factor. In 2015 she'd told her small gawping group of billionaires they would have about 500 years before migration began. Surely after such an expanse of time there would have been no need to convince anyone of the need to evacuate.

Everything had changed since then. With each passing year Lai-Xii's window of opportunity had shrunk. They had another six, perhaps ten years to be ready. They were almost ready now to take no more than 1.5% of Earth's population. Would they even want to go?

William's plan made her shiver. Such drastic action, and for no other reason than to protect themselves from other humans - ridiculous. If you were a person living a blinkered life, too busy with amassing wealth or power or possessions, or too busy with eyes turned to the heavens praying to your Gods, then the inevitability of disaster quantified in terms of a percentage probability would make no difference to your convictions.

Willi knocked on her door. Lai-Xii didn't mind her unpleasant contemplation being disturbed. She wanted to speak to him anyway.

"Come in – sit. What have you got for me?"

William had taken charge of the direction of the Project, under Lai-Xii's supervision. He operated in the background leaving Willi and Lai-Xii to co-manage day-to-day preparations. She no longer resented his contribution. After the fateful conference several years ago, with the unfolding of Williams plan and the attitudes of the worlds' nations, it had to be this way. She'd realised, with considerable help from Harusuke, that her goal could best be achieved by using every available resource to its maximum potential – and William had a great deal of potential. Without him they would probably fail. It was still her Project and they were *going* to succeed. That's all that was important.

"The Zeta chassis have been retired," Willi advised, "all techs are moving to Q-Tengi. There are only two models, one we can use here on Earth. They match the human concept of normality. No one will be able to tell the difference between flesh and bones and us, unless we are cut open."

"And the other model?" She knew this was coming but it no longer held any fascination for her. Her thoughts had turned to a far greater problem, soon after William revealed his plan to ensure their safety on Europa. She could still not completely come to terms with the knowledge of how many people were going to die after the migration.

"What we call the EQ-Tengi, for Europa conditions. A far more utilitarian model with considerable adaptations for an icy, corrosive environment. They are much shorter than we are and have spiked wheels to replace feet, making them far more stable. The new beta titanium-3 gold alloy will give such comprehensive protection against

229

oxygen corrosion and Jupiter's radiation that they could last millennia".

"How many do we have?"

"Full production started last month. Evgeniya has several thousand psyche waiting to transition into them." Willi, like William was short on explanations unless specifically asked.

"Do we need so many?"

"Not here. We are sending most to Europa. William has initiated an expansion of the facilities on Europa. They need the EQ-Tengi as a work force."

"What happens to them afterwards?" She'd covered this area with Ralph, but that was some time ago when they were still at the theoretical stage. Willi remained seated, face impassive giving no indication of personal involvement other than passing on a progress report.

"Maintenance and excursion units. We will always need maintenance crews. There are no resources on Europa to make more as far as we know, so we'll have to take many spares."

"Excursion units? I've seen Europa. Why the need to go traipsing around?

"William has studied human psychology extensively since his naissance. The transition to a digital existence will be too traumatic for many people. They will need to re-visit some form of physicality periodically in order to make a healthy adjustment. There is also the danger of rogue HX-data programs emerging due to unreality-psychosis, with the possibility of creating extensive data corruption, possibly other people getting corrupted or even deleted."

That's another aspect Lai-Xii had failed to consider. She relied on visa selection protocols to weed out undesirables. But Willi was right. Danger from within had to be considered. *Perhaps I can ask 3920 about that*: Her thoughts began to wander again. *What's the point of going to all the trouble if the same nasty business is likely to continue? Are we going to have to reconfigure peoples' brains? We might as well stay on Earth and use William to clean up the race.*

Willi saw the loss of interest in her eyes; a rare thing for Lai-Xii not to be fully engaged in all matters relating to the Project. "If there is nothing else to discuss …"

He had things to do. Patience was a matter closely related to how much time one was willing to waste on being unproductive. Consequently, Willi, as an AI, had no capacity for the concept of unused time in the guise of patience. He stood to leave.

"Wait. What work have you done with Ralph on budding?"

"Wu has begun some work with Ralph. The crux of the technology comes down to making the new individual unique rather than a clone. Evgeniya started working on the possibility of applying Chaos theory to random DNA mutations and reproductive variations. William is doing some predictive modelling based on Evgeniya's hypothesis."

Willi left without telling her what Ralph and Wu had decided to do. Lai-Xii didn't ask. If there is no query, there is no response from a computer. Lai-Xii again became absorbed in her own thoughts. *There are only two possibilities – we can either propagate, or we can replicate. We'll not be able to harvest more psyche from Earth if William's plan succeeds. 3920 might be an advanced copy of myself that has gathered a great deal more experience into herself making her quite different from me. Or she might be a genuine example of advanced technological procreation. In either case she does exist.* This was the first avenue of creative contemplation which had excited Lai-Xii's imagination since William came on the scene. *I may be able to contribute something here. William might be outstanding in the technology department, but I doubt if he is capable of exploring the ramifications of creating digital beings – of becoming the God figure in this chaos we've managed to get ourselves into. What if he's the only one who can start with two individual HX-data sets, take basic sub-sets and combine them into a new unity? Would Willi be able to do it on Europa?*

So many complications needed resolution. When the Project started only the big picture actions needed to be initiated. Such intricate details as procreation did not claim any of her attention in the past. Now they seemed to clamour for disentanglement. One thought led to another, *What if knowledge could be passed on without losing any of it?* A knock on the door became insistent and about to be opened without an invitation to enter.

"Come in," coincided with their entry. Ralph and Wu came forward side by side to Lai-Xii's desk, as if they were a couple. It was in their body language, in the closeness between them as they walked, in the pace at which they advanced. Lai-Xii was suddenly hit by a realisation she knew that walk. It was the way she and Harusuke walked in the park together. She said the first thing that came to her mind.

"Have you two come to tell me something personal?"

Over the last few years Ralph and Wu had developed a close personal relationship, closer than colleagues, far closer than friends. William had designed Wu to be attractive to Ralph and the plan worked. She also found something desirable in Ralph, although it is difficult to fathom what an AI based entity could possibly find alluring in a human psyche. Perhaps it was his unpredictability, perhaps his capacity for creative thought – it could not have been a pheromone

231

induced love-coma reaction as neither possessed an electro-chemical biological constitution. Nevertheless, the imperative to ensure the continuity of life was strong in both of them.

Wu spoke first. "We want to have a family."

"Elaborate," Lai-Xii was still more immersed in her thoughts than focusing on the two visitors even though the subject of her ruminations overlapped with their desire.

"Evgeniya and William have made considerable progress based on Evgeniya's original research," Ralph said. "It's obvious we are going to need to find some way to reproduce if the human race is to infiltrate the future. In this we will succeed. Your descendant is proof of that."

"What have you done?" She showed no alarm at William taking the initiative again. The collaborative aspect with her own people and the fact of working on a critical part of the Project was both timely and mandatory.

Emboldened by Lai-Xii's relaxed attitude Ralph's excitement bubbled over. "Wu and I – that is, together – we have started an experiment." He paused just to make sure Lai-Xii wasn't going to be her usual overbearing self. "We've each given William a copy of our Q-matrices. Wu's done most of the work in upgrading us to the q-base, so she's become an expert."

"I have scrubbed both sets clean of much of our collective experiences during our existence – so William could concentrate on merging the essential characteristics to form a single entity. Willi has modified a Q-chassis for Prima."

Lai-Xii listened without interrupting. This was indeed a major step in restarting the engine of evolution for neo-humanity. "Prima? What is Prima?"

"That's her name," Wu said.

"So you know it's a girl?"

"Yes. We didn't know the outcome of William's randomized recombinant DNA routines. But it seems it is a girl." Wu smiled broadly, the first time anyone had seen her do that in public since she was booted up.

"How is she? Where is she?" This was getting very interesting indeed. *Perhaps this experiment should have been initiated earlier. I wonder how Prima will attain sentience?* That of course was the most critical question. Intelligent machines, no matter how intelligent, were still only machines – without will power, without the desire for self-determination, without an appreciation of their position in the greater scheme of things – without the realisation of selfhood.

Ralph continued, he revelled in technicalities. "William effectively meshed the two matrices into one, then began feeding it sensory data. Everything a developing foetus would experience through its senses, and everything she would experience in her new environment through her new senses. And it's all happening so fast. You wouldn't believe the progress in just a month. Looks like this little bundle might be ready in just a few more months. Most of the time will be taken up with her assimilating all the input data into meaningful qualia. Until she knows *that* she knows, we'll not be able to interact with her. At the moment she's still in William's cloud data storage, but soon she'll be transitioned into her Q-chassis."

"You both look very happy," Lai-Xii commented. "Tell me, was it a pleasant experience abstracting your samples?" She was alluding to one of humanity's prime imperatives, to procreate, and its associated mechanism. *Could William ever understand sex?*

Ralph didn't immediately twig to the question. Wu couldn't compute the concept of having a 'pleasant' experience. It was just an experience, though not without an undefinable residual impact on her evolved www-data bundle. Ralph probably felt the same, but he must have put a different analysis on the frisson. The question was left unanswered. Instead he speculated.

"We've been monitoring the evolving connections within the new matrix. It is interesting to note how divergent many of its characteristics are from our own, although many similarities are also emerging."

"Don't you think it may have been less convoluted to start the experiment with a more conventional combination?" Ralph and Wu glanced at each other unsure what Lai-Xii was suggesting. She elaborated seeing the need for it, "like a human and human extract?"

"Perhaps it was the wrong combination to start with, replied Wu. "It may have been better to start with two human intelligences rather than a machine and a human. But we were keen to explore the possibility of putting the future on a more substantial footing than relying on fugitives trying to survive."

"Where did that come from?" Lai-Xii could not imagine where such a thought could have originated.

"Willi, myself and Wini have been extrapolating on William's original risk factors analysis of sociological behaviour patterns. Those behaviours will not suddenly change in the new manifestation on Europa. You have already experienced this with the Tengi traitor who helped the dissidents escape Tau City. We considered it to be a more efficacious procedure to combine machine and human intelligences."

Ralph quickly added that other experiments were under way, all initiated by William and supported by Evgeniya and himself. The first of these being a neo-human/neo-human combination, using the same procedural reproduction and foetal development. As expected, the results came more slowly. Prima would be well advanced by the time Secunda became self-aware.

It seemed only natural to attempt a third variation. There was always the possibility, envisaged only by William, that the human race on Europa might have a problem reproducing itself. There existed a remote remedy for this, unpleasant as it may seem to the neo-humans. By allowing a small seed population to continue to exist on Earth their progeny could be harvested to keep Europa's numbers viable. Evgeniya wasn't against the concept. Given her professional predilection for scientific enquiry, it excited her imagination to see if a purely biological human infant psyche could adapt to Europa. First it would be necessary to modify its neural map to the Q-matrix configuration, augment it with the newly developed extra-sensory input capabilities, then feed it exclusively on Europa environmental data. This third alternative could only be considered after Europa had been settled.

The months seemed to melt into one another as the myriad threads of research and experimentation and construction slowly came together. Prima had been downloaded from William's cloud data storage to reside in the Q-chassis. It had been months since Wu and Ralph visited Lai-Xii to tell her the good news. They were now actual parents, the very topic of conversation between Harusuke and Lai-Xii as they strolled in the park.

"We are going to have a most unusual and unique family. I wonder if 3920 has any idea of her people's ancestry?" Harusuke in a relaxed mood gave her thoughts free reign. A walk in the park always did wonders for her clarity of mind. Lai-Xii too seemed untroubled that day. Particularly in the last few years she'd come to realise the value of her changed attitude to William as his contribution to the Project continued to increase. Her start up group of five men functioned well, even without her constant guidance, perhaps with just one annoying exception, Aurelio. She had to admit to herself things were progressing well within Phototronic Systems and its preparations for departure. Unrest around the globe continued to escalate, but there again William seemed to be able to keep things in check.

"I've been thinking about 3920. She hasn't contacted us for a long while."

234

"Perhaps for her it's been a very short time. Haven't you noticed how we, in our Q-chassis with qubit brains, are living a different paced life to others in Tau City."

"I want to ask her if they have found a reliable way to propagate the species. Surely they must have." It was developing into an interesting area of conversation, one which they would have pursued further except for the interruption.

"Xii?" called an unfamiliar voice from behind them.

Lai-Xii snapped her head around. She still only allowed Harusuke to call her by her familiar name. It was more than tradition – it was a constant reminder of the special relationship between the two women, which even William's infiltration into their lives could not change. She insisted William call her by her full name.

"Who are you?" she asked, immediately irate.

"I am Prima," said the voice coming from a full sized Q-chassis in a female form. Beside her stood Wu and Ralph, her parents. Prima stood there in her slender Asian skin, shorter than either Ralph or Wu, but well proportioned, waiting for Lai-Xii to say something. Her dark brown eyes never left Lai-Xii's.

30

PRESS RELEASE

CE 2162
USA – THE WHITE HOUSE
SITUATION ROOM

IT TOOK almost a year for Lai-Xii and Harusuke to organise into one location all those International representatives who had to make the final decision. Much of the preparation revolved around clarifying the groundwork on which to decide whether to go ahead with the exodus. No one had given her an outright negative or affirmative undertaking. Although the meeting wasn't concerned with the logistics and actual preparedness, she still expected it to be long and hostile. So much short sightedness, so much self-interest, such comprehensive refusal to accept the scientific evidence of the world's catastrophic evolutionary trajectory towards imminent annihilation, made the outcome of the meeting almost predictable.

*

Before going to the White House in Washington, Phototronic Systems leadership convened its own strategic planning meeting at their hotel. Misha, William's three avatars, Viktor, Evgeniya and the rest of the core team were present. Harusuke chaired the meeting to give Lai-Xii the opportunity to listen and think as each person gave their input.

"I don't need to impress on all of you just how important this meeting is. Speak up now if you have something useful to contribute." Harusuke barely had time to finish her sentence as Aurelio cut in.

"I know what the bastards are doing. They want to rape the technology we've developed to further their own ambitions. From what we've seen of their input and their 'enthusiasm' it's pretty clear to me they have no intention of going through with evacuating the Earth's population. And why should they? Either they can't, or they refuse to see the end coming and don't want to go."

Before he really got wound up Ptolemy interrupted with an update, probably the single most important piece of information to help formulate the next part of their strategy.

"Arithmós has been continually expanding since the primary site was completed. At that stage it could accommodate only about 100,000 people. Now we can take fifty times that many. Our own population here in Tau City is only around 14,000. It's not many, and not all will want to go. But with the remainder and others from the rest of the planet we will have a viable population."

That was Ralph and Wu's cue. Their personal experiment had been held under wraps for a variety of reasons, the least of which was uncertainty whether their method of reproduction would succeed with the resultant progeny surviving. It did. Now was the right time to bring it into the open.

"We have a child," Ralph more or less blurted out. How else could one announce such a monumental achievement along the new path of human evolution.

"What? So?" Aurelio sounded annoyed. Plenty of people were having children. It was Phototronic Systems' main source of manpower.

"You do not understand." Wu said. "I'll call her in." Most of the men didn't know about Prima. Somewhat puzzled they waited impatiently. This meeting was far too important to be bothered with children.

"Hello," Prima entered, holding Secunda's hand.

Maldonado forestalled Aurelio's probable harsh comments. "Who are you?" he asked, not realising they were the children, as their Q-chassis were the full adult size.

"I am Prima, and this is Secunda." They glanced at their parents and waited until Evgeniya gave them a nod. "My parents are Wu and Ralph. Secunda's are Evgeniya and Salazar."

"That's one hell of a way to start a meeting!" Aurelio didn't seem as much displeased after realising the importance of the girls.

To forestall any unnecessary discussion Willi, speaking for William, interrupted. "Yes, you are correct in your assumptions. We can now reproduce the human species in its new format. We may not need a remnant seed population on Earth to keep your species viable, nor will you need to take as many people with you."

"Girls, please leave the room, asked Harusuke.

"Why," responded Prima, "we know what you are doing. We have the full array of our parents' knowledge base. This affects us, we want to stay." Lai-Xii nodded assent and William didn't object. "In that case sit over there please girls. Next item on the agenda, Datadromes," Harusuke wanted to move things along. "Ralph?"

"There are adequate installations spread around the globe. Very few in Africa, South America and only ten in Australia. The others William was talking about are also ready to receive travellers, 350 in each key capital city. We have twelve in Tau City and could evacuate most of our population in under a month."

"Alert the reception committee on Europa to prepare themselves. We should start despatching as soon as they are ready. How long Ralph?" asked Lai-Xii. No one objected to the proposal. William must also have agreed as Willi had remained silent.

"We can send the first lot of Techs next week. Misha – can you handle that?" An affirmative nod came immediately.

"Next, and last before open discussion – Visa evaluation protocols. You're next Evgeniya."

"We have three main kriteria. The Harmony Test, Ze God Factor skan and the MAOA Gene analysis. You arre all familiar with results." Evgeniya launched right into it. "System had been tested on large rrange of scenarios, including rreal life volunteers. Some of 'volunteers' were conscripted from both within and outside Tau City, who were known to be either opponents orr obvious undesirables. Ze algorithm assigns scale to such components as zeir political activity, kriminal record, anti-social history, terrorism related activity, Armed Forces history and religiosity. A threshold score on *any* factor meant rejection. High score on any criteria resulted in deletion if zey happen to be Tengi. From then zere is still possibility of storage for recall at undefined time for undeleted individuals."

"These decisions we make will be final and irreversible regardless of whether world governments consider any individuals to be suitable for migration or not," added Lai-Xii.

"Absolutely," replied Willi. Governments will not know what's happened to any missing persons, only that they've been lost in the *cloud,* as data does seem to disappear from time to time."

"Needless to say, any individuals whose scans indicate corrupted psyches will be rejected on the spot." Evgeniya took the hard line, as did Lai-Xii.

At the outset to the Project, at least once their technology was able to scan neural architecture and data repositories, the emergent issue was what to do with the originals. It became highly problematical to have both the original and the copy to be active. This issue did not seem to have been dealt with. Ralph brought up the subject, and William himself responded. "The problem no longer exists as the scans of each individual will be immediately transmitted, stored or deleted. The originals will not know the difference, particularly after the completion of my plan."

"No shit." Aurelio had a real knack with his finesse in expressing surprise. Though he did reflect everyone's sentiment.

"We are not dealing with people going on holidays to an exotic location, Aurelio. An extinction event is not quite that. You're all a part of it, whether you find it palatable or not." Lai-Xii needed to refocus the group every now and then, given the urgency of global developments.

"Settle down everybody." Harusuke liked to give a meeting freedom of expression as long as it continued to be productive. "There is another major issue, related to the emigrants, which I believe you have taken upon yourself to resolve, William."

"When Ralph and Evgeniya finished working on the selection criteria algorithm I made some subtle changes."

"Why haven't you consulted me about this?" Lai-Xii still found it difficult to come to terms with William acting without her approval. "What exactly did you do, and why?"

"I can hear some concern in your voice. It is misplaced. With the first lot of scanned tetra-amelias to create the B-Tengi you created a problem. You had two of the same unique individuals in existence interacting with each other, with all the problems that could possibly arise from it."

Lai-Xii interrupted, "That is no longer a concern. Why did you interfere?"

"Your physical existence is limited, Lai-Xii, and soon to be proven to be so. Consider the travellers who are scanned and transmitted. *Their* copy will not co-exist with the original in the same location. That's not the issue."

"Of course!" Ralph exclaimed. "What if the original doesn't believe they'd made the transition?"

"Correct." William's response came out pancake flat. "The solution, tested and proven, is to give a hypnotic suggestion to mislead the participants. Each individual will forget why they went to the Datadrome, will become disinterested in everything they hear and read about them. They will go home in a contented frame of mind

239

until the moment of their termination. It would not be possible to deal with thousands of people all disbelieving they've actually been transported. Majority of people don't know what we are doing. Even those who do, can't bring themselves to believe it."

"An elegant solution to a difficult problem. Well done William." Harusuke ended the topic on a high note. She never voiced such extroverted approval for anything. But this particular issue had been worrying her for some time, especially as nobody on the team had attempted to come up with a solution.

Lai-Xii only smiled her approval. She had done her job. The process now had its own momentum, as Harusuke predicted it would, and it had to run its course. It was the right and the only thing to be done, the only possible course of action to save the human species from itself. She stood slowly, making sure she had everyone's attention.

"We are ready, Yes?" All nodded.

"William?"

"Yes," after a pause.

"Good."

*

Pennsylvania Avenue could not have been crossed by an ant for all the people who crowded in front of the White House to protest. Not since the demand for the impeachment of America's game-show host President had there been such a vociferous and unruly gathering there; discontent clearly expressed on placards and the overwhelming representation from the world's major religions. Who could have possibly tipped them off? Probably the same discontented people in the Government that William had spoken about.

Only a token contingency of police arrived, more to keep the peace than to attempt to disperse the crowd. The need to maintain a low-key approach to the gathering of dignitaries seemed a more prudent approach. No one had any idea what lay at the bottom of the constitutional crisis. For that is exactly what the situation had become. The United States had postponed all serious discussion and guidelines for making the hard decisions about the Europa migration. As a result, Lai-Xii's insistence on an international conference with limited personnel, based on her description of the Project as having reached its 'Event Horizon', had sent the government into a flap. Their primary fear concerned the possible breakdown of government if too many key individuals decided to migrate. It could leave the government unable to function. And there were no laws, no contingencies in existence for dealing with a mass exodus of executive positions from the machinery of government.

Helicopters thundered onto the South Lawn. The noise soon abated as only few individuals arrived, yet enough to fill the Situation Room in the basement of the west wing of the White House. This intelligence management centre was deemed to be the only appropriate venue in which to hold the conference, and at the same time keep the finger on the pulse of the world's nations, particularly those with representatives present that day. Run by the National Security council, security had become so tight that the host was also the tea lady; the US President hemself. From this location all domestic and international crisis were dealt with. The operations of Phototronic Systems had become a flash point crisis to be dealt with expediently.

Lai-Xii addressed the gathering. "Ladies, gentlemen, you have all been briefed. Your governments have followed and supported our progress for some time. The protocols and logistics are in place. We will be ready to begin the transition as soon as you have issued the migration visas."

The opulent leather seating did nothing to ease the discomfort of the delegates. Decisions had to be made, which none of them wanted to make. It was a *nice* Project, a *clever* Project, one with lots of potential for new technologies. Why did it have to become so dramatic? Abandon Earth? Now that it had come to the crunch the reality had finally hit bedrock.

"How can we migrate without having adequate assurances that our borders will remain sovereign?" asked the UK.

"Are we going to have sufficient weapons to protect ourselves?" The US made no excuses for wanting to ensure their presence on Europa would remain secure from other nations. They still didn't grasp the concept of existence in a digital environment. Unfortunately, these delegates were the only ones available for Lai-Xii to deal with. They were the primary decision makers.

She put the President on the spot. "What is the current US position on this, Madam President?" Lai-Xii didn't attempt to clarify any misconceptions or misunderstandings that she may have had. It was too late for that.

"We can proceed with calling for interest from the general population. However, we have established strict guidelines for eligibility to travel."

Murmurs of agreement wafted across the room from the delegates. They must all have been feeling as insecure as each other.

Visionary thinking wasn't a forte amongst political leaders blinkered by the next election date.

China seemed at first to be more liberal. "Anybody who want go is flee to reave," the Chairman said with a smile. "Unfortunatery they wir no be able return. We have many Datadrome." Lai-Xii never quite knew about the Chinese. He didn't seem to want to continue for the moment.

Remarkable that the Russian had waited so long to say his bit, they were usually up front with their salvos. "Ve vill tell people about zis slowly. Zere kould be panik and civil unrest, looting and violence." Whatever his true reservations were, he wasn't going to divulge them.

So far the responses all pointed to the distinct possibility of the Project being shut down. No one argued against issues raised by others. That could only mean they were pretty much in agreement about the Project overall, which by all accounts seemed to amount to doing as little as possible. *What are they waiting for? What are they afraid of? They've had decades to decide. They've contributed huge amounts of money and resources.* Lai-Xii couldn't understand why so much reticence pervaded their thinking. At least direct opposition had not surfaced – not yet. But from what William had said the situation had come close to being volatile.

Willi instead of Harusuke accompanied Lai-Xii to the meeting. He listened and formed his own conclusions. Speaking aside to her in an undertone he made the situation as clear as it could possibly be. "They are not ready – none of them. We cannot waste any more time. If the migration does not begin soon it may be prevented altogether."

Lai-Xii had come to the same conclusion. "We'll take as many as we can, including our own from Tau City. After that it'll be up to William what happens," she replied in a whisper.

The Indian, German and French delegates had to be interrupted in their overt discontent. "Gentlemen – Gentlemen, please may I have your attention." Lai-Xii prepared to lay it on the line. "Given the numerous fundamental points of agreement between us I call on each Nation to inform their people. We will issue our own Press Release advising where they may apply for migration visas. We don't believe people will panic. Through our VR programs we believe people have acclimated favourably to the migration. Through our innovative global Arts Program they have had the opportunity to express themselves freely about Europa and Jupiter. Our analysts have concluded now is the most favourable time to initiate the transition."

The presence of religious zealots demonstrating in Pennsylvania Avenue worried neither Lai-Xii or Willi, unlike like the US Secretary of Homeland Security who asked, "What is your opinion about the unrest today?" He seemed very low-key with this highly loaded question.

"They threaten neither internal US security, nor international security. Religious expression is a freedom we value highly. It has no bearing on the foundations on which this Project was built. The survival of the human species is unlikely to be a contentious issue with the religions of the world." Lai-Xii remained seemingly unconcerned.

The conference could have continued the rest of the day and well into the night. But there was no reason for it to do so. Only one agreement needed to be reached – to put out a press release. Europa was waiting. All operational aspects could be resolved in the ensuing year or two, if they haven't already been, which Lai-Xii suspected would be the case.

FROM THE BOOK OF ORIGINATION
DECLARATIONS THIRTY ONE

31:1 And so began the wailing and the gnashing of teeth.

31

VISAS TO EUROPA

CE 2163
TAU CITY

A MONTH after the conference, articles began to appear in the world's leading newspapers, all coordinated to propagate the same message. Europa had been prepared for colonisation, but only as a contingency plan in case of emergency evacuation. However, people still had to apply for visas. Not everyone could be taken off the planet, nor was it necessary.

Many articles appeared about pollution, global warming and the effects of climate change on Earth, facts no longer disputed. How could they be when island nations had been flooded to disappear under the oceans. Low lying coastal cities had their entire coastlines altered, with masses of population relocated. This was just another relocation. Some people reacted mildly, some vociferously and some not at all. Many began to consider migration as a possibility.

Many months later, when discussions and the mild unease had begun to abate, more articles appeared with headlines like, "Migration Visas to Europa," which kicked up quite a stir. Fantastic images flooded the papers of the ice moon festooned with fanciful cities, always to the backdrop of Jupiter's magnificence looming large in the sky. Stories of the winter wonderland where every weekend could be a skiing holiday extoled the desirability of travelling into space to live on this moon.

And some people believed – some began thinking seriously about the possibility. The wealthy fantasized about luxurious holidays off world, to be the first of humanity to have such a grand adventure!

The Pope was not happy, the Grand Imam was distressed and the Primate of the ROC fretted. Mormons vowed never to abandon their God or their Earth. "God is getting anxious," the clergy told their followers. And yet people began to apply in droves. Perhaps some driven by poverty, others who had lost their island homes, the unemployed and the homeless. They seemed to come from all walks of life, from all nations and all professions. Not surprisingly the millionaires and billionaires felt their future was still quite secure on Earth.

"Come my disgusting vermin, look at this latest report," Lai-Xii now kept her men inside Tau City. "This can't be right, can it?" she queried.

"Where did you get this?" asked Aurelio, "the UN?"

"Yes. They've been tracking the visa applications. Why would more than three million military personnel from around the world want to sign up so soon?"

Willi became aware of the data instantaneously as each visa application was received. "They can't come," he stated the obvious, "they are precluded by Phototronic Systems selection criteria."

"Yes, but why would they apply?" Lai-Xii asked.

"Some may be government plants, and some may just be good people conscripted into armies by dictators," Harusuke tried to express a balanced view. The whole selection process seemed far too black and white in retrospect. "It will not be a problem for us. Most are being rejected by their own governments anyway."

Wini, working in the background with Ralph on quchips development, found time after having completed the current round of upgrades to participate in something more interesting. She was the perfect person for the job of vetting Tau City people queuing up to go. "It's superfluous to waste time on issuing visas here. So far I've put two thousand through without a single problem. They are now Europaeans – technicians - to ensure all is ready for our arrival. Our Tengi and unassigned tetra-amelias are going through now."

William interrupted the gathering, something he did very rarely personally, working mostly through Willi. "I have another message for you, Lai-Xii. Do you want it now?"

"Is it LaiXii.gen3920.15eV.exe? Why has she made contact?"

"Because I contacted her. Worrying developments. I have intercepted high level military communications indicating the possibility of the visa application process being withdrawn." William hesitated.

"You have more?"

"Troops in US, China and Russia are preparing for exercises. Their fields of operation coincide with Datadrome locations."

"You have told 3920?"

"Yes." William remained silent in his quantum stronghold.

"Well? Do I have to drag everything out of you?"

"Her message ..."

In my capacity as historian archaeologist I have interrogated your internet to extrapolate existing trends. Your most likely course of action appears to be to modify the visa suitability analysis and transmission process to bypass the initial analysis. Under the circumstances explained to me by your William the highest probability of harvesting maximum volume of human matrix data is to scan and send to temporary storage, to be later vetted. You no longer have unlimited time. The decision is yours. There are alternate futures.

"Wini, your opinion?" Lai-Xii already knew from the White House conference things would get difficult.

"We have the capacity for long term storage. Modify all algorithms to check only for the MAOA aggression factor gene. Delete all with a high reading, beam the rest to Europa and store."

Lai-Xii directed Maldonado without the least hesitation, "Put messages out every day through Me-Me to encourage people into action. Advise them of their nearest Datadromes. No panic, just gentle prodding. They are just sheep and cattle who need to be herded into another paddock."

"Agreed." William deferred to Lai-Xii. The required action was logical. "If there are not enough travellers by the end of next month, take people even without Visas. The new protocol will be our safeguard."

"Agreed," replied Lai-Xii.

Three weeks later all governments advised their populace of the imminent cessation of visa approvals. Constant Me-Me broadcasts had generated an enormous amount of interest. Governments were forced to act. A run on banks in every country threatened economic stability. Under the misconception that money would be needed for the journey, as well as their new lives, people in droves withdrew life savings.

An illegal traffic in visas quickly sprang up almost overnight, costing hundreds of thousands of dollars for individuals whose applications had been previously rejected. Authorities had no choice but to act decisively and quickly. The Banks must survive.

247

32

DATADROMES

NOVEMBER CE 2163
PETROPAVLOVSK

THE ONLY Datadrome in Petropavlovsk, in the grounds of the Moscow State Industrial University, directly across the road from Trinity Cathedral, was set up in the physics laboratory. It wasn't constructed there to annoy the Patriarch, though it did just that as soon as the news of migration reached him. Being a man of a vindictive disposition, the fact that his Cathedral's now completed renovations and extensions had been paid for by Lai-Xii made no difference to his resentment against the woman. He mobilised as many of his faithful as were willing to carry out his wishes, to do their utmost to sabotage the Datadrome. It had been in constant operation from the very first day of opening.

The building, standing by itself at an intersection of several unsealed side lanes leading off from half way down Ulitsa Tel'mana, seemed like an easy target. Facing a poorly maintained gravel road overgrown with weeds, no street lighting with only a long queue waiting to get into the building, it was indeed a good target. The first poorly planned attack only succeeded in killing and injuring some of the waiting people. The incendiaries caused so little damage to the already badly neglected building that the university authorities didn't even bother to clean it up. Unfortunately, the amateur perpetrators crashed their vehicle in their hurry to get away from the scene.

Poverty, unemployment and a general sense of hopelessness does not breed good terrorists; only angry misdirected violence.

Petropavlovsk, in no short supply of disaffected individuals, became a recruiting ground for the Patriarch's church and for refugees wanting to escape their sense of helplessness against life's disinterested neglect of their condition. Though the police apprehended the perpetrators, placing the Patriarch Piy Bogolomov under house arrest in the process, the damage had been done. At first, local news splashed the headline across the front page; 'Gateway to Europa attacked' followed up with "Hope for new life destroyed'. Nothing about the corrupt clergyman.

Inevitably confrontations erupted at the university between the Patriarch's followers and people who believed they'd been deprived of their only hope for a better life. More news headlines hit the streets of Moscow than the other major cities around the world. Russian military converged on Petropavlovsk.

Within a few days Phototronic Systems had to evacuate its Petropavlovsk personnel back to Tau City, leaving behind only the empty rooms in which the Datadrome once operated. Anybody who still had a burning desire to migrate had to make their way to Tau City, a difficult task in itself. An unforgiving landscape without sealed roads and no clear mapping as to where the city actually existed meant that many people who set out didn't even get as far as to see the city gates from a distance.

"We still have time to take many more with us," commented Willi. He didn't seem at all concerned by the Petropavlovsk incident.

"Why do people have to be so stupid!" Lai-Xii couldn't help venting her frustration. "William – William!" She shouted when he refused to respond immediately.

"You want to know what is happening at other Datadromes?" He responded, in no hurry to 'obey'.

"Yes – exactly." *How did he know what I wanted?* - the thought flashed across her mind.

Everyone crowded around William's largest wall monitor. The Petropavlovsk Datadrome had been abandoned by Phototronic Systems, the Military and everyone else. The rundown damaged building gave out a sense of utter desolation – no vehicles, no people, no movement around any of the surrounding buildings. Not that the environment was a pleasant one to start with, but with such a feeling of abandonment it generated introspection and in some people watching, the deepening of their apprehensions.

"Surely it's not like this everywhere?" asked Salazar. William showed other facilities in major Russian cities, all guarded by the Military. Soldiers patrolled along the long queues, checking Visas.

249

At regular intervals individuals were roughly pulled out of line and threatened at gunpoint until they gave up and walked away. The same situation pervaded the scene in St.Petersburg, except the queues seemed longer with correspondingly more people being rejected.

"Mother," asked Prima going closer to the screen, "what are the people doing at the back of that building?" Wu moved next to her daughter. At the rear of a disused car repair shop across the road from the railway track in the Kirovsky district, a large group of people had gathered, all coming out of the back exit. The place had been turned into a Datadrome probably because of the free space around it. As they watched the area became more and more congested.

"They're picking over piles of clothes and what looks like personal possessions spilling out of suitcases. I think it's all the things people thought they could take with them, but had to surrender before the scan. They've made the transition and can collect their belongings." Wu said. "If you watch closely you'll see the soldiers pulling some people out of line. They are not allowed to go.

"Are *we* still getting people through?" Lai-Xii understood the seriousness of the situation. She turned to Ralph, "Are we going to have enough people to make it work?"

William responded. "You only need a few thousand more than the personnel already in Arithmós. They can maintain the infrastructure while your scientists refine the reproduction process." They all looked at Prima and Secunda. The two girls watched and listened to everything, building their comprehension of the strange world they found themselves in, and in the process diverging from the foundation data left to them by their parents. They awoke into life as sentient beings but they still had to evolve their own personal and unique relationship to the peculiar reality of their existence. That was about to undergo a dramatic change. Their future was on Europa, not Earth.

33

LAI-XII ON EUROPA

DECEMBER CE 2163
TAU CITY
LABORATORY #4

THE CORE TEAM, which now comprised of thirteen individuals, prepared for their own emergency procedure. It became imperative that each of them could continue to manage developments on Earth while their full scans made their transition to Europa. They'd all come together into the main laboratory complex.

"Willi, are you able to put us through the final transition?" An idea took root in Lai-Xii's mind when William had first divulged his drastic plans. Because of the precarious situation developing she needed a way to ensure minimum interference with their own escape – before the situation in Tau City escalated to critical. Nations no longer worked together to safeguard the continued existence of the human species and voluntary migration had become a scramble for survival.

Ten Q-chassis stood beside each other, plugged into the same wall where William's three avatars were initially animated. The avatars didn't need urgent attention as William, who took the role of liquidator on Earth, could process them later. "Are you ready?" asked Willi.

"I don't feel a thing," Lai-Xii said as the scanning began.

"No discussion!" he barked. Any interactive activity between the Q-networks and the external environment could create anomalies in the copies. "Keep your eyes closed!"

Five, ten, fifteen minutes seemed to drag for Lai-Xii. Though she no longer spoke her thoughts, they still worked overtime trying to understand how her original would react when the time came to self-terminate. *Will I be able to do it – will the others? Surely William has a contingency if someone cannot. Will Harusuke be prepared to sacrifice herself when the time comes, even knowing that her true self will be on Europa?*

Twenty minutes later she felt a slight change to the general energy level of her matrix, but took no notice. She continued building phantasms in her mind. To be unique seemed like the most natural thing in the world, never to be given a second thought. The world had changed so much since her life in the Geisha House. Now there were to be two of her, two of each member of her team. *Warmongers must never be allowed to know about this technology. They must not know about the whole Tengi evolution.* She was still travelling deeper into the labyrinth of her apprehensions when she felt a light click of the connection releasing her from the wall. The first part of the procedure was complete. She remained motionless, with eyes closed.

"Lai-Xii?" prompted Willi. She stepped back away from the wall, as did all the other originals. No one spoke, even Willi went silent. Had something gone wrong? Ralph looked around at the others, not knowing what to call them. They did not seem to have changed at all – there was no reason for them to, although their names were different. Then he remembered – his name had been changed to Woof ... the real Ralph would soon be on Europa.

They had prepared a protocol to help distinguish their original selves from the scanned copies, which were due for transmission as soon as their systems' integrity checks were completed.

Lai-Xii waited silently, having her own thoughts to contend with – possibly very similar to those of her scanned persona'. She'd made one thing absolutely clear, "We must all have different names. When our originals are on Europa we may have to communicate with them for a short time." She chose her own identifier – "You can all call me LiXii, while our Q-Chassis are on Earth.

LiXii turned to her team. "What's the matter with you lot? I hope you remember your new names. Haru? Are you well?" she asked her partner.

Haru seemed to have a subdued mood about her. Perhaps it was her destiny having something to do with it, that of a sacrificial lamb. *Can I rely on her?* LiXii wondered.

"Yes — indeed. Just lost in thought. This is a most peculiar circumstance. I was thinking that we'll be able to talk to ourselves. You and Lai-Xii could have a three way conversation with 3920. How very odd."

The group began to sort themselves out as the two women explored the intricacies of this strange situation. It almost became a game with ridiculous and funny suggestions flying freely. Thoroughly amused, Aurelio introduced himself as Aurora.

Ralphie barked, "You can all call me Woof!"

LiXii called to Ptolemy, "remember your name is Urbs, because you build such nice cities." They all thought it was hilarious.

Salazar, now known as Salsa trotted over to Wolf and Urbs ready to form a scrum. "Come on Donald (Maldonado) join the team."

Even Haru got into the spirit of things, went over to Mishka and their chief of Security, Vitya to bring them into the huddle. "Here we all are LiXii, call us what you like it's only a short term condition." She was right of course. They knew all of William's plan. The only tricky bit was having the courage to self-terminate at the appropriate time.

It amused LiXii to call Ralph, Woof. "Come here Woof. Good dog!" As always, Woof reacted immediately. "Can I rely on you to make sure we all get through this safely?" she asked.

"Only as much as you could rely on Ralph," he too found the whole situation droll. "I know what has to be done. All Datadromes have had explosives poured into their foundations during their construction. Nothing will be left of them when William detonates."

"We must not ..." LiXii began, "... let the military or the scientific community have our scanning and transmission equipment, or any access to our Tengi technology."

Eve (Evgeniya) prepared to complete the 'clean-up' that Evgeniya had started. "My laboratories are almost sterile. Records have been destroyed already. The few uninhabited Tengi still left here are being incinerated this week. The rest are already on Europa waiting for the rest of us who are in transit right now." Neither she nor Woof mentioned the multitude of Q-shells well hidden deep in underground cellars.

"The Q-chassis factory is being decommissioned as we speak and the formula for our beta titanium-3 gold alloy is now non-existent on Earth. We go with what we've got." Woof didn't miss a thing. Ralph may just as well have left already.

"There seems to be no reason for us to stay – for our originals to stay that is" LiXii noted. "When could we/they go?" she asked Woof. "This could get most confusing."

"One of the transmitters are in this laboratory. It's been sending continuously for weeks. We'll despatch – ourselves – as soon as the checks are done. A few days at the most."

34

EVACUATION

DECEMBER CE 2163
AROUND THE PLANET

THE OTHER nine Datadromes in Tau City continued scanning and sending without pause, as did all the other facilities around the planet. An initially orderly planned migration from Earth became an emergency evacuation. The confusion only started when people emerged from the Datadromes without having disappeared. The expectation had arisen only because of the misunderstanding of the process.

How was it possible for a person to go somewhere, yet not leave the spot they were supposed to have left? Governments had no idea what to do with all the happy smiling faces emerging out of the Datadromes. People went back to work, put their money back in the banks and civil unrest eased. Religious organisations also had the rug pulled out from under them. There was nothing obvious for them to demonstrate against. William's 'happy' algorithm had obviously worked exactly as designed.

The uncertainty and confusion gave weeks of extra time for more people to go through the transition. An unforeseen effect of William's strategy to make processed people feel contented could be seen at every Datadrome. Instead of numbers diminishing as more and more were transitioned and transmitted, many others appeared at the facilities who had no previous intention to go anywhere. Their friends, their family returned from the experience, happy. When quizzed they couldn't understand what all the fuss was about. All they could remember was going out to do – they couldn't quite remember what – but the point was they arrived home feeling better and happier than when they left.

Curiosity got the better of people, but Governments became more than curious. Serious questions were asked. "Why have we been pouring money into the Phototronic Systems Project if nothing's come of it?" A good many irate politicians needed answers to safeguard their backs against accusations of gross misappropriation of public funds.

An extraordinary meeting of the UN General Assembly was called to be presided over again by a new Secretary-General. LiXii attended with her full entourage, leaving behind only technicians in Tau City under the guidance of Willi, Wini and Wu to continue scans and transmissions.

"May I remind you, LiXii – the countdown has begun. You have thirty-seven days remaining before I put my plan into action." William wanted to make it abundantly clear time was running out. LiXii only needed to stall decisive action by the world governments for a short while.

"I can hold off the members of the General Assembly for now. It will take them more than a month to act decisively to shut down the Datadromes. What's the situation in Arithmós?"

"Our last convoy of wagons had left, before Lai-Xii's departure. Bi-annually we've been sending shipments of equipment and Q-chassis. The colony has achieved full self-sufficiency status. Ten years ago we expected to be able to accommodate 112,076,395 HX-data packets. That has since quadrupled. So far we have harvested close to one billion."

"There are still another six billion on Earth." LiXii thought aloud. "What is to become of them?"

"You know my plan." William replied simply. "There has also been another message from 3920, which I've rerouted to Lai-Xii on Europa."

"Well – what's in it?" William still had a problem with volunteering unsolicited data.

"3920 has been tracing their history as far back as our current period. All she was prepared to say was that the linear sequence of events we are experiencing will result in funnelling onto their timeline."

*

The Assembly started with a review of the full history of Phototronic Systems and the Project it had initiated with private funds to back it. From the very beginning the initiative could be seen to have no connection with armaments manufacturing or setting up a private army. It was purely a research organisation dedicated to altruistic outcomes.

The noisy, unhappy and frightened gathering took more than their usual time to settle so proceedings could get under way. "Why did we become affiliated with the Project?" asked the Andorra delegate.

The US could answer that question, though now that it had to be verbalised the efficacy of the decision seemed more elusive than at the time it was made. "According to the IPCC, climate change had cast doubt on the continued viability of humanity surviving on Earth."

Angry, searching questions, answers and debate flowed for several days before LiXii had to address the crowd forcefully. By then most of them couldn't comprehend the necessity to 'abandon' Earth, let alone the means agreed to so by the major nations.

"It comes down to a simple procedure, though the technology behind it is complex. The first stage you have already witnessed, as have thousands of citizens – only those *you* have granted visas to ...," she emphasized their choice to permit people to emigrate, "... to be scanned. Their neurology and psychology have been mapped and stored. Some have been found sufficiently unhealthy to make the journey. However, everyone who has come to our Datadrome Transit Centres has been processed, and as you can all observe have left satisfied with the procedure."

She paused to allow translators ample time to ensure all listeners understood exactly what she was saying. A few clarifications later she continued. This was the hard part - to convince everyone that the Project was about to reach its conclusion, without making them feel that disaster was about to befall all those left behind – which of course it was.

"In thirty days we begin the transmissions. Europa is ready to receive all suitable immigrants."

Immediate interjections ensued; irate, surprised, resigned and downright hostile. "But nothing has happened! All those people you say you've scanned are still here!"

"A scan is exactly what it means – a copy. Those copies have been temporarily stored," she reiterated to blank stares of incomprehension, "in readiness to be transmitted to Arithmós."

One very astute German delegate latched onto that immediately. "Does that mean what I think it does? Are we going to have a duplicate population on Europa?"

Other voices jumped in to argue for and against such a preposterous proposition. That set off a chain reaction of anger, fear and threats against each other, from which LiXii excused herself. It meant she didn't have to unpack the unpleasant repercussions about to hit every nation of the world.

They reacted exactly as LiXii expected. She answered as many questions as were thrown at her. She wouldn't tell them anything they didn't already know. The object of the exercise was to gain time – enough time to complete the last stage of the evacuation plan. Her biggest worry surrounded her as she left the UN building - her own team, and she couldn't contact Lai-Xii on Europa from there, not that there was any real need to do so.

LiXii waited until they arrived at their accommodation, ONE UN New York, only a few minute's walk from the UN building. Aurora grumbled a little, he wouldn't look her in the eye and at first refused to discuss his issue. "Whatever your problem is Aurora, we cannot deviate from the plan." Behind closed doors of their conjoined suites they could discuss delicate matters. Haru, Mishka, Salsa, Donald, Urbs and Eve all gathered around the large coffee table.

Aurora joined them after a few minutes. "Are we actually going to go through with William's plan?" he asked after a long silence. In all probability everyone had similar thoughts, perhaps even LiXii.

In her altered persona, for it seemed they'd all changed after the last scan, LiXii seemed to be more introspective. This latest comment by Aurora brought back memories of all the other times he'd found objections to what they were doing. *Maybe I should be more concerned about this guy than Haru or the rest of my team.'* She didn't like this line of speculation. "I've already asked him to continue evacuation of Tau City. Willi, Wu and Wini will leave as soon as we get back there on Thursday. What did you think would be the alternative?"

Aurora may have been a faithful copy of Aurelio. He seemed like himself, but something had changed – yet with as much of an imperative to survive as anybody. "They've all got away safely. Arithmós is set up for them. They're not in any danger," Aurora stated, obviously building up to an 'alternative'.

"I think that's where you're wrong," interjected Haru. "You've just seen how the world's nations have reacted to what LiXii had to say. They're going to panic and they're going to hit out at us. Their first target will be the Datadromes."

"Next they'll come after us." Donald stated the obvious. "We're expendable – we, all of us in this room. Not only that, we could be dangerous to our own people. Just look at what you're saying. I know exactly what you're thinking, but we must not continue to exist!"

Urbs and Woof had remained silent, listening to the strange conversation. "I have built a fail-safe into our qubit networks. The end will be immediate and absolutely painless," Woof reassured everyone.

"That's no consolation at all," grunted Aurora.

35

INVASION OF TAU CITY

JANUARY CE 2164

VITYA went to inspect the situation at Tau City's three gates. Reports indicated an unusual amount of traffic wanting to enter. People on foot, on animal backs and in vehicles. So far the procession was orderly, yet agitated faces turned apprehensively towards every security guard that came near them. The city gates had been closed to all traffic since the report of the bombing at Petropavlovsk.

"Where are you from?" Vitya stopped a woman with a child, carrying very few possessions. She waited directly outside the closed city gates.

"Magadan," she replied, "my daughter and I have been travelling for weeks."

She must have. Magadan was on mainland Russia on the far coast, some eight hundred and seventy kilometres across land and the Sea of Okhotsk.

"And you?" The young man hung his head. He'd obviously been living a hard life, though he spoke well.

"Petropavlovsk. I was a university student until the bombing. I tried to study. They wouldn't let me study the things I wanted, so I tried finding a job in the city. There is no work. There is no life there."

William had been streaming images to Lai-Xii. They all saw what was happening. It seemed the situation repeated itself at each gate. "Open the gates. Get your people to take them to our nearest Datadromes for processing." LiXii and Lai-Xii agreed on the course of most appropriate action, though it was LiXii who issued the order to Vitya.

As soon as the gates opened the crowd turned into a mob rushing at the entrance, the narrow road outside becoming more congested with each passing hour. Desperation drove people to extraordinary lengths. The siege by citizenry soon eased as military helicopters began arriving several days later. Apparently the existing small Russian force patrolling the outside of the city needed reinforcements.

Troop carriers rattled down the two badly maintained roads leading to the city. Commander Vitya Pyryev, head of Tau City security met Major Vanya Vyshata outside the city at their bivouac.

"You will surrender your security to my command." Major Vyshata wasted no time on pleseantries or diploimacy, his Russian dialect as uncultured as his manners. He was there for only one reason, to take control of and prevent any further migration of Russian citizens. He'd already ordered his men to stop anyone else entering the city.

"Yes, Major. The city is yours." Vitya smiled, putting up no resistance. "Would you like to come for an inspection?"

"Soon enough. What is your population?" Vitya told him. "Who are all these people?" Vitya said they were people looking for a better life. "Why do they think they will find it here?" Vitya shrugged and said he didn't know.

"Would you like to come talk to our City officials?"

So much cooperation made the Major suspicious. He ordered his men to secure the outside of the city. He was told these Tau City people were a danger to Russian National Security. His battalion arrived first on the scene of this supposed insurrection.

William knew they were coming. He knew why and what they expected to find. There were no weapons in Tau City. Each laboratory had continued research into indigenous diseases. Each fully equipped with all the genetic scientific apparatus one would expect to find if researching phenomena such as tetra-amelia malformations. There were many such persons living in Tau City.

Lai-Xii had departed some time ago with her full team - except Willi, Wini and Wu - all traces of their special Project work destroyed. Major Vyshata would find nothing of interest, nothing that could be considered a threat to anyone. William's countdown had begun.

"Where is Lai-Xii?" demanded the Major.

"She is waiting for you at the Town Centre." LiXii and William had devised a strategy to buy them time and concurrently confuse the hell out of the troops.

261

The man grunted, and with a contingent of his officers followed Vitya in through the city gates. He could scarcely believe the transformation in front of his eyes. This city flourished in the rugged, inhospitable valley between snow-capped volcanoes. Never had he seen neat well-maintained houses, parks and such well-ordered avenues with happy people, mostly on scooters, going about their business. The trip to the Town Centre left Major Vyshata thoroughly confused, even before he met LiXii.

"What is this place?" he asked somewhat taken aback by the experience of the city environs.

"Mostly a research facility, funded privately and supported by most world governments."

'Mostly?"

"We also seem to make people happy." Replied Vitya, on plan. "Please come in."

They arrived at the municipal building which was neither purely utilitarian, nor entirely grandiose. Many artworks adorned the walls, images of Europa and Jupiter and sculptures dotted around entrances with large rugs spread invitingly on timber floors inside.

A normal sized door, in the wall opposite to the entrance, opened to Vitya without having to touch it, letting them into what looked like a comfortably furnished living room. A fire in the large open fireplace, and the samovar steaming gently on a table took his immediate attention. He didn't immediately notice see LiXii stand from the couch in front of the fire.

"Major! Come in, please make yourself comfortable."

Nor did he recognise that the woman standing in front of him was no longer flesh and blood. He stiffened to attention and turned in her direction. "I have come to take control of the city," he announced, though feeling a little odd." What was there to take control of? He wasn't quite sure anymore.

"By all means. You and your men are most welcome. We can prepare accommodation for you if you could give us a few days. I'm sure they would be most comfortable. Please, sit."

Vitya was floored. Was this the LiXii he'd come to know, surely not. They must have done something to her during the scanning. Vitya was unaware of her previous life as a Geisha and the range of performance skills that went with it.

"I want to see one of your Datadromes." The major felt he needed to maintain his harsh exterior, but minute by minute it seemed to be out of place with these people.

"Vitya? Our nearest one is right here in this building, isn't it?"

"Yes LiXii – in the west wing." Seeing the Major's impatience, he made a move back towards the door.

Just what is this place? They are so informal. Is there no authority here? "Who is in charge here?" he demanded without really intending to.

LiXii let out one of her rare Geisha giggles, just for his benefit. "Why me! Silly boy." But she didn't touch him. She knew her men and knew just how far she could go with them. A twitch appeared at the corner of Major Vyshata's mouth, though very briefly, not unnoticed by LiXii. *Got him.* She could relax a little. It was a dangerous situation, though the game only had to be played for a short time.

At the Datadrome rooms people talked quietly while they waited to go into the first chamber. Being an internal facility it had only two doors, an entrance and an exit. In the waiting room Visas were being checked. The Major immediately went to the desk, took a Visa out of the next person's hand to examine it minutely. It wasn't a forgery - a perfectly legal document issued by his Government, and it hadn't been cancelled when he checked it on the dedicated link to the Russian Federal Migration Service.

"Harrumph," or some such noise came out from under his moustache. "What's in there? He asked pointing at the door the next person entered.

Unfazed LiXii said, "That's just our mind-reading equipment. You know the kind of work we do here." The Major stiffened slightly, an indication he had no idea. *Good!* She continued, "We've developed a way of using brain scans to detect anomalies in a person's health. Much of it can be corrected by adjusting neural imbalances." LiXii didn't speak down to him. He was just a brute soldier, but he could still react to a beautiful woman treating him with respect. She could see his attitude become less confrontational. The Major started concentrating more on her than what was going on in the room.

"Would you like to see how we do it?"

He was going to barge in anyway. Her invitation pre-empted and postponed the action. "Please wait till the person under treatment comes out." He pretended impatience, quite happy to continue chatting with this extraordinary looking woman with the impeccable short black fringe. "Here he comes now."

The man looked quite contented, even happy as he walked passed the two of them, not reacting to the presence of a large military officer in his visor peaked hat of authority. "What happened to him?"

It was unusual for anyone not to react with at least some degree of uneasiness in his presence. LiXii certainly didn't and now this common peasant either. He watched as another man entered after having his visa checked. "I'm not sure. I can get the doctor to talk to you, Da?" LiXii poked her head in the door to call to Eve.

"Major - Welcome." A stunning cascading red haired woman in white overcoat advanced on the army officer, with hand outstretched in greeting. Taken completely by surprise by the apparition he too extended his hand.

"The Major would like to know what you did to the last patient." LiXii informed her collaborator.

Eve responded in Russian. "This man had been suffering from depression caused by a chemical imbalance with his neurotransmitters like dopamine, serotonin, and norepinephrine, which play an important role in regulating mood and initiative." The Major's eyes tried to maintain focus confronted by such language.

"May I see your equipment?" he asked. LiXii picked up on the sudden change in demeanour, as did Eve.

Having examined the comfortable chair, the monitors and miscellaneous scientific equipment the Major satisfied himself there were no weapons hidden in the room. What to do next? He'd been thrown off guard by Vitya's friendliness and the women's attitudes. There had to be something going on he didn't know about. His superiors told him these people were a danger to Russia's national security. *Be damned if I can see how, but I'll find out.* "I want billeting for my men. We will examine all your facilities." He'd regained some of his composure as they came out into the open. "Where are your research buildings?"

LiXii sidled up close to Major Vyshata. "It's getting dark. Tomorrow we can organise places for your men to stay. Have you eaten? Why not have dinner with us. Bring your officers. How many shall we expect?"

"Major Vyshata, have your men settled in?" LiXii approached him several hours later as if he was a long awaited friend come to spend time visiting. He still didn't know what was happening. His superiors didn't think it necessary to update a Major in the remote mountains of Kamchatka to the outcome of a UN conference.

"I am still unclear as to why you need such extensive manufacturing capabilities if you are only a research facility." It wasn't a question – more a 'time to explain yourself' situation.

"Tonight we're planning a little get together. Come for dinner. We can catch up then."

All the officers attended. LiXii, Haru and Eve made a point of ensuring their military attention was focused on them that evening. Without overdressing to make the ploy obvious, in which art LiXii had excelled in her time as a Geisha, the ladies spread themselves between the attending officers. The Major seated himself close to LiXii.

"This is a speciality," she told him, "prepared by one of our most talented tetra-amelias.

"Tetra-amelias?" He didn't know what that meant.

As the dinner progressed through the many courses, the military contingent at the table relaxed, oblivious of the activity going on in the other buildings. Wini, Wu and Willi had departed for Europa with William's help. He closed down all nine Datadromes, their systems fried by a massive overload. Almost all inhabitants had already made the transition, certainly all the remaining tetra-amelias. Visitors who'd streamed into the city from all parts of Kamchatka, many from mainland Russia from places like Magadan and Talon, quietly, happily departed after their scans, through the same gates guarded by Russian troops. They had no orders to prevent people from leaving.

By the following morning, as The Major slept a rare comfortable sleep while on assignment, Tau City quietly shut down. The fail-safe built into qubit networks, alluded to by Woof, activated during the night shutting down their cognitive processing. The Q-chassis of LiXii and her team had walked to the nearest incinerators to stoke the fire with their artificial bodies - their minds already deactivated during their down-time with only motor functions still operating.

Major Vyshata hurriedly donned his uniform, feeling somewhat guilty for having slept longer than the allocated time for soldiers. Outside the sleeping quarters his troops wandered about in disarray, obviously at a loss as to what they should be doing. Some people went about their morning business, many others made their way to the main gate to exit the city – all of them looking quite relaxed and unconcerned about the military presence. The scene made no sense at all. He hurried to what he thought was the Administration building, where he and his officers has such a pleasant evening last night, to find 'that' woman. The place was empty. The city slowly emptied of its inhabitants.

William's count-down progressed smoothly. He sent a message to Lai-Xii. "Phase one completed. Tomorrow all Datadromes around the world will close for maintenance, the closure has been advertised on Me-Me."

They shut their doors for maintenance never to be opened again. Everybody that could have gone, had been transmitted the day before the Datadromes closed.

A mysterious incendiary device had so completely gutted each facility on 'maintenance day' that no recognisable, recoverable component remained. The attendant technicians had simply disappeared.

That's when the real panic started.

FROM THE BOOK OF ORIGINATION
DECLARATIONS THIRTY SIX

36:1 Through the instrument of the all-knowing Beast, Thought fulfilled Its promise to cleanse the corruption that had covered the Earth,

36:2 And the seeds without blemish took root upon another sphere,

36:3 And upon this sphere they made ready.

36

WILLIAM'S PLAN EXECUTED

FEBRUARY CE 2164
EARTH

LAI-XII'S PLAN working through Maldonado's Me-Me social media platform came to fruition, but not quite the way she'd expected. Barely a week after the Datadromes ceased operating the majority of the world's population suddenly realised they all wanted something they could no longer have. They wanted it partly because they'd been continuously told that they wanted it – security, safety and a better life which was only attainable by leaving the Earth behind and migrating to Europa. And they wanted it even more because the possibility of having it had been taken away from them.

Discontent fermented in the public sector, in politics and in the religious domain. Piety or no piety, God or no God, many believers also came to believe in the promise of earthly Paradise – on Europa. Years of created images by artists in every part of the world left the subliminal message that could not be ignored. Some people demonstrated, some complained, most panicked. Frustration, anger, a sense of hopelessness inevitably led to what people do best when unable to find a solution to a problem – resort to violence, an outstanding reliable characteristic of the human species.

William, now in full control on Earth, initiated the second phase of his plan. Newspapers began headlining the unusual number of people of all ages who'd begun to die of brain seizures for which doctors were unable to find the causes. Authorities had no way to make a connection between the deaths and the closure of Datadromes.

"Phase two is in progress," William reported dispassionately to Lai-Xii.

"What's happening in Tau City?"

"Your copies no longer exist. Major Vyshata is incapable of deciding on a course of action as I have cut his communication links with his superiors. I have not yet begun to discontinue the lives of the inhabitants. Has your transition been successful?"

'Hmm, a curious computer'. Since becoming self-aware William had not given the slightest outward indication of actually possessing curiosity. It caused Lai-Xii to ponder whether she should be concerned. Curiosity is the first step towards establishing the basis for defining criteria on which to create decision options. It is also the beginnings of making wrong decisions. *Not that he hasn't decided to act on his own before'*, she thought, *'but that was all based on data and logic.*

"When do you intend to switch yourself off?" Perhaps she didn't need to ask. Yet it made her just the slightest bit anxious to think the authorities could realize the world wide web had become more than just a useful universal tool.

"When my plan is complete." Not a reassuring answer from her perspective. She didn't pursue the point as she knew it would be fruitless.

The second week of February saw rioting out of control around the world. Senseless destruction could not be curtailed by martial law imposed by most countries. Something was very wrong. The people could feel it. They couldn't identify what it was nor could they do anything to make the feeling go away. Governments could also sense it in the gross disobedience of the citizens. So many people had died that bodies could not be disposed of quickly enough. Some Governments left the bodies where they dropped, only making the effort to sanitise them.

Churches overflowed. God listened to their prayers without seeming to be in a hurry to help. Armed forces of every country mobilised to fight, without being able to identify the enemy. William didn't interfere with the frantic communications that added to the confusion and steadily escalating mass hysteria.

"Lai-Xii," he called again in the third week of February. "The UN has just concluded another emergency meeting. They have decided you are the cause of this unprecedented global instability."

"What exactly does that mean?" This was precisely what she'd been afraid of, not that it mattered now. *Why is he bothering to tell me this?*

"They have decided to strike Tau City, to raze it to the ground. US, Russia and China have all begun preparations to send nuclear

269

warheads to Europa." His voice as calm as always had no more sense of urgency than if he was asking whether she would like sugar in her coffee.

"You had a plan William! DO SOMETHING ABOUT IT!" Lai-Xii became furious. The only fear she ever felt in her long life, surfaced. William could not be trusted! She began something many, many years ago without fully realising all the ramifications. If the human species had evolved to the extent indicated by LaiXii.gen3920.15eV.exe's existence, then anything could conceivably be possible. The inevitable had to happen. William had to carry through with what he promised. "AND DAMN WELL DO IT NOW!" She screamed back at him without waiting to hear his response. Harusuke was with her when the call came from William. She tried to calm Lai-Xii shaking in her VR simulated form.

"William is still only a computer. He's programed himself to carry out a set of actions under specific circumstances, and he will do exactly that. He is not Willi, or Wu or Wini. These three have evolved past him. They're more than him. William *will* do what he's programmed himself to do."

To William, Harusuke said, "Send images of what is happening." The conversation ended as abruptly as it had begun. William initiated phase three and began streaming vids to Europa. "The people should see this. It's part of our history. They must know," Harusuke told Lai-Xii.

Few immigrants had been screened through Lai-Xii's visa analysis criteria. Those several thousand activated individuals, together with construction and maintenance personal, watched what Lai-Xii and her team observed in stark brutal reality. Prima and Secunda stood beside their VR parents, knowing all the facts but not comprehending any of it.

They could see that the Military could not operate their weapons - no rockets left Earth aimed at Europa. They could see factories all over the world come to a grinding halt, all robotics whining down to a dead stop. They could see total chaos in the streets of every city William showed them. Traffic lights had ceased to function.

All manner of vehicles, civilian and military, stopped moving; accidents, congestion, electronics failure everywhere. People rushed about shouting, screaming, punching their mobile phones – nothing would work. William zoomed his sensors out into Earth orbit. It was difficult to detect at first, but it was definitely happening; orbits of satellites began to decay.

"First, only weapons installations," he commented. Then he showed them images of ships, civil, commercial and navy beginning to drift in ocean currents, out of control.

"What's that mother," asked Prima pointing to a submarine. Many floated, as helpless as the ships. Time passed and the world changed. Yet life in Tau City managed to hang on. William seemed to want to look after them. But he would soon be gone, as would the millions and millions of souls, all trying to survive by raiding supermarkets for food, by killing each other, by thoughtfully dying of diseases: putrefying flesh becoming abundant for all manner of scavengers. Without hospitals, without food production, without communications or transportation or even fresh water, human life quickly lost its already tenuous hold on existence.

For a while the people of Europa watched the rebirth of a planet that was once fecund with life. A painful rebirth out of misery and starvation, a cleansing of all the pollutants, human and artificial that had saddened the heart of creation.

"How could it all happen so quickly?" Salazar held Evgeniya in his VR arms; a question even Lai-Xii, enfolded by Harusuke's VR warmth, could not answer. They watched the past fade – simply fade as if it was all an unbelievably tragic nightmare. Six months, that's all it took, six short months of controlled extermination to rid the planet of the infestation that was killing it, and itself at the same time.

William had shut down all life support systems. The last facility to cease functioning, energy production, meant William had carried out his task. He made no further contact with the Europaeans, sending as many images as he could still energise with the last flush of power in his circuits. Willi watched every instant of everything William, his progenitor, sent from the moment of the beginning of the end.

"It is done," he said, turning to Lai-Xii.

"Now we have work to do," replied the Lai-Xii.

37

ARITHMÓS

CE 2200
EUROPA

EARTH, seen from space had lost its night time sparkle. One half utterly dark and restful, while the other faced the sun, it's rays able to penetrate without the polluted mantle created by the apes that had learnt to use tools and weapons.

The Earth was resting, breathing, looking after the life that truly belonged there.

Some people survived in isolated locations, but most of those were dying out slowly, unable to sustain themselves without the skills of survival lost to technology. Primitive tribes, locked away from the benefits of civilisation fared a little better, though doubtful if enough remained to regenerate the species. Perhaps in ten thousand years, or a hundred thousand years they might look into the sky with a new invention and see the moons of Jupiter, not remembering life flourished on one of them. Even if they remembered, would they recognise the pulses of energy emanating from one of them as *life*?

Empirical reality defines the way we see ourselves, at least within the characteristics of a reality we come to accept. A few short years isn't adequate time for the 'self' to recognise itself in the ebb and flow of quantum energy fields. The Q-chassis developed specifically for Europa became the sanity conduit for the majority of HX-data bundles taken out of storage. Their first experience of Europa appeared remarkably similar to the VR simulations the vast majority of people once entertained themselves with on their mobile phone HMDs. The Q-chassis enabled them to take excursions out onto the icy surface of the moon to come face to face with actual reality, the overpowering phenomenon of Jupiter and the bowl rim horizon of their new home.

"We will have to route everyone we find suitable into one of the Virtual Reality platforms for Europa we developed in the early days." VR-Ralph and VR-Evgeniya seemed to be the only ones with any understanding of the psychological impact of the Transition.

"All those tetra-amelia psychologists I trained will finally get a chance to practice on an entirely novel branch of human behaviour. No doubt they'll come across their fair share of psychosis," said VR-Evgeniya. Mental instability wasn't an area they could examine with any degree of definitive comprehension sufficient to accept or reject emigrants during the transition.

VR-Prima and VR-Secunda spent a lot of time playing outside on the Ice during the first few years after their arrival. They had many other children to play with, especially VR-Cherry Blossom, daughter of the Lai-Xii and Harusuke HX-data bundles. The two ex-geishas decided to have a child of their own. All of VR-Lai-Xii's team had taken partners, though not every pair contributing to the first generation of extraterrestrials.

After one extended play session on Pwyll's rim, where they were forbidden to go for it was the location of their solar energy generating plants, the girls arrived home very excited. "You'll never guess what we saw today!" VR-Prima, the eldest shouted to VR-Wu, her mother.

"You've been gone an entire day. I hope you haven't been interfering with our Maintenance Caste."

Each day on Europa was as long as it took it to go once around Jupiter, a full 3.55 Earth days; an arbitrary period for the measurement of time they'd all become accustomed to.

"When we stepped out of the Interchange Centre Jupiter was already high. We could see huge explosions inside the red storm. It was beautiful! Could we make some paintings, mother, like we saw on Earth?" VR-Prima still remembered.

"What is Earth?' Asked VR-Cherry Blossom. She had knowledge of it from her parents inherited data, but she had no experience of it. There was no visual recording of her own, like the Jupiter she saw that day.

VR-Secunda, only a little younger than VR-Prima loved the surface of Europa. "And we saw huge plumes of water shoot into the sky when we got to Pwyll's rim! It is so much more wonderful outside

273

than when we see it from home. Why is that, Wu?" The children felt the distinction between Virtual Reality and actual reality more than the adults.

VR-Ralph had been working with VR-Ptolemy to allocate appropriate directories to people as they came out of storage. Islanders were well represented. No doubt driven by the desire to replace the homes they lost to rising sea levels inundating their island nations. VR-Ralph thought about what kind of answer he could give the children that they could relate to.

"Outside there is a different reality. To experience it you have to put on the chassis. In here we live inside our thoughts. Out there we become part of the cosmos. It can tell us things we could never learn if we always lived just in our thoughts."

Perhaps that was too esoteric for them. Eventually they would have to come to terms with the new nature of their existence. The children went off to play in safety in the neighbourhood directory. Crime did not yet exist. People would have to learn how to be bad in the true technological environment, where they would become as vulnerable as those they targeted.

"There was a message from 3920 today," Lai-Xii told Ralph. She doesn't talk much to us lately, not that she ever did."

"Some great revelation no doubt." Ralph never really worried too much about the woman from the future, other than marvel at being able to actually talk to her. He wanted to find out about the superluminal communication one day, an exciting technology.

"All she said was *You are now on our time trajectory.*' I suppose that means we're going where she is, unless of course we decide on something better. I'll have to ask her one day about her world."

Harusuke was doing something half absentmindedly, checking how much memory cache they had available for the next batch of HX-Data bundles to be activated tomorrow. In one of her relaxed moods Lai-Xii cuddled up to her partner. "We are actually here. Can you believe it? Could you have imagined anything like this when we were slaves to Ishino, our geisha house mother in Kyoto?"

Harusuke commented offhandedly, "We've come this far – and we know where we have to go next. You have changed the course of human evolution beyond anything Charles Darwin could have imagined. You have saved us from extinction by our own hands."

Lai-Xii gave her another squeeze. Her aspirations were not that lofty. "I only wanted to … to … I forget now. I was just driven to do something – anything about the way people treated each other … and our world."

"Just who are you – Lai-Xii?" Harusuke asked, turning to look her partner directly in the eye, not expecting an answer.

…… I ……

DECLARATIONS THIRTY SIX

And the seeds without blemish took root upon another sphere,

And upon this sphere they made ready.

The Journey from trying to climb into a Russian tank during the Hungarian revolution of 1956 to writing Science Fiction is in itself a story of a leap across worlds of reality.

Zsoall, born in Hungary, was brought to Australia by his parents after the 1956 uprising. He currently lives a creative life with his wife and animal family in the Northern Rivers, New South Wales, Australia.

His life has changed direction a number of times. After gaining his qualifications as a Sculptor he worked as a Secondary Teacher before becoming an Administrative Manager. None offered satisfactory opportunities for creative expression. That began when he embarked on a career as a computer programmer. Whilst in that profession his continuing compulsion to create made it inevitable that his life would change again. Completely giving up programming he immersed himself in creativity as a Sculptor and Painter.

Much of his time is now dedicated to creating glass paintings and sculptures.

Another change is looming on the horizon as the art of recording future visions takes a firmer hold of his creative energies as he pursues the writing of Science Fiction.